SKEPTIC

HOLDEN SCOTT

D0709927

St. Martin's Paperbacks

NOTE: If you purchased this book without a cover you should be aware that this book is stolen property. It was reported as "unsold and destroyed" to the publisher, and neither the author nor the publisher has received any payment for this "stripped book."

SKEPTIC

Copyright © 1999 by Holden Scott.
Excerpt from *The Carrier* copyright © 2000 by Holden Scott.

All rights reserved. No part of this book may be used or reproduced in any manner whatsoever without written permission except in the case of brief quotations embodied in critical articles or reviews. For information address St. Martin's Press, 175 Fifth Avenue, New York, N.Y. 10010.

Library of Congress Catalog Card Number: 98-40617

ISBN: 0-312-96928-7

Printed in the United States of America

St. Martin's Press hardcover edition / March 1999
St. Martin's Paperbacks edition / March 2000

St. Martin's Paperbacks are published by St. Martin's Press, 175 Fifth Avenue, New York, N.Y. 10010.

10 9 8 7 6 5 4 3 2 1

OVERWHELMING ACCLAIM FOR *SKEPTIC*

"Intriguing . . . [A] promising debut novel."
—*Publishers Weekly*

"The cover of SKEPTIC is crowded with accolades from researchers and writers, and this is one time a novel is worthy of exuberant praise."
—*Hartford Courant*

"Gripping! SKEPTIC grabbed me in the first chapter and pulled me into the fascinating story line. The medical/science premise was ingenious and based on enough scientific fact for me to accept the story line and enjoy the ride."
—Peter G. Traber, M.D., Chair, Department of Medicine, University of Pennsylvania Health System, and Frank Wister Thomas Professor of Medicine

"SKEPTIC is a riveting adventure story in the best tradition of popular medical thrillers. Scott mines current biomedical research for highly imaginative scenarios, while his sound comprehension of the motives and workings of biomedical research institutions gives the narrative an aura of plausibility."
—Thomas P. Stossel, M.D., Professor of Medicine, Harvard Medical School, and Director of the Experimental Medicine Division, Brigham and Women's Hospital

"SKEPTIC is one of the cleverest and most exciting medical stories that I have read since Michael Crichton first appeared on the scene."
—Leonard Jarett, M.D., Simon Flexner Professor and Chair, University of Pennsylvania Department of Pathology and Laboratory Medicine

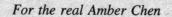

For the real Amber Chen

Acknowledgments

My deepest thanks to Dr. Jack McConnell, without whom this novel would not exist. I am also indebted to Jennifer Enderlin, Matthew Shear, and the continuing wisdom and foresight of Aaron Priest. Thanks also to Or Gozani, Katrin Chua, Jon and Josh Mezrich, Scott Stossel, Lisa Erbach Vance, Dee Dee Zobian, and most of all, my parents.

SKEPTIC

CHAPTER ONE

Teri Pace wanted to tear off her clothes and run naked through the basement laboratory. She wanted to leap into the air, scream at the top of her lungs, careen through Metro's hallways. Instead, she let out a tiny yelp of joy, then quickly looked over her shoulder to make sure she was still alone.

She turned back to the glass maze and stared down at the tiny white mouse. Sightless eyes stared back at her from behind twitching whiskers. She picked up the mouse in her hand, feeling the creature's lilliputian claws against her skin. Then she carefully placed the mouse back at the start of the maze.

Without thought, without flaw, the animal rushed through the tiny glass hallways, once again making all the correct turns, arriving at the end in record time. Teri sat down hard on a metal stool next to the maze, fighting to catch her breath. *She had never expected the experiment to actually work.*

She ran a hand through her tousled mop of auburn hair, forcing herself to calm down. There was still plenty of work left to do. She had to run the experiment a dozen more times. She had to prepare a paper on the results, something good enough for the hard-nosed editors at the major journals. She had to make sure she had covered every detail. "The particulars!" her mother used to shout at her. "Never forget the particulars!"

Suddenly, she started to laugh. She felt light-headed, like a diabetic on a sugar low. She thought about what her mother would say when she saw Teri's name in *Science, Nature and Cell*. When she saw her interviewed on *Nightline, 60 Minutes,* even *Oprah.*

She quickly shook the thoughts of her mother out of her mind; this was not about *her.* This was about a tiny white mouse and a scientific discovery that was going to change the world. A discovery so enormous, it was going to challenge fundamental beliefs and basic assumptions that stretched back to the beginning of time. A breakthrough so immense it would turn science upside down. Trembling, she rose from the stool, picked up the mouse, and started across the dimly lit basement lab.

For three years, this place had been her second home. The lab was a cinder-block rectangle, four thousand square feet lined with equipment cabinets, pewter sinks, test-tube racks, and sealed glass animal cages. Puke-green tiles covered most of the floor, and long fluorescent tubes bounced flickering orange light off the polished white walls.

Ballantine's Batcave, the graduate students called it. The underground lab presented a stark contrast to the shiny modern look of the hospital upstairs. Originally, the basement had been the site of Boston Metropolitan's pathology lab. Then the cinder-block cavern had slumbered unused as Metro brightened its image, clawing ever upward along the flat of Beacon Hill. Five years ago, in the midst of Metro's reconstruction, Dr. Ballantine had somehow convinced the hospital to let him use the space for his own virology lab. Since then, the lab's funding had remained steady, despite Dr. Ballantine's lack of publishable results.

Teri skirted a long row of sinks and arrived at the far corner of the lab, still gently clasping the mouse in both hands. A tall steel shelving unit rose up behind a large mahogany desk. The six shelves were cluttered with unmarked vials, Bunsen burners, boxes of latex gloves, and small-animal cages. Dr. Ballantine had loaned Teri the shelving unit for her personal use, and over the years she had developed a carefully determined sense of disorder. The clutter was actually a disguise, meant to further hide her efforts from Dr. Ballantine and the four other graduate students who worked in the Batcave. As far as anyone knew, Teri was just a quiet, almost painfully shy third-year Ph.D. virology candidate assisting Dr. Ballantine in his study of cytotoxic T cells.

She smiled as she carefully placed her mouse back in its cage on the top shelf. Next to the cage were two glass vials filled with thick, clear liquid. To the right of the vials stood a black cylinder, twelve inches tall, dangling a long electrical cord. Next to that, another wire mouse cage. Teri hadn't bothered to name the four mice inside the second cage, simply referring to them by the plastic tags on their tails: Mouse A, Mouse C, Mouse D, and Mouse E. The cage had once housed the entire alphabet. Before her experiment was finished, she was going to need at least a dozen more of the little critters.

That thought in mind, she turned away from the shelving unit and opened the top drawer of Dr. Ballantine's desk. She found the stack of equipment request forms and began scripting a viable story. Over the past three years, Dr. Ballantine's lab had been going through mice like popcorn, perhaps five dozen in the last five months alone.

As Teri worked on the form, a familiar hiccup echoed off the cinder-block walls, followed by a dull hum. Teri glanced at the metal ventilation cabinet that stood by the elevator on the other side of the lab. For years, the hum had been nothing but background noise, the sound of a complex system of rotating fans and mechanical filters. Now it was music, a wonderful symphony in her ears.

She finished filling out the request form and headed toward the elevator, her eyes still pinned to the humming ventilation cabinet. She hit the button for the elevator, then held one hand over the cabinet's vents, feeling the rush of warm air.

The Batcave was a Biosafety Level One lab, with its own self-contained oxygen recycling system. In accordance with Level One requirements, the sealed elevator was the only entrance to the lab, and the ventilation cabinet was the only source of fresh air. This system was primitive compared with the high-tech filtration units in place in the more modern virology labs upstairs—but that was par for the course where Dr. Ballantine was concerned. It was no secret what Metro's administration thought of Mike Ballantine—and Teri had serendipitously benefited from that resentment.

She had stumbled on the key to her experiment completely by mistake. She had been carrying a vial of her latest R-E solution past the ventilation cabinet when the elevator had suddenly whirred to life, signaling that someone was on the way down. Startled, she had spilled some of the R-E solution into the air vent. She had tried to clean the vent, but some of the transparent, viscous liquid had dripped inside the metal cabinet, making it nearly impossible.

The spill had occurred exactly three weeks ago. This morning, Mouse B had run the maze for the first time.

Teri had a very good idea why the accidental spill had made the difference. It had to do with oxygen diffusion and the olfactory centers in the tiny mouse's brain. It would be an entire section in her paper, though the editors at *Science* would probably cut the breakthrough down to a single appendix entry.

When she finally told Dr. Ballantine about the spill, he would rebuke her for keeping it a secret. After all, she had put the entire lab at risk of inhaling an unknown substance. But she hadn't had a choice. She had been determined not to tell anyone about her experiment until she was ready.

Besides, there had been only one noticeable side effect to the R-E spill. Everyone who had spent significant time in the virus lab had come down with a slight cold.

Teri doubted Dr. Ballantine would be thinking about his trivial cough and stuffed nose when she showed him what she had accomplished. As a scientist and a doctor, he would grasp the significance of her work immediately. He would realize that in one sudden stroke, she had changed the future of science. He would know that in time, her work would overshadow everything else in the history of the profession, and change the lives and beliefs of every person on earth.

Her stomach flip-flopped as she pictured Dr. Ballantine's reaction to her revelations. His blue eyes would sparkle at her from beneath those wonderful brown locks, as his lips turned up at the corners—

Teri chided herself for thinking like such a fool. It was a schoolgirl crush—even if the schoolgirl was twenty-five and halfway to her Ph.D. Dr. Ballantine barely knew she existed. To him, she was just a quiet, green-eyed woman who puttered around behind him while he worked at his desk. She was young, pretty, with an athletic body, two legs, and appropriately perky breasts. But she had hardly spoken three words to him in as many years—in fact, she doubted he would even recognize her voice.

The elevator doors *whiffed* open, and Teri rushed into the carpeted cube, her stomach churning despite the thoughts running through her head. True, Dr. Ballantine had no reason to like her the way she liked him—not yet.

But would that all change when she showed him her mouse?

Thirty seconds after the elevator doors slid shut, a brief whirring filled the deserted lab. A fluorescent light panel in the direct center of the lab's ceiling shivered, as tiny gears hidden inside the panel reacted to the commands of a computer chip roughly the size of an insect's brain.

A transparent hair-thin wire descended through a minuscule pore in the plastic panel. The wire consisted of two cylindrical fiber-optic cords supporting a perfectly concave lens one millimeter wide. The lens rotated in a silent 360-degree arc as the wire descended, capturing a three-dimensional video image of the deserted lab. A second computer chip, no bigger than the first, instantaneously converted the megabytes of digitized visual information into packages of light, which were in turn transmitted in continuous cone-shaped pulses through a fiber-optic antenna strung through the wall of the basement lab. Twelve miles away, a third computer chip reconverted the light-packaged information into digital bits. The bits were fed into a receiver attached to a Pentium processor, which analyzed the visual information, adding shadow and contrast. Seconds later, a crystal-clear picture of the basement lab appeared on a flat high-resolution screen located above the Pentium. As the concave lens revolved, the picture on the screen shifted, displaying more detail and depth.

The entire process continued for less than three minutes; then the tiny gears again whirred to life, and the transparent surveillance wire disappeared back into the fluorescent light panel.

CHAPTER TWO

Mike Ballantine watched the motorcade from the passenger seat of the ambulance, a mixture of emotions rising behind his chiseled Irish features. It was, after all, an awesome sight. A writhing, reptilian convoy of vehicles, plying its way through the throngs of screaming fans. The rhythm of the celebrating crowd was almost sexual, shouts and applause reverberating against the staid brick townhouses that lined the far side of the street. Mike tried to count the faces behind the barricades, but quickly lost track. "Christ. Looks like they're three deep all the way to the top of the hill."

"It must be nice," Joel Kaplan responded from behind the ambulance's steering wheel. "Everyone lining up just to see you. So much goddamn love."

Mike laughed, not out of jealousy, really, but because it was funny. A thousand people standing outside on a cold November morning just to cheer as his best friend rode by in a limousine. Millions and millions more watching on television as the limousine crawled up Beacon Street toward the statehouse, trailing a peacock's tail of police motorcycles, bulletproof sedans, and network vans.

The whole damn city at his feet. Mike pictured the expression on Andrew's face as his friend looked out through the limousine's tinted windows. He imagined the wide smile, the round, sincere eyes; if anyone deserved the accolades, it was Andrew. Mike felt the pride wash through him in waves. Once upon a time, they were two Irish kids playing kickball in a tiny backyard in Cambridge, Massachusetts. Two Irish kids sharing their first beer, first cigarette, first *Playboy* magazine. Now Andrew was riding in the back of a stretch limousine as the entire city applauded. And Mike was right there with him—riding support, but still part of the party. It was one hell of a moment.

"Look at 'em," Kaplan continued, shaking his head. "You'd think he was some sort of rock star. Probably gets panties in the mail."

"That a good thing, Joel?"

Kaplan grunted. He was barely three years out of his EMS-B paramedical training course, probably twenty-three, twenty-four years old. Short blond hair, blue eyes, and an ever present cocky grin. No wrinkles, no worries. *Still* just *a kid.* Mike felt ancient next to the young paramedic, even though he himself had just recently turned thirty-six. Sure, he still had his college varsity body— wide shoulders, muscular limbs, tight stomach and chest—but his face had finally begun to mature. He hadn't been called boyish in more than ten years, despite his dark curly locks of hair and his youthful smile. Aging like a fine wine, was the way Andrew put it. Mike didn't know the first thing about wine; but as long as he could still run five miles before breakfast without his knees giving out, he didn't care about the cracked eggshells at the corners of his eyes. "What's a guy supposed to do with a mailbox full of panties, anyway?"

"I'll get my girlfriend to send you a pair," Kaplan responded, still grinning. "Let you figure it out for yourself."

"Why don't you just send me the pair you're wearing now?"

"That's real funny, Doc."

"On second thought, you'd better keep the panties. I wouldn't want you getting arrested for male fraud."

Kaplan groaned, and Mike turned his attention back to the crowds besieging Beacon Street. College students in leather jackets, businessmen in heavy overcoats, old ladies with toothless smiles. Row upon row, pushing up against the blue barricades as the motorcade rumbled past. It had been this way throughout the ten-mile journey from the outskirts of the city to this, its center—Beacon Hill, the historic seat of the state's government.

"They say he'll probably be president one day," Kaplan continued, one hand on the wheel while the other tapped out a thoughtful rhythm on the dashboard. "Then it'll be raining panties for sure. Some guys have all the luck."

Mike wondered if it was really possible—*president?* Certainly, there had never been a more beloved governor in Massachusetts history. This thought made Mike laugh again, his face pressed against the cold glass window as Kaplan maneuvered the ambulance ten yards behind the last police motorcycle. Crazy, how life worked out.

To Mike, Governor Andrew Kyle would always be the fat kid with glasses and a widow's peak who lived two doors down, the kid Mike protected in Mrs. Carrol's third-grade homeroom because their moms played bridge on Tuesday nights. Even when Mike made the switch from bodyguard to best friend, his image of Kyle never changed: dumpy, helpless, but smarter than hell and blessed with the most genuine smile in history. Neither of those things mattered in the *Lord of the Flies* atmosphere of Cambridge Public High School—but life wasn't high school.

"President Kyle. It does have a nice ring to it."

"You'd be sitting pretty, wouldn't you?" Kaplan said. "High school chums, college roommates. He'd probably set you up at some posh hospital in Washington. Play with senators' colons all day long."

"Dream come true," Mike said, pausing to cough into his hand. For three days, he had been fighting the beginnings of a nasty head cold. "Why I spent nine years learning medicine."

"You've got to admit, it can't hurt having a friend like Andrew Kyle."

Mike wasn't going to argue. If not for Andrew's influence, he would have lost his prestigious post as associate director of internal medicine at Boston Metropolitan years ago. Mike also suspected that Andrew was funding his virology lab in the basement of Metro—perhaps out of his own deep pocket. In exchange, Mike continued in his role as protector; he was Andrew's private physician, never more than a phone call away. And when Andrew went out to greet the people, Mike was always there as a precaution, ten yards behind the motorcade. The ambulance and the paramedic were paid for by the state government, but Mike was there out of friendship. Just as Andrew had always been there for him.

"Not a bad set of coattails to ride," Mike conceded.

"Forget the coattails. I'd like to ride that wife of his. You can keep the prestigious career in Washington, just give me a few minutes in the Lincoln Bedroom."

"You bleed class, Joel."

"Just making a point, Doc. Your friend's got one hell of a wife."

Anne Kyle was arguably the most attractive woman in the city of Boston. A former runway model turned patent attorney, from one of the wealthiest families in

Mobile, Alabama, she had married Andrew four years ago. Mike had been the best man at the wedding, and he could still remember everything about the evening, down to the details: the color of his cummerbund and the cut of his own wife's matching burgundy dress— Kari's favorite, because of the slit down the left side and the way it fell off one shoulder. Mike hadn't been able to take his eyes off her during the entire ceremony.

Mike shifted against the vinyl passenger seat. It was a strange feeling—smiling and sad at the same time. He had buried Kari in that same burgundy dress two years ago. Andrew and Anne had stood by his side while he sprinkled dirt on the coffin.

Just months ago, the memory would have stabbed at his heart like a scalpel. He knew that somewhere inside him, the pain was just as fresh, but he had trained himself not to go there.

"Yeah, I guess some guys do have all the luck." Mike coughed again, rubbing at his eyes with the back of his hand. His cold was definitely getting worse.

"You want to grab a cup of coffee after this is over?" Kaplan asked, changing the subject. "Or are you backed up at the hospital?"

Mike was about to answer when suddenly Kaplan screamed, throwing both hands in front of his face. The entire ambulance rocked backward and Mike grabbed at the dashboard. What the hell was going on? He focused his attention forward, through the trembling front windshield.

The explosion happened so fast it seemed to split time. Fifty feet ahead, in the direct center of the motorcade, a plume of bright orange flame ripped upward through Andrew Kyle's bulletproof limousine, instantly vaporizing its back half. The pavement underneath the plume of fire rippled outward in concentric circles, chunks of melting black asphalt erupting into the air. The two police cars directly behind the limousine lifted ten feet off the ground, then suddenly disappeared into a cloud of swirling black smoke.

The wall of sound seemed to lag a heartbeat behind the explosion, and for a second Mike felt as if he were floating in silence, staring at something that wasn't real, a single frame in an imaginary roll of film. Then the sound hit him and his eardrums popped. He was slammed backward into his seat. He stared in horror as the police motorcycle directly in front of the ambulance lifted off the pavement and windmilled toward his face, two flaming rubber tires spinning closer and closer and closer—

Mike's reflexes flickered to life and he dove beneath the dashboard. The windshield shattered above him as the motorcycle burst through. Glass rained down against his shoulders, and something white-hot touched the back of his neck. He rolled to his right and slammed into the ambulance door. His fingers found the latch and suddenly he was lying on the pavement, staring up at the gray November sky.

He tried to catch his breath as he pushed himself to his knees. The ambulance was tilted forward on two flat tires, surrounded by a three-inch pool of broken glass. The police motorcycle was halfway through the shattered front windshield, one flaming tire embedded in the passenger seat where Mike had been sitting. Kaplan was hanging out the open driver's side window, both hands limp, blood streaming from somewhere above his hairline. The motorcycle cop was nowhere to be seen. Mike could only guess how far he had been thrown by the explosion; it was doubtful he was still alive.

Mike's entire body began to shiver as he forced himself to his feet. The back of his neck stung, and he gently

reached for the spot with his fingers. A nasty burn, perhaps third degree, where the motorcycle tire had nicked
him. Other than that, he seemed uninjured. Relief flowed
through him, and then his body started to shake even
harder. His eyes moved back to Kaplan.

Christ. He rushed around the destroyed ambulance
and straight to the unconscious kid's side. Thankfully,
Kaplan's pulse was strong and his breathing stable. Mike
gently probed around Kaplan's neck and head, searching
for any serious injuries. Nothing screamed out at him,
and he felt another tinge of relief. The gash across the
top of Kaplan's scalp was messy, but not life threatening. If he was lucky, the kid would come out of this
with nothing more than a concussion and a few stitches.

Mike gently reached underneath Kaplan's arms and
eased him out of the ambulance. As he worked on the
kid, sounds of the aftermath began to trickle into his
ears. Cries, moans, screams, sirens. The patter of a helicopter up above, the shouts of police officers, shocked
television reporters, and injured bystanders. Mike's
trauma training began to kick in, and his mind started
to clear. He had to focus, to fight back the shock and
take control of the situation. There would be more doctors and paramedics arriving by the second. The worst
was over. Then, suddenly, a single thought hit him.

Andrew. I have to help Andrew. He laid Kaplan down
on the ground, making sure the kid was still stable. Then
he spun in the direction of the horrible blast.

As he rushed forward, he could hardly believe the
devastation around him. He had seen the effects of
terrorist-style bombings before—on television, and during his short rotation through the ER after medical
school—but he had never experienced anything as
ferocious as this. The explosion had slammed down Beacon Street like an angry fist. Bodies lay scattered at

every angle, macabre accessories to the wrecked remains of the still-burning motorcade. It looked like a scene from Bosnia or Beirut, not Boston, Massachusetts. As Mike got closer to the center of the explosion, he had to struggle not to stop and help the wounded he passed; letting them lie untended went against every inch of his training. But Andrew needed him.

He put one foot in front of the other, maneuvering around the burning vehicles and injured bodies, stepping over the chunks of pavement and piles of broken glass. *Focus,* he screamed at himself, *focus!*

Finally, he arrived at what looked like ground zero. The degree of damage was beyond imagination: the strange plume of flame had formed a ten-foot crater in the pavement, ringed by a half-dozen concentric circles of melted black asphalt. The asphalt was speckled with shiny patches of translucent crystal; Mike guessed it was some sort of mineral precipitate, formed by the immense and sudden heat.

As he gingerly picked his way forward, he could still feel the heat resonating through the soles of his shoes. What the hell could have caused such a blast? The thought vanished, as he saw what was left of the bulletproof limousine, lying upside down a few yards beyond the edge of the crater. The back half of the limo was melted beyond recognition, a twisting mass of metal that seemed to spring right up out of the still-smoking pavement.

Mike leaped toward the car, and his left foot caught on the edge of the dark crater. He toppled forward and suddenly found himself kneeling in a cloud of red-gray mist. He coughed, trying to catch his breath. Then his eyes centered on something on the charred ground directly in front of his knees.

At first, the object didn't make any sense; the shape

was familiar, but the context was all wrong. Then Mike's eyes somehow found perspective, and the object came into focus: a thumb and forefinger, attached by tattered strings of burnt flesh to a four-inch section of wrist. He was looking at the partial remains of a human hand.

Then Mike noticed the leather watchband embedded in the burnt skin below the disembodied thumb. He remembered picking the watch out of a catalogue less than two months ago. A congratulatory present for his best friend, on the verge of his nomination for a second term. Mike's eyes widened, and he slowly raised his head. The strange red-gray mist suddenly seemed even thicker, and he could make out tiny bits of flesh suspended in the air, intermingled with flecks of burnt clothing and blackened strands of human hair.

Oh, God. Realization hit Mike, and he stumbled back, starting to choke. He bent forward at the waist and retched uncontrollably. Then he crawled away from the crater, his mind spinning, tears biting at the corners of his eyes. The truth continued to sink in. He rubbed the tears out of his eyes and stared at the spot where he had found the disembodied hand. Then he let out an anguished, helpless wail.

There was nothing left of his best friend but a thumb, a forefinger, and a noxious cloud of red-gray vapor.

CHAPTER THREE

Six hours later, Mike was sitting in the back of a police cruiser, battling a growing sense of numbness. It was the same cruiser that had dropped him off at his apartment after the madness on Beacon Street; the two officers had barely made it two blocks down Commonwealth Avenue before Mike had dialed the number on the card one of them had given him, explaining that he had changed his mind and wanted to accept their offer of a quick lift across town. Even so, Mike had nearly gone stir-crazy waiting for the cruiser to navigate the circuit of one-way streets back to his front steps. Home was supposed to be a sanctuary, but in Mike's state, it felt more like a coffin, and pretty soon he knew he'd be clawing at the walls. Although it seemed callous to be heading back to work the same day his best friend had been killed, he needed to be surrounded by people he knew, by his routine, by things that had order. He needed to be distracted from his thoughts and memories while he struggled to make sense of what had just happened.

In the back of the cruiser, he rubbed a sweat-soaked sleeve across his forehead, trying not to think. He closed his eyes, his mind flashing back nearly twenty years. Suddenly, it was the day before his senior year of high school, and he and Andrew were tossing empty soda bottles at the wall of an abandoned gas station somewhere near the line between Cambridge and sprawling, blue-collar Somerville. As the bottles shattered and the glass piled up, Mike watched his chunky friend struggling to get a throw within ten feet of the makeshift pitching target they had painted on the cement wall.

"Why the hell do I hang out with a sorry shit like you?" Mike had asked, good-naturedly but with a hint of real curiosity in his voice. Andrew had pointed a chubby finger in his direction, his signature smile twice as large as usual.

"Doesn't take a psychiatrist to figure it out. Two lonely Irish kids on the poor side of a rich neighborhood. One's got a shithead for a father, the other never had a chance to hate his own. Face it, Mikey boy. We need each other."

Mike had laughed like it was the biggest joke in the world. But inside, he had known Andrew was right. Andrew had always been smart that way. Not like Mike, who needed a bulldozer to get to his emotions. *Or a fucking bomb.* Back in the police cruiser, he breathed deeply, feeling the numbness beginning to fade. In its place rose a violent red anger, a fierce, voracious feeling that sent chills down Mike's spine. He clenched his teeth, refusing to let the anger take hold. He hated the anger—because he knew where it came from. *One's got a shithead for a father . . .*

Mike chased the thought away, as the police cruiser pulled into Metro's receiving circle and slowed to a stop in front of the sliding glass emergency-room doors. The officer in the front passenger seat looked back through the divider, sizing Mike up with a concerned gaze. "You sure you don't want a lift somewhere else? Maybe a friend's place? Or even the Commons? Seems like we could all use the rest of the day off."

Mike shook his head. With the motion, the sterile

white strip of gauze taped over the tire burn on the back of his neck tickled his skin, and he held back a wince. "I'm going to try to lose myself in my normal routine. But thanks for the offer."

The officer slid out of the cruiser and opened Mike's door. "You did good today, Doc. Saved a lot of lives."

Mike stretched his calves as he rose to his full height. He was at least two inches taller than the police officer, with an intimidating, muscular physique. He had played football in high school, then lacrosse at BU. Since college, he'd kept in shape through his morning run and in Metro's pickup basketball league. But today, he felt every second of his age.

"We all did our best. In some cases, it wasn't enough."

"I'm sorry about the governor, Doc."

"Me, too. He deserved a lot better. Your captain said he'd keep me informed on the investigation."

"We'll get the bastard," the officer said through his teeth. "I can promise you that. The FBI and the Secret Service will have a hundred men in Boston by tomorrow morning. But between you and me, I hope it's an Irish cop who finds the monster who did this."

Mike nodded, despite himself. Violence—along with the anger that provoked it—had been a part of his life from a very early age. As much as he hated to admit it, he understood the officer, the same way he understood his cousins and uncles who hung out in the South Boston bars drinking Guinness and talking about the English. But understanding the anger and violence didn't make Mike detest it any less.

"I'm sure everyone will do his best to see that justice is served," he said, quietly. The officer looked at him curiously, expecting something more. Then he shrugged, sliding back into the front passenger seat. A second later the cruiser pulled away from the curb, slipping between a pair of incoming ambulances with flashing lights.

Mike turned toward the glass doors. For a moment, his legs stopped working and he just stood there, his gaze wandering up and down the monolithic entrance. He let the last vestiges of his own anger trickle away, as he surveyed the architectural wonder—a site that had graced the cover of more than thirty design magazines since the "great reconstruction" five years ago: the New Face of Metro.

Huge Doric pillars rose up on either side of the high glass sliding doors, casting geometric shadows across the cement glade of the receiving circle. Above the pillars, reddish brick gave way to marble, dotted at irregular intervals with oval windows, tinted against what little light managed to slip over Beacon Hill to the flat. Metro's main building continued backward, behind the receiving circle, for close to a quarter-mile of brick and marble, like a petrified dragon wriggling up from the banks of the Charles.

Truly, Metro was a horrific sight. It was supposed to mix modern architectural style with the city's historic charm; instead, the great reconstruction was an obvious failure—obvious to everyone except the man behind the billion-dollar blunder: Douglas Stanton, Metro's administrator. Stanton had overseen the entire project, using money the hospital didn't have to chase a modernity the hospital didn't need.

Mike rubbed his eyes, finally forcing life back into his paralytic muscles. He started forward, watching as his reflection split in half with the *whish* of the electronic sliding glass doors.

The ER was hopping, stretchers and interns and nurses pirouetting across the shiny marble floor. The waiting area consisted of a huge semicircle lined with cushioned movie-theater-style chairs. The semicircle was bisected by a long teak admission desk, staffed by a half-dozen nurses.

Three ER interns and five fourth-year medical students roamed the open semicircle in search of the more seriously wounded. Those fortunate enough to have only minor problems were given numbered cards and ushered to the cushioned chairs. The major players were placed on stretchers and squired to curtained cubicles behind the admission desk, where the med students got a chance to practice under the interns' bleary eyes. Somewhere in the fray danced a resident or two, guiding the morbid cotillion from behind a clipboard and emergency X-ray contact sheets. As in every other ER in the country, the name of the game was turf: get the patients stable and then send them somewhere else—to surgery, radiology, oncology, anywhere—just get them out of the ER and into the damn elevators that led into the belly of the dragon. Or better yet, send them home, away, to the old-age homes or the rehab centers. The Word reverberated through the ER like a heart beat: turf, turf, *turf*. Get them the hell out of mine and into somebody else's.

Mike passed through the center of the ER, looking straight ahead. In his peripheral vision, he saw faces from the tragedy on Beacon Street, people he had helped patch up on the scene. The faces set his thoughts chugging backward, and he grimaced, tasting bile at the back of his throat.

Mike had spent three hours trying to put people back together—sometimes literally, as in the case of a woman whose left leg had been blown ten feet from her body—with nothing but his bare hands and his medical training. Trauma teams had arrived in droves as the morning progressed, but Mike had refused to step back, barely pausing to allow a paramedic to cover the burn from the motorcycle tire. By the time rescue workers had bagged the last tattered body, the count stood at thirty-six dead, nine critically wounded, and at least sixty more with minor injuries. It was the worst terrorist attack in Boston's history, and a sure candidate for the nation's top ten. *So much goddamn blood.* Splotchy cauliflowers had covered Mike from his neck to his knees, and even though he had changed his scrubs twice in the back of an ambulance on the scene, he still felt as if he were bathed in blood.

He passed the admission desk, catching concerned looks from the nurses. Mabel Cross, Althea Hemper, Laura Smith, three more he didn't recognize. Mabel reached out with dark fingers and grabbed his hand, giving it a warm squeeze. "You did what you could. You're a hero, Mike."

Maybe she had seen him on television, the distraught tears streaming down his cheeks. The camera had caught him on his way into the police station for the inevitable Q&A. The police interview had been exhausting, lasting for more than an hour; the investigating officers had wanted to know everything Mike remembered, from the seconds before the blast to the moment he stepped into ground zero. Mike had tried to be helpful, but his mind had already lost focus, and the details had begun to slip away.

After the Q&A, things had gotten a little strange. Mike had been moved to a soundproof room in the basement of the police station, where he was joined by a woman in a dark gray suit. She didn't look like any police detective he had ever seen before: tall, even statuesque, with long sable hair and almond eyes. Her origins were Chinese or Korean—but she was much taller than any Asian woman Mike had seen before.

She had introduced herself as Amber Chen, a federal

agent from Washington. She then began to ask Mike questions that made no sense to him: Had Andrew visited China in the past two years? What were Andrew's opinions on American foreign policy toward China? Did Andrew have any business relations with Chinese firms? Had Andrew accepted any campaign contributions from Chinese sources?

The questions had come completely from left field, and Mike had been unable to answer most of them. Andrew had never spoken to him about China. As far as Mike knew, Andrew had never been there, had no intention of going. As for campaign contributions—Mike guessed it was possible. But Andrew had never discussed the financing of his campaign.

The tall woman had thanked Mike, then excused herself. No explanations, no words of sympathy, just a curt nod as she shut the door on her way out. A strange end to a terrible morning.

Mike let go of Mabel's hand, then continued past the admission desk and squeezed into the elevator at the back of the ER. A few minutes later he stepped out into the inpatient ward, and he paused, letting the antiseptic air brush his cheeks. The sounds here were very different from those in the ER; the frantic, cacophonous battle against time and disease had been replaced by a controlled, pedagogical rhythm: Examine; Diagnose; Cure. Every step guided by immutable laws and hard-and-fast rules, the result of centuries of study and proven systems of belief.

That was the thing about medicine—and, more sweepingly, all of science. There were always hard-and-fast rules. Cause and effect, replicable results, clues that led to a logical, acceptable answer. Mike had always followed those rules. Even when Kari died, he had tried to stay rational, to accept that it was all part of the order of life. Commuter planes crashed. Men buried their wives.

And political figures got assassinated. Mike plodded down the main inpatient hallway, heading toward the unit's assignment desk. His small group of interns, residents, and fourth-year medical students had already gathered by the coffee machine, stethoscopes over their shoulders, charts in hand. Nine of them altogether, the same group that had been leading him through his patient list for three months.

As he approached, the senior third-year resident broke away from the coffee machine and ushered the rest into a small semicircle. Mike could see that the group was uncomfortable; his charges didn't know how to react, or whether they should react at all. Perhaps they were surprised that he had returned to work so soon after the accident. Perhaps they had expected him to take a week off, to work through the pain somewhere quiet, somewhere safe. What they didn't realize was that this was the safest place Mike knew: a controlled environment, guided by strict rules. Mike knew he wasn't ready to digest what had happened to Andrew.

"I know you've all heard what happened on Beacon Street," Mike finally said, keeping his voice as composed as possible. "I appreciate your concern. But I'd like to keep to my routine for the rest of the afternoon. So, Tascha, if you're ready, we'll begin rounds with Mr. Pomerand."

The senior resident stepped forward, quickly flipping her chart as she walked. Tall, lanky, with caramel skin and short, kinky hair, Tascha Field had two of the sharpest diagnostic eyes Mike had ever known. She had been his prize medical student five years ago, and he liked to think that he had something to do with her choice to pursue internal medicine over surgery. With her leading the rounds, he was certain that things would go smoothly. And, he hoped, smooth rounds would give him the time he needed to "think without thinking," as the therapists called it. He would let his psyche sift through the horrible morning—slowly, patiently, gently. He wasn't ready to face the tragedy head-on, so he would come at it from an indirect angle, like a jeweler chipping away toward a fragile core.

They headed into the first patient-care room, and Mike tried to keep his mind focused as Tascha presented the case. Sixty-two-year-old male, run-of-the-mill CHF—congestive heart failure—with pulmonary edema. Even the med students knew how to handle this one, and Mike carefully let himself drift. *Andrew's dead. Blown into a fine mist.*

"ACE inhibitor, digitalis, nitroglycerine," Tascha continued, listing the medicinal cocktail she was using to manage the CHF. Mike noticed a trickle of sweat running down from above his eyebrows, and he rubbed at his forehead with the back of his hand. The temperature in the hospital room seemed like a thousand degrees. He glanced at the med students and interns; none of them were sweating.

As Tascha led them to the next private-care room, Mike felt the beginnings of a piercing headache. Either his cold had suddenly taken a turn for the worse, or the morning's shock was affecting his body more than he'd realized. *Stay in control,* he told himself, *think without thinking.* He bit down on his lower lip, determined to finish out his rounds.

The next patient was as routine as the first. Fifty-six-year-old woman with a forty-pack-a-year smoking history, presenting with shortness of breath. Mike interrupted Tascha halfway into her description, asking one of the interns to make the diagnosis. After a quick glance at the chart, the intern nailed it: COPD, chronic obstructive pulmonary disease. Mike was about to ask the intern to get an arterial gas to check out the woman's oxygen and carbon dioxide levels, when a wave of nausea caused him to clamp his mouth shut. He swooned backward, catching himself on the shoulder of one of the med students. Tascha quickly moved toward him.

"Dr. Ballantine?"

"It's nothing. Just a bit of a head rush. Let's continue on."

Mike swallowed back the nausea, then asked the intern for the arterial gas. As the intern ran the numbers, Mike did an internal check. Nausea, fever, headache. Christ, he was a mess. Perhaps his plan wasn't working. Maybe work was somehow even *worse* than home. One more case, he decided. He would let Tascha handle his patient load for the next twenty-four hours. And there was no need for him in his virology lab. The lab hadn't produced anything worthwhile since his wife's death, anyway. Beginning around the time of Kari's funeral, he had come to find the quiet isolation of his basement lab claustrophobic, and he had shifted more of his time and attention to his medical practice. His research, once promising, had languished over the past two years. In fact, he had hardly set foot in his lab in more than a week.

With Andrew gone, it wouldn't be *his* lab much longer. The thought seemed trivial, almost hard-hearted, but it struck Mike nonetheless. Even though Andrew had never admitted it, there was no doubt in Mike's mind that his best friend had kept his unproductive lab afloat. The anonymous grants had begun to trickle in shortly after Kari's death, as if to soften the blow life had dealt Mike. Andrew couldn't have been more obvious if he had signed his name to the checks.

Mike clenched his jaw, struggling to stay alert as Tascha brought the group to the next private-care room. "Mr. Charles Acton," she began, pausing at the foot of the hospital bed as she studied the chart in her hands. "Fifty-four-year-old Vietnam vet with adult-onset diabetes. He presented this morning with loss of sensation in the lower and upper extremities and shortness of breath; he was hyperglycemic and acidotic."

Mike was barely able to keep his mind off his own worsening physical condition. "What's your diagnosis, Tascha?"

"Diabetic ketoacidosis, with peripheral neuropathy."

Mike nodded, scanning the patient with his eyes. Everything seemed in order. He was about to congratulate Tascha on her good work and dismiss rounds, when he noticed a tiny lick of motion from the patient's left cheek. Something dark and red flickered by, then disappeared.

Mike stepped forward for a better look. Charles Acton was thirty pounds overweight, with thick jowls and scruffy gray hair. Mike leaned close to the man's face and watched as a bloody tear dripped out of the corner of Acton's left eye, tracking across his cheek. There was another pearl of dark blood pooling under his right eyelid. Mike cleared his throat. "Mr. Acton? How are you feeling today?"

The only response was a muffled grunt, followed by two more bloody tears. Mike quickly turned back toward his group. "Tascha, we need to start him on IV amphotericin B immediately. Then we've got to get someone from surgery here right away to see if we can get rid of some necrotic tissue."

Tascha rushed to initiate the IV, while Mike started to explain his diagnosis to the rest of the group. Perhaps because of the adroit diagnosis, he felt a little better.

Maybe he could last a bit longer. "It's a classic rhino-cerebral mucomycosis—"

He stopped. He stared past the group of students, his eyes growing wide. There was a horse standing in the doorway of the private-care room.

"What the hell?"

The horse was charcoal gray, with a pitch-black mane and dark, piercing eyes. There was a streak of white above its right eyebrow. The creature took up most of the doorway, pawing at the tiled floor with its two front hooves.

Mike took a step forward, pushing past Tascha and the other members of his group. He couldn't believe what he was seeing. The horse was truly a magnificent animal; coat glistening, nostrils flared, muscles long and swelling. Mike had been near horses only twice before in his life. On a trip to Dallas, where Kari was born. And on a high school expedition to the headquarters of the mounted park police. He didn't know what to say or do to keep the animal calm, so he raised his hands, palms out, a gentle expression on his face.

The horse stepped backward out into the hallway. Mike slowly followed, his palms still out ahead of him. "Of all the crazy shit you see in this hospital," he whispered to Tascha as he left the room. "This takes the cake. And on today, of all days."

The horse turned in the narrow hallway, barely avoiding an EKG cart and a nurse carrying a pile of unused bedpans. Then the animal started forward, its hooves clicking against the hallway floor. Mike followed after it, beckoning nurses and other doctors out of the way with his hands. He didn't want to make any sudden noises—the animal was big enough to cause considerable damage, and no doubt it was scared out of its mind. What was it doing in the hospital? Mike guessed there was a park policeman lying on a stretcher in the ER, or some misguided polo player in the ICU.

The horse turned a corner at the end of the hall and continued toward the bank of elevators that led to the rest of the hospital. There were two nurses by the elevator doors, arguing about something in loud, heavily accented voices. Mike tried to shush them with his eyes, but they didn't seem to see him or the horse. One of the nurses hit the button for the elevator, and the steel doors whisked open. She was about to step inside when suddenly the horse charged forward.

"Look out!" Mike shouted, chasing after the animal. "Watch the hooves!"

The two nurses looked up just as the horse hurtled past them. The huge animal squeezed into the elevator, and the steel doors clanged shut.

Mike stopped, chest heaving, and stared at the closed elevator doors. He shook his head, shocked laughter rising in his throat. *Of all the crazy shit.* He noticed that the two nurses were staring at him. He smiled back at them.

"Guess he wanted a tour of the hospital."

Then he saw the expressions on their faces. They were looking at him as if he were insane. He turned, slowly, and saw his students coming toward him. Their faces were equally concerned. Tascha stepped forward, nervously clutching her clipboard. "Dr. Ballantine? Are you feeling all right?"

Mike's stomach constricted. He turned back toward the elevator. He could see his reflection in the shiny steel doors. He looked pale, almost anemic. He felt his knees quiver.

Nobody else had seen the horse. The huge animal had walked right past them, and they hadn't seen it. How was that possible?

"Dr. Ballantine?"

Mike swallowed. A hallucination. Brought on by the shock of Andrew's death, or his worsening cold. But it had seemed so real. The details had been so vivid, from the animal's flaring nostrils to its beautiful black mane. Still, there was no way the others could have missed it. Such a huge animal, wandering through a crowded hospital hallway.

Mike rubbed his eyes with the back of his hand, his cheeks burning. He was still sweating profusely, but at least the headache and nausea were gone. He decided his plan of keeping things routine was misguided. It was definitely time to go home. He turned back toward Tascha. "I think I need some rest. Tascha, I'd be grateful if you'd finish rounds for me."

Mike ignored the eyes that followed him as he headed toward his office on the other side of the inpatient ward. He was too startled to be embarrassed. He had heard patients describe hallucinations before; but he had never really believed the images could seem so real. All his senses told him that the horse was real—

"Dr. Ballantine? Could I speak to you for a moment?"

At first, Mike didn't recognize the voice. Then he saw Teri Pace rushing toward him from the direction of his office. Even so, it took him a moment to place the perky dervish whirling toward him. Then he remembered: she was one of his virology graduate students—the quiet, shy one who worked behind his desk in the basement lab. Except now, she didn't look quiet or shy. Locks of her short, auburn hair fluttered in every direction, like a demented halo. Her gray Harvard sweatshirt was disheveled and hanging slightly off her left shoulder, revealing a curve of porcelain skin. And she was wearing a skirt, even though it was forty degrees outside and getting colder by the hour. She looked as if she had spent the night in the basement—or maybe the week.

But her green eyes were on fire. In three years, Mike had never seen her so animated. *Wonderful.* This was just what he needed. He rubbed his jaw, wondering how he was going to get rid of her.

She skidded to a stop in front of him and brushed a lock of hair out of her eyes. "Dr. Ballantine, there's something I need to show you—"

"Teri, could it wait until tomorrow?"

"Well, yes, but I don't think—"

"Good. I'm not feeling well and I really need to get home."

The truth. Minus the horse and the fact that his best friend had just been murdered. Mike continued down the hallway, leaving the flustered young woman bobbing in his wake.

Teri Pace watched Dr. Ballantine until he had escaped around the next corner. *Gee, that went well.* She cursed herself for being such a wimp. She should have grabbed him by the arm and dragged him down to the Batcave. He would have forgiven her after she showed him her mouse.

Then again, Dr. Ballantine hadn't looked well. She wondered about the bandage across the back of his neck, whether it had anything to do with his curt behavior or his bloodshot, tired-looking eyes. She had the sudden worry that his cold had somehow turned into something worse; but then she remembered that she, too, had the slight cold, that everyone who had been in the Batcave had the same set of symptoms. She was sure there was something else going on. Perhaps it had to do with the commotion down in the ER; some sort of accident had occupied half the hospital staff all morning. It had taken

Teri close to two hours to get the requisition forms for her new mice through administration.

Finally, she shrugged, straightening her old college sweatshirt. She would be waiting for Dr. Ballantine in his office tomorrow morning. And this time, she would be wearing her best outfit, not a silly black skirt she had found at the bottom of her locker. She would dress for the occasion: the beginning of a whole new life.

As Teri straightened her skirt and headed toward the elevators, a tall, gaunt man watched her from the doorway of a vacant patient-care room. The man was wearing dark blue scrubs, and his face was partially covered by a sterile white surgical mask. But his eyes were clearly visible above the mask; piercing, velvety black oil spills, focused on Teri with ferocious intensity.

The gaunt man remained stock-still as Teri passed within a few feet of him. Then he slowly started after her, his brutal black eyes locked like fangs into the back of her skull.

CHAPTER FOUR

It was a quarter to five by the time Mike arrived back home, and his third-floor apartment looked as if it had been sprayed in liquid rust. The oversized church-style living room windows dribbled brown-orange light across the fading oriental carpet. There were three volcanic stacks of unopened mail on the low glass coffee table, and an avalanche of dirty laundry crept across the herringbone couch from Crate & Barrel. The small color television was blanketed by dust, and the rattan bookshelf was half empty, piles of books and magazines at its feet.

Mike stood in the doorway for a few minutes, his heavy wool jacket rolled up under his right arm. He could hear the cars rumbling by on Commonwealth Avenue, the late-afternoon euphony of young people traversing the quaint, tree-lined streets of the Back Bay. Mike and Kari had moved into the apartment a week after their wedding. It had been a geographic compromise, halfway between Metro and the town of Brookline, where Kari had worked for a small biomedical research firm. Mike had never felt entirely at home in the posh Back Bay, infested as it was with wealthy European college students, overpaid yuppies, and overextended retail clerks. But over the course of three years, the apartment had become a haven, if not a home.

Mike closed his eyes and imagined a vase of yellow tulips on the polished glass table, puffy embroidered pillows positioned amicably across the couch, a bowl of bright green Granny Smith apples on the ledge by the window. He breathed deep, pretending that Kari's mosaic of scents still lingered in the apartment. Her perfume, her shampoo, the lotion she used on her skin. A loose smile touched his lips, and he sighed, shaking his head. If only his memories of her could be as real as the hallucination he had experienced in the hospital.

A shiver moved through his shoulders as he thought about the horse. During the ride home from the hospital, he had convinced himself that the hallucination had been a product of his cold; his fever had spiked, and his mind had played a trick on him. A sort of waking dream, a product of dehydration and overheated brain cells. If the symptom recurred, he would begin to worry; but for now, he was determined to put the episode behind him.

He crossed the living room and entered the kitchen. The electric stove was barely recognizable under a clutter of unused Teflon pots and pans, and the small rosewood kitchen table peeked out from beneath a Rorschach test of empty Tupperware containers, discarded pizza boxes, and glossy magazines. Mike spotted his college lacrosse stick leaning against the refrigerator and took it with both hands, spinning an imaginary ball in the triangular net. The stick always helped him think. At the moment, he needed to think.

Mike had listened to news reports on the ride home; the rest of the city seemed as shocked by the assassination as he was. There was no discernible motive, and the method of the horrendous murder—some sort of unidentified high-powered explosive buried three feet under Beacon Street—had investigators baffled. How had the terrorists known the exact route and timing of the motorcade? And why kill a governor? *Why kill Andrew?*

Mike leaned back against the kitchen wall, his chin resting on top of the lacrosse stick. He didn't know whether to cry or break something. He had called Anne Kyle from his car phone, wanting to connect with her sorrow, to share what he was feeling. But she had been curt on the phone, obviously too broken up to talk. She had finally invited him to dinner at the mansion tomorrow night—an event that would most likely be unbearably awkward for him. In retrospect, the call had been a mistake. The only thing he had in common with Anne was Andrew. She was a rich, beautiful, accomplished socialite, and Mike was an ex-jock who had clawed his way to a medical career with the help of his best friend. Although Mike had grown up in Cambridge, he'd been born in South Boston, the son of a mechanic who had married above himself. Compared to Mike, Anne was royalty. Andrew's queen.

Andrew's widow.

Mike's entire body suddenly felt weak. Kari and Andrew, both in the space of two years. No wonder he was seeing horses—

"You're lucky your mother ain't alive. She'd swat your ass for this mess."

Flannery Ballantine was standing in the doorway to the kitchen, hands jammed into the oversized pockets of his forest green windbreaker. His burly form was slightly hunched forward, his craggy, unshaven face partially obscured by a pair of thick-lensed plastic glasses. Mike stared at him for a long time, wondering what to say. Finally, he found his voice.

"What the hell are you doing here? Run out of whiskey?"

"Damn fine way to greet your father, boy."

"And a damn fine father, too." Mike pushed past the

old man and into the living room. The heavy smell of cigar smoke licked at him as he slipped by, bringing back brief memories of childhood visits to South Boston—visits that always ended with Mike in tears, begging to go back across the river to Cambridge. "So how did you get inside? Break a window?"

Mike's father stopped cold at the words, jamming his hands deeper into his pockets. Mike hadn't meant his thoughts to come out like that, but he didn't have the energy to edit them.

It had happened when Mike was five years old. The memory was emblazoned in his mind, because in many ways it was the defining moment of his childhood. His parents had been three weeks past their seventh wedding anniversary, and his father had come home drunk, another late night at the machine shop working on other people's fancy cars. As usual, Mike's mother had lit into him about the alcohol and the late hour—but that night, Flannery did something that changed everything. He hauled back and hit her. Hard enough to send her right shoulder through a downstairs window.

A shattered pane, a row of stitches—and the next morning, the beginning of a separation that had lasted twenty years. When Alice Ballantine died of breast cancer at the early age of forty-three, Flannery had cried at the funeral; but Mike had sat two rows away, next to his cousins from the Cambridge side of the river. Flannery and Alice reconciled near the end of her life—but in Mike's mind, the Charles would always stand between the two remaining Ballantines.

"You got an old lock," Flannery grunted. "Any fool with a screwdriver can get inside."

Mike crossed to the window, his hands hard against the lacrosse stick. His father had broken in several times in the past—why was he even surprised to see him now?

He could see Flannery's gray pickup parked between two BMWs on the street three stories below. It was the same truck his father used to park outside the house in Cambridge when he came to visit. Once or twice a week, more in the later years, then every day when Alice got sick.

Mike hated that truck. It reminded him of the yelling and the drinking, of the sour smell of whiskey and vomit, and most of all, of the terror. Never knowing what words might set the old man off, what subtle utterance would send him into a fit of wild rage. Even though his father had never actually hit Mike during his drunken fits, the anger had gone deep, infecting him like a contagious viral disease. Mike knew the disease would always be inside him; even today, he had seen a hint of it in the police cruiser. *A fatherly gift I can never return.*

"So what are you doing here?" Mike asked, turning away from the window. His father was scanning the piles of unopened mail, the chaos reflected in his thick glasses.

"I'm here because of Andrew. Heard about it on the news. A tragedy. He was a good man."

"You didn't know him." Mike set the lacrosse stick against the rattan bookshelf and crossed his arms. He was too tired for this. He wanted to go into his bedroom, shut the door, and sleep for a dozen years. A part of him knew he was being unfair. He had held onto his hatred for nearly thirty years. But he certainly didn't have the strength for a reconciliation. Not today.

"He was your friend," Flannery responded. "And I know you're hurting. It isn't fair. You've lost too much already."

Mike looked at the man. The hunched shoulders, the barrel chest, the hands still jammed into the deep pockets of the windbreaker. He imagined his dad driving through the Back Bay in his pickup truck, a cigar clamped in his yellow teeth. On a mission of love. Of sentiment. *No, of duty.* The one thing an Irish father knew how to share was suffering. Mike felt his head growing hot again, and suddenly he wanted this day to end.

"You didn't know *her,* either. And you certainly don't know me. You don't have any reason to be here."

Mike kicked the lacrosse stick, sending it clattering across the floor. His father stared at him through his thick lenses, then turned and headed for the door. Mike felt a surge of regret. He had been too harsh. His father was not a bad man—just a bad father.

"Look," Mike began, "I appreciate your wanting to help. But you can't. Not now. I need to go through this alone."

Flannery paused with one hand on the knob, looking over his shoulder. Even from behind the glasses, his eyes were piercingly blue. "Boy, I know we ain't close. I know you hate me for something that happened a long, long time ago."

"Dad—"

"Just shut up and listen. I got only one more thing to say. I'm your father, no matter what you might think of me. That's it. That's why I came over here. When you need me, I'll be there. You just remember that."

The door clicked shut behind him. Mike stared at the cold wood for a long time. Then he shook his head and walked heavily toward his bedroom.

Four hours later, Mike came awake suddenly, a stabbing pain ricocheting behind his eyes. He was lying in a pool of sweat, and waves of nausea crashed through his stomach. He flung the covers off his body, bringing his hands up to his head. His hair was thick with sweat, sticking to the material of his pillow. Christ, he felt like he was going to die. His fever was raging, an inferno inside his veins. He clamped his palms over his eyes, breathing deeply, trying to slow his beating heart.

Then he heard a noise and froze. A sudden cough from the foot of his bed. He wasn't alone.

His first thought was of his father. But then a new sound touched his ears. Laughter. Unfriendly—even cruel; building toward a sinister crescendo. Mike swallowed, slowly moving his hands away from his eyes. Then he sat up.

There was a man standing at the foot of his bed. The man was tall and gaunt, of indeterminate age, wearing some sort of white smock buttoned at the throat. His facial features were decidedly Asian: narrow, almond-shaped, jet-black eyes, high cheekbones, small nose, angled jaw. There was a hand-shaped acne scar under his right eye, the mangled skin rippling upward as his lips opened and closed. His crude laughter echoed through the dark bedroom, reverberating in the pit of Mike's stomach. Mike dug his fingers into his sweat-soaked mattress.

"Who are you? What are you doing here?"

The gaunt man laughed even harder. He crossed his arms against his chest, then arched his head back, his Adam's apple leaping up and down beneath the skin of his thin neck. Mike felt himself starting to shake. "Who the hell are you?"

Suddenly, the gaunt man vanished. Mike's eyes went wide. His chest heaved and he leapt forward, his hands clawing at the empty air. He tumbled headfirst through the bedroom, crashing into the oak dresser that stood by the far wall. Kari's vanity mirror toppled off the top of the dresser, shattering against the floor. Mike struggled to his feet, his breath coming in short gasps. He whirled through the room, searching frantically for some sign of the gaunt man. But his visitor was gone. Vanished into thin air.

Mike's mind started to spin. It wasn't possible! The man had been real! Mike kicked the bedroom door open and raced through the rest of the apartment. He searched the kitchen, the bathroom, even the closets. He pulled open the front door and searched the hallway. Nothing.

He stumbled back into his apartment and collapsed onto the floor, his head resting against his cluttered couch. His nausea and headache were gone, but his body was weak, as if he had just run a marathon.

Another hallucination. Visual and auditory, lasting at least a minute, maybe more. So real. So vivid. Mike could still picture the gaunt man. He could still see the hand-shaped acne scar rippling before his eyes. He needed to get help. There was something wrong with him—something much worse than a bad cold.

CHAPTER FIVE

"Looks like a freakin' disco," Karl Bader mumbled, flicking a cigarette toward the pavement as he lumbered forward. "Enough colored lights to dress a Christmas tree."

Amber Chen remained two steps behind him, her hands hidden in the pockets of her heavy black overcoat. Bader was burly—huge—with a thick brown mustache and frizzy dark hair. Not exactly ugly, but far too bearish for Amber's tastes. Muscles that large came from weights, steroids, and vanity. The only thing working in Bader's favor was a suave, if clichéd, sense of style. He was wearing a tan trench coat, a blue tailored suit, and leather Armani loafers. Agent chic—but appropriate for the evening's business. He also wore a gun, strapped under his left arm. From the shape of the bulge and the way Bader carried himself, Amber guessed it was a Heckler & Koch HK4, chambered in 9mm Short. The heavy artillery went with Bader's macho exterior; it was a man's gun, brutal and inelegant.

"BPD, bomb squad, Fibbies from Andover," Bader said, listing with his fingers. "Probably some Secret Service, maybe even statehouse security. But the guy we're going to have to deal with is Dick Leary, BPD's chief of antiterrorism, and a real bastard. Territorial as hell. Hates outsiders—and I guess you're about as much outside as a person can get. So you better let me do most of the talking."

Amber listened to Bader's rough, almost guttural voice in silence, tugging her overcoat closed against the stiff November wind. Her silk shirt was too thin for the Boston weather, and her gray slacks felt transparent against the icy cold air. She could feel her nipples hardening beneath the soft material of her shirt, and she took special care to make sure the folds of her overcoat covered the high, round curves of her breasts. She knew how her looks affected men like Karl Bader; she wanted him subservient, not anesthetized. She had learned *that* lesson during her first year in the Company. Twice, she had watched investigations fizzle while her underlings wasted time and effort competing for her affections. She fastened the overcoat closed almost to her neck, concentrating on the scene up ahead.

Even though it was past two in the morning, Beacon Street was alive with motion. Pinwheels of red and blue light cavorted up and down the gutted blacktop, casting ghostly shadows high into the cloudless sky. A dozen police cars and bomb squad vans squatted unevenly by a police barricade at the bottom of the street, while no less than fifty officers—most in uniform—milled up and down the roped-off slope. Their flashlights danced like glowing daggers across overturned motorcycles, chunks of pavement, and chalk outlines of the dead and wounded. Amber followed the flashlights with her eyes, approximating ground zero from the damage, imagining the plume of flame and the rippling, concussive waves.

"Of course," Bader rattled on, as they approached the cars and vans, "it might help if you at least told *me* why you're here. I'm security cleared, and I'd have a better idea how to handle Leary if I knew something of your purpose."

Amber shifted her attention back to the man in front of her. She had to be firm, right from the beginning. Karl Bader was the director of the Boston field office, a competent agent but by no means an equal. Amber had met him for the first time two days ago; he had picked her up at the airport, wearing the same shoes and trench coat. He had greeted her with a wide smile and a thick hand on her shoulder. She had cringed inwardly at the contact, but her face had betrayed nothing, her body language already adjusting to the difference in culture.

"As far as Leary is concerned, I am simply a federal representative observing the investigation into Governor Kyle's assassination. You needn't tell him anything more." Amber knew that her clipped upper-class Hong Kong accent made her words sound even more severe. But she did not have time to play nice. She needed to get her point across before Bader made any judgments of his own.

"I understand. I just thought it might be easier—"

"Agent Bader, if you have any questions as to my authority, please direct them to your superior at Langley. Otherwise, I would appreciate it if you would follow protocol. I expect full cooperation from your office without question—and without confrontation. Is that understood?"

Amber watched the back of the man's neck turn red. In another situation, she might have chosen to be gentler, instilling loyalty with smiles and kind compliments. But the current circumstances called for a whip, not a smile. She was a woman—and a foreigner—placed in a position of authority, and it was important that she set the tone of their relationship. Bader's overfamiliarity was not conducive to her mission. Amber had to be in total control. In high-risk cases, that was how she felt most comfortable. "It is extremely important that the nature of my visit .remain on a need-to-know basis. I'm sorry if that makes your work as liaison more difficult."

Bader shrugged, his wide shoulders hunching forward. He did his best to keep the resentment out of his voice. "You're the boss. I certainly didn't mean to question your authority. We'll do it your way."

Amber nodded. He didn't like her, but he would follow her orders. Good enough. She had not traveled halfway around the world to make friends. She returned her concentration to the scene around them. They had already passed the first set of parked police cars and had begun to draw stares from the nearby uniformed officers. More accurately, *she* had begun to draw stares.

It was something Amber was used to. In her native Taiwan, it was her height that turned heads. At nearly six feet tall, her thin lines, long black hair, and unending legs only added to the visual effect. At the boarding school in Hong Kong where she had spent most of her teenage years, it had been her bearing and her family's wealth that had drawn stares: her fancy imported clothes, the limousines with the diplomatic plates, her entourage of servants, tutors, and bodyguards. At Oxford, it had been her model-sharp looks: the high angles of her face, her silken hair, the cinnamon glow of her skin.

In America, what drew attention was her race—and her sex. Combined with the badge she carried in the pocket of her overcoat, these things made her an anomaly, a sight difficult to ignore. She kept her head high as she strolled behind her massive escort, emanating calm and respect. She remembered her father's words, the traditional teachings of a thousand years: "Control of the outside begins on the inside."

"As if this night could get any worse," a harsh voice blared out from somewhere up ahead. "Now I got a couple of fuckin' spies crawling up my ass."

An overweight man in an ugly polyester suit separated himself from a group of uniformed officers and thundered forward. The man was short, perhaps five six, balding, with a big nose and thick, wet lips. His jaw was covered with stubble, and curly brown hairs peeked out from beneath the ill-fitting neckline of his rumpled white shirt. Two of the uniformed officers raced to keep up with him; one had a clipboard under his right arm, and the other, the younger-looking of the two, clutched a small metal briefcase with curly black wires running out the bottom. Amber recognized the briefcase as a GE Mark-7 satellite receiver. Unlimited range, easily portable, a favorite Pentagon toy. She wondered how many political officials were following the investigation as it progressed.

"Evening, Dick," Bader said, stopping short as Leary and his entourage approached. "I promise, we won't take up much of your time."

Leary parked himself a few feet away, his hands on his oversized hips. He looked like an angry bulldog, and Amber could smell his fetid breath even at that distance. Old tuna fish, mixed with something tangy; she fought the urge to cover her nose.

"You're damn straight you won't," Leary growled. "I got three hundred men under me, an investigation in full throttle, and the last thing I need is the CIA sticking its nose in here. When I got the call from headquarters that you guys would be here, I was surprised. I thought you only handled foreign shit."

Bader glanced at Amber, wondering whether she was

going to take the lead. She ignored his gaze, her hands clasped behind her back. She had worked alongside large operational task forces before, and there was always someone like Dick Leary involved. She had spent two years studying psychology at Oxford, and she could deconstruct the overweight bulldog just by looking at his face.

Leary was a walking insecurity complex; somewhere in his childhood lurked an abusive parent, an overbearing sibling, or a schoolyard bully, and his personality had never fully recovered from the blows to his ego. As the investigation progressed and slipped beyond his meager grasp, he'd grow more territorial, more angry, and especially more threatened. Day by day, he'd start to mimic the bully from his nightmares, trading swagger for ability, praying nobody noticed the difference.

Amber could already see it in his eyes; he wanted her to challenge him, he was daring her to turn his bark into a bite. It was almost funny, his nearly animal bravado. With one phone call, she knew, she could take his investigation away from him. But that would not serve her interests, only her ego. For now, she was content to remain on the outside, a silent spectator.

Finally, Bader deciphered her intention and raised his palms out ahead of him. "Dick, we're not here to get in your way—just to help out if you need us. This is Agent Chen, a terrorism expert from our overseas division. She's already introduced herself down at the BPD. She happened to be in town, so Washington has asked her to step in and observe."

Leary looked Amber up and down, a sneer spreading across his oversized lips. Maybe his investigation had already begun to break down. The stench of schoolyard bully was overpowering. "*Observe*. Yeah, I like that.

The CIA's sent a pair of spooks in to 'observe.' Just like the FBI's got a hundred agents coming down tomorrow to 'consult.' "

"I assure you," Amber said, quietly, "Agent Bader and I won't put any demands on your staff."

"Won't even know you're here, right?" Leary laughed, the sound unkind, even obnoxious. He cocked his head to the side, one eye locked on Amber's face. "So you just *happen* to be in town when the governor gets his ass blown to hell in front of a million people?"

"That's right. I flew into Logan two days ago." Amber thought about adding more—a cover story, a colorful lie—but decided it wasn't necessary. Leary did not rate the effort. Besides, she was in the CIA. She was supposed to be mysterious. "I'll be in town until next Friday, when I go to Washington for an antiterrorism conference at Langley."

Leary chewed his lower lip. Slowly, his eyes roamed down Amber's body. Her stomach crawled under his lascivious gaze, and she could feel his imagination tearing through her overcoat and silk shirt. She considered saying something, but instead chose to control her anger by focusing her own eyes on the fatty tissue surrounding Leary's head and neck. She counted seven pressure points she could reach with minimal effort—three that would cause permanent disability, four more that would cause immediate, painful death—before he finally finished surveying beneath her clothes.

"What are you, Chinese?"

She responded stiffly. "Taiwanese, yes. Is that important to you?"

"Hey, don't get fucking PC on me. I just ain't never seen an Oriental as tall as you. Spent two years stationed in Korea during my Army days, made me feel like a giant. But hell, you're nearly a six-footer. Didn't know they grew that big."

Ang mo, Amber thought. Red beard. Less benignly *Yang gui.* Foreign devil. She had been unfair to the schoolyard bullies of the Western world. Leary was a step below—loud, overbearing, without class. The stereotypical ugly American, a brother to the arrogant, vulgar men who walked the streets of Taipei and Hong Kong, ogling the women and trampling on a culture older than anything they knew. She took a deep breath, remembering another of her father's favorite sayings: "Pity the unenlightened. They do not deserve hate."

She smiled, coldly, then nodded toward the flashlights creeping up and down Beacon Street. "Have you found any remains of the explosive device?"

Leary ran a hand through what was left of his hair. "Not a fuckin' trace. And we're up to our ears in experts, so I don't expect you to pick out anything we've missed. Whatever it was, it's got us stumped."

Bader exhaled, his eyes exaggerating his surprise. It was obvious he was glad the conversation had moved to an area more comfortable than Amber's race. "You haven't found anything? Not a signature? A fragment?"

"Nothing at all. It doesn't make any sense. I've been in this business thirty years. When something this big goes off, there's always something left behind. There's no such thing as a perfect explosive."

Amber was no longer listening. She had already heard enough. "I'm sure something will turn up. In the meantime, you won't mind if we look around."

Without another word, she stepped past Leary and started up the hill toward ground zero. Bader and Leary followed a few feet behind, nattering on about explosive signatures. Inside, Amber knew the truth. Leary and his men could spend a year going over every inch of this hill, and they would find absolutely nothing. No trace of the explosive device. No hint of a detonation mechanism. Absolutely nothing.

Leary had been correct: it was no coincidence that Amber had flown from Beijing to Boston two days before Beacon Street turned into an asphalt inferno. And although she would never divulge the information to Leary, Bader, or anyone else involved with the investigation, she knew exactly what had caused the explosion. In fact, she knew more about the device than anyone alive.

She had spent the past three months studying the Valhalla XT-7 Experimental Oxygen Compression Mine. She had interviewed its inventors, watched video footage of the explosive in action, had even detonated one herself in a laboratory in Germany. In simple terms, the Valhalla was an incendiary device that used pure, compressed oxygen as its payload. The device was cylindrical, approximately three feet high and a foot in diameter, encased in an extremely flammable plastic derivative. The encasement was designed to be completely consumed upon detonation, along with every other trace of the detonation mechanism. The Valhalla left no signature, no evidence, and no clues. It was a highly effective, immensely powerful explosive, and there were only nine—now eight—in existence.

Three months ago, six of the nine Valhallas had been stolen off the back of a truck in Seoul, South Korea, by twelve members of an elite division of the Chinese military. It was nearly a perfect crime; the thieves had faked their own deaths and the destruction of their plunder in a spectacular explosion shortly after the heist. But a well-placed informant had tipped Amber off to the ruse, and she had secretly given chase, using a combination of high-tech toys and a handful of discreet operatives under her command.

She had tracked the Valhallas over the border into North Korea, then up into mainland China. She had followed them through nine cities and across two thousand miles of terrain. She had watched them loaded onto a freighter in Shanghai and had tracked them by satellite across the Pacific Ocean. Then, two days ago, she had lost the trail. And that single slip had been enough.

When she had heard about the assassination from her hotel room in the Back Bay, she had known immediately: one of the Valhallas had been used to murder the governor of Massachusetts.

Amber stepped over the charred remains of a motorcycle tire. The scent of burned flesh still hung in the air, and she thought of the governor's spirit rising up out of his destroyed limousine. Why? Why kill a newly elected governor in such a public fashion? Why Andrew Kyle, a man with no known ties to China, with no documented policy on Chinese foreign relations, with hardly any influence on U.S. foreign policy?

The murder made absolutely no sense. And, more significantly, it did not correspond to the Chinese Way. The fiery explosion was too showy, too ostentatious. China's military "black" forces were masters of subtlety and patience. *Dao,* the Way, was more than a tradition; it was a revered guide to action and to life. If the Chinese were behind the assassination, there had to be a good reason. It was up to Amber to find out what that reason was.

Her hands turned into fists as she hardened her resolve. She had never failed at anything in her life. Failure meant dishonor, loss of face. To an *ang mo,* that was a meaningless concept. To Amber, it meant everything. She quickened her pace, pretending that she could not hear Leary's coarse whisper from a few feet behind.

"Good-lookin' spook," the *ang mo* sneered. "But I wouldn't trust her, Bader. Problem with Orientals, you can never tell what they're thinking."

At that moment, Amber was thinking about a dead governor and a trail that led deep into the heart of mainland China.

CHAPTER SIX

Liu Deng had never felt pure terror before. He could see his own naked body reflected in the curved Plexiglas, his flesh glistening because of the conductive jelly they had rubbed over his tan skin. His sinewy muscles contorted as he fought against the leather straps, but his efforts were useless; the leather bit deep into his wrists and ankles, pinning him against the cold steel chair. He could feel the conductive jelly pooling under his nude thighs and buttocks, and his terror swelled, piercing his thoughts like wild talons. *Have mercy, ancestors! Please have mercy!*

But Liu knew his ancestors had deserted him. Miserable, he shifted his head forward, staring down at the strange jungle of copper wires beneath his bare feet. The frayed ends of the wires tickled his soles, and he curled his toes inward, trying to push the wires away. Above him an identical tangle of copper wires hung from a circular plate a few inches above his shaved head.

Liu trembled, dull moans tumbling from between his lips. He didn't understand what was going on, and that made it much worse. He was nude, glistening, strapped to a chair with naked wires above and below him. The chair and wires were encased in a transparent cylinder, which in turn was suspended in the center of a huge steel chamber. The chamber was ringed by pitch-black windows. The windows stared at Liu like black eyes, reflecting the terror in his soul.

Worse still, Liu knew who watched him from behind one of the black windows. Gui Yisheng, the Devil Doctor. The demon who came late at night and stole children from their mother's breast, the old beast who tore off men's ears to get at their brains. In the village where Liu had grown up, Gui Yisheng was a tale parents used to scare disobedient children; but he was also real, flesh and blood, and this was his laboratory. Liu knew it was true because he had seen it from the back of the armored truck. The laboratory was unmistakable, described in half a dozen fables and campfire stories. Liu had known the minute he had seen the monstrous yin-yang circle dug into the foot of the Great Mountain like an angry burr; they had brought him to Mogue De Ghong, the Heel of the Demon. And now Gui Yisheng was going to rip off his ears and eat his brain.

Liu's mouth opened at the thought, and a feral scream echoed inside the cylinder. Four days ago, Liu had been working his uncle's portion of the Xinshan Collective Peasant Farm, pushing a heavy wooden hoe through freshly irrigated mud. Then he had heard the helicopters, and the thunder of the trucks tearing down the dirt road that ran parallel to the farm. At first, Liu had not been afraid; the military had a substantial presence in the nearby city of Xining, and they often sent units far into the peasant villages that squatted by the banks of the Yellow River. But then Liu had heard the shouts of his fellow farmers as the uniformed men rounded them up. Liu could not believe what was happening; these men had committed no crimes. They were not students, they were not political, they were certainly not radicals. Most of them could not even read. But the soldiers had dragged them all to the armored trucks, and the long journey into terror had begun.

For four days, the trucks had moved eastward, scraping the southern edge of the Gobi, then jagging upward into the living mountains that housed the sky. Liu and the other peasant farmers had spent the time talking in quiet voices, sharing stories of the hardships of the past, of the fifties and sixties. Liu was too young to remember the camps and reeducation exercises of Mao's early years, but he had heard the stories from his uncle, and he knew his father and mother had died deep in the East, a year after he was born. When he saw the giant yin and yang and the Heel of the Demon, he realized that his own destiny was something much worse than Mao's death camps.

As the armored truck approached the Great Mountain, the yin-yang circle had split in half, revealing a long gaping throat. Liu had gone numb with fear as the armored trucks descended into near darkness. But the nightmare had only gotten worse. Liu had been dragged out of the truck by more soldiers and taken to a tiny steel cell in the deep belly of the mountain.

An hour later, he had been visited by the monster himself. Short, stocky, bald, toothless, as old as the Great Mountain herself, Gui Yisheng had come dressed in his trademark Mao-style white smock, buttoned tight against his wrinkled rooster's throat. The sleeves of his smock had hung uselessly at his sides; as the myth told it, Gui Yisheng had lost both arms trying to pluck the ears from a white tiger. When the tiger had bit off his arms, he had used his feet instead, killing the tiger with two blows. Then he had sucked up the animal's brain with his toothless mouth.

But Gui Yisheng hadn't come for Liu's brain. Instead, he had come to poke and prod Liu's body. A second doctor in a matching white smock had stuck Liu with many needles, taking vials of his blood and studying the color and thickness of his urine. Then a strange ritual had begun. The second doctor had shown Liu a series of colorful flash cards with pictures of animals on them. The animals all had names, and Liu had been forced to memorize the names, matching them to the pictures on the cards. Lin-Lin the potbellied pig. Yoon the wolf. Ching the green monkey. Whenever Liu had missed a card, two thick-necked soldiers entered the cell and beat him with a heavy rubber truncheon. Once, when Liu missed two of the flash cards in a row, the men beat him so badly he lost consciousness. But when he awoke, the second doctor was back again with the flash cards, and the strange game had continued. All the while, Gui Yisheng had watched in silence, his toothless mouth half-open.

Twelve hours ago, Liu had played the game for the last time. He had gotten all the names correct, and Gui Yisheng had smiled, his mouth a disturbing moon lying on its side. Then the thick-necked soldiers had returned—but this time, instead of the rubber truncheons, they brought with them electric shears and a bucket of thick, transparent liquid.

One soldier had ripped away Liu's clothes as the other went to work on his hair with the electric shears. Naked and bald, he had been forced to spread the jelly over his skin. When he had asked why, Gui Yisheng told him that the conductive jelly was food for his *ling hwun*, his life spirit. Without the jelly, his spirit would become an *e gui*, a hungry ghost, impossible to control. Liu had not understood, but he had spread the jelly on his skin.

Then Gui Yisheng had brought him to the steel chair

and the Plexiglas cylinder. The soldiers had strapped him in, and the terror had taken hold.

Alone in the vast chamber, Liu Deng stared at his own reflection and bemoaned his terrible fate. He knew that at any moment, Gui Yisheng would come for his brain. Perhaps the strange copper wires beneath his feet would somehow help the old monster tear off Liu's ears—

Liu stopped abruptly halfway into the thought, as a new sound filled the chamber: a low hum, like a dozen electric fans spinning simultaneously. The hum grew louder, rising up from deep within the Great Mountain herself. Liu opened his mouth to scream.

Suddenly, the copper wires beneath Liu's feet spasmed upward, and there was a magnificent burst of blinding white light. The entire chamber shook as one million volts of pure electricity poured through Liu's glistening body.

A second later, all that remained of Liu Deng was a Plexiglas cylinder full of red-gray vapor.

CHAPTER SEVEN

Mike spent the last few hours before dawn pacing the hardwood floors of his apartment, poking at the walls and ceiling with his lacrosse stick. His decision to seek medical help as soon as the sun came up went against something deep and vital in his psyche; beyond his Irish stoicism, he had a doctor's fear of doctors, a logical apprehension induced by years of watching a stream of sick and dying patients course through the halls of Metro's ICU. He knew his fears were hypocritical; when someone else showed acute symptoms, he was the first to point the way to the nearest hospital ER. But where his own body was concerned, he followed a different Rule: procrastinate. Ignore and dismiss symptoms as long as humanly possible. As foolish as the policy seemed, Mike knew his attitude was based on a secret shared by doctors around the world: the best way to avoid finding something wrong was to resist the urge to look in the first place.

But this time, Mike knew he had no choice. Two hallucinations in the space of twelve hours was something he simply could not ignore. As much as he disliked the idea of checking into the hospital for a slew of diagnostic tests, he was more afraid of the laughing gaunt man and the disappearing horse. Something unusual was happening to him—something he simply did not understand.

That, in itself, was worse than the fear or the physical discomfort surrounding the strange visions. Mike was a scientist—a staunch and stubborn skeptic concerning all things beyond the rule of scientific reason. Many times in his career, he had been faced with situations that had seemed inexplicable. Patients dying without warning, other patients recovering from the edge of death, without the help of chemicals, surgery, or medical machines. But beneath the surface, there had always been explanations, from undiagnosed ailments to exaggerated symptoms. Mike had never been willing to take the unexplained at face value; he had always struggled to seek out the logic and the science, no matter what the cost.

Even when Kari had died, he had been unable to think of her passing in nonscientific terms. Andrew, among others, had tried to comfort him with religious talk of an afterlife, of heaven beyond death. But even for Kari, Mike had found it impossible to truly believe. As much as he had wished for the comfort of blind faith, his very nature had made it unattainable. Every inch of his world had to be grounded in scientific fact.

And his recent hallucinations were no exception. There had to be a rational explanation. The key was to know where to look. And when it was time to start looking.

His decision firm, Mike clutched the lacrosse stick in detached silence, waiting for the first trickle of morning sunlight.

Almost nine hours later, Mike lowered himself into a high-backed leather chair, rubbing his right arm. His eyes flickered across the oversized hexagonal room, and he marveled at the quiet decor and the sense of ordered calm.

The seventh-floor office was an oasis perched high above the bustle of the rest of the hospital. A thick oriental rug covered most of the tiled porcelain floor, and the standard hospital walls were obscured by tall mahogany shelves. A huge oval window overlooked the hospital's receiving circle, but the tinted glass was thick enough to shield the tranquil sanctuary from the sirens far below.

The leather chair exhaled as it accepted Mike's weight. He continued massaging the skin of his right arm, avoiding the patchwork of Band-Aids that ran from his elbow to his wrist. He had been poked and prodded so many times since leaving his apartment, he felt like a human pincushion. The Band-Aids served as a reminder of his long and awful day.

Beginning sharply at eight A.M. he had subjected himself to a full medical workup, including consults with more than a dozen of Metro's top experts. At first, he had picked his consults carefully, in the feeble hope of keeping his condition moderately quiet; but by the end of the day he had become desperate for answers, calling on colleagues from nearly every department. Sadly, the thicker Mike's chart grew, the more confusing his condition became. The hexagon on the seventh floor was his last hope for a simple answer, and a fitting place to finish his search, considering his exceedingly frazzled state of mind.

On the huge mahogany desk in front of his chair, a bright green, high-rimmed fishing hat, bristling with colorful bass tackles and beveled hooks, sat jauntily atop a marble bust of Freud. Next to the bust was a framed picture of a sailboat, the S.S. *Neurosis,* parked in Boston harbor. A few years ago, Mike and Kari had spent a stormy afternoon vomiting over the brass railing of the *Neurosis,* and just the sight of the picture made Mike queasy. He looked past the picture to the other side of the desk, and a smile touched his lips.

Arthur Feinstein was Metro's chairman of psychiatry, and one of the leading psychiatrists in the country. He'd been a classmate of Mike's in medical school, and they had shared a bunk bed during their third-year surgery rotation. Arthur was a certified genius, miles above Mike in the hospital hierarchy, but Mike trusted him as a friend and respected him as a professional. Still, the chief psychiatrist's appearance always caught him off guard.

Arthur was the most spherical human Mike had ever met. Draped in his mammoth white doctor's coat and matching oxford shirt, he looked like a freakishly large snowball. He weighed more than three hundred pounds, and his head was a jellied ellipse, mounted atop rolls of pasty white fat. At the moment, his round face was buried in Mike's medical chart, his saucer-shaped blue eyes darting through the numbers and opinions at a pace incongruous with his gargantuan exterior.

Mike had gone through the chart a dozen times on his way to Arthur's office, but he wanted to reserve comment until the psychiatrist had surveyed the results himself. A full minute ticked by in silence, when finally Arthur's thick hands slapped the chart down against his desk.

"I'll take the sirloin and a side of mashed potatoes."

Mike laughed, feeling some of the tension run out of him. Despite Arthur's appearance—or perhaps because of it—the psychiatrist had a way of putting others at ease. Mike guessed it was part of the reason Arthur had risen so far in his profession.

"Maybe I could conjure something up for you," Mike responded. "You sure you don't want horsemeat? It's my specialty."

"Seriously, Mike. Your insides look okay to me. But guts ain't my thing. I don't touch anything below the neck. You can ask Samantha."

Samantha was Arthur's ex-wife. She had dumped the psychiatrist after having a series of adulterous affairs, leaving Arthur more relieved than upset. Mike had always suspected that his obese friend was actually a repressed homosexual—another incongruity in a man who was an expert at extracting secrets from his patients' symptoms.

"You're the authority on insides," Arthur continued. "Anything jump out at you?"

"I've gone through my chart with a fine-toothed comb. No signs of kidney or liver trouble. No signs of any hallucinogenic substances in my blood or urine. And of course no drugs and no alcohol."

"What about your cold symptoms? I see there's a fairly high serum antihemagglutinin count in your values. Wouldn't that be compatible with a fierce bout of influenza?"

Mike shrugged. Hemagglutinin was a protein found on the surface of a number of viruses, most notably influenza A and B. Hemagglutinin was responsible for the virus's ability to attach itself to a healthy cell, so the presence of a high number of antihemagglutinin antibodies suggested the presence of a robust viral infection. But Mike's other symptoms were weak; if he had the flu, it was certainly not a severe strain. His guess was that his immune system was simply overreacting to a mild infection, and he doubted that influenza was the sole cause of his hallucinations. But that left him back where he'd started, without answers.

"I've had the flu before. And I've never experienced anything like this."

"But you've also got a bandage on the back of your

neck from a burning motorcycle tire. Your body has gone through hell in the past twenty-four hours."

Mike touched the gauze bandage with his fingers. The burn still stung, but he had already learned to ignore it. Still, Arthur was right: it was possible the strain on his body had exacerbated his flu. But his head cold didn't *feel* like severe influenza. And although he had experienced fever, headaches, and nausea directly before his hallucinations, the symptoms had been short-lived. There had to be something else going on, something worse.

"I guess it's a possibility. But for now, let's shelve influenza."

"And turn to matters above the neck," Arthur finished for him. He took off his glasses and began rubbing the lenses with a white sleeve. "Sensory hallucinations, both visual and auditory. First, the horse in the hospital. Vivid, extreme, causing marked anxiety as you watched the animal move through the crowded hallway. And then last night, what we call a hypnagogic vision, one that arises before or during sleep. The laughing gaunt man. Asian, you said."

"Correct." It felt so strange, talking about it to another scientist. Mike wanted to blush, even though he knew that an unexplained vision was no less relevant a symptom than a spiked blood pressure reading or a high white-cell count.

"Well," Arthur continued, "as you know, hallucinations arise when brain metabolism is somehow altered from its normal level. After we rule out the more common physiological causes—liver failure, renal failure, high fever, drugs, and alcohol—we're left with a few interesting psychiatric conditions. But from what you've told me, one screams out much louder than the rest."

Mike nodded. After his hallucination the night before,

he had spent two hours reading through his old med school textbooks. He had a pretty good idea what Arthur was going to say. But he was hoping for something else, a burst of genius, an angle he hadn't thought of. At the very least, he wanted to hear it from the expert.

"The most likely candidate is PTSD," Arthur said, putting his glasses back over his nose. Mike exhaled, looking down. No great revelation; Arthur had responded exactly as Mike had expected. Post-traumatic stress disorder.

"I'm sure my diagnosis comes as no surprise to you," Arthur said. Mike nodded; he had worked on patients with PTSD many times in his career, and was familiar with the broad strokes of the syndrome. He had even spent a month in a VA hospital during his residency, and he had seen firsthand what trauma could do to the human brain.

"Considering what happened to your friend," Arthur continued, "and the memories the tragedy opened up for you—of Kari, and perhaps even of your mother—I'd say PTSD is a solid guess. Your friend's murder was a hell of a shock to your system. And you had your first hallucination about six hours later."

"True. But as you alluded, I've been through tragedy before."

"That's just my point. These things build up inside you. They cause tiny fault lines in your mind. Sometimes, something happens to set off a little earthquake. You see a dress your wife used to wear, and you break down in tears. Or you smell your mother's perfume, and you can't sleep for a week."

Mike was amazed at Arthur's choice of examples. He had experienced both "little earthquakes" numerous times. Arthur heaved his huge body forward in his seat, his heavy elbows bumping down against his desk. "And sometimes, something sets off the Big One. Your friend dies in a horrible way, and your mind can't deal. PTSD. Agitation, fever, headaches, exhaustion, and hallucinations. These are all textbook symptoms."

Mike knew Arthur spoke the truth. But still, he was not convinced. Like many internists, he had always thought of PTSD as something of a "tabloid" disease. A trendy, useful label for a variety of misunderstood symptoms, just flashy enough for the popular journals and magazines. A "disease" of Vietnam vets who murdered their wives and of homeless men who chased joggers through New York's Central Park. Mike was an educated man, a doctor; stress and tragedy were nothing new to him. Even though he had lost his wife and his best friend, his mind should have been able to cope.

"So you think I'm cracking up."

"Not cracking up. Reacting. It's a physiological process, Mike, like renal failure or diabetic shock. Your brain is trying to understand an impossible situation, and the stress has altered your cerebral metabolism."

"But why a horse?" Mike asked, frustrated. "Why the Asian man? I feel like I'm going insane."

"You have to understand: these things you've seen, these hallucinations—they don't have to *mean* anything. As I tell my Freudian colleagues, sometimes a dream is just a dream. The images come from somewhere in your memory, and your brain spits them out because they're available. Don't focus on the images, focus on the cause. The tragedy itself, the losses you've endured. There isn't any cure for PTSD, no drugs I can give you or therapy that truly works. But I promise, when you come to terms with your underlying pain, the PTSD will fade."

Arthur was halfway out of his seat, his blue eyes focused intensely on Mike's face. Mike suddenly felt uncomfortable. He knew where Arthur was heading.

Arthur was a psychiatrist, and he wanted Mike to open up—to show his scarred insides. And maybe he was right; maybe that's all it would take. A fountain of tears in a psychiatrist's office.

But for Mike, it would never be that easy. Mike suddenly thought of his father, clutching the wheel of his gray pickup truck. He remembered his father's words from the night before: "When you need me, I'll be there." The irony was so thick Mike wanted to vomit. It was true, his father was there—in the walls that surrounded Mike's emotions, in the insurmountable barriers that kept the anger and everything else in check. Mike wasn't a psychiatrist; but, as Andrew had once said, it didn't take a psychiatrist to figure this out. Mike's fear of the anger and violence that had wrecked his parents' marriage had forced him to build a shell around his feelings. The shell had helped him survive the deaths of his mother and wife—but now it had started to fracture. He was still the product of that broken window, nearly thirty years ago. An Irish father. An equally Irish son. He broke away from Arthur's gaze.

"So there's nothing I can do but wait, and hope the hallucinations don't come back?"

"Not wait," Arthur said, breaking off his intense gaze, his hands cupped over his bulbous stomach. "*Mourn.* Your friend died in front of you. You have to gently accept your loss. Is there a planned funeral service?"

"Tomorrow morning," Mike said, quietly. The thought of Andrew's funeral made his throat heavy. Then he remembered the dinner only hours away. He pictured himself and Anne Kyle sitting in that great big mansion on the Hill, talking about his dead friend. He swallowed, closing his eyes. At that moment, he missed Kari more than ever before. He wanted to hold her hand, to borrow her strength. He took a deep breath, then rose from the leather chair. He had gotten as much as he could from the doctors at Metro. No simple answers, no clear explanations. He tried not to sound as disheartened as he felt. "Thank you, Arthur. I appreciate your help. And I'm sure you understand why it's important for me to keep this quiet. Stanton would love to get something like this on my record."

Arthur snorted. Douglas Stanton, the hospital administrator, was the bane of most of Metro's staff. At the time of the "great reconstruction," he had cut salaries and staff bonuses across the board, while spending millions on tinted glass and tiled floors. "Douglas Stanton is a prick. If it were up to him, there wouldn't be any doctors at Metro, just lawyers and cashiers."

It was common knowledge that Stanton saw doctors as little more than exchangeable, expendable gears in the Metro machine. It was especially true in Mike's case; ever since he had clashed with the administrator during the reconstruction—over a plan to trade an entire floor of ICU patient care rooms for a new surgical ward— Stanton had been searching for ways to knock him down a few pegs. It was only because of Andrew's influence with the hospital board that Stanton had failed to do any real damage.

"Anyway, thanks for the consult. I'll name my next vision after you." Mike smiled, shook Arthur's hand, then headed toward the door. He could hear Arthur's chair groaning behind him, as the huge psychiatrist teetered dramatically backward, raising his heavy legs to his desk.

"One more thing, Mike. The simple truth is, even without PTSD, experiencing hallucinations after the death of a loved one is not uncommon. In fact, it's a symbol of the most common reaction to death: denial."

Mike paused at the door. He wanted to believe Arthur, but something inside him resisted. "So you've really seen this sort of thing before?"

Arthur offered him a comforting smile. "More times than you can imagine. And they aren't all ghost stories. I'm talking about real, educated people seeing loved ones one last time. It may not make any scientific sense—but it's a real phenomenon. The only surprise here is that, instead of Andrew or Kari, you saw a horse."

Mike wasn't comforted by Arthur's words. He didn't believe in ghost stories. He was a scientist—and he knew that somehow, somewhere, there had to be a scientific explanation.

Ten minutes later, Mike's shoes clicked against ugly green tile as he stepped out of the over-air-conditioned elevator. Part of him was surprised to find himself in the cinder-block basement; after Kari's death, his laboratory had lost much of its appeal, and he had refocused his life on the day-to-day routine of patients and medical students. It had not been a small decision: at the time, his research had been considered groundbreaking. Twice, he had been nominated for major scientific prizes—and if his work had continued uninterrupted, there was no telling how far he could have gone. But when Kari died, everything changed. Mike had found it impossible to lock himself in the lab for the long hours necessary to continue his work at such a high level.

Still, after his conversation with Arthur, he had felt the old urge rising up—a desire to chase something solid, to surround himself with science and its hard-and-fast rules. He had taken the elevator straight from the fifth floor, purposefully avoiding the inpatient ward and the area around his office on the third floor. After his performance the day before and his barrage of medical tests, he had no doubt that he was the highlight of the hospital rumor mill, and he wasn't ready to face the prying eyes or sympathetic ears.

He walked through the deserted lab, listening to the hum of the Biosafety Level One ventilation cabinet. Thankfully, there was no sign of Mike's graduate students, nobody to interrupt him as he searched for refuge. His eyes danced across the beakers, test-tube racks, and pewter sinks, and the nervous energy drained from his body. Maybe he had been wrong to forsake his lab research for so long. Maybe he should have fought back against the claustrophobia and loneliness. In a strange way, *this* was sanctuary. As far away from Arthur's hazy ghost stories and unexplainable symptoms as one could go. This was the realm of pure, unadulterated science.

Mike headed directly to the white-tiled work area a few yards to the left of his mahogany desk. The cluttered countertop was exactly as he had left it, a montage of gel plates, petri dishes, and test tubes. Everything he needed to run the quick and dirty experiment he had in mind.

He reached the counter and began organizing the items he would need. He found his culture plate in the small refrigerator built into a shelf beneath the counter, along with a marked solution of protein antibodies and a fresh gel plate. He also retrieved a thin, papery nitrocellulose membrane and a series of variously sized pipettes.

As he worked, he forced his mind to focus on the instruments and the science behind them. It was an experiment he had run a dozen times before, but he pretended it was a virgin experience, fantasizing that it would somehow push his research back into the limelight. He knew it was a foolish fantasy, but he indulged himself anyway.

The most promising angle of his research into cytotoxic T cells concerned a discovery he had made three years ago, just days before Kari's death: he had isolated by flow cytometry and gradient centrifugation a population of T cells he'd never seen mentioned in any textbook or journal article. If he could prove that these cells played some significant role in the human immune response to disease, he might breathe new life into his research.

That goal in mind, he opened up his refrigerated culture and used a pipette to transfer a small quantity of his cells into a lysis buffer to solubilize the cellular proteins. Aliquots were placed on a polyasylamide gel and electrophoresis was carried out to size fractionate the cellular proteins. He would next transfer the proteins onto a nitrocellulose membrane. The proteins in the membrane would be stained with dyes and separate gels would be incubated with antibodes to specific proteins with known cell surface receptors. That would allow him to determine the similarities between his new population of T cells, and the already documented populations from which the protein antibodies were derived.

As he worked, he lost track of time and place. The hum of the ventilation cabinet filled his skull, and his fingers seemed to be working of their own accord, following the rote procedures embedded deep in their muscular memory. The minutes ticked by as Mike floated deeper and deeper into mental serenity.

He was in the process of putting the nitrocellulose membrane into a phosphorimaging machine attached to a Dell laptop computer, when he felt the hairs on the back of his neck suddenly rise, as if touched by a cool breath. He turned, looking around the lab. Of course, no one was there. Still, Mike couldn't shake the strange sensation that he was being watched. He shook his head, telling himself it was the old claustrophobia coming back, and returned his attention to the membrane and the laptop computer. But the strange feeling wouldn't go away. It multiplied, became something incessant, unavoidable—an almost rhythmic sensation of something crawling up and down the back of his neck.

Finally, Mike slammed down the membrane and whirled around. The lab was gone. In its place was a plume of bright orange flame. Mike screamed, crashing back against the cabinet. The plume of flame rolled toward him, and he could feel the heat pressing into his face, stealing the breath out of his lungs. He tried to leap out of the way, but he was gripped by a paralyzing terror, the likes of which he had never felt before.

Suddenly, the plume was on top of him, and his skin caught fire. The pain was immense, searing, driving across every inch of his body. He felt his eyelids tear away and his eyeballs swell and rupture. The hair on his chest erupted outward in flame as the skin peeled off his muscles, revealing his rib cage and the organs underneath. His lungs sizzled and suddenly split open, the oxygen inside catching fire in a burst of bright red. His throat closed and his mouth opened and his tongue melted against his teeth. Then the flames touched his groin. The pain ricocheted up into his brain, and he dropped to his knees, his screams becoming guttural, feral.

And then something happened. It was as if he'd been cloven in half, part of him separating from his burning, blazing body and rising toward the ceiling of the lab. He saw himself crouching on the floor, the licks of flame eating away his skin, his hair, his organs. He saw the plume of fire reach his head; he saw the hair and skin ignite; he saw his skull crack open under the intense heat and his brains burst upward in a geyser of steam. Then he watched as his body collapsed against the floor. He watched as the last tremors gripped him beneath the flames. He watched himself die.

And suddenly, it was over. He was lying on the floor of the lab, his body still jerking spasmodically. He gasped, his eyes wide, and slapped at his skin. But the fire was gone. The pain had vanished. He scrambled to his feet, his heart pounding furiously. *My God, my God, my God!* He leaned forward and started to retch, but nothing came out. *My God, my God!*

Slowly, the tremors stopped. He leaned against the cabinet, staring down at his half-finished experiment, watching the beads of sweat roll off his face and splash against the cabinet surface. *What* had just happened? A seizure? Some sort of epilepsy? It was certainly more than another hallucination. A hallucination couldn't burn you, could it?

Mike's hands trembled as he leaned against the cabinet. He knew it was futile to try to work more on his experiment, but he didn't know what else to do. He was unsettled now, much worse than he had felt after leaving Arthur's office. Time and place rushed at him, and he closed his eyes, trying to control his thoughts. But the effort was useless. He thought about Andrew, about what Arthur had told him, and about Kari. He thought about the disembodied hand lying in the black crater on Beacon Street. He thought about the plume of flame that had ripped at his flesh, and the plume of flame that had killed his best friend. One real, one in his head, both equally horrifying.

Then he thought about the night ahead. In a few hours, he would meet Anne Kyle at Andrew's mansion. And everything would get churned up, all over again.

He swallowed, opening his eyes. He felt lost, terrified, helpless. What was he supposed to do? How could he fight something he couldn't understand?

What the hell was wrong with him?

Four floors above the laboratory, Teri Pace tapped her glossy black heels against the oak leg of a scuffed antique desk as she nervously scribbled a note on the top page of Mike Ballantine's prescription pad. Sitting in the sparsely appointed office sent excited chills down the skin of her back. She periodically glanced at the closed door as she wrote, half expecting the solid wood to somehow manifest his face, like a charmed tree from *The Wizard of Oz*. Even though it was now obvious he had taken the day off, Teri could feel the nervous sweat trickling down her neck. She was sitting in *his* chair at *his* desk. The small gray Crate & Barrel couch crouching against the far wall came from his apartment in the Back Bay, and the books on the shelf by the door were a window into his daily thoughts: *Methods of Internal Medicine, The Joy of Diagnosis, The Complete Works of Ayn Rand,* two volumes of Hemingway, and the latest Frommer's guide to Ireland.

Not to mention the clutter on his desk. Daily newspapers, yellow pads of paper, pens and pencils from numerous drug companies—and the framed pictures. Mostly of Kari, so exceptionally beautiful, with her long honey-blond hair and her smiling blue eyes. She had been much taller than Teri, and thin enough to slice bread. But Teri pretended she could see similarities—in the shape of her ears, the pout of her lips, the curves of her small breasts. Teri knew how much Dr. Ballantine had loved his wife; she had watched him cry at the memorial service after the tragic crash. It was then that Teri had truly fallen for him.

She brushed away a tear and turned back to the prescription pad. Her note was brief, but she wanted to get the words right. She had to tell him enough to get his attention, without giving anything away. She did not want to miss the expression on his face when he heard the full story. Teri had already waited so long, she felt as if she were going to burst.

She had stopped by Ballantine's office more than twenty times before his senior resident—the tall, gangly black girl with arrogant eyes and absolutely no hips—had explained, curtly, that *Michael* had taken a sick day. Of course, Teri had immediately distrusted her. The girl had seemed almost catty.

Even so, on a normal day, Teri would have shrunk away in silence. But this morning her confidence had been soaring. Late last night, three more mice had run the maze in record times. Teri knew that her moment was approaching; she could already hear the applause of the Nobel Prize committee echoing in her ears.

And besides, today she looked great. After yesterday's brief hallway rendezvous with Dr. Ballantine, she had gone shopping, something she hadn't done in months. She had found a beautifully cut dark blue sheath that accented her high breasts and made her legs look twice as long. She had found shoes to match, and a red Chinese silk scarf that echoed the shine of her moussed-up auburn hair.

So Teri had ignored the senior resident's assertion, and had spent the rest of the day wandering back and forth through the hallway outside Dr. Ballantine's office. Eight hours later her feet were killing her, and her hair had drooped a few inches under the weight of the mousse, but she still looked pretty good. She wished she had a Polaroid to leave on Dr. Ballantine's desk along with her note.

She blushed at the foolish thought. It was much easier to be daring when she was alone. That had been the

same when she was younger, waiting until her mother
had left for work to respond, shouting at the imitation
wood paneling of their tract house in Marlborough.
Once, in her rage, she had broken an ugly faux-Ming
vase one of her mother's many boyfriends had given her,
and she had spent hours searching for a duplicate, scouring the flea markets and ninety-nine-cent stores. She had
not even had the guts to tell her mother that she hated
the stupid trinkets. In fact, sometimes the gifts were
worse than the lusty gazes and the groping hands, because the gifts she had to accept, smiling like a fucking
jack-o'-lantern in front of her mother. At least the hands
usually came late at night, when her mother was asleep
two rooms away—

There was a sudden snap. Teri stared down at the
broken pencil in her right hand. She blushed, then
found another pencil and quickly finished her note.
Now Dr. Ballantine would know that tomorrow, she
would be waiting for him in the Batcave, ready to reveal a discovery so important it would change both
their lives. She took one last look at the pictures of
Kari, then started to rise from Dr. Ballantine's chair.

Something caught her eye. Under a framed photo of
Kari in a burgundy dress lay yesterday's *Boston Globe*.
Smack in the center of the front page was a picture of
the governor of Massachusetts. Teri recognized the
widow's peak and the oversized ears immediately; in the
past few weeks she had seen Governor Kyle numerous
times in the hallways of Metro, and she knew he was
Dr. Ballantine's best friend. Teri hadn't seen a newspaper or a television screen for months; she wondered
why the governor was back on the front page, so soon
after his election.

The headline above the picture was obscured beneath
a pile of Merck pens. Teri pushed the pens aside, and

stared at the oversized type. Her heart jumped as she quickly read the lead article. *Christ.*

No wonder Dr. Ballantine had called in sick. First his wife, now his best friend. Teri felt new tears building behind her eyes. She finished the article, memorizing the time and location of Governor Kyle's funeral. If Dr. Ballantine didn't call her at home, she knew where to find him.

As she headed for the door, a strange thought touched the back of her mind. Governor Kyle's death, Dr. Ballantine's odd behavior in the hallway, his sick day . . . she quickly pushed the thought away. It was an impossible, laughable idea. There were too many variables. The conditions were too unrestricted.

Mike Ballantine was not a mouse in a maze.

CHAPTER EIGHT

Cool wind licked at Mike's cheeks as he barreled forward, his sneakers churning against the curving strip of blacktop. He could see the Mass Ave bridge two hundred yards ahead, a sparkling tongue hovering above the serpentine Charles. Bright headlights pulsed across the bridge like neurons leaping along a massive synaptic network, casting a rainbow of glimmering light against the choppy waves of the dark river below.

Mike picked up his pace, focused on his goal. His sweatshirt stuck to his chest and his shorts clung to his legs as the blood pounded through his brain. His stomach muscles were tight and sore over his laboring diaphragm, and his calves felt like rocks under his skin; but his mind remained lodged in that special place known only to true athletes: the burn.

Mike had learned about the burn during his football days at Cambridge Public High. The burn was the place you went when your body had given everything and you still wanted more—when your muscles had stretched past their limits and your lungs threatened to tear right through your chest. A doctor would say it had something to do with endorphins and adrenaline and caloric release—but at the moment, Mike Ballantine was not a doctor. He was an athlete, nothing more, nothing less. And he was deep in the burn.

Pure fucking freedom. An animal unchained, a co-ordinated symphony of muscle, spirit, and flesh, locked in a battle with gravity and fatigue. It was an extremely personal sensation—and a secret Mike had never shared with anyone in his life. Andrew would not have understood. And Kari, though fit and a weekend athlete, could never have experienced it for herself.

But it was the one thing that truly came easy for Mike. His abilities in medicine were the result of years of ass-breaking hard work and late-night memorization. His grades at BU and Tufts had been the product of his Herculean will, not any innate ability. But the sound of his sneakers against pavement, the dance of his muscles beneath his skin: this was his inborn gift.

If he had stayed with football instead of choosing the more intellectual sport of lacrosse, there was no question in his mind that he could have gone pro one day. But to him, it wasn't about the competition or the glory—it was about the feeling he got when he reached the burn. The feeling of absolute and total freedom.

He barely felt the pavement as he took the last hundred yards at a dead run. The paved footpath along the Charles was deserted, owing to the cold weather and the encroaching darkness. But Mike didn't give a damn about the weather or the night. He was too far gone to notice.

He reached the base of the bridge and finally let his body stop, bending at the waist as he fought for breath. Spikes of fire worked through his lungs, but he felt good, truly alive, for the first time in days. He put his hands on his knees, feeling the hot cartilage and the hint of scar tissue just beneath the caps.

He remembered the morning after the surgeon had cut him up, nearly sixteen years ago. It was during his sophomore year at BU, two weeks after a minor lacrosse injury involving an opposing lineman and an overturned goalpost. The surgeon had warned Mike that he might never be the athlete he once was, that the scar tissue would take away some of the freedom, perhaps even end his college lacrosse career. Mike had been determined to prove him wrong.

Within two months, he had been back in the game— and stronger than ever. Somehow, the rest of his muscles had learned to compensate for his weakened knees, his thighs and calves proudly absorbing the changed angles of impact.

Mike gritted his teeth as he pulled his sweatshirt up to wipe the sweat from his eyes. The cold air made his abdominal rack ripple beneath his skin. Sometimes, when the rest of his life went to hell, he forgot about the burn and the freedom. Most of all, he forgot about the scar tissue in his knees. But that was exactly the point: His *body* didn't forget. His body *endured*.

Mike stretched down, touching his palms to the cold pavement. He could feel the muscles expanding along the insides of his legs. He could see huge teardrops of sweat splashing into a dark pool beneath his solid, square jaw. Sometimes he had to remind himself: this was also Mike Ballantine.

He rose, listening to the clamor of the traffic reverberating across the Mass Ave bridge. He had just enough time to get back to his apartment, shower, and shave.

Forty minutes later, Mike's cab rumbled across smooth cobblestones as he shook shampoo out of his right ear. His knees ached, but it was a wonderful pain, a pleasant contrast to the dull throb of his fading head cold. "This is good," he shouted over the cab's engine. "Right at the entrance."

The cab pulled to a sudden stop, and the driver

cocked his head toward the front windshield. "Nice digs. You a Cabot or a Lodge?"

Mike laughed at the driver, then responded in his heaviest Irish accent. "Which do I sound like?"

The driver winked at him through the divider. "You sound like you're here to mow the lawn. The fare's on me. After all, we mighta come over on the same boat."

Mike tossed him a ten anyway, and stepped out onto the cobblestone sidewalk. Louisburg Square stretched out ahead of him, two opposing rows of massive brick town houses overlooking a private, gated park. The area was synonymous with old money; generations of Boston Brahmins had hatched inside the lavish brick buildings, and to many this was still the soul of Beacon Hill, a throwback to the age of colonial aristocracy.

Mike strolled along the wrought-iron fence that enclosed the immaculately groomed park. The high, opulent mansions around the square exuded arrogance and Old World panache, from their oversized arched bay windows to their turrets chiseled out of imported Italian stone. Mike absently ran his fingers along the cold black fence, wondering how many security cameras watched him from the recessed doorways on either side lest he vault the fence and sully the sacred park that stretched like a probing finger down the center of the square. Only the owners of the mansions had keys to the fence and access to the center grass; that way, the children of the Cabots played only with the children of the Lodges. There was no place on that emerald glade for an Irish kid from South Boston.

Not even one who had grown up across the river. After all, Cambridge was just a place the Brahmins visited for four short years before migrating back to their mansions on the Hill. Mike's childhood in his mother's house on the cheap end of Brattle Street did not entitle him to walk these sidewalks as a native, and it certainly didn't erase his true lineage. The cabby had been right; Mike's kind kept the grass nicely trimmed, patrolled the streets, and repaired the brick townhouses. No amount of money would change that, because it was a matter of blood.

Mike had tried to explain this to Andrew when his friend bought the town house on the far corner of the square. It will never be a home, Mike had warned. You can throw money at the marble walls and the frosted French windows, but you'll always be a stranger when you walk out the front door. Andrew had laughed at him, calling him a throwback. And maybe Andrew had been right. A year later, he had been elected governor of Massachusetts. Then he had met Anne, the toast of the Boston social scene. No doubt, had he lived long enough, his children would have played behind that high black iron fence.

But that didn't change the way Mike felt as he walked past the enormous mansions. He could see the flicker of fireplaces reflected in the windowpanes, and the smell of burning hickory filled his nostrils. Chandeliers winked at him from second- and third-floor ballrooms, and he fought the urge to gawk at the grand pianos and antique furniture he could see through countless open drapes. Even though he had been earning a doctor's salary for years, he had nothing in common with the people of Louisburg Square.

Least of all with Anne Kyle. She was sitting on the front steps of the mansion on the corner, her long legs covered in sheer black stockings, her triangular face resting on her hands. As Mike's footsteps echoed off of the cobblestones, she raised her head, and a thin smile broke across her carefully drawn lips. At first glance, her face seemed unreal, like something molded out of pure porcelain. Her cheekbones were Colorado ski slopes, and her eyes were the color of an overchlorinated swimming pool. Her long blond hair flowed down around her shoulders, a glowing contrast to her black jacket and skirt. She was royalty in mourning, still perfect but adjusting to the part, like one of those dolls that leak tears when you pull the string in its lower back. As Mike approached, she rose.

"Thank you for coming." Her heavy Southern accent reminded Mike of dripping paint. "It's been a horrible two days."

Mike didn't know how to respond, so he leaned forward and gave her a hug. She felt like a bird in his grasp, so angled and thin. At five ten, she couldn't have weighed more than a hundred and twenty pounds. Her body shook as she turned her head to the side, but when she broke away, there was no trace of her anguish. She brushed an errant lock from her right eye.

"We're quite a tragic pair, aren't we?" There was a sharp edge to her voice, and Mike felt sweat break out across his back. He had always felt like this around Anne. During college and after, he had never been intimidated by women. But Anne was different, and the difference had little to do with her striking looks. She was intelligent, confident, and honed by years of being the center of attention. At thirty-four, she was already a managing partner at one of the most prestigious law firms in Boston, but despite her intellectual achievements she had never shed the glamour of her former career on the runways of Europe. As a teenager, she had appeared on the cover of magazines around the world, and she still had the innate ability to dominate a room—or a conversation—without saying a word.

At the same time, there was a fragility to her that Mike had never understood. Andrew had once described

Anne as a steel spring wound up inside a beautiful glass figurine. He had meant it as a compliment, describing the complexity of her personality, sometimes obscured by her own good looks. But Mike had taken the description to mean something else entirely: if you touched Anne the wrong way, she wouldn't simply shatter; she'd explode. "Maybe people like us just attract death. My father went when I was five. Did Andrew ever tell you that? A skiing trip in Aspen. Killed by an avalanche. Kind of ironic, when you think about it. Growing up in the deep South, then getting killed by snow. At least Andrew had the decency to blow up just a few blocks from home."

Mike swallowed, unsure whether she was joking. Then he saw a tear clinging to the corner of her right eye, and he realized she was in pain, too. She just had her own way of dealing with one of the few situations she couldn't control.

"It's a part of life," he finally responded, weakly. She nodded, taking him by the hand. He followed her through the front door and into the marble foyer. As she hung his frayed gray overcoat in a closet by the door, his eyes accustomed themselves to his posh surroundings. Gilded sconces hung from the white walls, casting cones of orange light onto the polished slabs beneath his feet. Each marble stone had been imported from Italy at a cost of more than ten thousand dollars; Anne had expected the best, and Andrew had never disappointed her.

Mike followed her into the narrow hallway that led to the dining room, his eyes gliding over a progression of Renaissance oils that lined the walls: all originals, all presents for Andrew's porcelain queen. The long hallway continued past elegant sitting parlors, plushly appointed libraries, and museum-style showrooms, finally ending in the mansion's vast main dining room. Above the mahoganied walls, the high ivory ceiling was detailed with tiny winged angels and trumpeting cherubs, carved over a period of two years by an artist imported from the southern tip of Greece. A huge chandelier hung from the center of the ceiling like an inverted wedding cake, three descending layers of crystal teardrops and ruby hearts. When Anne flipped a switch on the wall, the chandelier lit up like a supernova. Mike remembered what he had said when Andrew had brought the monstrosity back from Paris: "Why don't you just save some time and import the whole damn continent?"

"I've sent the cook and the servants home," Anne said, as she ushered Mike toward the long oak table in the center of the enormous chamber. "I'm tired of them buzzing around like flies. At first, I thought it was important for me to be surrounded by people, but now they just remind me how alone I am. I know you've been through this before—I just hope I can be as strong as you were after Kari passed away."

Mike looked at her, surprised by the sudden admission; in the past, she had always spoken to him as if she were reading from a script. Her frankness made him wonder: why *had* she asked him to dinner? At first, he had assumed it was a formality, a gut reflex from her Southern upbringing. But the way she was now looking at him made him think there was something else at work. Nothing sexual, of course. But there was a determined glint behind her gaze.

He lowered himself into a plush chair at one corner of the table, trying to force the sudden suspicion out of his thoughts. It was impossible to read anything from a face that had been applied in front of a mirror with strokes as practiced as a neurosurgeon's. If Anne wanted something from him, he would have to wait for her to spell it out. "People told me it would get easier. But it never did. You just learn to raise your threshold a bit, learn to live with the constant ache. You start to expect it when you wake up in the morning. And after a while, it becomes such a part of you—you don't really remember what it was like before."

"That's strange. When I was with Andrew, I never remembered the time before we found each other. Now you say I'm going to forget what it was like to have him as my partner."

Anne sat down directly across from Mike, her hands flat on the mahogany table. Her enormous diamond engagement ring sparkled under the chandelier's reddish glow. Mike guessed the ring had cost nearly as much as his virology lab. Most of Boston would have agreed that Andrew had gotten what he had paid for—a stunning, cultured, vibrant ornament, a successful, vivacious woman to go with his meteoric political success. But a *partner?* Mike had never really thought of her that way. Not the way Kari had been to him.

Andrew had tried to explain it many times: the depth of his attraction, the substance behind Anne's blue eyes. She was smarter, he said, than Mike could imagine, as strong and confident as any Irish mother he had ever met. And sexually, Andrew had said, she was like an angry cat: ferocious, insatiable, creative, so intent on pleasing herself that he had thanked God every night, just for letting him go along for the ride. Mike had always known the description had revealed more about Andrew than his wife; his friend, who had so dominated the world, needed someone who could dominate him while, in public, adding to his thunder rather than stealing it. *A steel spring inside a glass figurine.*

Anne waved a thin hand toward the end of the long table, and Mike noticed a small pile of silver trays wrapped in cellophane. There was no such thing as Tupperware in Louisburg Square. "As you can see, people have been dropping food by all afternoon. I'm like a stray kitten everyone wants to feed. But I haven't felt like eating since it happened. I haven't been able to do anything, really, except sit here and think."

"Where were you when you heard? About Andrew?"

"I had just landed in Logan. One of our Secret Service men met me at the airport with the news. I almost fainted. I was supposed to be in that limo, you know. But my sister was in the hospital. She had ruptured her spleen skiing in Utah. It's hard to believe she skis, after what happened to my father. But my sister has always been the idiot of the family. And certainly the least agile. I went to visit her after the surgery. Otherwise, I would have died with Andrew."

Her hands shook as she spoke, and Mike realized how difficult this was for her. She needed to be in control—to keep the steel spring from tearing through the glass—but death was uncontrollable. He thought of his own recent meltdown, and wondered if he had been too hard on the Southern belle. Were they really that different? He had his own walls to protect.

"I guess I should feel lucky," she continued, looking down at her hands. "But I just feel numb. I don't understand how this could have happened. Or why. Everyone loved Andrew. I used to tease him about it. More people wanted to fuck him than had ever wanted to fuck me, even during my modeling years. He had the fan mail to prove it. Nobody had any reason to do this."

"Sometimes there doesn't have to be a reason."

"I saw you walking into the police station—they showed it on the news. Did the officers tell you anything about whom they suspect? Or why someone would want to kill Andrew?"

Mike was surprised by the questions. No doubt, Anne

had already spoken to the police. Why would they tell him something they hadn't told her? "They didn't have any answers. Just a lot of questions."

"What sort of questions?"

Mike noticed that Anne's eyes had suddenly turned a shade of azure he had never seen before. And her voice had changed. The lawyer in her was leaking through. He coughed into his hand. What was she driving at? "They asked about the explosion. What I saw when the bomb went off. If there were any suspicious people hanging around the motorcade, or any visible threats from the crowd."

He thought about describing the interview with the tall Asian woman in the basement of the BPD, but decided it was too strange; he doubted that foreign policy had any relevance to Andrew's death. "Basically, they asked a lot of routine questions, which makes me think they have no idea why it happened. But you can't focus on the investigation, Anne. You'll go crazy trying to find someone to blame."

This was the same thing Andrew had told Mike after Kari's plane crashed. Mike had spent thousands of dollars on lawyers, bringing suits against the commuter airline, the mechanics' union, the air traffic controllers, even the local weather bureau that had underreported the speed of wind gusts in the Logan area. But all the lawyers had gotten him nowhere. As usual, Andrew had been right.

Of course, this was a different situation. Andrew *had* been murdered. And Mike could see why Anne would want to find out who did it. But why was she asking him? "You've spoken to the police, haven't you?"

"And the FBI, and the Secret Service. But I get the feeling they know more than they're telling me."

"That's the way they do their job."

"Frankly, I don't give a damn. That's what I told them when they tried to use that crap on me. With my best Mobile accent: Frankly, I don't give a damn. He was my husband. I have a right to know what they've uncovered. Whom they suspect."

It was the second time Anne had used the word "suspect." Mike looked at the red splotches that had appeared on her cheeks. Rage? Or fear? He suddenly felt uncomfortable, as if being used. "I'm sure when they know something concrete, they'll tell you."

"Will they? When Kari died, did they keep you in the dark? Did they ask you hundreds of questions about your wife—about why you weren't on the plane next to her, why you didn't die holding her hand?"

Mike paused, stunned. He took a deep breath. "It was a different situation. Andrew was the governor of Massachusetts."

"And I'm the governor's widow. My sister's spleen was bleeding into her abdomen, and I wanted to be by her side. That shouldn't make me a suspect."

There it was, out in the open. Now Mike knew why he was sitting in Andrew's dining room. Anne had wanted to pick his brain for information about the police investigation. Perhaps the police had treated her harshly; Andrew had made enormous donations to the BPD, and as an Irish governor, he was one of their own. Anne was a blueblood from Mobile, Alabama. She'd been on an airplane instead of sitting in the limousine with her husband. And as the governor's wife, she was probably one of a handful of people who knew the route and time of Andrew's motorcade. But Mike was certain all that was just coincidence. This was Anne, Andrew's glass figurine.

"I'm sure you're not a suspect. The police just have

their own way of doing things. They're only trying to find the truth."

Anne exhaled, closing her eyes. Then she moved her hands off the table, clasping them together in her lap. When she reopened her eyes, she seemed to have gained control over her anger. "You're right, of course. And I'm sorry I said that about Kari—it wasn't fair. I know how you've suffered."

Mike shrugged it off, but the words had hurt. For months after Kari's death, he had wished he had been on that plane. He would happily have traded his life just to see her one last time. The thought reminded him of the meeting with Arthur Feinstein. Ghost stories. Seeing loved ones one last time.

"It's just too much to accept," Anne continued. "I'm finding it hard to believe he's really dead."

Suddenly, Mike felt the need to splash water on his face. Sweat was building up beneath his collar, and feverish chills ran down his spine. *Not now,* he hissed at himself. Not again. He shakily pushed himself up from his chair.

"Mike? Are you all right?"

"I'm fine. I just need to use the bathroom."

"You remember where it is?"

Mike nodded, heading toward the main hallway to the rest of the mansion. He felt a little better standing up. Maybe this time, the feelings would pass without incident. He breathed deeply, calming his frantic heart.

"On your way back," Anne called out as he reached the hallway, "stop by Andrew's study. I think there are some pictures of the two of you together. I have all of his albums, so you can take what you find."

Mike stood for a long moment in the doorway to the study. After his trip to the bathroom, his fever seemed to have vanished; there was no sign of emergent nausea or impending headache, and he prayed the episode had passed. He forced his mind to relax, while he regarded the familiar, memory-filled room.

Brass banker's lamps bounced warm light off the paneled study walls, giving the room a homey golden hue. Andrew's mammoth antique desk stood by the far wall, cluttered with papers, plaques, and computer equipment. Most of the rest of the room was taken up by a regulation-size pool table, covered in light green felt. Mike and Andrew had spent many evenings hitting balls around the table, though pool was just an excuse to drink whiskey and talk about high school. Two rows of unopened bottles of Johnnie Walker sat on a shelf behind the antique desk, and Mike guessed there were more hidden in the desk drawers; Andrew always believed in keeping a month's worth of whiskey handy, in case of emergency. What sort of emergency lasted a month, Mike never asked.

Aside from the desk and pool table, the only other piece of furniture was a tall oak shelving unit straddling the far corner. The bottom three shelves were filled with books and magazines, while the top shelf contained a row of framed photographs.

Mike's fingers bounced across the green felt of the pool table as he moved toward the shelving unit. He pretended he could still hear Andrew's laughter and the clink of the pool balls searching for the corners; certainly, he could still smell the Johnnie Walker. Its scent would probably stay in the study until the green carpet was ripped out and burned.

Mike studied the framed pictures. The first group were of Andrew and Anne—two from their wedding, one from somewhere in Europe, two more from inside the gated park in the center of Louisburg Square. Andrew's smile was the same in each picture, his entire face alight with unconstrained happiness. Mike marveled at how mature the pictures made Andrew look; his memories of the fat kid with glasses and a widow's peak were years out-of-date, and he wondered why he still clung to them.

In the next picture, Andrew stood with his arm around Mike's shoulder at Mike's graduation from Tufts Medical School. At the time, Andrew had been almost two years out of Harvard Law, already on his way to building his vast fortune. Certainly no more little fat kid, he emanated confidence and authority.

The next few pictures chronicled his meteoric rise. First a shot of Mike and Andrew after Andrew was elected the first twenty-eight-year-old senior partner at Ropes & Gray, Boston's most prestigious law firm. Then a photo from a party two years later, celebrating his ascension to CEO of Macaw Industries, one of the largest corporate finance institutions in the Northeast. Thirty years old, with a net worth in the tens of millions, while Mike struggled through his excruciating medical residency. But any jealousy Mike had felt at the time had been brotherly; he had been proud of Andrew's success, and prouder still to be a part of it.

The next two photos marked the loftiest of all Andrew's accomplishments: they'd been taken at his first inauguration. Mike smiled as he saw himself standing in the background of one of the shots, a smile creeping across his face. He reached for the photo, gently lifting the frame with both hands—

—and saw something that made his heart freeze. Beneath the frame was another photo, lying face up against the shelf. He leaned close, his eyes widening in shock. Then his fingers went numb, and the inaugural photograph slipped out of his hand, the glass shattering against the floor.

"Mike?" Anne called from the hallway. "Are you okay?"

He didn't answer. His head was on fire. His fingers shook as he lifted the photograph off the shelf. The picture was unmistakable. A magnificent charcoal-gray horse, with a streak of white above its right eyebrow. Christ. Was he hallucinating the photograph? But he could feel it with his fingers, he could see his thumb covering the horse's pitch-black mane.

"Black Betty. His second love. I know it's ridiculous, but sometimes I was jealous of that horse."

Mike turned his head. "Sorry?"

"The picture," Anne said, pointing from the other side of the pool table. He hadn't heard her enter the study. "Andrew bought her about three months after we were married. I'm not surprised he kept her a secret from you. He didn't tell anyone. He was fulfilling a childhood dream. I think it embarrassed him."

A childhood dream. Mike remembered a day during his freshman year of high school. Two seniors had picked on Andrew for being fat and slow, tearing his favorite jacket and throwing his books in the mud. Mike had walked him home, then sat with him all afternoon watching cowboy movies. Andrew's face had lit up when the cowboys rode in on their horses. A strange obsession for an overweight little Irish kid. Mike wet his lips, still staring at the horse in the picture.

"He kept her in a stable in Marblehead," Anne continued. "He took riding lessons twice a week. He was getting pretty good at it. Then about a month ago, there was a fire at the stable. Black Betty died of smoke inhalation. Andrew was pretty upset."

Mike started to shake, fighting to digest what he had

just learned. The photograph in his hand was not a vision. It was a picture of a recently dead horse. A dead horse Mike had watched stroll through Metro's hallways yesterday afternoon.

Trickles of hot sweat ran down Mike's back. He closed his eyes, his fingers tightening against the photograph. How would Arthur explain this one? The plume of fire in the basement laboratory could have come from his memory, but Mike had never seen Black Betty before. He had never even been to Marblehead. It was absolutely impossible. Arthur had said it himself: hallucinatory images have to come from somewhere in your memory. But how could you remember something you had never seen?

A familiar nausea rose in Mike's stomach as he grappled with the thought. Then the nausea was joined by a sharp pain behind his eyes. Christ. It was happening again.

Suddenly, brutally familiar laughter echoed in his ear. He jerked his head around, his eyes wild. Anne, still standing on the other side of the pool table, watched in confusion as Mike's face went stark white.

The gaunt man was standing in the doorway, his arms crossed against his chest. He was wearing the same white smock, buttoned to his throat. His mouth was wide open, his head back; his eyes were black slits. The hand-shaped acne scar under his right eye seemed alive with motion, as the cruel laughter rocked his body.

"My God," Mike whispered, "who are you?"

"Mike?" Anne gasped, turning toward the doorway. "What's wrong?"

But the doorway was empty. The gaunt man had already vanished. His laughter hung in the air a moment more, then slipped away.

Mike's entire body started to shake. He knew he was

going insane. No psychiatrist could explain what was happening to him. The picture of the horse was real. But the gaunt man had been a vision, some sort of walking nightmare.

"Mike?"

"I have to go," Mike whispered, shoving the picture of the horse deep into his pocket. "I'm not feeling well."

He rushed past Anne and out into the main hallway. She chased after him, her long legs keeping her just a few feet behind. "What's wrong? You looked as if you saw something—"

"I didn't see anything. I'm not well. I haven't been well for a few days." He didn't even know what he was saying. The words had a life of their own. "Thank you for the invitation. But I've got to get out of here."

"Do you need a ride? Should I call a cab?"

Mike had reached the door. He found his overcoat in the closet and draped it over his right shoulder. "I think I'll walk. I need the fresh air."

It was more than four miles to his apartment in the Back Bay. But he didn't care. He was rapidly losing control. He felt as if someone were playing an enormous hoax on him. A horrible, impossible hoax. He needed to get outside, to walk, to think. He needed to regain control.

Anne leaned forward and kissed him on the cheek. "Please feel better, Mike. And I'm sorry I sounded so crazy—about the police investigation. I'm just having trouble dealing with what's happened."

Mike almost laughed out loud. If she only knew. He squeezed Anne's hand, then pushed out into the night.

"Ta zai waimien. He's outside. Start the engine."

A dark brown Infiniti sedan parked two hundred meters from the edge of Louisburg Square rumbled to life.

The headlights remained off, the engine muffled. The windows were tinted completely black. Two men, both tall, thin, and wearing white smocks buttoned at the throat, sat silently in the front seat. A third man, taller and thinner than the others, sat alone in back. His gaunt face was obscured by a pair of high-tech infrared goggles.

"He's alone. The woman remained inside. He's probably returning home." The gaunt man's Adam's apple lifted up and down as he watched the *ang mo* descend the high stone steps. Through the infrared goggles, the figure looked like a floating red ghost; waves of magenta floated around his centers of heat—his head, heart, groin—and a cloud of pink lifted out of his open mouth.

The gaunt man adjusted the distance meter on the goggles, and the figure finally shivered into focus. Tall, wide-shouldered, with dark curly hair and long, muscular legs. A handsome man, by Western standards. The gaunt man studied the way he walked, measuring the length of his muscles and the looseness of his joints. Athletic, capable, strong. But there was something wrong; his *chi* was out of balance. He was a jumble of nerves, and his skin trembled in a mixture of fear and confusion. The gaunt man wondered if it was significant.

"He's reached the edge of the square. Prepare to follow. But keep a distance of two hundred meters." The gaunt man lowered the infrared goggles. The figure was now close enough to watch without the expensive military technology. The gaunt man liked it better that way.

As he watched the Westerner exit Louisburg Square and head toward the park, he wondered: Was this a waste of time? He did not think the man knew anything. But the orders had been clear. Both the girl *and* the doctor.

The gaunt man knew there was a better way to get

the answers they needed. It would be foolishly simple to take the girl. And even simpler to break her.

But he would never disobey his orders. That would be unthinkable. And certainly fatal. He leaned close to the tinted window, focusing his black eyes. "He's almost out of sight. It's time to move."

The brown Infiniti slid forward, and the gaunt man smiled. He could be patient. Like a desert viper in the eastern Gobi where he had been born, thirty-nine years ago. Waiting day after day for the right moment. *Dao,* Patience, the Way. Soon, he knew, his orders would change.

CHAPTER NINE

It was close to midnight when Amber finally stepped through the threshold of her hotel suite on the far side of the Back Bay, but her body still felt fresh, the muscles of her legs responding as if they were loaded with springs. It was always like this when she was on a case; sometimes, when the stakes were high enough, she went days without significant rest. And unlike other operatives she had worked with in the past, she hardly ever turned to the small bottle of CIA-issue amphetamines she carried in her inside coat pocket. The thrill of the hunt was enough to keep her going.

She heard the door click shut behind her, and immediately kicked off her low heeled shoes. The Eliot Hotel was a Back Bay landmark. The walls of her suite's small sitting room were delicately papered in an off-peach color, and the floor was covered by a woolly white carpet. There was a camelback sofa against the far wall, facing an antique colonial armoire. On top of the armoire squatted a twenty-inch color television, the curved screen reflecting the soft light emanating from the two covered lamps that flanked the uncomfortable, if stylish, couch.

On the other side of the armoire stood a small secretary table, shouldering a Hewlett-Packard fax machine and a four-line speaker-phone. Amber was surprised that the Eliot's decorators hadn't come up with some way to make the high-tech items fit in with the room's staid archaism; at the very least, they could have hidden the television behind one of the Audubon paintings that covered more than sixty percent of the peach wallpaper. Ducks, ducks, more ducks.

Amber took a step forward, her bare feet sinking into the thick carpet. She reached up behind her head, removed the pair of ivory pins that held her long hair in place, and shook her head back and forth, enjoying the cool sensation as the silky strands licked the skin of her cheeks. She could feel the muscles of her face relaxing as she moved past the armoire. Her shoulders lost their stiffness, and her stomach loosened a few centimeters against the rope fastening of her slacks. A former boyfriend had once told her it was like watching ice melt. Truth be told, it wasn't easy to be stared at twelve hours a day. And it took an enormous amount of energy to maintain the daily image of a hard-assed bitch.

Amber smiled at her own joke. She had borrowed the label from another former boyfriend, the only one significant enough for his name to remain in her emotional memory banks. Alec Constantine had been a classmate at Oxford, her first white lover and the only Western man she had ever let inside her body. He had lasted almost two years, a marathon in comparison to the half-dozen other brief liaisons in Amber's romantic history. In the end, the relationship had ended like the rest: the moment he fell short of her expectations and needs, she had walked. With Alec, it had been more difficult than with the rest, because her love for him had been sincere. But it went against her nature to settle; if her standards were impossibly high, then that was just too bad.

She took the speaker-phone in both hands. The cord was barely long enough to reach the couch. She settled against one of the too-firm pillows and dialed an eleven-digit number from memory. There was a series of high-pitched beeps as electronic signals relayed a packet of coded information through a tangle of fiber-optic lines located twelve feet beneath the basement of the hotel. As the electronic signals were transformed into tightly cropped microwave pulses en route to a relay satellite hovering above the eastern U.S. seaboard, Amber slipped her overcoat off her shoulders and undid the top two buttons of her shirt, running a fingernail across the caramel flesh above her breasts. She had been cooped up in the task force's tiny strategy room for most of the evening, breathing a smog of cigarette smoke and hot air. She had gone over dozens of transcribed interviews from Leary's investigation, but had uncovered nothing pivotal. She had conducted phone interviews of a handful of witnesses herself—but always under Dick Leary's watchful eye, so, of course, she had been forced to avoid the important questions. Still, unlike Leary, she was not yet frustrated or worried by the pace of her investigation. While Leary tossed foam coffee cups against the task force strategy board and kicked over metal folding chairs, Amber calmly contemplated the facts of the case, searching for answers they might have somehow missed.

The biggest question yet unanswered had to do with the time and place of the assassination. The terrorists had known the exact route and timing of the motorcade—which hinted at the possibility of an inside agent. Dick Leary was convinced that there was someone working on the inside; in fact, he was suspicious enough to blame even the investigation's slow pace on some nebulous infiltrator, some unnamed betrayer in the pay of the terrorists. Although Amber had not yet found any sure proof, such internal deception would certainly fit the Chinese mode of operation. Despite her initial impression of Leary and his grating personality, she was slowly accepting the fact that he was fairly intelligent, and undoubtedly good at his job.

Finally, the series of beeps ended: the microwave packets had reached their final destination. A few seconds later, the phone line chirped, telling Amber she had connected with her international voicemail system. She dialed in her number and password and listened for the tinny English voice. It told her she had two messages waiting, and she punched in another multidigit code.

The international voicemail system was shared by the three major federal agencies, and was considered one of the safest locked-line networks in the world. The fiber-optic lines had been installed beneath the Eliot Hotel by a team of National Security Agency specialists, working in conjunction with the CIA and FBI; the list of hotels with similar fiber-optic systems was available only to the highest-ranking operatives and was itself encoded on a computer disk that could be read only by a specially provided program.

However, Amber did not believe in unbreakable codes. So she used her voicemail sparingly, never entrusting truly important information to the satellite-based relay system.

After her code was accepted, the phone chirped again, and suddenly a nervous American voice echoed out of the receiver. Amber hit the speaker button, and listened to the message reverberate through the small sitting room.

"Ms. Chen? Benton Crow, at the governor's office. You left me a message this afternoon. I'm not sure how I can help you, but please try me at home. It's about eleven now, but you can call as late as you'd like."

The weak voice cracked halfway through the number. Amber touched her fingers to her lips, contemplating the tone of the message and the fact that Crow had returned her call at such a late hour. The young man had been one of the governor's most senior aides, and Leary and his people had already gone over him with the verbal equivalent of a rubber hose. Still, Amber had a few questions of her own—and there were much more efficient ways of obtaining answers than rubber hoses.

Amber memorized Crow's number, then erased his message and waited for the second. There was a brief pause, before a loud voice erupted through the speakerphone, intermixing Chinese with broken, heavily accented English. Amber could hear high-tech music in the background, the kind of synthesized Europop that currently dominated the French and German disco scenes.

" 'Ey, *jie jie*! You missin hell of rockin' good party! I think Paris. No, might be Marseilles. Either way, chicks got hair under arms, but they still look great! Big love, Am-jiang. Ciao."

Amber rubbed the skin above her eyes. A loud dial tone suddenly echoed through the hotel room. She didn't know whether to laugh or curse. She replaced the receiver, picturing the little fool as he made the call. Standing in the corner of some high-priced disco, strobe lights splashing across his wide, handsome face. Probably a drink in one hand, a young blond socialite-party whore in the other.

Wei-sun. Or Winston, as he now called himself. Toast of the Hong Kong elite. One of the hundreds of Chinese playboys living off trust funds in the fast-paced Euro scene, hopping from city to city in search of the ultimate party. Shaming himself and his culture with his blatant disregard for his breeding, his body, and his family name. Choosing his atrocious broken English over his native tongue, proud of his refusal to learn correct grammar or pronunciation—because to do so would entail studying, and study was the equivalent of work, the greatest playboy sin of all. Amber wouldn't have given a damn about any of it—except that Winston Chen was also her father's son. Her little brother, raised in the same house and sent to the same private school—but symbolic of a Taiwanese tradition dating back thousands of years. As the only son, he was the heir to their family's fortune. And, like heirs all over the world, Winston had been warped by the chance of his birth. Amber was only thankful that he had waited until their father's death, seven years ago, to embrace the playboy way.

At least he had the decency to check in, once or twice a month. When Amber heard "*jie jie*"—"big sister"— on her voicemail, followed by "Am-jiang," the pet name her father had given her when she was a child, she knew Winston wasn't floating facedown in the Seine, or lying OD'd in an alley in Berlin.

The hardest part of the situation with Winston was that he was still so damn likable. As much as Amber hated his irresponsible ways, she always felt like smiling when she heard his voice or thought about his big, endearing eyes.

She considered trying to track him down in France— he owned at least one penthouse apartment in Paris and another somewhere near the beach—but decided it could wait. She was about to reach for the phone to call Benton Crow instead when a shrill ring exploded from the plastic speaker. Amber scooped up the receiver and pressed it to her ear.

Karl Bader's voice was muffled, but bursting with excited energy. Amber could tell he was trying to control his enthusiasm; she guessed he was still in the task force strategy room, keeping tabs on Leary's investigation. She listened carefully as he spoke, asking a handful of questions when he paused for quick gulps of air. It didn't take her long to realize why Bader was so excited; the new development wasn't case-breaking, but it was a step in the right direction.

She waited for him to finish, then cleared her throat. "We'll let Leary get a head start on the scene, so he won't think we're muscling in. You can pick me up here, at my hotel."

"I can be there in ten minutes."

Amber tossed her hair back over her shoulder, balancing the phone against her ear while she looked at her sleek quartz watch. "Make it twenty. I need to make a phone call. And I haven't had dinner yet. I'm going to order something from the restaurant downstairs."

There was a pause, and she could imagine Bader's surreptitious grin. She knew what he was thinking: *The ice queen eats.* She smiled, amused at how thoroughly she had laid on the façade. "Yes, Agent Bader, I need food like everyone else. Pick me up in twenty minutes."

She hung up the phone, her hands tingling, thankful that there was still no trace of tiredness in her limbs. Her night was just beginning.

"This doesn't look good."

Amber ignored Bader's statement as she stepped out of the dark blue Mercedes sedan. It was an unfortunate Western habit: stating and restating the obvious. Amber wasn't blind; she could see the stricken looks on the policemen's faces as they stumbled down the front steps of the apartment complex. She could hear the noxious retching coming from the other side of the nearest police cruiser, where a newspaper reporter crouched over a trash bin. She pushed the Mercedes's door shut and followed Bader down the narrow alley, avoiding the football-sized rats that scurried around her comfortable suede boots.

"Looks like Leary's already inside. And at least one FBI agent." Bader was pointing at two cars parked perpendicular to the curb, directly in front of the decrepit apartment building. One was a souped-up cruiser with the garish Anti-Terrorist seal emblazoned across its front hood. The other was an oversized Chevrolet with federal plates. Amber wondered how the FBI agent had managed to arrive before her and Bader. Bader had met her at the Eliot barely fifteen minutes after they had spoken. Still, she didn't blame him for his eagerness; she had a strong feeling that at least one of the mysteries surrounding Kyle's death was going to be solved tonight.

"Used to be a lot of college kids living around here," Bader rambled on, as they came into the shadow of the five-story brick building. "Then it went gay for a few years. Now it's catching the runoff from the South End. Every trendy café that opens on Tremont Street means another welfare case shipped off to the Fens."

Amber watched a rat run into an overturned trash can as it tried desperately to avoid Bader's expensive leather shoes. The rats and the rundown atmosphere of the alley did not bother her; in Taiwan and Hong Kong, she had chased leads into areas that would have made the Fens look like Beacon Hill. But this four-block neighborhood of crumbling apartment buildings and overgrown vacant lots did seem inconsistent with the charm of the rest of the city. Still, the poor had to live somewhere. Why not in the shadow of the Green Monster?

"Might look like shit, but you could catch a home run from your bedroom window." Bader laughed as he started up the apartment's front steps. He had spent the ride over barraging Amber with Red Sox war stories. As they had driven past the legendary baseball park that gave the neighborhood its name, Bader had glowed with near religious zeal; in Boston, baseball *was* religion, and the Fenway was its shrine.

Amber had glanced at the high green wall at the back of the park, trying to understand Bader's state of rapture. China had the Great Wall and the Forbidden City; Boston had the Green Monster.

"Here we go," Bader announced, opening the door. "They discovered the bodies less than an hour ago. But they've been dead for more than forty hours, so the smell should be pretty fierce."

Amber grimaced as the odor swept into her nostrils. There were two police officers on the other side of the door, searching the walls and floorboards with heavy rubber flashlights. A third officer was unrolling a spool of yellow crime scene tape, blocking off the entrance to a descending cement stairwell. The officer with the tape had bushy red hair and an unlit cigarette hanging out of the corner of his mouth. His cheeks were a pasty green. He looked up as Bader and Amber approached.

"If you think you're gonna throw up, do it before you get downstairs. The chief's so pissed off, he's threatening to clear the place. The forensic boys have had to restart twice on account of that fuck from the *Globe*."

He held up the tape so Bader and Amber could squeeze underneath. Once they were on the other side, Bader looked back at him. "Is it really that bad?"

The police officer rubbed the back of his hand across his lips. "Remember when that Swedish nanny got sliced in half up by Boylston a while back? I was on duty that day. Saw the garbage bag in the Dumpster, all the chick pieces sticking out. Didn't puke, though. Held it in until the coroner arrived."

He shivered, pointing past them, down the stairs. "Puked three times tonight. Think the chief's the only one who's kept his dinner, besides the two feds, of course. Take a nuclear bomb to crack those bastards. Still, I think this came close."

His face turned a darker shade of green, then he shifted back to his tape. Amber had already started down the stairs. "Holy mother of God." Bader's exclamation echoed through the hushed room. Amber did not react as she carefully navigated over the bottom step, landing on a patch of fresh newspapers that covered a corner of the filthy tiled floor. They were in a dingy studio apartment, a low-ceilinged, poorly lit rectangle with cracked plaster walls and no windows. There was a bright orange seventies-style couch in the center of the rectangle, facing a small black-and-white television perched on an overturned plastic milk crate. In a tiny kitchenette off to the right were a stainless-steel sink and a pint-sized refrigerator.

Three uniformed officers huddled by the refrigerator, talking in low tones, as a fourth officer dusted the sink with fingerprint powder. Another man, dressed in a heavy tan overcoat, stepped gingerly around the couch, his face hidden behind an oversized evidence camera. Every few seconds a flash of bright light exploded off the walls, giving the scene a surreal, dramatic edge. Amber watched the forensic photographer as he slowly rounded the far corner of the couch, finally focusing his attention on the horror itself.

Amber held her breath against the overwhelming odor, as the bright flash illuminated the right half of the room. She took in the queen-sized steel-framed bed and the small wooden dresser, cluttered with half-empty bottles of vodka and ashtrays overflowing with ancient, lipstick-stained butts. Dick Leary stood at one side of the bed, his hands on his fleshy hips. Next to him stood two FBI men, both blond and wide shouldered, wearing expensive gray suits. One of the men was talking into a cellular phone while the other made notes on a yellow legal pad. At one point he stopped writing and extended his ballpoint toward the body on the bed. Leary said something and the agent nodded, turning back to the legal pad.

Amber felt no emotion as she walked across the apartment. She had struggled through five years in CIA special training camps in Southeast Asia, where she'd spent many nights studying the work of some of the worst butchers in modern history. She had seen classified pictures from Burma, Libya, Iraq, Vietnam, Cambodia, and of course China. She had graduated at the top of her class, and had since refined her abilities in countless operations in the eastern hemisphere. Although she had never witnessed physical torture up close, she had seen the results, and she knew how to depersonalize a corpse. Still, it took all of her faculties to remain in complete control as she approached the bed.

The man had been tall, Caucasian, with short blond hair and an athletic physique. His body was stripped completely naked, his wrists and ankles handcuffed to the steel posts at the four corners of the bed. It was an intensely vulnerable position—legs spread wide, hands incapacitated—and someone had taken full advantage of the situation.

Although decay had already set in, Amber had no trouble recreating the torture scene. The first focus had been the man's chest. Small incisions had been made above each nipple, and the skin had been peeled downward to reveal the sensitive pockets of nerve endings. Both nipples had been removed, and the area just beneath had been scooped out, possibly with a tool specifically created for the task.

From there, attention had shifted downward to the man's exposed genitalia. Amber heard Bader retching behind her as she stared at the violated place between the man's legs; even for a woman, it was a gut-wrenching sight. The man's flaccid penis had been split down the middle, and a tiny shard of clear glass jabbed upward from between the peeled sections of skin. An incision had been made in the scrotum, and both testicles had been plucked out, trailing twisting spaghetti cords of blood vessels and nerves. The intact testicles rested obscenely on the man's right thigh. Worse still, a pair of metal pliers was tightly clenched around one of the spherical glands.

Amber drew to a stop next to Leary and the two FBI agents, pulling her eyes back to the dead man's face. The flesh around his eyes had already started to swell and blister. She could see streaks of purple under his outstretched arms and legs, where the blood had pooled. By the drooping skin tone, gas swelling, and marked lividity, she guessed the actual time of death was even more than forty hours, perhaps closer to three days. It would take a medical examiner and a forensic entomologist to tell for sure.

"Christ," Bader said, as he finally stopped retching. "Someone did a number on him."

Leary turned, noticing the two CIA agents for the first time. "Wonderful. The cavalry's here. But you're two testicles too late."

Amber glanced at him, then back at the corpse. She didn't know which was worse, Bader's obtuse comments or Leary's sense of humor.

"Agents Bader, Chen, meet Agents Rickman and Nozicki. Hey, if we get one more of you guys down here, we can field a spook basketball team. I know where we can get a couple of balls."

"That's just about the most appalling thing I've ever heard," the taller of the two FBI agents grunted, nodding at Amber. He had striking blue eyes and a moon-shaped scar on his left cheek. Fairly attractive, in a Neanderthalish way. "I'm Frank Nozicki. This is my partner Dave Rickman. It's an honor to meet you, Ms. Chen. You're something of a legend at the Bureau."

Amber lowered her head a fraction of an inch, the custom of her culture showing through. In Asia, it wasn't proper to accept a compliment at face value. "An exaggeration, I'm sure. But I appreciate your kindness."

"No exaggeration. Your name appears in half the footnotes in our foreign field texts at Quantico. Twenty-six collars in five years of foreign duty, more than any other antiterrorist agent in field history. There's an entire chapter on the capture and coerced 'extradition' of Kaola Sen—the Mongolian Butcher—from North Korea. Ninety-two, wasn't it?"

"Ninety-three," Bader answered. Amber was surprised by both men's knowledge of her accomplishments. She was not driven by a need for respect or accolades. Nor was she ambitious, in the Western sense. Her success was simply a matter of honor. Her father had been one of the greatest terrorist-hunters attached to the British forces in East Asia. At the age of twenty-two and fresh out of Oxford, Amber had chosen to follow in his footsteps. After his death on a deep mission in the mountains of eastern China seven years ago, she had striven to pay homage to his memory, and bring "face" to her family, even as her brother, Winston, did everything in his power to achieve the opposite. At thirty-two, Amber was not yet half the hunter her father had been; but as Nozicki had correctly noted, her obsession with detail and her stubborn endurance had caused fate to smile on her twenty-six times in the years since she had left the CIA training camps.

"Well, shit, Bader," Leary said, an irritated smirk on

his thick lips. "You didn't tell me your new friend was a celebrity spook. Maybe our Oriental superspy can tell us something about the corpse with the split dick stinking up this rathole."

Amber ignored his sarcastic tone, turning her attention back to the body on the bed. She could feel the two FBI agents watching her, and she wondered how careful she had to be with her information. It wasn't simply a matter of interagency competition; she was dealing with a highly sensitive situation. No doubt the FBI agents were already suspicious of her presence. She had to be careful not to feed those suspicions; her orders on the subject were extremely clear. Any evidence of a Chinese connection to the governor's assassination had to remain strictly confidential. At this stage a leak suggesting Chinese involvement could have massive consequences.

She did not want to hinder the FBI's investigation, but in many ways, it was in competition with her own. "I think it's obvious this man suffered a great deal at the hands of a professional," she finally responded. "In the end, he probably gave up whatever information he had."

Leary rolled his eyes. "Good thing we got an expert with us. I thought he had slipped and cut himself on a butter knife. Of course he gave 'em what they wanted! They cut his fucking dick in half!"

"Actually, no. It was much worse than that." Amber knew she was responding to Leary's baiting style, but she wanted to wipe the smirk off his face. She could be careful and dominant at the same time. "After the nipple procedure had proved ineffective, a glass rod approximately six inches long was inserted through the tip of the victim's penis. The rod was thrust down the length of his urethra, causing immense discomfort, to say the least. After the rod was fully inserted, the side of his penis was struck with a blunt object, snapping the glass and causing the shards to slice the organ in half."

Leary's face had turned pale, and the two FBI agents had turned away. Bader was moaning softly, his right hand pressed tightly over his mouth. Amber continued, her voice a stiff monotone. She was leaving out pertinent information, but still giving enough to justify her involvement in the investigation. "Somehow, the victim managed to hold out through this procedure, so the professional began to improvise. The skin of the testicles was cut away, and pliers were used to crush one of the glands, at which time the victim gave up his information."

There was a brief pause, then Leary wiped sweat from his forehead. "I bet you're a hell of a first date."

"Once the identity of the victim is confirmed," Amber continued, "the nature of the revealed information becomes academic. According to what Agent Bader's told me, you've already made a preliminary identification. Is that correct?"

"Although we still need visual confirmation," Nozicki answered for Leary, reading from his yellow legal pad. "We're pretty sure it's Peter Mattison, a Secret Service agent assigned to Governor Kyle's personal safety. He was supposedly in the limousine with the governor during the motorcade—impossible, since he's been dead for approximately two days."

"So where does that leave us?" Bader asked, his voice weak.

Leary kept his eyes trained on Amber as he answered. "With one less mystery—and at least one less inside suspect: Scarlett O'Hara didn't kill Rhett after all. Anne Kyle already knew the timing and route of his motorcade, and wouldn't need to torture the information out of our corpse. So that's one betrayal theory gone to hell."

A fitting place for a foolish theory. Amber had known Leary was grasping at straws when he first proposed an adulterous-wife scenario to the investigating task force. Even without the Valhalla connection, the case against Anne Kyle· was absurdly weak. The only evidence of her alleged adultery was a record of late-night phone calls from her private line to a real estate mogul in her hometown of Mobile. And even if the calls *were* evidence of something more than a close friendship, she had no real motive for killing her doting husband. She came from a long line of money, and Andrew Kyle had never kept her on a short leash.

Anne Kyle had never been a viable suspect. But the terrible glass rod had solved the mystery of the timing and location of the waiting Valhalla. Perhaps there was no one on the inside after all.

"You called our target a professional," Nozicki interrupted, and all four sets of eyes turned back to Amber. "And you seem to know a lot about his method of interrogation."

Amber shrugged, still focused on the corpse. "Whoever did this is patient, methodical, and obviously enjoys his work. His torture technique, though carefully refined, is not unique; similar methods have been used in Bolivia, Burma, South Africa, and Colombia."

She purposefully left out the key piece of information: *bo pi*—literally, "the flesh peeling"—had been used effectively by the Chinese military as early as the 1950s. During the Korean War, the Chinese shared the technique with their struggling brethren, and after that the secrets of *bo pi* spread through the rest of East Asia. In the early 1980s, an enterprising Colombian drug lord learned the technique while on vacation in Bangkok, and within a few years, terrorists around the world were touting its effectiveness.

The use of *bo pi* on the Secret Service agent did not prove that the Chinese were involved, but it certainly strengthened Amber's suspicions. She wondered what other clues she would find in the dingy basement apartment.

"Judging by the lipstick stains on the cigarette butts and the vodka-bottle necks, I assume there's more to this story."

Leary glanced at her, surprised. Then he threw a fat thumb over his left shoulder. "In the bathroom off to the left. The mistress of the household. Paulette Clooney. Thirteen priors for solicitation, six months in Walpole for propositioning the underage son of a local judge. Worked the Combat Zone and the Fens, sometimes wandered the Back Bay when the weather was good."

Amber noted the past tense. "I assume she won't be wandering the Back Bay anymore."

"See for yourself. You'll find most of her in the bathtub. Everything but the head. The head's an interesting twist—"

Leary was interrupted in midsentence by a commotion coming from the stairs. A short, pale man with dark hair and glasses was standing on the bottom step. He was wearing an expensive blue suit and had a notebook under his left arm. His mouth was wide open, a look of sheer revulsion on his face. "Christ. Is that Mattison?"

Then his eyes digested the scene in front of him and he dropped to his knees, adding his own vomit to the puddle on the bottom step.

"Aw, great," Leary snarled. "Benton Crow? The governor's little prick? Who invited him?"

Amber started toward the stairs. All four men were

staring at her. "I did. Now you've got your visual confirmation."

The temperature had dropped ten degrees outside, and the cold wind felt good against Amber's skin. She leaned against the side of Bader's Mercedes, watching the political aide as he struggled to compose himself. Benton Crow was sitting half inside the Mercedes's front seat, his head almost to his knees. His pale body was shaking, and Amber felt a touch of sympathy for the little man. It was an old Company trick, but incredibly effective. Crow would answer any questions she asked, truthfully and without thought. The shock to his system was as good as any CIA truth serum.

"That was horrible. What they did to him. Just awful."

Amber ran her hands along the cold surface of the Mercedes. Her overcoat was open, her white shirt unbuttoned to her collarbone. She had picked up the new suit at a chic store on Newbury, to replace the light silk outfit she had brought with her from Hong Kong. She had already adjusted to the cold weather and the time change, and she felt alive, bristling with inner energy. She was on the hunt—and it felt good. "Mr. Crow, I'm sorry you had to see that. I hadn't known the details, or I never would have asked you to meet me here."

"Why did they do that to him?"

Amber did not like to think of her quarry as a "they." She was not hunting the Chinese government or any subset of China's vast military. She was hunting an operative who had committed a terrorist act on American soil. "For information."

"But why? Who would do such a thing?"

"That's what I'm trying to find out. I see you brought the information I asked for."

Crow nodded, pulling the notebook out from under his knees. It was small, with a black leather cover. Amber took it from him and flipped through the pages. She saw lines of coded writing separated by blank spaces, perhaps ten lines per page. "And this is the driver's complete log?"

"Depends what you mean by 'complete.' The notebook contains a record of Governor Kyle's use of his limo over the past four weeks. I've already given a copy of the log to Detective Leary, and also to the FBI. But as I was telling you over the phone, the governor had a real independent streak. He took his own car out three, maybe four times a week."

Amber watched the small man's face carefully. Sweat ran down from his dark hair, and his glasses were partially fogged over. The torture scene had shaken him considerably. Amber shut the small notebook and placed it inside her overcoat. "Perhaps the governor was more independent in the past few weeks than usual?"

Crow looked up, his lips twitching at the corners. Amber had read the man correctly when she had finally spoken to him over the phone. There was something he hadn't yet told the police. She needed to get him to open up. "Benton, I'm not with the BPD. My only concern is catching the animal who killed Governor Kyle."

Crow took off his glasses and rubbed sweat from his eyes. Then he glanced around the edge of the Mercedes. The nearest police officer was twenty feet away, searching the thick hedges in front of the apartment building. "Ms. Chen, I could get in a lot of trouble for telling you this, and it's not the police I'm worried about. But I think it might be important. Two weeks ago, Governor Kyle initiated a project on his own time—a private investigative project, one that won't be reflected in that driver's log."

Amber could hear the blood rushing through her ears. "What sort of project?"

Crow replaced his glasses and lowered his voice. "He was investigating rumors of illegal foreign contributions both to his own office, and to a number of other municipal institutions in the Boston area. Mind you, in the governor's case these contributions were not solicited. But they came from unresearched sources, and involved an enormous amount of money."

Amber wondered if this was the break she was looking for. She knew that China had taken heat in the past few years for contributing to political campaigns in Washington and elsewhere. But she couldn't conceive of a contribution scandal that would lead to torture and murder. "So you're saying the governor's office had accepted illegal foreign funds."

"Actually, no. Governor Kyle investigated every contribution to his last two campaigns, and found no basis for the rumors. But in the course of his inquiry into *other* municipal institutions, he discovered something interesting. A flow of funds from a foreign source into Boston Metropolitan Hospital."

Amber raised her eyebrows. She knew very little about Metro, except that it was considered one of the best hospitals in the country. "Is that unusual?"

"Not normally. Hospitals with large research facilities often get funding from foreign sources, but these sources have to be reported, logged, and carefully monitored if the hospital wants to remain federally accredited—in other words, entitled to accept Medicare. The influx of foreign money into Metro had not been reported, and Governor Kyle had wanted to know why."

Crow reached into his suit jacket and pulled out a slip of computer paper. "This is a record of the funding, added in annual increments to Metro's research budget.

Governor Kyle had intended to make this information public next week, after he completed his investigation. As far as I know, he had not yet figured out who was making the investment or why. But, I didn't speak with him much in the few days before his death."

Amber took the sheet of computer paper and looked over the figures. Someone had been making contributions of more than $5 million annually to Metro's research coffers, beginning a little less than three years ago.

"You can see why I've been careful with this information," Crow continued. "If the media found out that Governor Kyle had investigated his own office because of foreign-contribution rumors, they would have had a field day. Lieutenant Governor Robertson—Kyle's running mate and the likeliest candidate to replace him—has already forbidden me to speak to the police, or anyone else. But I know it might be significant."

"You did the right thing," Amber said, folding the sheet of computer paper and storing it next to the notebook. "If you think of anything else, you have my number."

She stepped away from the Mercedes and headed back toward the apartment building. She wasn't sure what the new information meant, but she had a gut feeling that it was significant. Kyle had been investigating foreign funding and had discovered an influx of money into Metro. He had been about to go public with his information—and had been abruptly assassinated. Crow had not mentioned China, but that didn't mean China was not involved.

The key was Metro. Why would China pour money into a hospital in Boston, Massachusetts? Amber didn't know where Kyle's investigation had led him, but she knew where her own was going to begin: with the natural link between Andrew Kyle and Boston Metropolitan. Dr. Mike Ballantine.

She had already interviewed the governor's best friend once, when she first arrived at the BPD and before she had introduced herself to Leary and the rest of the task force. She had found him handsome, intelligent, and genuinely grieved by his friend's sudden death. She had spoken to him only briefly, but in that short time she had attained a fairly clear impression of the man. If she had needed a single word to describe him, she would have chosen "solid." Both physically and emotionally. It was a word she had once heard used to describe her father, and she did not employ it lightly. Alec Constantine had not been solid—brilliant and unique, but not solid. And Winston was as far from solid as any man Amber had ever met.

But Dr. Ballantine had shown that quality, and Amber couldn't help but feel intrigued at the thought of a second meeting—

"Excuse me, Ms. Chen. Wouldn't want to drop this." Nozicki was carefully descending the front steps of the apartment complex, an opaque plastic coroner's bag held out in front of him. The bag was tied at the top, and Nozicki was staring at it as if it was full of spiders. "We're taking it to our lab in Andover for a workup, since we've got better facilities than the BPD. I'll fax you a report at your hotel the minute we're finished."

Amber stopped in front of him, gauging the size and weight of the object inside the bag. Round, the shape of a cantaloupe or a small watermelon. "May I take a look inside?"

Nozicki scrunched his blue eyes. "I'm not sure you really want to. But go ahead."

He turned his head and untied the top of the plastic bag. Amber peered inside—and gasped, her eyes going wide. Nozicki looked at her, surprised.

"I warned you it was bad. Our perp is one fucking butcher. The worst part is, Paulette Clooney was probably just an innocent bystander. Wrong place, wrong time."

Amber ignored him, stepping back from the bag. Her heart was suddenly racing in her chest. She fought for control, unable to digest what she had just seen.

"Ms. Chen? Are you okay?"

Vivid memories rushed through Amber's mind. She was dragged back seven years, to the day of her father's funeral. She pictured the closed casket as it was lowered into the incinerator. She remembered the reason the coffin had been kept closed, in stark contrast to her father's Daoist tradition. Then she stared at the plastic bag in Nozicki's hands, and her entire body started to shake.

The head inside the bag was missing both ears.

CHAPTER TEN

Trinity Church rose above the undulating crowd, ancient stone spires clawing like spastic fingers into the face of the indigo sky. The great arched doorways were propped open, and waves of organ music splashed down the white stone front steps. Above the doorways, shadows wrestled behind the painted glass church windows, as flickering holy candles struggled against the incessant flash of camera bulbs. Cacophonous platoons of reporters from the local television stations and national networks had bivouacked on either side of the steps, their cameras and microphones aimed like howitzers at the steady stream of overdressed mourners. The crowd extended out behind the reporters, an ocean of bodies severed by two flimsy bright blue police barricades.

The irony was not lost on Mike as he staggered through Copley Square toward the steps of Trinity: two days ago, the same bright barricades had lined Andrew's motorcade route. Mike had the sudden urge to kick the nearest wooden horse into splinters, to fling its shattered pieces into the throbbing crowd. This was not a funeral; this was a show, put on by the city of Boston and Anne Kyle, the former model in mourning. Trinity wasn't even a Catholic church; it was Episcopalian. Mike could hear the Irish officers grumbling as they held back the crowds. They knew why Anne had chosen Trinity instead of the church in Southie where Andrew had been confirmed. The spot had been chosen for the cameras and the crowds. Next week, Andrew would get a real funeral, away from the fanfare and the telescopic lenses. An Irish priest would cry real Irish tears, and no one would care what Anne Kyle was wearing or what the ceremony would look like on the evening news. The scene at Trinity was a spectacle, a circus starring an empty coffin and a teary eyed bride. Mike lowered his head, concentrating on the cement beneath his black leather shoes.

He could feel each step reverberate through his knees. He had spent most of the night walking, his mind spinning through the events of the past two days. He had finally returned to his apartment after three and had spent the remaining hours before dawn lying on the couch in his living room, jabbing at the ceiling with the tip of his lacrosse stick.

As he moved between the barricades, his eyes burned with exhaustion, and the sweat built up beneath his dark wool suit. It was the only suit he owned that Kari hadn't picked out; consequently, it was a size too big and the thick pants chafed the insides of his thighs. He had bought the suit for her funeral, never expecting to wear it again. He had prayed that the next funeral he attended would be his own. As his mother had told him a week before she herself passed away, it's abundantly harder to mourn than to die.

The short walk over to Copley Square had been a painful blur, and Mike had stopped twice to catch his breath. The fever and the nausea had not been back since Louisburg Square, but the memories of the gaunt man standing in the study doorway had plagued him incessantly throughout the past twelve hours. After finding the photograph of Andrew's horse, Mike could no longer think of his visions as mere hallucinations; they were something more, something haunting and impossible to accept.

He slid his hand down the side of his pants, feeling the photograph through the rough wool. The picture defied science. It went against all the rules that held Mike's world together. Without those rules—without science—Mike knew he could not survive. He could no longer trust any of his senses. The pressing crowds on either side, the cement beneath his feet, the other mourners moving with him toward the stone steps, Trinity Church itself—were any of them real? Or were they all part of the cruel hoax, waiting to vanish in front of his eyes?

"Dr. Ballantine? May I have a word?"

Mike looked up, startled. He was still ten feet from the steps of the church, caught behind a cluster of minor Boston celebrities mugging for the cameras from CNN. The voice had come from directly behind the barricade to his right. He squinted against the sun, and saw a tall woman with long black hair and dark sunglasses standing next to a red-faced police officer. The police officer was checking the laminated security card hanging around the woman's neck, the same bright orange card that dangled against Mike's suit and allowed him to walk unmolested between the blue barricades. The cop shrugged, and the woman climbed over the nearest wooden horse, her interminable legs stretching the black, velvety material of her expensive slacks.

Mike recognized her as she came toward him: Amber Chen, the federal agent who had questioned him at the police department. But her appearance seemed even more striking now, her long lines and confident posture immediately setting her apart from the thousands lining the barricades. Her sable hair was tied behind her head in an elegant bun, revealing the smooth curve of her neck. Her lips were full and glossy red, even beneath a minimal lick of carefully applied lipstick. Behind the dark glasses, Mike could see the edges of her almond eyes, carved as if by diamonds into the caramel glass of her face. She drew to a stop at Mike's side, removing the sunglasses and sliding them into the pocket of her overcoat. Her irises were pitch black, her cheekbones high and perfectly symmetrical.

She was exotic, flawless, and intimidating. Mike had never met anyone, Asian or not, who looked like Amber Chen. She had stopped shoulder to shoulder, and he realized they were within an inch of the same height. Her lithe body, small waist, and almost elastic legs made her seem even taller, like a late-afternoon shadow stretching up the side of a marble building. She pulled out the badge Mike recognized from the other morning.

"I'm sorry to intrude on this solemn occasion," she said, showing him the shiny seal that identified her as a federal agent. "I know this must be difficult for you. But I have a few questions that simply can't wait."

Her accent was as abrupt and direct as her words. Mike guessed she had been schooled in Hong Kong or Singapore, someplace where the majority of teachers were from England. He started forward again, his eyes on the looming church steps.

"Your timing isn't very appropriate," he responded. At the moment, it was a struggle to stay on his feet, much less answer questions from a federal agent. He was afraid of his own mind, of anything that might set off another one of Arthur's "fault lines." "Can't it wait until after the funeral?"

Amber covered her face as a CNN camera swiveled past. "An investigation is a lot like a dying patient, Dr. Ballantine. Every minute lost is a minute you can't get back. And if I'm not mistaken, this isn't the real funeral, is it? Your friend was an Irish Catholic. I don't think he'd mind you taking a few minutes away from this circus."

Mike glanced at her, surprised. She was looking at the mob of expensive dark suits crowded around the arched doorway of the church. Anne Kyle was barely visible in the center of the mob; but her well-tailored black dress seemed to glow in the flash of a dozen newspaper cameras. "It's interesting," Amber continued, almost to herself. "Where I come from, white is the color of death, red the color of celebration. Brides wear red; coffins are draped in white. Some of us hope to avoid both colors. We do not relish the attention, happy or sad."

She turned back toward Mike. "Anne Kyle would not have made a good Chinese."

For the first time in days, Mike felt like smiling. He tried to look into Amber's dark eyes. She was unreadable—yet for some reason, he felt connected to her. And something in her face told him he was not alone in his feelings; there was something sudden and intriguing traversing the air between them. Or was it just another figment of his fevered imagination?

Mike smiled inwardly, surprised by the sudden rise of interest in a woman he hardly knew. He realized with a start that somehow, her appeal went beyond her exotic physical beauty; for some reason Mike could not fathom, Amber Chen fascinated him.

He cocked his head toward a less crowded area to the right of the church. "Why don't we talk over there, where you won't have to worry about the cameras."

Amber raised her eyebrows. "I didn't know if you noticed. Appearances on CNN are frowned upon in my line of work."

Mike could not tell if she was serious or joking. "I

thought you were just shy. Or embarrassed by the company."

"I'm sure you're aware of the Asian stereotype. It's our nature to be embarrassed and demure."

Mike watched as she flashed her ID at a nearby police officer, ordering him to move one of the barricades so they could push through. Amber Chen was anything but demure.

Mike sat across from her on a cold stone bench. Beyond her, Boylston Street was packed with parked television vans and groups of gawkers. The funeral had shut down an entire section of the Back Bay, and the lieutenant governor had made the day a statewide day of mourning. Mike had met Robertson only once, at a party at Andrew's mansion. He was a slick, handsome man bristling with ambition, a lawyer like Andrew but with a pedigree that stretched back hundreds of years. Robertson's ancestors had been waiting on the shore when the *Mayflower* touched Plymouth Rock, and the Robertson family had been entrenched in Massachusetts politics ever since.

"This would not exist where I come from. It would never be allowed."

At first, Mike thought Amber was talking about the spectacle surrounding them, but then he realized she was talking about Copley Square itself. Mike glanced around the stone glade perched between the gothic public library, Trinity Church, and the Hancock, the tallest building in the city. He looked back at Amber, confused, and saw she was glaring at the high glass of the Hancock. Mike had never seen such a reaction to an inanimate object before. He followed her gaze up its reflective face. At this angle, the Hancock seemed almost two-dimensional, a glass knife rising high into the sky.

"You don't like the Hancock? It's just an insurance building. And it has a great skywalk. You can see the entire city."

Amber pulled her eyes away from the towering glass dagger and turned to the gray stone library on the other side of the square. "Have you ever heard of *feng shui*, Dr. Ballantine?"

Mike recognized the term. "Some sort of Asian religion, isn't it?"

"Not a religion—more a spiritual science. Literally, *feng shui* means 'wind and water.' It is the art of achieving proper harmony in your physical surroundings."

She shifted back toward the Hancock, then shivered. Mike couldn't help noticing the way her breasts shifted under her shirt with the involuntary motion, her nipples two dark dimes pressing up through the white material. "In the East, it is believed that the physical and spiritual worlds are connected; that spiritual energy flows between inanimate and animate objects, and therefore physical surroundings can truly affect mental and physical well-being. The desired state, at all times, is a state of harmony, internal and external."

Mike swallowed, watching her eyes. She was truly stunning—and wildly enigmatic. He didn't know what to make of what she was saying. It seemed absurd and unscientific, but she did not strike him as the type who put stock in fantasy. He realized they were separated by an enormous cultural chasm; still, science was an objective entity. It had nothing to do with culture. Looking at her striking features, he wondered what other truths cut across such disparate cultures. Then he lowered his eyes, feeling strangely guilty about the sudden thoughts crossing his mind. It wasn't the memory of Kari that bothered him; it was the situation. He was sitting outside his best friend's funeral, becoming aroused by a woman he had met in a police interrogation room. It didn't seem right. It certainly didn't seem Catholic.

"Before a building goes up in Hong Kong or anywhere in China," Amber continued, "the architect must consult a *feng shui* expert. An expert is also called on when you decorate an office or apartment."

"Sounds like a serious business," Mike said, doing his best to compose himself. Amber didn't seem to notice his internal struggle.

"*Feng shui* is a *very* serious business. When companies go to war, they use *feng shui* as both a defensive art and a method of attack. Some people believe that entire businesses have failed because of the poor placement of a mirror in the CEO's office, or the angle of an antenna on the top of a nearby building."

Mike raised his eyebrows, wondering if she was playing with him. Her intensity seemed sincere. She waved a hand at the square behind him.

"Look at the way the Hancock Building slices through the sky. The triangular corners cut like a dagger through the energy pooled in the square. There is no harmony here. It is impossible to have a clear thought anywhere near that atrocious building. The entire Back Bay is threatened by a state of confusion as long as the Hancock pierces the skyline."

Mike almost laughed. The Back Bay *was* locked in confusion; it was a chaotic neighborhood with so many voices that they amounted to nothing but noise. Lack of spiritual harmony was as good an explanation as any. Mike rubbed his eyes, thinking of his own confused state. He wished he could simply blame it on the Hancock Building.

"Well, we could lobby the state government," he said, still pawing at his bleary eyes. "Maybe get the thing torn down. Too bad you didn't tell me about this a week ago. I used to have a friend in a high place."

There was a moment of silence. When Mike looked up, he realized Amber's expression had changed. It was as if an icy sheet had been pulled across her face. Any interest he had experienced slithered away, replaced by a sudden, irrational tinge of fear. What the hell was with this woman? One minute she was almost making eyes at him, the next minute she looked as if she was about to accuse him of murder.

"Dr. Ballantine," she asked, her voice cool and clipped, "who funds your lab at Metro?"

The question seemed to come out of nowhere. Mike shifted forward against the stone bench. Behind him, he could hear the shouts of the reporters as they tried to get Anne Kyle's attention. The service inside Trinity was going to begin at any moment, and the crowd in front of the stone steps was already beginning to disperse. "My lab? What does my lab have to do with anything?"

Amber lowered her voice. "It's a simple question. Five years ago, Boston Metropolitan allocated four thousand square feet in the basement of its main building for your research. At the time, your annual budget was half a million dollars. Three years ago, your funding increased to more than five million dollars, despite the fact that you have failed to publish anything scientifically viable since your lab's inception. So I ask you again, who funds your basement lab?"

Mike was staring at her in shock. *Five million dollars?* The number was absurd. His funding had not changed in the past five years; it had remained at half a million annually, which was far more than he needed. "I don't know where you get your figures, but my lab doesn't receive anywhere near five million in funding. And besides, a lot of young labs have yet to produce publishable results. That's the nature of research."

Amber's dark eyes seemed to drill into his skull. He realized she was trying to gauge his sincerity. A few seconds passed in silence, then she broke off the intense stare. It was as if he had passed some sort of test. The ice left her face, and once again her expression turned warm. "Dr. Ballantine, I spent the morning sifting through Metro's computer banks. Despite what you might have been told, your lab has been budgeted at over five million dollars annually. What does your research concern?"

Mike shook his head in disbelief. "There's obviously some sort of mistake. My research doesn't cost anywhere near that much. I've been studying the action of cytotoxic T cells, and their role in cellular immunity from certain forms of viruses. It's not the kind of high-profile work that generates that sort of funding."

He suddenly remembered the short scene from two days ago; Teri Pace, his shy graduate student with the bright green eyes, trying to tell him something. Then he shook the memory away; he doubted it had anything to do with Agent Chen's $5 million.

"If I've been budgeted for that kind of money," Mike continued, "I certainly haven't received it. And I damn sure haven't spent it. And what does it have to do with Andrew's death?"

Amber paused, as if trying to decide how much to say. "Maybe nothing. Governor Kyle had been investigating some discrepancies in Metro's funding. I picked up his trail late last night, and traced the influx of funds to your lab's research budget. If you didn't receive the money, then obviously someone else did. Any idea where I should look?"

Mike felt lost in her words. He had always assumed that Andrew had been funding his lab—but certainly not to the tune of $5 million! And now he was supposed to believe that Andrew had been investigating his lab's funding? Why hadn't Andrew said anything?

It dawned on Mike immediately: Andrew *would* have said something—unless he thought Mike was involved in some sort of scandal. He wouldn't have wanted to implicate Mike in anything illegal. After discovering the $5 million discrepancy, he would have continued his investigation in secret, trying to determine Mike's involvement before going public.

"He was investigating my lab? He should have told me."

"He was more interested in finding out where the money was coming from than where it was going. And that's what interests me, too. Kyle believed it was flowing from a foreign source. To get to that source, I need to track the money backward. I believe you didn't spend it. The question is, Who did?"

Mike's stomach hurt as he began to realize what she was saying. Andrew had discovered there was money pouring into Mike's lab, but he hadn't been willing to blow the whistle on Mike. He had intended to find out where the money was coming from, and take aim at the source. *Andrew. You should have trusted me. You should have told me.*

"The place to start is Douglas Stanton," Mike said, his teeth coming together. "If there was something improper going on at Metro, you can bet he was involved."

"The hospital administrator. That would make sense. He has access to the computer system, and he approves the allocation of research funds."

Mike had already stopped listening. Andrew had been surreptitiously investigating his backyard, not knowing if Mike was taking money illegally and then embezzling it. The thought made him sick. He shifted uncomfortably against the hard bench, turning his face away from Amber. For some reason, he didn't want to look at her. He felt embarrassed and betrayed by Andrew's tacit accusation: his own friend hadn't trusted him; why should a woman he hardly knew? He focused on the back of the disbanding crowd and watched a reporter interviewing a nameless mourner. He told himself it was irrelevant, now. There was no way to reach beyond the grave, no way to tell Andrew it wasn't true.

"Dr. Ballantine." There was a brief pause, and her voice softened. "Mike. I have only one more question."

Mike was barely listening, his eyes still focused on the reporter. "Go ahead. But I doubt I have an answer."

"Is there any reason why the Chinese military might be interested in your lab?"

Mike couldn't help himself. He laughed out loud. "The Chinese military? Why the hell—"

Mike's face drained of color, and he leaped up from the bench. The hallucination was back: the gaunt man, standing five feet behind the reporter, staring directly at him. For some reason, the apparition was trying to conceal itself within the dispersing crowd—but the dark eyes and hand-shaped acne scar were unmistakable.

"Mike?"

"No more, damn it. I won't take it anymore!"

Mike felt himself crack on the inside as sudden anger tore through his body. Before he realized what he was doing, he leaped over the stone bench and hurtled forward. His knee connected with a wire trash can, but he ignored the pain, running as if he were carrying the winning goal in a close lacrosse match. He didn't care if he was going insane, he didn't care if the thing he was chasing existed only inside his skull, he didn't care if he was giving in to the anger he hated more than anything else in the world—he had been pushed too far. He wasn't going to accept it anymore, he was going to kick and scream until they carried him away!

He reached the edge of the crowd and began shoving people aside. He felt a hand grab his shoulder but he kept moving, using his wide shoulders and strong arms to carve a path. He passed the reporter, smacking an oversized foam microphone to the ground—and suddenly found himself face-to-face with the gaunt man.

He stopped, stunned. The man hadn't disappeared. A look of pure shock had swept across his features. His long arms twitched beneath his white smock, and his dark eyes darted back and forth. The scar under his right eye was violent and pitted, five fingers of tortured skin curling across a dark brown cheek.

"Why are you persecuting me?" The words tore into the gaunt man, and he cringed backward, his mouth wide open. Without thinking, Mike reached out and grabbed the front of his white smock.

My God. It wasn't a hallucination. The gaunt man was real! Mike yanked him forward, staring into those dark, malevolent eyes. He could feel the man's wiry muscles through the soft material of his smock. The man was well built, like some sort of desert animal, perfectly toned and proportioned.

"Who are you?" Mike hissed through his teeth.

Then something in the gaunt man seemed to snap; the shock and fear left his face. His black eyes turned cold. Mike let go of the smock and stumbled back, terrified. Staring into those black eyes was like looking at pure, liquid violence.

Mike's mind fluttered back more than thirty years. He could hear the windowpane shattering as his mother's shoulder crashed through; he could see his father standing by the door, fists balled, eyes burning with the same liquid violence. Mike swallowed, his throat constricting. His own anger fled as the fear took over.

"Who are you?" he whispered again. Suddenly, the gaunt man smiled; it was as if his face had split in half. Then he turned and sprinted through the crowd.

Mike's shoulders sagged as he let the man disappear. He heard Agent Chen's voice over his shoulder. "Mike, are you all right?"

He closed his eyes, a shiver moving through his spine. He felt her hand on his arm. Her fingers were tender and warm. "Mike, who was that?"

Mike didn't answer, because there was no answer. He looked at her exquisite face and shook his head. A part of him wanted to try to explain, but it was too insane. He gently lifted her hand off his arm, then pushed his way forward through the crowd. He was thankful that she didn't try to follow.

The pretense was over: his mind had finally cracked. First, the horse. And now the gaunt man. His hallucinations had turned real.

Amber stood rooted to the ground, watching Mike Ballantine recede into the crowd. Part of her wanted to follow him, but she felt paralyzed, too stunned to follow her brain's commands.

She had only seen the gaunt Asian man for a brief instant—but that had been enough to set her insides on fire. She couldn't be sure; it had been years, and the only pictures that existed had been taken at great distances by men who had not lived long enough to develop them properly. But the scar and the malevolent black eyes tore at Amber's already provoked memories.

A little over seven years ago, her father had gone on a deep-cover mission into eastern China. Denshow Chen, England's top spy-hunter at the time, had been tracking one of the most brutal terrorists in China's history, a freelancer known only as Sheshen—literally, "the Snake Spirit." Sheshen's very existence was wrapped in myth and rumor, linked to nightmarish peasant stories that had risen out of the necklace of villages squatting along the eastern banks of the Yellow River. Amber had often heard the stories during her childhood—ghastly tales of medical experiments, ghost doctors, and bodies rising from the dead. At the center of these tales was the legend of a Devil Doctor—Gui Yisheng—who tore off men's ears, then reached inside and dined on their brains.

According to the myths, Sheshen was Gui Yisheng's only son. Gui Yisheng had traded him to Mao Zedong, China's Great Leader, in exchange for the use of a secret mountain laboratory. Sheshen had been raised and trained by Mao's elite guard, subsequently running missions for the Chinese military in locales around the world.

As with everything in China, it was difficult to know where rumor ended and reality began. In 1978, the British M1 and the American CIA began tracking a mysterious, brilliant, and vicious operative calling himself Sheshen; the Chinese agent's first act was the murder of three Taiwanese diplomats on a pleasure trip to Thailand. All three had been found with their ears and the central portions of their brains removed.

Sheshen's career had flourished in the years that followed. According to the CIA's files, he planned and executed forty-nine more assassinations over the next decade. By the late eighties, his kills had grown so many and so far-reaching, the British had begun calling him the Chinese Jackal—and some believed that perhaps a number of agents were working under the name Sheshen, borrowing his vicious signature to increase his international reputation.

At first, Amber's father had gone after Sheshen reluctantly; Denshow Chen had been a skeptical man, and he had understood the Chinese penchant for mythic hyperbole. He did not believe the stories of the Devil Doctor and his mountain laboratory. But when the son of a British Parliament member had been discovered in a bathhouse in Kowloon—missing his ears and the central portion of his brain—Denshow Chen had taken the case.

Amber had been two years into her CIA training when her father first began tracking the elusive Chinese Jackal. She had chosen the CIA instead of M1 for practical reasons: since Mao's death, the CIA had been extending its reach into China, and the opportunities for plum cases had been much greater in the American sector. So she and her father had already been in only limited contact when he set out for the mountains of the East. As was usual when he disappeared on a deep-cover mission, Amber had focused on her own work, trusting the ancients and her mother's *gui*—spirit—to look after her father. It wasn't until a year later that her father's supervisor from M1 had told her what had happened.

Six months after Denshow Chen had left in search of Sheshen, a package had been delivered to the offices of M1 in Hong Kong. Inside the package had been Denshow's head—missing both ears and the central portion of his brain.

Amber stood in the center of Copley Square, trying to shake away the memory of her father's brutal death. She took deep breaths, listening to her own heartbeat, chasing her inner harmony. She consciously avoided looking at the shadow that ran down the middle of the square—the dark, disharmonious line cast by the arrogant glass Hancock Building. Her thoughts were already unsettled enough.

Since the night before, her investigation had taken on

new life; Benton Crow's revelations had led her into the depths of Boston Metropolitan's financial machinery. It had taken hours to familiarize herself with Metro's computer system, and hours more to locate the discrepancy in research funding. When she had finally discovered that the money had been designated for Mike Ballantine's lab, Crow's story had begun to make more sense. Of course Governor Kyle would have focused his investigation on the source of the errant funds, rather than simply calling on Metro's administration to explain. He had wanted to protect his best friend.

Which brought Amber back to Mike Ballantine. His responses to her inquiry had been sincere. He still struck her as intrinsically solid, and she trusted him without question. More than that, she had *felt* something during the brief conversation—an indefinable kinship, a connection at a very complex and significant level.

It wasn't merely his looks: his strong Western features, his piercing eyes, his wide shoulders. There was a unique depth to him, a sense of pathos that she found intensely stirring. She knew from the file Bader had constructed in the early hours of the morning about Ballantine's dead wife and mother, and his father's struggle with alcoholism. She also knew about his sensitivity toward his patients, and his abilities as a healer. Her father would have called him *jen xin jen shu*, a sensitive and caring heart. In his patient suffering, he was as close to Chinese as any *ang mo* she had ever met.

But there was a mystery to Mike Ballantine. Amber pictured him as he sprang up from the bench, his face a pallid sheet. It was clear: he had recognized the gaunt man and had reacted with both terror and relentless anger. Even though Amber believed he knew nothing about the foreign money, he was somehow connected.

Amber clenched her fists as the energy built inside

her. She was suddenly ravenous. In the past ten hours, her investigation had become intensely personal. First the earless head in the plastic bag, and now the gaunt man with the hand-shaped acne scar. If Amber was right—if the gaunt man was Sheshen—then by some twitch of sister fate, Amber was hunting the same beast who had brutally murdered her father.

CHAPTER ELEVEN

The naked lightbulb cast shadow demons across the cracked plaster ceiling as the first needle twisted deep into the skin above the gaunt man's left eye. There was no pain, just a sharp sucking sensation at the point of puncture, a subtle signal that the needle had pierced the correct meridian. The gaunt man reached for a second needle from the plastic case by his cot, while using two fingers of his left hand to massage the next puncture point, a spot two inches above his nose. The second needle went in as easily as the first; this time the essential *teh-chi,* the sucking sensation, was less intense, more a general heightening of awareness than an actual feeling. The electromagnetic energy that flowed in circular fashion through the gaunt man's *Tu-Mo* meridian had been diverted; as long as he left the long needles embedded in his skin, his life energy would pool in the deep gray matter beneath his skull.

He had learned the six-thousand-year-old art from his father. Not the Great One, his adopted ancestor; but his real father, the demon who had brought him into the world. The lesson had taken place one year before his father had cruelly shipped him off to the Special Elite Red Guard Education Camp in Beijing. He could still picture the moment as if it were yesterday. The gaunt man had not yet earned the name Sheshen, but his father had always been Gui Yisheng. As ancient as the stars, as cruel and twisted as his decaying, armless body.

"*Zhenjiu* is the art of control," the Devil Doctor had whispered as he had forced his nine-year-old son to insert the needles into his own skin. "Master the meridians, my worthless seed, and be like the spirits: unchained from the weakness of flesh." The blood had run freely as the needles missed their marks, but Gui Yisheng had been relentless. "Swallow your tears, whelp, and concentrate. You must never accept failure. Rats eat the souls of failed little boys."

More than thirty years later, Sheshen used the needles to try to control his rage, as the rats gathered around his sweat-soaked cot. He lay prostrate against the hard mattress, his eyes open but not seeing. The *ang mo* had his lacrosse stick; Sheshen had his needles. The diverted electromagnetic energy enhanced his ability to think, numbing his nervous system while slowing his circulation. It was a purely scientific process, unlike the *ang mo*'s mystical fetishism involving the netted stick.

Finally, as his spirit hovered inches above his skin, Sheshen felt his mind focus. He could see himself lying naked against the mattress, his long tan limbs quivering as his muscles constricted, following the flow of energy. He forced his thoughts backward, his spirit rising out of this small room above a grocery store in an alley deep in Chinatown, back to the confusing moment two hours ago.

Something had gone seriously wrong at the funeral. The doctor had recognized Sheshen from across the crowded square. It was impossible, but true. Sheshen had been so surprised, he had felt an emotion that had not touched him since his first days in the Red Guard camp: fear. He had quickly beaten back the emotion, but in its place rose a deep, fetid shame. He had lost face in the grip of a *yang gui*.

The scalding anger returned like a firestorm, and Sheshen's spirit leaped back into his trembling body. His eyes narrowed, and he rose to a sitting position, reaching for a third needle. He could still see the look on the doctor's face, the bewildering frustration and madness, as he asked the strange question: "Why are you persecuting me?"

Sheshen wondered if he had understood the English words correctly. He wasn't sure how his surveillance qualified as persecution, but the mere fact that the doctor was aware he was being watched was disturbing enough. Sheshen was a professional, one of the best in the world. Mike Ballantine was a civilian, a Western doctor with no training in surveillance. It made no sense.

Had Sheshen underestimated him? Was the innocence an act? Another possibility suddenly dawned on Sheshen, and he pressed his lips together. He twisted the third needle into the skin directly below his hairline, watching as the toes of his left foot began to twitch.

Did the *ang mo* recognize him for another reason altogether? Was it possible? Sheshen realized immediately what he had to do. Even if there was the slimmest of possibilities that it was true, the time for patience was over. Sheshen's beastly father would have to understand. A viper that struck two seconds too late was also food for the rats.

Sheshen rose to his feet. In his nakedness he was an awesome sight; each muscle looked like a burrowing snake beneath his skin, and he moved with the grace of a deadly animal, his joints reacting in perfect, practiced harmony. Although he was thirty-nine years old, he felt ageless, inexhaustible. The four cement walls barely contained him, and his callused feet seemed to float on a cushion of energy above the dirty cement floor.

Aside from the cot, the room contained a steel desk, a swivel chair, and a set of wooden drawers. A single window looked out over the grocery store's green vinyl awning to the alley down below. This was a part of Boston that Westerners never saw, a dark, dingy matrix of alleys where tourists weren't welcome. The six-block section in the center of Chinatown was tightly controlled by the Triad, the infamous Chinese "Mafia" known for its vicious brutality and incomparable criminal efficiency. Even the Boston police, out-organized and severely outgunned, were reluctant to tread on the Triad's turf.

This small room had previously belonged to a Triad High Officer; when Sheshen and his men had arrived at the High Officer's combination grocery store–heroin dealership, the High Officer had immediately moved his operation two blocks away. Sheshen had watched with amusement as the sweaty, overdressed gangster had nervously covered his ears, then quickly turned over the keys to the store and its network of cell-like rooms. Even officers of the Triad knew to fear the son of Gui Yisheng.

Sheshen moved silently toward the desk, the acupuncture needles trembling at each step. He lowered himself into the swivel chair and looked up at the wall above the steel desktop. A huge, beaming face stared back at him. The face seemed three-dimensional, etched into a dripping crimson background. The features were as familiar as Sheshen's own: the high, rounded forehead, the receding black hair, the pursed lips, and especially the dark, omniscient eyes.

There were no words that could explain Sheshen's feelings when he looked into those eyes. *Divine Father, Right Hand of God.* Mao Zedong, the architect who had built modern China out of the bones and blood of an entire generation. Sheshen felt his lips quiver as a near orgasmic wave of pure devotion filled him from the inside. The Great Leader was the polar opposite of his putrid blood-father; Mao was a true master, worthy of total piety.

Sheshen's earliest memory of his surrogate father was still as clear as a desert morning: it was the summer of 1968, barely a day after Sheshen had turned eleven. Chairman Mao had arrived at the special Elite Red Guard Education Camp, and all the young boys had been ordered to line up in front of his Jeep, heads bowed in deference to the great man. The Chairman had walked down the line of boys, slapping a leather riding crop against his military trousers with each step. Sheshen could still hear the sound of the leather crop. The crisp *snap, snap, snap*. Then the Great Leader had come to a stop directly in front of Sheshen. He had cupped his thick hand under Sheshen's jaw. Their eyes had met, and everything had changed. From that day forward, Mao had made the boy his personal project. For the next nine years, Sheshen had lived beneath the Great Leader's right fist. Proud, privileged, adoring, pure in his belief and his loyalty.

Mao had called Sheshen his greatest experiment, and Sheshen had been honored by the label. Day and night, he had been trained by Mao and his cadre of Red Guard teachers. Under Mao's gaze, he had vowed to become a vessel unmatched in skill and strength—and he had succeeded beyond even Mao's expectations. Within five arduous years, he had grown into a human weapon with only one purpose: to serve his living god, the Great Leader of the eastern world.

Sheshen smiled as he remembered his "graduation," nine years after Mao had touched his chin at the Red

Guard camp. After a dinner of specially prepared dumplings dipped in honey, Sheshen had been given his first assignment by the Great Leader. In a voice reminiscent of howling Siberian wolves, Mao had ordered him to liquidate all of his Red Guard teachers, each by means of his own teachings.

At first, Sheshen had been stunned by the task. But looking into Mao's deep black eyes, he had suddenly been filled with an ecstasy beyond anything he had ever experienced. Mao had shown him the way to true loyalty! There could be no false masters. None besides the Great Leader himself!

Sheshen had leaped to the task. Within three days, he had murdered fourteen of Mao's top generals, finishing what the Cultural Revolution had begun. As he dragged the corpses past Mao's bed, where Mao lay weakened by the illness that had become part of his life in his latter years, the Great Leader had explained that Sheshen had finally become the true embodiment of his endless revolution: a tree that had happily destroyed its own roots.

But a bare three months later, the living god died. And Sheshen's world collapsed. Even now, in Boston, his smile turned to a snarl as rage enveloped him at the memory. He remembered climbing into the bed next to the corpse, holding Mao's lifeless body against his chest as the tears ran down his face. He remembered the generals trying to drag him from the bed—how he had lashed out at them, how they had cowered from his rage. He remembered how the rage had eaten out his insides, filling him with thoughts of vengeance, of violence, of rivers running red with blood. But vengeance against what enemy? Where could he aim his rage?

As China's top operative, he'd had no lack of victims—but no worthy enemies, either. Frustrated, he had grown creative with his kills. In the process, he had found a way to stifle the rage if not make it disappear. The violence itself fed him in ways his mind could not explain.

As his violence progressed and his bloodlust grew, he was soon labeled unmanageable, a threat to the party he had once loyally served. In an ironic, hateful twist he could not have possibly foreseen, he was duly returned to the only one who could still control him: the beast who had traded him away in the first place.

Sheshen pulled his eyes away from the poster's gaze and reluctantly reached into the top drawer of the steel desk. He retrieved a small leather briefcase with two compartments. He unzipped the smaller of the two compartments and pulled out a rectangular device with a tiny concave dish attached to one end. He hit a series of levers on the bottom of the device, and a flat screen the size of a credit card slid out next to the dish. The dish rotated a quarter turn to the left, then paused, emitting a sequence of high-pitched tones.

Sheshen exhaled as the flat screen flickered to life. The figure in the center of the tiny screen was partially hidden behind clouds of gray static, but still the face was unmistakable. Wrinkled, toothless, completely bald, with a rooster's throat and pitted black eyes. How Sheshen hated that face. It took every ounce of inner strength to keep from smashing the small screen to shards.

The image shivered as strange sounds emerged from the rectangular device. Sheshen waited for the satellite receiver to decode the garbled code, a mixture of seven different dialects arranged in a complicated, seemingly random semantic structure. Even if the NSA's computers somehow intercepted the transmission, they would find the cryptogram impossible to break.

The voice that finally emerged from the satellite receiver was deep and slightly metallic. Sheshen sat stock-still as he listened, responding at the appropriate moments with a quick nod. A tiny fiber-optic camera embedded in the credit card-size screen relayed his motions around the curve of the world, where he knew Gui Yisheng hovered over a similar portable screen.

When it was time for Sheshen to speak, he chose his words carefully. He had to mask his hatred and embrace the Confucian doctrine of *syau shwun;* selfless filial devotion. Gui Yisheng was a traditionalist with a vicious sting. "Honorable father. Your worthless servant must report a dangerous development. And though I am without your vast knowledge, I believe this development suggests that it is time to act."

There was a brief pause; then Gui Yisheng's face shifted closer, one eye taking up most of the tiny screen. "You are an impatient whelp," the metallic voice croaked. "We have not yet been able to replicate the girl's results. We must continue to wait."

Sheshen exhaled, unable to hide his frustration. He longed to reach through that tiny screen and scratch out his father's black eyes. "Distinguished father—are you not sick of watching the child play with mice?"

Sheshen knew he was walking a dangerous line. He was Mao's great experiment, but Gui Yisheng commanded a network of more than three thousand men, all former Red Guards who had remained in the People's Army. As the director of Unit 199 of the Scientific Branch, Gui Yisheng held indisputable authority. Sheshen had heard the stories from the old days, when his father had commanded the Ninth Academy, the complex of laboratories in Qinghai where Chinese scientists had struggled to build their first nuclear bomb. Gui Yisheng had ordered five hundred of his own men drowned for sharing rations with the starving peasants in a nearby village. Still, Sheshen was his most valuable operative. That alone endowed him with special privileges. As long as he did not push too hard—or pretend that their blood relationship carried any weight with the demon beast.

"Esteemed father," Sheshen begged, "let me take her. I am a worthless cur—but I will find her secret."

There was a pause, and Sheshen touched the ends of the long needles sticking out of his face. He could imagine the thoughts running through his father's ancient head. He, too, was becoming impatient. His men had been watching the girl and her laboratory for nearly three years. And still, somehow, this little Western child had accomplished what Gui Yisheng—and all the vast resources of Unit 199—could not achieve. It was a travesty, a tremendous loss of face.

"You spoke of a development," the metallic voice finally rasped. "Explain."

Sheshen took a deep breath. His father had sent him a verbal signal. It was time to dispense with the traditional formalities. "The *ang mo* doctor saw me at the funeral. Somehow, he recognized me."

"He *recognized* you?"

"He knew my face. And yet he could not have seen me before." Sheshen knew his father would not question his statement. Sheshen had arrived in Boston barely two weeks ago. He had not been involved in the three years of surveillance, only in the planning and execution of the recent security operation. He had been following the doctor for the past twenty-four hours, but he was too skilled to have been spotted in that short time.

"And what do you think that means, Sheshen?"

Sheshen shivered at his father's use of the name Mao had given him. He concentrated on the terrible face in the center of the small screen. "Perhaps the Western girl is no longer playing with mice."

There was a long silence. Then Gui Yisheng's tooth-less mouth opened and closed. There was a three-second delay before the metallic voice reverberated through the room. "It is a possibility we must consider. If you are correct, we do not have much time."

"I await your orders, magnificent one." Sheshen was inwardly pleased. The conversation was going exactly as he had planned. His hateful father could not be goaded into action, but he had too much at stake to ignore Sheshen's concerns.

"For now," Gui Yisheng responded, "you will step up your surveillance of the doctor and the girl. But proceed with caution—and be prepared to strike. Once we discover the secret to her success, we must move like the viper for which you are named."

The tiny screen went black. Sheshen pictured Gui Yisheng's ugly face receding in reverse around the curve of the world, riding a ghostly stream of pure light. He leaned back in the swivel chair, his stomach churning. He knew it was unhealthy to keep so much anger inside. In the first few days after Mao had died, the rage had warped his soul. Remembering that rage, and the hunger that soon followed, he felt his eyes drifting toward the briefcase's second zippered compartment.

The zipper came open slowly, revealing the shiny steel instruments beneath. Sheshen took them out one by one, turning them over in his hands. First the oversized surgical scalpel, with the specialized serrated edge. Then a pair of steel scissor-clamps, spring-loaded for precise, leveraged control. Beneath the clamps, a long telescoping steel pole, with a hooked spoon attached to one end. And last, the gun-shaped pneumatic drill. Sheshen lifted the drill with both hands, gently pressing the trigger. He watched as the scored quarter-inch bit ripped through the air. Satisfied that the cadmium battery was still well charged, he took his finger off the trigger and replaced the drill with the rest of the surgical tools.

If Sheshen was a viper, these were his fangs. He longed to hear them tear through another Western skull. Gui Yisheng and the other scientists of Unit 199 might have crafted the tools for purely scientific reasons—but for Sheshen, they were the perfect way to feed his rage.

He closed his eyes, reaching for the needles embedded in his skin.

CHAPTER TWELVE

Mike dropped to his knees inches from the edge of the cold water. He pretended he could feel the earth revolving beneath him, and wondered what would happen if the revolutions suddenly stopped. He imagined himself hurtling off the beach and across the cold water, crashing like a fleshy missile into the stone-and-glass turrets of the airport two miles away. He pretended he could see himself on the air traffic control computer screens, an unidentified glowing blip speeding across the concentric radar circles, a dagger of motion exploding straight out of South Boston. He could almost hear the air traffic controllers screaming at one another as he hurtled toward them. He knew what they would say, because he had listened to the tapes before: "She's losing altitude! She's not going to make the runway! Christ, she's going down in the bay! Scramble the Coast Guard and the emergency teams! *Repeat, she's going down in the bay!*"

Mike gritted his teeth, staring at the choppy waves of the watery break that stretched between the tip of South Boston and the airport. A cocktail of scents filled his nostrils: the salty spray of the ocean, tainted by a noxious mixture of engine exhaust and jet fuel. He watched as a black shadow appeared in front of him and sprinted across the waves, quickly traversing the stretch of water on its way to Logan's runways. Looking up, he saw a heavy silver coffin lower itself out of the blue sky, a glint of bright sunlight reflecting off a huge, rectangular tail. The Boeing 727 drifted lower and lower over the water, its wings tipping left and right as it fought a gusty breeze coming in from the east. For a moment it seemed to hang frozen in the air, and its shadow raced to catch up, doubling and tripling in size. Then the airplane dipped even lower, until it was barely above the water's surface, speeding toward the asphalt glade of the peninsular airfield.

Mike leaned forward on his knees, focused on the landing plane. His chest constricted as the airplane seemed to skim the edge of the strip of ocean—but at the last instant the rubber tires skidded against pavement, sending up a puff of white smoke. Mike knew it was partially an optical illusion; even from the air, it was hard to see where Logan ended and the water began. But it still sent chills through his body when he watched the audacious display of technology: one wrong calculation, one misjudged yard, and a dozen husbands lost their wives.

Mike closed his eyes. He had walked for three hours before arriving at this spot at the edge of South Boston, just beyond the docks and warehouses that marked the end of the Irish section of the city. Without thinking, he had staggered down the gravel beach, his eyes pinned to the airport two miles away. He had not been to this place in three years.

He was kneeling in roughly the same spot where the Coast Guard's dredging crews had gathered with their amphibious cranes and rubber boats, where the ambulances and medevac helicopters had parked, lights flashing, rotors spinning. He closed his eyes and pictured the row of yellow coroner's bags stretching the entire length of the gravel beach. He felt his insides churning, and realized with a start that he hadn't returned to the spot to mourn. He was there to vent.

He lowered his head, his hands clenching into fists. This was the feeling he had held back his entire adult life. This was the reason he hated his father so thoroughly. This was the side of his personality he had buried so deep inside, it was finally cracking him open. He wanted to hit something, to scream, to pummel the gravel into dust—

There was a sudden noise behind Mike, and he whirled, his muscles taut. He intended to tear the next vision, real or hallucinated, to shreds. But the surprised face in front of him was a different sort of vision: a pretty young girl, wearing lipstick and an expensive black sheath.

Teri Pace stepped back, shocked by the expression on Mike's face. Mike stared at her, not knowing what to say. She looked even more out of character than she had during the interlude in the hallway outside his office. Her short hair was pulled back in chic waves, and her green eyes sparkled. Her nubile body pressed out against the silky sheath, her nipples abrupt and unavoidable in the crisp air.

"Dr. Ballantine"—she spoke in a rush—"I'm sorry, but I followed you from the funeral. I need to talk to you about something I've done. Something incredibly important."

Mike's hands went limp and he turned his head, embarrassed and ashamed. It was impossible to explain away the anger. He stood in silence as another plane began its descent over the strip of ocean. The unnatural shadow shimmered over the choppy waves. Finally, he cleared his throat. "I'm not sure I'm going to be much help today. Actually, I'm thinking of taking some time off from the hospital. Effective immediately."

"You can't," Teri said, her voice pitched higher. "I mean, not yet, not until I've shown you my work. Please, Dr. Ballantine. It won't take long. My car is right over there."

Mike saw the beat-up off-yellow Volkswagen Bug parked fifty yards away, in the shadow of an abandoned wooden dock. He looked at Teri's face, the determined cast to her features. She'd followed him from the funeral. He suddenly realized what that had entailed: driving behind him as he wandered across the entire city, the VW weaving in and out of midday traffic. He looked at her hands, watching the way her fingers nervously pulled at the soft material of her dress. So shy, so unsure of herself—the exact opposite of Amber Chen.

The thought of the federal agent brought a flush to Mike's cheeks. He wondered what she thought of him now. He had probably looked like a psychotic fool, taking off into the crowd without the slightest explanation. If anything *had* passed between them, he was sure he had killed it with his maniacal performance. "Teri, I haven't been myself lately. Isn't there anyone else you can talk to?"

For a brief second, Teri looked as if she were about to cry. Then she shook her head, her full lips tightening. It was obvious she had worked up all her strength for this moment. She was not going to be pushed away. "Dr. Ballantine, just give me an hour. I promise, it will be worth your time. Please, my discovery can't wait any longer."

Mike thought for a moment, then shrugged. What was the difference, anyway? If the living visions returned, it didn't matter if he was alone or in the company of a pretty young girl. "I guess I can postpone my retirement a little longer."

In truth, Teri had aroused his curiosity. For three

years, she had avoided him—and everyone else—with almost religious fervor. When he thought about her, and he seldom had, he always pictured an incredibly shy, insecure young girl, quietly chasing her Ph.D. in the dark corners of his lab.

The young woman in front of him was attractive, energetic, and strange. Something had brought her out of her shell; Mike wondered: what sort of discovery had the power to change Teri's personality so thoroughly?

He followed her toward the car, watching her perky, athletic form as she navigated the gravel in her high heels. He felt a reflex stirring as he noticed the way her body pressed out against the material of her dress, but quickly pushed the feeling away; she was ten years younger, and emotionally still a girl. Attractive, but just a child. Nothing like Amber Chen.

"Where are we going?" he finally asked. Teri gave the car's side door a solid kick, and it popped open. Then she crossed toward the driver's side.

"The Batcave," she answered. Then she looked across the top of the car, blushing. "I mean, your virology lab. Where I've been working on my experiment."

Mike laughed. He knew what the graduate students called his basement lab. He slid into the front passenger seat and heard something crack under his left thigh. A shattered test tube dug into the already torn vinyl. Luckily, the glass hadn't been able to pierce his heavy pants.

"Shit, sorry." Teri quickly dusted the glass away with a rolled-up *New England Journal* from the backseat. "The car's kind of a mess. Did it cut you?"

Mike shook his head. Hearing another crack, he noticed a large pile of test tubes by his feet. "I see you bring your work home with you."

"Recently," Teri said, still blushing, "it's sort of taken over my life. And certainly my car."

Mike laughed again. Despite her peculiarities, she had a way of cheering him up. Maybe it was simply her good looks. "I guess that makes this the Batmobile."

Teri glanced at him, then smiled. Gravel spat up from the tires as she gunned the car backward, away from the strip of beach. Mike dug his fingers into the dashboard, hanging on for dear life as the VW sped off toward Metro and the basement lab.

CHAPTER THIRTEEN

Time did not exist in the virology lab. Outside, the sun hung just above the peak of Beacon Hill, attacking the narrow brick alleys and cobblestone streets with a final volley of bright orange light. But in the Batcave, it could have been three in the morning, noon, or midnight. Instead of the sun, the dim fluorescent lights flickered off the green floor, turning the cinder-block walls a nauseating shade of hepatitis yellow. The only clock in the low-ceilinged room lay drowning in a sea of old medical journals and unused equipment-request forms congesting the bottom drawer of Mike's mahogany desk.

Mike inhaled the antiseptic air as the elevator *whiffed* shut behind him. He felt a surge of fear as he remembered his last visit to the lab, and the strange seizure or hallucination that had gripped him, but he forced the incomprehensible memory out of his mind. The familiar sounds echoed in his ears: the hum of the self-contained ventilation cabinet, the flicker of the lighting panels up above, the constant drip of a half-dozen filtered sinks. Cutting through these familiar sounds was something new; the click of high heels, as Teri hurried across the lab.

"Have a seat at your desk," she called over her shoulder, her voice excited. "It will just take me a moment to get the right maze."

Mike raised his eyebrows. This was the first real hint Teri had given him since picking him up at the gravel beach: "the maze." He knew she had a collection of white mice on her shelves in the back of the room, but he had assumed she was using the mice to rehash the immune-system experiments he had shown her when she first joined his lab. He couldn't begin to guess why she would need a maze.

In truth, he had not been a very good Ph.D. supervisor to Teri and the other graduate students who worked in his lab. Before Kari's death, he had taken an interest in his grad students, helping them with their doctoral projects, sometimes even assisting them in their oral defense preparations. But as his own research languished, he had focused on his work upstairs in the internal medicine wards. He had pretty much left the graduate students to their own devices, assuming they would come to him with any real problems. At least, none of them had ever complained.

He lowered himself into his chair, tapping his fingers against the cool mahogany as he listened to Teri digging through the shelves behind him. An array of knick-knacks cluttered a corner of his desktop. Most were souvenirs he and Kari had gathered from Boston landmarks: a small brass Paul Revere; a tiny porcelain Bunker Hill monument; a wooden model of the *Constitution*, the oldest commissioned warship in the world, still docked in the Charlestown Navy Yard. As he looked at the souvenirs, he felt his concentration blurring; thankfully, Teri finally reappeared, carrying a heavy glass maze three feet square. Teri placed the maze in front of the souvenirs with a dramatic thud, then quickly headed back toward the shelves. Mike looked down at the glass, trying to trace the correct path with his eyes. He failed three times before giving up. It was a seemingly impossible tangle, even from his vantage point.

"Level Six, right?" Level Six was the most difficult maze rating. It took weeks of training and pounds of cheese for a mouse to learn to run a Level Six maze correctly.

"That's correct," Teri answered, crossing back from the shelves. She had a metal cage in her hands. "I borrowed the maze from the Alzheimer's lab upstairs. It's the most difficult one I could get my hands on."

Mike felt the exhaustion pulling him deeper into his chair, as Teri placed the wire cage next to the maze. Inside, one of the little rodents was climbing excitedly up the wire, while the other sat in a corner, seemingly asleep. Both had white tags attached to their tails, labeling them with bright red letters: Mouse A, Mouse B.

"I've been through a few generations of mice in the past couple of months," Teri continued, as she opened the top of the cage and reached for the more animated mouse. "So I've been reusing the labels. I always try to run the important experiments with an 'A' and a 'B.' It will help keep my *Science* article simple."

Mike thought she was kidding, then noticed the seriousness of her expression. Her *Science* article? She didn't even have her Ph.D., and already she was talking about getting an article in one of the most prestigious magazines in science? Mike's curiosity was piqued: Teri's confidence as she placed the jittery mouse at the start of the glass maze was more than a little intriguing, considering her shy personality. He watched her determined green eyes, partially hidden behind a lick of auburn hair. Somehow, she looked even prettier in the dim fluorescent light of the lab. Mike wondered if it was because this was where she felt most comfortable, surrounded by the trappings of science.

She glanced up, noticing his attention. Her cheeks turned bright red, and she smiled. For some reason, Mike felt himself blushing, too, as if his gaze had been inappropriate, or misinterpreted. But before he could say anything, Teri had turned back to her mouse.

"Okay little fellow. Go for it." She removed her hand, and the little mouse took off. It skidded through the tiny glass hallways, cutting left and right at incredible angles. In a matter of seconds, it had arrived at the finish. No mistakes.

"As you can see," Teri said, picking up the victorious mouse, "Mouse A knows the way. It took me almost three weeks to train my 'A' series, and this bugger is the last one left."

While Mike stared at her, bewildered, she exchanged the excited mouse for the more sluggish of the pair. She lifted the second mouse high above the desk, pointing its tiny triangular face in Mike's direction. "Mouse A knows the way—but Mouse B cannot see."

Mike saw that the second mouse's eyes were a dark black. He recognized tiny marks around the rodent's pupils, the signature of chemical blinding. Teri placed the blind mouse at the start of the maze, then removed her hand. The mouse lumbered a few centimeters to the left, then stopped, sniffing a glass wall. It certainly wasn't going to make the finish line. "Mouse B has never run the maze before, and he's completely blind. His chances of guessing his way to the end of a Level Six maze are practically nonexistent."

"Teri," Mike finally interrupted, leaning back in his chair, "where is this leading?"

"Just another few minutes, Dr. Ballantine. Please, I'm almost at the good part."

She left the blind mouse in the glass maze and retrieved Mouse A from the cage. Then she headed back toward the shelves. "Over here." She beckoned. "I need to use the high-voltage outlet."

Mike followed her, his bewilderment growing. The high-voltage outlet was mounted behind a Plexiglas safety hood, tucked into a recessed alcove in the far corner of the lab. In the five years since Metro's administration had granted Mike the basement laboratory, he had never opened that hood. The specialized outlet provided access to more than fifty thousand volts of electricity, generated directly by the massive power plant that fed Metro's electrical needs.

Teri stopped halfway and turned back toward Mike. "Could you hold Mouse A for a moment? I need to get one more piece of equipment."

Mike took the mouse from her, letting it run around his hand while he held it firmly by the tail. He watched as Teri grabbed a strange-looking device off the steel shelving unit. The device was a metallic cylinder about two feet high and eight inches in diameter. It trailed a long, rubber-lined cord, fitted with a five-pronged head. Mike recognized the head from the pamphlet that had come with the high-voltage outlet.

"What the hell is that thing?" he asked.

"I designed it myself. It doesn't have a name." Teri reached for the Plexiglas hood and flipped it open, ignoring the bright red warning labels and voltage-to-amps calculation tables.

"Teri, are you sure you know what you're doing?"

"My mother was an electrical engineer." She made a face. "When my father left us—I was about four at the time—she converted his study into a workshop. She was hardly ever home, so I got to spend a lot of time playing with diodes and circuit boards. I built this myself six months ago."

Mike raised his eyebrows, impressed. He realized

how little he knew about Teri. He hadn't know that she, too, had grown up without a father. And he was quickly discovering that behind the shyness was a brilliant, creative mind.

Still, he took a slight step back as she plugged in her device. She pointed to a small black switch near the base of the cylinder. "As long as the switch is to the right, nothing happens." She carefully unscrewed the top of the cylinder. Mike saw that the inside was hollow, like an oversized electric thermos.

"Okay," Teri said. "Now I need the mouse back."

She held out her hand, and Mike gave her the energetic creature. She lifted it by its long tail—and dropped it into the metal cylinder. Then she closed the top, tightening it with three quick twists. She looked back at Mike, concern in her eyes. "I promise, you'll understand in a moment."

She flicked the switch at the base of the device. There was a loud crackling sound, followed by a gigantic pop. Teri flicked the switch off with a shudder. Mike stared at her, shocked. Although he was no engineer, he could guess what fifty thousand volts would do to a tiny mouse.

"Teri—"

"Mouse A has been completely immolated by a burst of close to ten thousand amps." She set the cylinder on the floor and headed back toward Mike's desk. Mike remained where he was, staring at the sealed cylinder. *Completely immolated.* Scientific words for a very unscientific procedure. "Mouse flambé" was more like it. Of course, Mike was a lab researcher; the death of a mouse didn't bother him. But the grisly method of Teri's experiment raised some questions. He held up a hand as Teri returned holding the second mouse by the tail.

"Hold on a minute," he said. "How many mice are you going to fry?"

"Don't worry. The hard part is already over." She unscrewed the top of the cylinder and dropped the second mouse inside. Then she closed the top and checked her watch. Mike waited patiently for thirty seconds, then shuffled his feet. "Teri, what the hell are you up to?"

Teri gave him a sly smile, then unscrewed the top of the cylinder. She reached inside and pulled out the second mouse. Mike noticed that its fur was tinged with pink.

"It's a little gross," Teri said, "but necessary."

She started back across the lab. Mike followed her, his eyes pinned to her; his exhaustion was gone, replaced by concern. He was beginning to believe Teri was unstable. The shy researcher had been replaced by a perky Dr. Frankenstein. And Mike still had no idea where her experiment was leading. She had immolated an energetic, intelligent mouse, and had dipped a lethargic, blind rodent into its vaporized remains.

"Now for the kicker," Teri said, as she reached Mike's desk. "Watch closely."

She placed Mouse B at the start of the glass maze. Suddenly, the creature lurched forward. Without pause, it dove through the glass corridors. It avoided the blind alleys and dead ends, racing around the corners at an incredible pace. In a few seconds it had reached the finish. It skidded to a stop on tiny claws, its little whiskers churning the air.

Mike stared in utter shock. He could not believe what he had just witnessed. He reached past Teri to pick up the mouse. He looked at the tag on its tail, then stared down into its tiny eyes. Black and scarred, completely useless. He put the blind mouse back at the start of the maze—and again it lurched forward, choosing the correct path. A moment later it was back at the finish, sniffing for cheese. Mike shook his head, flabbergasted. "Teri, I'm lost. Is it some sort of trick?"

"No trick, Dr. Ballantine. As I said before, Mouse B is completely blind, and has never run the maze before."

"Then I don't understand. How is this possible?"

What Teri said next blew Mike's mind.

"Dr. Ballantine, do you believe in ghosts?"

CHAPTER FOURTEEN

As he waited for Teri to return from the bathroom, Mike concentrated on the coffee cup braced in his hands. He could feel the concentric circles of warmth emanating from the cup, and he inhaled deeply, forcing the heavy aroma deep into his lungs. His head was on fire. He didn't yet know what Teri had meant by her cryptic question; but something told him it was going to be the most important revelation of his life.

He shifted uncomfortably against the hard wooden stool, spinning the half-filled paper cup between his fingers. He was sitting in the window of a Starbucks located across the street from the hospital. The huge Doric pillars of Metro's receiving circle were directly on the other side of Cambridge Street, and he imagined he could hear the squeal of gurneys over the din of the early evening rush-hour traffic.

He took another sip of his steaming hot coffee and turned toward the bathroom door. The coffee shop was almost empty; two medical students in sweaty blue scrubs sat at the counter in the center of the shop, and an elderly man was by the door, his head buried in a *Boston Globe*. In a few hours, the place would be swarming with nurses and interns, as the hospital switched over to the night shift. But for now, Mike and Teri had the privacy they needed.

They had traded the confined, sterile atmosphere of the Batcave for the trendy setting of the Starbucks out of necessity: two of Mike's other graduate students had stepped out of the basement elevator, carrying a piping-hot pizza and a six-pack of beer. They had stood frozen in the entrance to the lab, staring at Mike in surprise; obviously, his recent absence from the lab had changed the atmosphere of the Batcave considerably. Mike had contemplated berating the two frightened students for breaking the biosafety rules, but had instead taken a piece of their pizza as punishment. Then he had offered to buy Teri a cup of coffee, so she could explain her experiment.

The bathroom door finally swung open, and Teri hurried out into the coffee shop. She had straightened her hair and done something to the makeup around her eyes. Mike saw the two medical students gaping at her as she passed the counter, and smiled to himself. It was amazing what the sight of a pair of nice breasts could do to the male endocrine system.

Mike's thoughts drifted momentarily to Amber Chen. *Pure fantasy,* he chided himself. *She thinks you're insane—and she's probably right.*

Teri dropped onto the stool next to Mike and reached for her cup.

"You're going to have to start from the beginning," Mike said, watching her sniff the coffee apprehensively. "I know I've been out of the research loop for a while, but I don't remember reading about ghosts in any of the recent medical journals."

He meant the comment as a joke, but Teri didn't laugh. She sipped her coffee carefully, and Mike had the sudden feeling that she was trying to appear older than her years. It wasn't just the makeup and the dress; it was the way she was controlling the muscles of her face, fighting the pertness of her features. She hid a grimace as the coffee went down, then touched the corners of her lips with a napkin. "Well, it doesn't start with ghosts. It starts with viruses."

"Viruses," Mike repeated. Of course that made sense. Teri was earning her Ph.D. in virology. But he couldn't guess what viruses had to do with the blind mouse's ability to run an impossible maze. He took another sip of his coffee, letting the caffeine add to the fire in his brain. "I take it your experiment isn't some sort of extension of my work with T cells."

Teri shook her head, embarrassed. "I'm sorry, no. I was only pretending to work on T cells. I was more interested in the viruses themselves. In fact, I've always been fascinated by viruses. And during the course of my studies, I began to realize that the common thinking on viruses was basically flawed."

Mike raised his eyebrows. Earlier, she had talked about her *Science* article as if it were destined—and now she had the hubris to challenge years of study with the flick of her auburn hair. Instead of being annoyed by her overconfidence, Mike was pleased. This was the sort of rebellious thinking he had always encouraged in his students. "What do you mean, flawed?"

"Well, common thinking defines a virus as a tiny parasite, consisting of proteins and strips of genetic material, which attacks host cells and co-opts them for its own purposes. Neither alive nor dead, the microscopic parasites need the cells they attack in order to reproduce. First, they trick their way inside; then they turn the cellular machinery into virus generators, spitting out copies of themselves in a selfish, endless quest for immortality."

Mike listened to her description as he clutched his aromatic coffee. Teri's depiction was straight out of every med school microbiology textbook, and he didn't see anything wrong with it. Viruses used host cells to reproduce. They inserted their own DNA into that of the host, forcing the cellular machinery to create new virus copies. "Okay, so where's the flaw?"

"The flaw is in the *attitude* of the description, not the description itself. See, when most people think of viruses, they think of disease—influenza, herpes, Ebola, HIV—but in truth, from an evolutionary standpoint, these are very *weak* examples of viruses. All of these disease-causing parasites eventually destroy the cells they invade. For them, replication is a suicidal process."

Mike watched an ambulance pushing its way through the traffic outside. He held back a slightly condescending smile. "And you don't agree with this common view of viruses?"

"Dr. Ballantine, you know as well as I do that the disease-causing viruses actually make up a very small portion of the virus species. There are literally millions of nonthreatening viruses. Every living creature has thousands of these viruses living inside its cells: symbiotic, peaceful interlopers that replicate quietly, without causing any cellular damage at all. In fact, sometimes these viruses even help the cells by repairing damage and storing cellular information. It's in the best interest of the symbiotic parasites to keep the cells healthy—to keep the cellular machinery intact."

Mike nodded, feeling the young graduate student's intense excitement as she talked deep science. He remembered how excited he used to get, puttering around his lab. He wanted to grab Teri's hand, to feed off her exhilaration. In truth, she had already helped him forget some of the trauma of the past two days. "So you began to study these peaceful viruses."

"Exactly. I focused on a subset I've named mirror viruses. They reside within animal cells and are completely harmless to the cells' inner machinery. Their nucleocapsid contains both their own viral genome, and a copy of the genomic material of their hosts. In many ways, they are a tiny mirror of their hosts, only without the cellular machinery necessary to reproduce. Their symbiotic relationship with their host cells is almost touching to observe. Due to the hosts, they are able to reproduce. In return, when the host cells are damaged by an outside force, the mirror viruses give up segments of their mirror DNA, allowing the host to repair itself."

Mike was looking at her with new respect. The idea of mirror viruses was innovative, but it made perfect sense. "And you've found these mirror viruses, located throughout animal cell structures?"

"Well, they appear to be most concentrated in the brain cells. Particularly in the anatomical structures located roughly in the center of the brain—the structures most commonly associated with memory."

Mike felt his energy rising. His mind was jumping ahead—but he told himself to slow down and let Teri finish. She was about to continue when a siren echoed through the coffee shop. Bright flashing lights played across her face, and she turned to watch another ambulance pull in to Metro's entrance. "From what I've read, the animal memory system consists mainly of the hippocampus, the limbic system, the thalamus, and the basal ganglia. Essentially, my understanding is that it works like this: The flashing ambulance lights hit my eyes, and my optic nerve sends signals into my temporal lobe. From there, the signals are projected onto the entorhinal cortex. The entorhinal cortex communicates the signals to the hippocampus, which recognizes them as something to remember, and stores them in a sort of electronic matrix. Is that about right?"

She had turned back to Mike, who was staring down into his coffee, listening carefully. It was a simplified description, but accurate. "Correct. The mechanism's not entirely understood, but you've covered the basics. Signals pass from the sensory organs to the entorhinal cortex, then to the hippocampus. The hippocampus then sends signals to the other sections of the brain, enabling perception. Your eyes see the flashing ambulance lights, your hippocampus stores the image as a memory, and then the rest of your brain perceives the memory—and recalls the flashing lights."

Teri smiled, glad she had gotten it right. "Now, back to my mirror viruses. Millions of them live peacefully within the cells of the memory structures—they don't cause any harm, and consequently, the immune system leaves them alone. In some ways, they represent the peak of viral evolution."

Mike was impressed. "Happy viruses living happy lives inside the center of an animal's brain."

Teri smiled. "Cute, isn't it? But here's a question: What happens when tragedy strikes? What happens when the animal's cells are ripped apart violently?"

Mike remembered the high-voltage pop and the incinerated mouse. "Mouse A. Its brain—along with every other cell in its body—was exploded into trillions of pieces."

Teri nodded. "Not only were the host cells torn apart; *so were the mirror viruses*. The peaceful parasites that lived in the mouse's cells were shattered into tiny pieces, viroles. These viroles carried with them fragments of the original cells' DNA—the mirror portion of their nucleocapsid—"

"—and then Mouse B inhaled those virole particles."

Mike saw where Teri was going. "My God. The olfactory bulb. It's brilliant."

Teri's expression was almost ecstatic. Mike's words of praise had obviously affected her deeply. "That's right. It *is* brilliant. You see, smell is the key. Smell is an amazing, simple, wonderful process. When you inhale through your nostrils, microscopic particles floating in the air stimulate a combination of contact points, called odorant receptors. These receptors trigger neurons, which transmit information down neural channels to the olfactory bulb, which is located in the frontal lobe. From the olfactory bulb, it's a short hop over a tiny strip of membrane to the *entorhinal cortex*—the launchpad of memory! You see, there's a direct path between the nose and the memory centers of the brain!"

Mike's fingers had tightened around his cup. "So when one animal inhales another animal's mirror viroles—"

"—he's on his way to 'infecting' his own hippocampus with another animal's memories. The mirror codes in the virole particles are the codes from the original animal's memory cells. Anything imprinted in those cells can be carried by the viroles. In other words, the shattered viruses carry with them the images stored by the original animal's brain cells."

Mike felt as if the wind had been knocked out of him. "So Mouse B ran the maze—"

"—*because Mouse A showed him the way.* Mouse B inhaled Mouse A's memories, and used them to find his way to the finish line. The fact that Mouse B was blind—that his eyes couldn't see—made no difference. The images had been deposited directly into his brain. The mouse's blind eyes were completely bypassed."

Mike's stomach started to churn. Something was at

the back of his thoughts. "That's what you meant when you mentioned ghosts."

"Mind you, I don't want to threaten my science by couching this in terms scientists won't ever accept. But when you think about it, there are some interesting parallels. From what I know about them, ghosts are usually 'seen' where violence has taken place. Suicides, murders, train wrecks, house fires—these are all events that could cause the violent rending of cells *and* the tiny viruses that live inside them. Even strangulation causes the rupture of brain cells; and to be released into the air, all a virole needs is a tiny tear in a cell's membrane, certainly not something as spectacular as immolation. Head trauma, drowning, even chemical poisoning—all of these things compromise brain function and destroy brain cells."

"And when something violent like this happens, you believe the viroles are released immediately? How do they get from the ruptured cells into the air?"

"In the case of explosions and the like, the viroles are immediately thrown into the air like any other microscopic fragment. In other types of violence, it probably takes a little longer. Once released from their home cells, the viroles can move pretty easily through the bloodstream to the more porous organs of the body, and, finally, out through the skin. And remember, viroles don't die—they're not really alive to begin with. So even if a violent act occurred hundreds of years ago, there might still be viroles floating around, waiting to be inhaled."

"Teri, we're talking about memories here. Remembered images—not visions." Mike's teeth chattered at the word. The tug at the back of his mind was growing stronger. Teri shrugged.

"I'm not sure that's right. Memories are more than

just stagnant images. Think about my experiment. Mouse B's brain had no way of knowing that the new inputs were nothing more than the shattered memories of Mouse A. Mouse B's brain didn't know that its eyes weren't working—to Mouse B, the images were *real,* as real as any visual memory stored in its hippo-campus."

She was on a roll now, her entire body behind her words. "We can take it even further. You want to pre-suppose that the memories embedded in the viroles are like images recorded on a roll of film. But that just isn't true. As I said before, mirror viruses contain the same DNA codes—the basis of the cell's machinery—as their hosts. Not only were the stored images transferred to the new host cells, *so are the mechanisms for understanding and manipulating those images.*"

"So what you're saying—"

"Mike," she interrupted, using his first name deli-cately, as if the moment were enormous to her, "what I'm saying is that it's possible to catch a ghost. The same way you catch a cold, or influenza."

Mike gripped the bottom of his stool with his shoes, keeping himself steady. It began to dawn on him: the visions he had been having, the gaunt man and the horse, the plume of flame in the lab . . . he quickly shook the thought away. It was impossible. It couldn't be true. Her science had to be flawed.

"No, Teri, it doesn't make sense. Violence is a com-mon phenomenon. Cells are torn apart every day. Why aren't we constantly bombarded with memories?"

Teri smiled, an ingenious glint in her eyes. "Mike, why aren't we always coming down with the flu? Why doesn't everyone catch AIDS when they have unpro-tected sex with an infected person? Viruses are not per-fect; they can only insert themselves into host cells when the conditions are right. I knew from the very beginning that ghosts were rare occurrences—in other words, mirror viruses are normally very difficult, almost impossible, to catch. If one thousand people were exposed to the same virus, maybe one would catch it. And that person would catch it because they happened to have the correct susceptibility at the correct time. This was the key obstacle to my experiment. So I created a reception enhancer—an R-E solution, a cocktail of proteins including hemagglutinin and neuraminidase—which made the mice better able to receive the virole particles into their cells. In other words, a solution that made the 'ghosts' more *infectious*."

A mixture of relief and disappointment flowed through Mike. The insane explanation could not fit his situation; he was not one of Teri's mice. "So you injected them with something that made the experiment work?"

Teri shook her head. "Not exactly. I tried that, but it didn't work. I tried aerosol sprays, edible pills, intermuscular shunts—I tried everything. It took three years before I stumbled on the answer."

She leaned close, as if telling a grave secret. "It happened by accident. I spilled my R-E solution into the ventilation cabinet. It diffused in the rush of air."

Mike's heart jumped. His face went pale. Teri continued. "See, rodents have enormous olfactory bulbs. In fact, relative to their size a mouse's olfactory bulb is more than ten times as big as a human's. The key was getting just the tiniest amount of R-E solution into their tiny nasal passages."

"You spilled the solution into the air vents?"

Teri looked suddenly nervous. "Three weeks ago. I know it's not proper lab procedure. But there weren't any side effects—well, except one. But it was minor."

"What side effect?" Mike hissed through his teeth. Teri pulled away, frightened.

"Well, anyone who was in the lab during the next few days came down with a slight head cold. But it should have cleared up by now."

Mike's mouth opened and closed. His mind was whirling. *A slight head cold.* His flulike symptoms. The high levels of antihemagglutinin antibodies he and Arthur had discovered in his blood. And it was true; his symptoms *had* pretty much disappeared in the past few hours. He considered the ramifications of what Teri had just revealed.

He had been in the lab three weeks ago. He had inhaled her R-E solution. Then he had charged right into the middle of an act of sheer, explosive violence. Andrew Kyle had been immolated like a mouse in a high-voltage cylinder. Mike had inhaled Kyle's shattered cells, along with millions of airborne virus particles.

He had inhaled his best friend's memories. *He had caught a ghost.* Mike shook his head in disbelief. But then he understood: this was a scientific answer to a seemingly impossible phenomenon. He *had* been seeing visions. And the visions had turned out to be based on reality.

He had asked himself how he could remember images he had never seen. Teri had given him the answer: they were someone else's memories. Because he been infected by someone else's ghost. The plume of flame he saw in the lab could have been Andrew's last memory, the final, horrible seconds before his death.

But why the horse? Why the gaunt Asian man?

Mike thought about what Teri had said: the images

embedded in the shattered viroles were not like pictures recorded on a roll of film. They were dynamic, active—because the viroles also carried copies of the cellular genetics responsible for understanding and manipulating those images.

A sudden, insane thought entered Mike's head. The images he had picked up were not necessarily random. The cells of the hippocampus and related structures did not merely store images—they decided which images to send to the rest of the brain for perception. The cellular machinery embedded within the mirror viroles could analyze and choose specific images. In other words, the mirror viroles contained the basic mechanisms behind deliberate thought. These were not stagnant images; they were quite possibly the products of Andrew Kyle's thoughts.

Again, Mike's mind asked the questions: Why the horse? Why the gaunt Asian man? Was it possible that the images had a purpose?

It was an insane idea. But Mike had been on the verge of insanity for two days. If there was a chance that there was meaning behind the visions, he owed it to Andrew—and himself—to find out what that meaning was.

He looked at Teri. She was watching him with her brilliant green eyes, trying to gauge what he was thinking. He smiled at her, and had the sudden urge to grab her in a tight embrace. Two hours ago, he had been on the verge of losing his mind. When she had found him on the gravel beach, he had just about given up. Now that despair was gone; in its place was a fiery determination.

"You really are a genius, you know. Absolutely brilliant."

Teri's entire face lit up. "I was worried you'd think I was crazy. Even with my data, it seems hard to accept."

Mike took a deep breath; Teri's data were just the beginning. Now he was going to tell her about his own data, gathered over forty-eight hours of sheer hell.

And when he was finished, with her help, he was going to try something *really* crazy.

CHAPTER FIFTEEN

"Separated. Fourteen months. I miss the kids—but we're all a whole lot better off. When something doesn't work, cut and run. That's a lesson my father taught me."

Amber placed the framed picture of the mousy brunette and the two overweight young children back on the expensive glass desk. She masked the bitter taste in her mouth behind a sympathetic smile. She had been inside Douglas Stanton's office for less than three minutes, and already she was repulsed by the man. He was endowed with all the worst attributes of the Western stereotype, as well as a handful of repugnant traits with a more universal "charm." Amber watched as he leaned back in his oversized leather chair, his massive paws clasped over his potbelly. "Don't know how it works over in China. But here, a man relishes his freedom most of all. Especially a busy, successful man like myself. Can't be tied down by a woman with low self-esteem. I'm a mover and a shaker—Miss Chen, wasn't it?"

Amber forced a nod, still playing the part of the polite China doll. She had asked a simple question about the picture on the administrator's desk, not expecting a barrage of sexist philosophy. Again, the difference in culture had placed her in a painful position: in the West, even the slightest hint of interest could turn a conversation into a psychoanalyst's nightmare.

While she waited for Stanton's next unguarded revelation, she let her eyes analyze the piggish man in his natural habitat. Stanton was short and stocky, with thick, stubby arms and oversized hands that reminded Amber of baseball gloves. His head was square and covered with black, oily hair that had been greased back to cover an encroaching pancake of pink scalp. He was dressed in an expensive gray herringbone suit, and he was constantly checking the line of his slacks, his thick fingers pulling at the soft material, revealing the white socks beneath the carefully tailored cuffs.

Neither money, nor vanity, could hide the man's lack of class. His office was a case in point. The red Persian weave that covered most of the tiled floor had no doubt cost a small fortune; but Amber knew from her own grandfather's collection of antique fabrics that it had actually been designed as a wall hanging, not a floor covering. While the natural pounding of feet against a proper oriental carpet enhanced the material's luster, years of leather heel prints would make Stanton's rug utterly worthless.

The decor of the rest of the huge office situated in the back corner of Metro's tenth floor was likewise inappropriate. The glass desk was too large and stood off center, cutting off the huge bay windows that looked out over a manicured enclosure set between two wings of the hospital. The white walls on either side of the bay windows were covered in framed photograph originals; Amber recognized two Herb Ritts nudes and three Ansel Adams landscapes. Although Amber had nothing against these American photographic artists, Stanton had chosen the five pieces seemingly at random; they did nothing to complement each other or the rest of the decor.

Stanton's office wouldn't have been complete without a final touch of vulgarity: a six-foot-tall cigar-store Indian, standing with crossed arms in an alcove by the door. Amber assumed that either none of Metro's two thousand employees was American Indian, or Stanton was so oblivious or so powerful that the racial makeup of his underlings made no difference.

Amber refocused her attention on the administrator, the acrid taste growing in the back of her throat. After studying Bader's file on the pig-man and seeing his hideous office, she agreed with Mike Ballantine's assessment: if something was amiss at Metro, Douglas Stanton was the best place to start looking. She only wished she could have spoken to Mike again; she was finding it surprisingly difficult to push her concern for the troubled doctor out of her thoughts. But the hunt came first. Her growing feelings for Mike Ballantine would have to wait.

"The thing about us movers and shakers," Stanton finished, his gaze drifting to Amber's legs, "is we're never satisfied with the status quo. That's Latin, by the way. I'm sure there's a similar concept in Chinese—but my Mandarin's a little rusty."

Stanton laughed. The grating, high-pitched tone was somewhat muffled by the transparent plugs Amber had placed in her ears during the elevator ride up to Metro's administrative floor. Even so, the image of sparrows being brutally strangled filled her thoughts. She watched the pig-man as he leaned forward over his desk, attempting to muster a wolfish grin. "Anyway, you get my drift. A man like Douglas Stanton can't be tethered. I keep the picture for appearances' sake. But I'm certainly available."

His eyes made it to her waist, then slid back down. She crossed her legs, letting her long skirt slip open at the knee, revealing the curve of her firm brown calves. She wanted him off balance, and she had often found

that the best way to set a man off balance was to chase
the blood out of his head. Of course, when that didn't
work, there were other methods. She patted the small,
pen-shaped device in her front jacket pocket, then
moved her hands back to the two manila folders on her
lap.

"You told my secretary you're some sort of federal
agent," Stanton continued, finally looking at her face,
"and that you're investigating Governor Kyle's tragic
death. But I still don't understand why you're interested
in talking to me. I hardly knew the governor. Met him
at some local functions, but we certainly weren't close.
Not to say we didn't travel in similar circles."

Amber understood what he was implying; she knew
more about Douglas Stanton than that he was separated
from his wife. She knew about his mansion in posh Wes-
ton and his apartment on Beacon Hill. She also knew
about the ski condo in Vermont and the house in
Miami—both of which were paid for by the hospital,
and were thus not reported on Stanton's annual financial
forms. The same went for the new BMW convertible
parked in Stanton's spot in the hospital parking lot. No
doubt, somewhere there was a Swiss or Bahamanian account that went with the BMW; Stanton's kind was as
predictable as the seasons.

"We're just being thorough," Amber responded, her
head tilted slightly toward the floor. It was another trick
from the East, a way of appearing submissive, luring the
victim in. "We've uncovered some reports that document a number of visits the governor made to Metro in
the last few weeks of his life. Would you know anything
about that, Dr. Stanton?"

Stanton's face flashed red for a brief second, then
turned back to its original pasty white. "I'm not actually
a doctor, Miss Chen. I have a law degree from Yale and

an MBA from Harvard. *Mr.* Stanton will do fine. And no, I didn't realize the governor had visited Metro. Was he ill?"

"Oh, nothing like that. Actually, he was following a lead of his own."

"At Metro?" Amber detected a slight tremor in Stanton's irritating voice. "I'm sure there must be some sort of mistake. If the governor had wanted to investigate something at Boston Metropolitan, he would have come to me first. It's proper procedure. Did the reports indicate what sort of lead we're talking about?"

Amber raised her head, looking right at him. "Mr. Stanton, what kind of car do you drive?"

Stanton coughed, staring at her. The demure China doll had suddenly vanished. In her place was a hungry tigress. Amber remembered what she had been taught during the first months of her CIA training: "An interrogation is like a street fight: there are no rules, only winners and losers." She would use everything at her disposal to get the information she needed. "There's a late-model BMW convertible parked in your spot in the Metro parking lot. And yet, according to the DMV's computers, the only car registered in your name is a '96 Volvo station wagon."

Bright red cauliflowers had exploded across Stanton's cheeks. "The BMW is the property of the hospital. It's loaned to me for business use—"

"You manage a very generous hospital, Mr. Stanton. Along with the car, I believe, you have use of a ski condo and a beach house. Am I correct?"

Stanton looked as if he had swallowed something ugly. "I'm not sure what this has to do with Governor Kyle. What exactly are you investigating, Miss Chen?"

It was time to play rough. "Five million dollars, Mr. Stanton. Annual installments, made over the past three years. The money was earmarked for a lab located in the basement of Metro—but somehow the lab never received the funding. Nor was the money reported in Metro's research budget. I don't care what you did with the money. But I want you to tell me where it came from."

Stanton was not a good poker player. His face had turned milk white. His hand shook as he rubbed his fingers across his jaw. Then he slammed his palm against the glass-topped desk. The picture of his wife and two fat kids toppled over with a clank. "How dare you make such an accusation? My lawyers will eat you alive."

Amber had expected the resistance. Stanton was a lawyer. He would hold his ground for as long as possible, and Amber didn't have time for a standoff. She leaned forward and placed the first folder on the desk in front of him.

"Mr. Stanton, you might think this is just a matter of money. But you're dead wrong. My agency has reason to believe that you're mixed up with some pretty dangerous characters."

Stanton kept one eye on Amber while he opened the folder. He tipped it toward the desk, and two black-and-white photographs fluttered out, landing upside down. He turned them over with his left hand, then gasped.

The shots had been taken from two different angles—one from directly above the body, the other from the headboard of the steel-posted bed. Amber had borrowed them from the police photographer on her way out of the Fenway apartment.

"What the hell is this?" Stanton whispered.

Amber placed the second manila folder on the desk. "Inside, you'll find a description of what we believe happened to the man in the picture. You'll also find something else—something we found in the front seat of your BMW."

Stanton opened the second manila envelope and shook it over the desk. A sheet of computer paper spilled out, followed by a transparent glass tube, approximately six inches long. The tube hit the top of the desk and shattered, sending shards in every direction.

Now it was time for the kill. As Stanton reached for the sheet of computer paper, Amber slid her hand into her jacket pocket. She waited until Stanton was fully engrossed in the description of the horrible torture technique; then she flipped a tiny switch on the end of the pen-shaped device, and began counting seconds.

She had barely made it to ten when a thin sheen of sweat broke out across Stanton's forehead. By twelve, his hands were shaking against the sheet of computer paper, and his eyes were jumping back and forth. By fifteen, his face had gone a greenish hue, and his entire body had slumped a few inches forward. All of the arrogance and bravado were gone.

Amber smiled inwardly. She could feel the device vibrating against her right breast, even through the lining of her jacket. She had picked up the device—along with a handful of other interesting playthings—at a CIA base in South Korea. The base was not listed in any roster of agency outposts, and in fact had no official name. It was a scientific research compound, specializing in the development of NLWs, nonlethal weapons. The object in Amber's jacket pocket was one of their greatest success stories.

The idea that sonic waves could damage objects located a short distance away was not a new concept. During World War II, the Germans had developed a weapon called the Vortex, which reportedly could knock a B-17 Flying Fortress out of the air with a short burst of concussive waves. After the end of the war, American scientists attempted to recreate the Vortex—and succeeded, to a degree, with a sound-wave "gun" that could shatter cement at a distance of one hundred yards. But when the gun was turned on a human "volunteer," an interesting phenomenon occurred. Instead of causing any damage to the human subject, the sound waves induced nothing more than a feeling of extreme discomfort. Apparently, organic cells could sustain much stronger sound vibrations than cement or steel. But that seemingly innocuous discovery opened up an entirely new direction for sonic weaponry.

The pen-shaped device in Amber's pocket was the latest descendant of the Vortex technology. The low-level sound waves emitted by the small device caused the inner ear to vibrate, sending confusing messages to the brain. The first sensation was an intense feeling of unease. As the brain attempted to interpret the sensation, the unease grew, rising to unbearable levels. Despite the transparent plugs in Amber's ears, she was experiencing a mild ache; she knew that within a few minutes, Stanton would have no defenses left. And, more important, he would have no idea why; the low-level sonic waves could not be heard, only felt.

She leaned close to the desk, gesturing toward the splintered glass tube. "The tube we found in your car was analyzed by our experts. The glass was blown in the same factory as the tube used on the man in the photograph."

Stanton looked up from the torture description, his face a mask of anguished terror. Amber had a slight feeling of guilt, but quickly pushed it away. *An interrogation is a street fight.* "We believe the second glass tube was meant for you. The suspect was waiting for you in your car, but was somehow scared away. We believe he'll be back. Unless we find out who he works for."

Amber had invented this story two hours ago, after Bader uncovered Stanton's undeclared wealth. She had purchased the tube from an eyeglass store across the street from the hospital. It was actually the arm of a designer frame. She had guessed that, combined with the effects of her pocket-sized Vortex device, the story would be enough to scare Stanton into talking. The logical connections were weak, but Stanton's brain had by now lost all knowledge of logic. He rubbed his palms into his eyes, groaning softly. "I didn't want to hide the money. I wanted to report it, go through the normal channels—but they wouldn't let me. They said they would find another lab if I didn't do it their way."

"So you kept most of the cash for yourself. As long as nobody knew about it, you figured you could get away with it. Why were they interested in Dr. Ballantine's lab?"

Stanton's neck was swaying back and forth. Amber knew she couldn't leave the device activated much longer. Stanton spoke between sobs. "I have no idea. They didn't tell me. The arrangement was simple. They funded his lab and, in return, they had free run of the facilities whenever they wanted. They also received copies of any equipment requests or interhospital reports coming out of the lab. Even the grad students' Ph.D. reviews. It was unconventional—but I didn't see the harm. Many of our labs are funded by outside sources. The only real difference was that this time it was kept secret. My God, are they going to torture me for using their money? Ballantine didn't need it! He hasn't produced anything in years!"

Stanton was nearly apoplectic. Amber reached across the desk and grabbed his wrist. She made him focus on her eyes. "I can take care of this, Mr. Stanton. First, you have to tell me who they are. Where did the money come from?"

Stanton shook his head. "I don't know. I never met anyone—it was all done by phone. The money was wired in from an account in the Cayman Islands. It seemed so easy."

Amber let go of his wrist and stepped back from the desk. Her disappointment was palpable. She had tortured the piggish man for nothing. She was about to shut off the device in her pocket when Stanton began rummaging through the top drawer of his desk. He pulled out a small slip of paper.

"Here," he sputtered, throwing it toward her. "Here's the fax number they gave me for the request forms and Ph.D. reviews. You've got to stop them. Take away their glass tubes!"

Amber retrieved the slip of paper. Next to the number was a scrawled company name: Cortech Industries. She read the name aloud.

"Cortech," Stanton repeated. "That's what the man on the phone called them. He had an accent, some damn foreign accent. I thought they were some sort of genetics company. They're all throwing money at the research labs. Christ, I thought they were just another foreign fucking company."

Amber pocketed the slip of paper and headed toward the door. She paused in front of the hideous wooden Indian. "What sort of accent did the man have, Mr. Stanton? Like mine?"

Stanton groaned, laying his head flat against the desk. His voice was weak, muffled by the cold glass. "No, his was Chinese. I mean *real* Chinese—like he had just jumped off the boat."

Amber headed out of the administrator's office. She

didn't turn off the sonic device until she had reached the elevators at the end of the hall.

Forty minutes later, Amber slowed Bader's black Mercedes to a precise crawl and turned in to a narrow, poorly paved alley. She knew she was taking an enormous risk driving such an expensive car through this particular area of Chinatown, but she hoped her thick scarf, wool hat, and oversized glasses sufficiently hid her race.

She wasn't worried about theft or random violence; she knew these streets were Triad territory, so petty crimes such as car theft and assault were nonexistent. She was concerned about being identified by one of the hundred unseen pairs of eyes that undoubtedly watched her from recessed doorways and second-story windows. She knew how the Triad operated; nine of the twenty-six terrorists she had captured had been trained as Triad officers before enlisting in more militant endeavors. She also knew what the Triad would do if they caught a Chinese federal agent snooping around their territory.

The Triad didn't fear the CIA or any other government agency. Their network was too vast and too profitable to be threatened by an organization funded by mere tax dollars. The CIA, FBI, and other American agencies had long ago learned to leave the Triad to itself; as long as the Triad kept its focus limited to heroin, prostitution, and the illegal immigrant trade, the U.S. government allowed it to rule Chinatown unmolested. In exchange, the Triad rarely menaced Westerners—keeping the infrequent outbreaks of violence in the family, so to speak. But Amber was a different story; to the Triad, she was a turncoat, working for a species they despised.

She was running an enormous risk, but she had no

choice. A few minutes after plugging Stanton's fax number into the CIA's computer system, she had obtained an address for Cortech Industries; it had not taken her long to locate the tiny alley in the direct center of Chinatown. She had then checked the location against a special FBI map she had borrowed from Agent Nozicki, which detailed the territories of Boston's various gang and otherwise criminal elements. She had not been surprised to discover the alley smack in the middle of Triad territory. There had always been a strong relationship between the Chinese military and the Triad organization. Considering China's enormous black market operations—both domestic and international—it sometimes seemed they were two names for the same creature.

Even without Nozicki's map, Amber would have known she was driving deep into Triad territory. She watched an old Chinese man walking a pug dog alongside her slow-moving Mercedes; the man kept his head down, his eyes keeping pace with his feet. She could see the colorful edge of a vast tattoo crawling up the back of his weathered neck. Tattooing was a tradition of many Asian cartels, most notably the Yakuza in Japan, the Tongs of Vietnam, and the Triad. She quickly looked away as the old man entered a decrepit building to her left; there was a small blue cricket cage hanging above the building's doorway, another Triad symbol. The cricket cage was a sign to any law enforcement agencies foolish enough to even contemplate surveillance in this part of town; policemen murdered by Triad operatives were often found with dead crickets shoved down their throats. Amber felt sweat building beneath her palms, and she tightly gripped the steering wheel.

Finally, she saw what she was searching for: a bright green awning, hanging over a small Chinese grocery store. A row of strangled roosters obscured the front window of the store, and there was a little Chinese child, about six, sitting in the doorway, playing with a spotted kitten. Completely enthralled by the little animal, the boy didn't look up as the Mercedes rumbled past.

A minute later, Amber exhaled as she neared the end of the short alley. She hadn't learned much, but it would have to do for now. If Sheshen—or whoever was behind the governor's death—was running his operation from this grocery deep in Triad territory, it would make her next step extremely difficult. Somehow, Amber had to find a way inside.

She tightened her hands on the steering wheel, casting a final look into the rearview mirror. What she saw sent a shiver down her spine.

The little child and the kitten were gone. In their place was a small blue cricket cage.

CHAPTER SIXTEEN

The emergency room throbbed with the electric energy of a Friday night. Most of the waiting room seats were filled, and gurneys lined the walls—a macabre chrome procession leading all the way from the sliding glass doors to the curtained cubicles on the other side of the teak admission desk. The residents and interns bobbed like fishing corks across the blood-spattered marble floor, trying in vain to keep up with the rush of patients. For most of them, the night was just beginning; they'd go through three or four pairs of scrubs before sunrise, and still the ambulances would whirl through the receiving circle, a never-ending carousel of flashing lights and private tragedies.

"Christ," Teri whispered, following Mike past a pair of jackknifed gurneys just inside the glass doors. "It's crazy in here."

"Friday night," Mike responded, stepping over a small pile of discarded latex gloves as he moved toward the admission desk. "The Knife and Gun Club gets going at sunset, and the drunks join in after ten. Couple more hours, the bars let out, and then the fun really starts."

He grimaced as he passed a bloodied homeless woman clinging to the edge of a stretcher, while an intern fought to get an IV line into her right arm. Next to her, a kid who looked no older than thirteen vomited into a bag as a nurse held his forehead; the nurse's eyes had that vacant, glazed look common to trauma professionals—she was a woman who had seen it all and stepped in most of it. Mike's mind wandered back to his own rotation through the ER, during the first few months of his internship. Even after so many years, his memories were vivid and difficult; he had never understood how people could choose to spend large portions of their careers in the frantic, violent atmosphere of a trauma center.

"I guess there's something exciting about it all," Teri ventured, delicately stepping past an elderly man in a wheelchair. "Working on the edge between life and death. Or is that too dramatic?"

"No," Mike said, smiling at her. "It's accurate. But I like to stay a few steps away from that edge. I like to be able to catch my breath now and then."

Even as he said the words, he felt his heart racing. Teri's comment about the edge between life and death had set his mind working. In the past few hours, that edge had blurred. Mike still hadn't digested all the ramifications—but he knew Teri's work was going to change science and medicine in ways he could not yet comprehend. Her work was still in an embryonic stage— mice running mazes, glimpsed images from beyond the grave—but already, Teri's and Mike's own experiences had pushed the boundaries of modern science. At the very least, they were going to redefine what was currently known as the paranormal.

Mike shivered, as he thought about how crazy his own thoughts sounded. He reminded himself that all breakthroughs of such magnitude seemed insane at first. The idea that tiny, invisible creatures existed that could make people sick must have once seemed lunatic. Viruses, bacteria, and even smaller protein-based parasites were now considered undebatable fact. Science was objective and open-minded—if something could be proved and replicated, it didn't matter how absurd it seemed. Still, that didn't make it any easier to believe. Teri's discovery—and Mike's own experiences—extended beyond anything anyone had achieved before. When Mike thought about what they were going to attempt next, he was staggered. A week ago, it would have seemed like fiction, impossible, even laughable. But now he knew: they were going to question basic beliefs and fundamental truths. They were going to stretch their own imaginations and turn science on its head.

Mike reached the admission desk, Teri a few steps behind. There were only two nurses behind the teak desk, Mabel Cross and Althea Hemper. Mabel gave him a concerned look as he approached, and he tried to mask the excited turmoil gripping his thoughts. "Understaffed, and on a Friday night. More of Stanton the Horrible's cutbacks?"

Mabel shook her head, surprised. "You haven't heard? Stanton's gone. Took a leave of absence, effective tonight. The others are out at the Hill, toasting his departure. I'd be there too, if it weren't so crazy in here."

Mike paused, Teri nearly walking into him. There was a brief, frightening moment as she juggled the sealed beaker of clear liquid in her hands, but then she found her grip. Mike turned back to the ER nurse. "Stanton's taken a leave? Do we know why?"

"Nope, and we don't care. He's gone. A letter circulated, some bullshit about an undefined sabbatical. But according to the hospital rumor mill, he had some sort of fit—full-out sobbing and screaming. Then he just crated up half his office, and left. His secretary told a nurse down in path, who told one of the radiology techs, that he headed straight for the airport. Left his BMW in its spot, took a taxi—and didn't even use a hospital voucher. Nobody knows where he went after that, but the farther the better."

Mike exhaled, surprised. He would never have figured Stanton for a breakdown. Then he remembered his interrupted conversation with Amber Chen, outside Trinity Church. The $5 million she had traced to his lab. He had suggested she question Stanton, and that if something was wrong at Metro, he was the likely suspect. Maybe Mike had been right. Maybe Stanton's sudden departure solved the riddle—he was either on his way to a federal prison for some sort of embezzlement scam, or on the run from Amber Chen and whoever she worked for. Either way, it was good news; Stanton was no loss to Metro.

But the $5 million puzzle—and even the possibility that Andrew had thought he was involved—seemed unimportant now, compared to the experiment he was about to attempt. And if that experiment worked . . .

He glanced back at Teri, noting her flushed cheeks, the way her eyes flickered back and forth, how she awkwardly clutched the oversized beaker. She was frightened and excited, as astonished by what he had told her as he was by her revelations. After the conversation in the coffee shop, they had spent nearly two hours wandering up and down Beacon Hill, talking about the discovery, about Mike's visions and how they might have been connected to Andrew's death. Then Mike had told her his idea: how he wanted to try to reach out to Andrew, to find out if there was a purpose behind the visions.

He had broadly sketched his plan, asking her for input into the technical details. It had been strange at first—a teacher seeking approval and assistance from a student—

but Mike had quickly adjusted to the role. Teri was the genius behind the scientific breakthrough, and Mike had been the unwitting guinea pig. Or little white mouse. The next step, however, would be a shared experiment. Mike had been relieved to find Teri agreeable to letting him take her research to the next extreme. She was game for anything, as long as it wouldn't interfere with her New England *Science Journal* article, which she had already half-finished and intended to send in the following morning. They had returned to the Batcave to retrieve what they needed, and then come to the ER. Teri hadn't even asked the details of what he intended—she seemed content to follow quietly.

Mike reached the back of the ER and pushed through a set of double doors that led to a tiled hallway. The hallway was lined with unmarked wooden doors.

"I've never been back here," Teri said, as Mike stopped in front of one of the doors. "Is this still part of the ER?"

"Those three doors lead to intern rooms," Mike responded, pointing. "Bunk beds, refrigerators full of Jolt cola and rotting Chinese food, and a few zombies dressed up as doctors. These doors over here lead to equipment rooms. Linens, folded stretchers, gloves, gowns, and all the disposables we use in the ER."

He pushed open the door in front of him and reached for a light switch on the inside wall. Then he ushered Teri through. The room was twenty by twenty, lined with steel shelves and cluttered with plastic rolling carts. On the carts were old ultrasound machines, EKGs, and defibrillators. Most were out of use, replaced by newer models stored in the corners of the ER itself. "I guess you'd call this the miscellaneous room. A lot of out-of-date junk, but a few items we still use in the ER and upstairs."

He stepped past an EEG cart and toward the back of the room. "Here we go, just what we need."

In the far corner stood a waist-high wine rack filled with bright red portable oxygen tanks. Mike reached the rack and chose a tank from the center shelf. The tank, roughly the size of a loaf of bread, weighed about eight pounds. It was rectangular, with rounded corners and a one-way rubber gasket at one end. Attached to the gasket were a plastic knob and a volume gauge. The little red arrow inside the gauge indicated that the tank had recently been refilled. Mike knew from experience that the tank contained four hours of compressed oxygen, locked in a pressurized state by the rubber valve.

"Ever try scuba diving?" he asked over his shoulder. Teri was still standing in the doorway of the storage room, watching him. Although he had told her his basic plan, she did not yet know how he hoped to achieve his results.

"Once," she finally answered. "During spring break my senior year of college. Brad made me try it."

Mike raised his eyebrows. "Brad?"

Teri flushed, looking away. "Nobody, really. We dated a few months, until graduation. He's in med school in California. We still talk on the phone, but we're just friends. He's very quiet, and not all that exciting."

Mike ignored the irony of her statement, his attention fixed on the oxygen tank in his hands. He twisted the plastic knob, and a fierce hiss filled the equipment closet. He watched as the red arrow swept across the gauge, tracking the declining O_2 volume. When the arrow reached the three-quarter point, he twisted the knob shut, cutting off the irritating hiss. "Well, these portable tanks are pretty much the same thing you find in scuba shops, except that they're filled with pure oxygen instead of a nitrogen-oxygen mix. We use them with patients with compromised respiratory function. Unlike scuba tanks, they aren't designed to be the sole source of air, just an enhancement."

He set the tank down on the floor, then began searching the shelves along the storage-room walls. It took only a few seconds to find what he was looking for, a small package of hypodermic syringes, with fresh plastic-wrapped needles. He opened the bag with his teeth and pulled out a syringe, then unwrapped and attaching a sterile needle. Then he retrieved the oxygen tank and crossed back to Teri. She was staring at the tank, hesitation in her eyes. When she spoke, it was obvious she had been thinking of the right words since they had reentered the hospital.

"Mike, do you really think this is going to work? I know what you've told me—the visions you've been having, how they're related to the spill in the Batcave ventilation cabinet. But that was an accident, not a predicted result. I can understand wanting to recreate the dispensation level with my mice; that's something I'll have to do to prove and recreate my results. But this . . ."

She stopped, waving one hand at the oxygen tank while holding the beaker with the other. "Well, maybe this is a little crazy. There's a lot we don't know about the process behind these viroles, and their manner of infection. Even with my mice and your . . . ghosts, we're still just working off a theory."

Mike nodded. "You're right. But we've also got evidence that the theory is sound. And I don't just mean my visions and your blind mice. You also mentioned that everyone who entered the lab during the days after the R-E spill came down with a slight cold, correct?"

Teri paused, looking at the beaker in her hands. "Yes, that's right. Rhinoviruses are among the most common viruses, found just about everywhere. With the help of the R-E solution—"

"It was no wonder we all got infected. True to its design, the R-E solution helped the rhinoviruses bind to our nasal and epithelial cells. Since rhinoviruses are so common, and so infectious even without help—it didn't take much of the dispersed solution to make the difference. But your mirror viroles are different. Violence happens all the time, but people rarely see ghosts. So it makes sense that it would take a higher concentration of R-E solution to catch the full effects of these viroles."

Mike was surprised at how easily he had adapted to the new terminology. It cheered him, reminding him that this was indeed science, not science fiction. "When you spilled the R-E solution, it dispersed quickly through the air. Mice have huge olfactory centers, relative to the size of their brains, so the tiny amount of R-E in the air was enough to produce a full-blown virole infection. But in my case, the dispersed R-E solution might have done only a partial job. When I inhaled Andrew's viroles, I didn't catch a full infection, just a mild dose. Like a mild flu, or a mild pneumonia. I'm seeing visions, but they're weak, disjointed."

"And now you want to up the dosage."

"You said it yourself—viruses are pretty much immortal. There may still be viroles present in the spot where Andrew died. I want to find out what would happen if they had a real chance to infect me, in the same degree that the viroles of Mouse A infected Mouse B. If there's a possibility the visions are trying to lead me to the end of a maze, I want to give them a fighting chance."

Mike felt the heat rising in his face. He was truly determined. Andrew was dead, but he was trying to communicate. Mike's vision's weren't just random images; they'd been chosen by mirrors of Andrew's own hippocampal cells, the decision and processing system located roughly in the center of the human brain.

Mike held up the syringe and pointed at the beaker in Teri's hands. She unscrewed the sealed top carefully to keep the contents from sloshing over the edges. Mike filled the syringe to the top, more than 200 cc. He and Teri had worked out the proper dispension level on the way back to the hospital, calculating the ratio from the volume of air in the basement laboratory and the distance from the ventilation cabinet to the mouse cages on Teri's shelf. When the syringe was full, Mike stuck the needle into the one-way rubber gasket on the top of the oxygen tank and depressed the plunger, emptying the syringe into the pressurized container.

"The pressure will break up the liquid particles," he explained, as he watched the rising gauge. "The molecules will be suspended in the gas, like a fine mist or fog. It's the basic process behind aerosolization. It won't affect the makeup of the R-E solution, but it will produce a similar concentration to the ventilation cabinet spill."

"How are you going to inhale it? Some sort of scuba mask?"

"Better than that." At the bottom of the oxygen-tank rack was a plastic container full of what looked like yellow rubber tubing. Mike lifted out one of the tubes, showing Teri the twin nose plugs at one end. "Nasal channels. Most of the respiratory patients we move from the ER to the ICU get a tank fitted with these, to assist in the dispensation of oxygen without interrupting the medical interview. I got the idea from an experiment I once witnessed—a cystic fibrosis protocol that used one of these tanks to 'infect' a patient with a genetically altered retrovirus. It was an innovative gene therapy method, though it was only partially effective. But the dispensing process was a success."

He attached the nasal tube to the rubber gasket and checked the gauge again, noting that it was near full. He imagined the R-E solution sifting through the pressurized container. "Hemagluttinins and neuraminidases. Brilliant."

Teri flushed. "I scavenged them from influenza samples, then let them breed in specialized gels. They help the viral and cell membranes fuse, permitting viral invasion. Once inside the cells, the viruses replicate. The more viroles get inside, the more thorough the infection. At least, that's the theory."

Mike smiled. "That's all we need for now. A good theory. That's all Watson and Crick had to go on, and Louis Pasteur, and Galileo."

"And Marie Curie," Teri added, her eyes sparkling.

It was close to four in the morning when Teri pulled her VW Bug to a stop at the edge of the Commons, two blocks from the bottom of Beacon Street. They had been driving around for the past hour, waiting for the last few carloads of drunken barflies to disappear from the dark streets. Now that Beacon Hill was deserted, they were ready to proceed with their experiment.

Mike stepped out of the bug and shut the door gingerly, watching as Teri did the same. His limbs creaked from the close quarters of the tiny car. He stretched his calves and thighs, hitching the oxygen tank up under his right arm. "Looks pretty quiet."

Teri nodded. The Commons stretched off behind the high wrought-iron fence to Mike's right, a rolling stretch of green broken by snakes of pavement. Across the street from where Teri was standing, the Public Gardens squatted behind a similar black fence; Mike could barely make out the Mother Goose bridge that spanned the duck pond in the center of the Gardens, where the sleeping swan boats waited patiently for summer.

Mike and Teri started forward between the two parks, moving quietly toward the base of Beacon Street. Mike knew he should have been dead tired from lack of sleep and overexertion, but his muscles pulsed with excitement. Even if the experiment didn't work, at least he had an explanation for his hallucinations. An amazing, thrilling explanation.

"Look," Teri whispered, as they neared the end of the iron fences. "At the bottom of the hill."

There were two police cars parked at the base of the dark street, next to a pair of blue barricades and a line of yellow tape. The tape closed off one lane of the road. There was no sign of traffic at this late hour; still, the police cars were going to be a problem. Mike did not relish the idea of trying to explain the oxygen tank or his late-night visit to a pair of Irish cops.

"Let's double back and cut through the park. We can reach Beacon Street higher up, closer to ground zero."

Teri followed him back past the VW and through the entrance to the Commons. They walked quickly over the grass, Mike's eyes scouring the darkness for any moving shapes. The Commons was nothing like Central Park in New York, but it had its share of dangers. That was the problem with working at a big-city hospital; it was hard to ignore the statistics, when the statistics were your daily work.

Thankfully, they reached the next Beacon Street gate without incident. Mike stuck his head around the iron fence. The yellow tape ran all the way up the hill, but there was no sign of more police officers. Mike couldn't see the top of the hill, but he assumed there would be another pair of cop cars by the stone statehouse steps.

He guessed they were patrolling between the cars, but he hoped the late hour meant fewer patrols, and more time in between.

"We'll just have to hurry," he whispered. He reached out and squeezed Teri's forearm. "Don't worry. They can't arrest us for trying to inhale a ghost."

She smiled, and Mike started forward, reluctantly forcing his mind back to the horrible morning of the explosion, trying to calculate the exact point where he had stumbled upon the crater and the destroyed limousine. He guessed it was twenty more yards up the hill, and he jogged quietly, the oxygen tank nestled tightly in his arms.

He and Teri stayed along the yellow tape until they reached the approximate spot. He took one last look up the hill, making sure he didn't see any shapes in the darkness. Then he pulled up the tape, beckoning Teri underneath.

The street on the other side of the tape was as Mike remembered it: gutted, pitted, pocked with chunks of melted black asphalt. Mike nearly tripped in a hole at least three feet deep, next to a chalk outline with only one arm. He heard Teri gasp as she avoided another chalk outline.

Standing in the gutted street, Mike's mind returned to thoughts of Andrew and the plume of flame that had torn him to shreds. The plume of flame that had split his cells into pieces, releasing tiny virus particles that carried with them—what? Images? Memories? Thoughts? *Andrew?*

Mike found the huge crater a few feet in front of him. He could almost see the pink mist floating above the crater, could almost smell the strange, burning scent in his nostrils.

He quickly unfurled the yellow rubber tube from his

forearm and stuck the plugs in his nose. He reached for the knob as he stepped forward, steeling himself as he reached the edge of the crater. Then he turned the knob, took a deep breath, and stepped over the edge.

The pressurized oxygen felt cold in his nostrils; a strange, wet sensation moved down the back of his throat. He inhaled deeply, fighting the urge to cough. Then he took the plugs out of his nose, and took a deep breath of the night air. It was strange, chasing invisible particles in the darkness, trying to bridge a distance that had never been intentionally crossed before. Again, he asked himself: *What am I chasing? Hallucinations? Or a dead best friend?*

He put the plugs back in his nose. Teri stood a few feet away, watching with nervous eyes. Mike could see she was scared, and he wondered what it was that was scaring her. The darkness, the enormity of her own discovery—or the thought that they were pursuing a ghost, visiting the spot of a recent murder in search of a dead man's soul? Mike breathed deeply, the cold, liquidy feeling moving up his nose. "It's going to be tremendous— the effect on modern science. You're going to force us all in a direction we've been reluctant to go."

Teri looked at him, confused. "What do you mean?"

Mike took another breath, then removed the plugs and leaned close to the ground, breathing through his nose. "Think about it. We doctors and scientists talk endlessly about the structures, organs, and pathways of the human animal. We talk about cell membranes, neural networks, circulatory channels—every bit of machinery that makes the human organism work. But as soon as someone tries to turn to matters beyond the machinery, we scientists shut our mouths, and our ears. I admit it, I'm as bad as anyone. I've never believed in the paranormal. I'm Catholic, but I'm not religious, and I never put much stock in the idea of a soul, or anything even remotely related."

Mike replaced the plugs, his voice turning nasal as the R-E-laced oxygen poured into him. "But the truth is, things exist beyond the grasp of medicine and biology. People are more than their organs, networks, and cells. There is an entity beyond the machinery. Science simply hasn't had a way of studying it—until now."

Teri was looking at him as if he were the center of her world; it made him suddenly uncomfortable. But he continued anyway, caught up in the magic of his thoughts. "Teri, you've opened up an entirely new avenue of experimentation. The possibilities are endless. It's not just reaching beyond the grave—it's redefining the human organism. In a way, your research is proof of the hardware-software concept of human biology."

"The hardware-software concept?"

Mike nodded, still breathing deeply through his nose, stepping gingerly across the upturned blacktop. "It's basically a comparison between the human animal and a modern computer. A person's physical body is the hardware; the soul is the software. The body is made up of definable structures, all connected, cell to cell. And the soul is the software that inhabits the hardware, giving the cells life and purpose."

He paused, pulling the plugs out of his nose. "These viroles of yours—they might just be the bridge between the hardware and the software. A part of Andrew might be floating around this deserted street, a part that I can download into my hardware. And if your theory is right, it's more than just static images; it's a fully evolved program, a program that can manipulate and process those images, give them sense and meaning."

"Andrew's soul," Teri whispered, staring.

Mike shrugged. "Soul, ghost, viroles. I'm starting to

wonder if the difference between the paranormal and the scientific might just be a matter of semantics. The point is, you've touched on something that's going to turn an entire world of thought upside down. It's a bit frightening."

He rolled the rubber tube back around his forearm and took one more deep breath. Teri moved closer to him, and he could see she was trembling. He put a fatherly arm over her shoulder and felt her muscles tense under his touch. It dawned on him that she might not be thinking of his touch as purely fatherly; but he didn't pull away. He could feel her fear, and her need for closeness.

They stood like that for a while; then Mike led Teri back toward the yellow tape. "We should get moving. If our experiment worked, I've still got some time to kill before anything happens. From what you've told me about your mice, and from what I've experienced, I'm guessing I've got about four or five hours."

"Where are we going?"

Smiling, Mike said, "I'd guess my place will be more comfortable than your car. Marginally—but at least we won't have to dodge any test tubes."

Teri laughed, still happily tucked under his extended right arm.

Fifty yards away, hunched beneath the bent branches of an overgrown fir tree, Sheshen lowered his night vision goggles, his dry lips pressed together in muted excitement. He pressed his face against the Commons fence, his eyes following the two shapes as they passed under the yellow police tape. Now there was no doubt in his mind. The girl and the doctor were working together—and they had moved far beyond little white mice.

Worse yet, they had turned their interest in a dangerous direction. Sheshen had the sudden image of a snake chasing its own tail, and he shivered, a bitter taste rising in his throat. He could feel the hunger inside him, the daggers of need moving through his twitching muscles. He wanted to snuff out the problem, to expunge the danger of failure and shame from his thoughts and his world. He felt Mao's eyes watching him from high up in the darkness, and he wanted desperately to leap over the fence, to solve everything in a flash of brilliant violence.

But he couldn't, and that fed the hunger, turning it into something savage, barely controllable. He slung the night goggles over his right shoulder and turned away from the fence. Then he started across the Commons, toward the waiting brown Infiniti sedan.

From the backseat, he would contact his father with a detailed report of the new development—and in particular a description of the oxygen tank the doctor had attached to his nose. Sheshen had a strong suspicion that this was the key they were waiting for.

Sheshen's heart pounded as he rushed through the darkness. Now he felt more than just hunger; he was excited by the thought of final, permanent success. If he was right, Unit 199 was an enormous step closer to its true goal.

Sheshen broke into a wide smile at the thought.

CHAPTER SEVENTEEN

The darkness dripped down the curved windshield in viscous sheets, obscuring the blacktop that stretched forty feet ahead of the Mercedes to the rest area. The rest area looked like a World War II bunker, a shadowy cube barely illuminated by a single orange street lamp; Amber could imagine leather-coated Nazis huddling behind the concrete walls, drawing up plans and torturing captured American GIs. A forbidding beginning to this late-night operation, but Amber had a feeling it was only going to get worse.

Tonight, she was heading deep undercover for the first time since her journey to the West. She was going to infiltrate the Triad-controlled section of Chinatown and find out for sure whether Sheshen—or whoever was behind the governor's assassination—was indeed using the small grocery with the green awning as a base of operations. It was a dangerous but necessary step in her investigation, and she had spent the past few hours preparing herself mentally for the ordeal. Still, no amount of preparation could chase away the mounting tension. Or the fear.

"It's getting late," Bader said from behind the steering wheel. "Early, I should say. You sure you got your shit straight?"

The question was aimed at the rearview mirror, and

Amber looked over her shoulder at the two men sitting in the back of the Mercedes sedan. One was tall, lanky, with wispy brown hair and a two-day stubble covering his triangular jaw. The other was short—almost dwarf-ish—with stubby limbs and thick plastic glasses. Neither looked happy to be in the Mercedes; the lanky one scratched nervously at his jaw, while the dwarf squinted out the front windshield, his eyes twitching behind his thick glasses.

"My shit's solid," the lanky man said, glaring at Bader in the rearview mirror. "Give it a few more minutes. He has to find the turn-off on I-95. And he might have to elude a tail. The Triad doesn't even trust its own."

Amber shivered involuntarily, then focused her dark eyes on the lanky man. "Nestor, you're certain about the driver?"

The lanky man turned toward Amber, the anger quickly dissipating from his face. The simple fact that he was in the Mercedes at four in the morning because of a series of phone calls she had made was proof of her status and the priority of her operation. "We've used him twelve times before. Nothing as dangerous as this, but he's trustworthy. He's Tibetan; lost three brothers and his father in a suppression raid by the People's Army five years ago. He's loyal to the Triad, but he hates the military and the Chinese government. We pay him well and give him a chance to strike back at the people who killed his family."

Amber nodded, studying the man's long, unshaven face. Nestor Paresi had come well recommended by her superiors at Langley. He was considered the top deep-cover agent in the Immigration and Naturalization Service, the agency that monitored the flow of illegals into and out of the United States. His turf was Asia, specifically Asian illegal immigration operations. He knew everything there was to know about the Triad's trade in refugees from the East.

At first, Amber had just been seeking information from him. But as Paresi described the Triad's recent smuggling endeavors—specifically, the recent upswing in their Boston-based flesh trade—she had realized he was providing her with the perfect means to get inside the Triad controlled area. Paresi had assuredly been shocked when his own superiors at the INS had ordered him to schedule the pickup, but of course he had not contested the orders. It wasn't his skin at risk.

"The truck left the Triad holding center in New York's Chinatown at eleven forty-five," Paresi continued, glancing at the dwarfish man twitching nervously next to him. "It will pull into the rest area up ahead within the next ten minutes. The driver will get out, let you into the back of the truck, and continue on to Boston. After that, you will be treated exactly like the rest of his cargo. Under no circumstances will the driver acknowledge your true identity. Once he drops you at the receiving center in Boston's Chinatown, you'll be on your own."

Amber nodded, a chill riding down her back. Although the heat was already misting up the windows of the Mercedes, she was chilly in her thin blue one-piece smock. The smock was fastened tightly up to her throat, in traditional peasant fashion. She could feel each breath pressing her skin against the stiff collar, and she glanced at her reflection in the side window, feeling a momentary jolt at the face that stared back at her. It had taken her twenty minutes to carefully apply the thick mascara, dark blue eyeshadow, and bright red lipstick, and another ten to wrap her hair in the tight knots popular in the country villages of the deep East.

She took a deep breath, turning away from the window. She could see Bader watching her out of the corners of his eyes. He couldn't hide his apprehension at the upcoming operation. Despite how she had been riding him the past few days, he had grown protective toward her. In truth, a part of her, too, wished he could participate. She did not relish the idea of infiltrating Triad territory on her own. But there was no better way. She steeled herself, thinking of her father, of all the dangerous missions he had executed, of the honor he had brought her family. She had a chance to bring the same honor to his memory. She had to control her fear, as her father had taught her to do.

She turned toward the two men in the backseat. "All right, Nestor; once the truck drops off the cargo, what can I expect?"

"The receiving center is located above a pawnshop two blocks from the target structure. According to information we've bought from our driver, the receiving center consists of a large lounge area and about thirty adjoining bedrooms. The cargo will be led into the lounge for the *xuan*, the breaking-in ceremony."

Amber noted the INS man's perfect Mandarin accent. It took years of study to master the subtle tones, especially of the more archaic terms. "The bulk of which, I assume, will take place in the adjoining bedrooms."

Nestor glanced at her, then nodded. "From our information, the breaking-in is done by a handful of high Triad officials. They take turns with the cargo, usually well past dawn. The highest official has first pick, and access to the best adjoining bedroom—a large, well-appointed room with its own stairwell entrance."

Amber shifted her eyes to the dwarfish man. It took him a few seconds to realize that this was his cue. He coughed, then reached into his jacket and pulled out a rolled-up blueprint. Peering nervously out from behind his thick glasses, he spread the blueprint out on the center seat between himself and the INS man.

"As per the information I faxed to your hotel room," he began, his voice high and nasal, "the tunnel marked 'A12' runs directly from the basement of the pawnshop to the target structure. It's pretty much a straight line, with a slight leftward bend to avoid a water main."

Amber watched as the man dragged a stubby finger across the blueprint. Beneath his finger was a series of crisscrossing black lines, indicating underground tunnels, superimposed on an aerial photo of Boston's Chinatown. Amber had studied the blueprint in her hotel room; she knew most of the tunnels by heart. She also knew it would be enormously different when she was actually down there, in the darkness, feeling her way through the reinforced dirt passageways. She had tracked terrorists through similar Triad tunnels in Taipei and Hong Kong, so it had been more than an educated guess that had led her to create the current operation. The minute Paresi had told her that the cargo would be dropped inside Triad territory, she had known there would be some physical link to her target, the grocery with the green awning. That was the Triad mode of operation.

Still, when her hunch had been proved true by the NSA satellite blueprint, she had felt more anxious than satisfied. Alone in the dark tunnels, she would need every ounce of willpower to stay in control.

"That's some fancy shooting," Paresis said, looking at the blueprint. "Radio waves? Ultrasound?"

Amber glanced at the dwarfish man, assuming he would ignore the question. Tarrance Glendale was a high level com-ops agent in the ultrasecretive NSA; he answered to only a few people in the entire country, and an operational agent in the INS certainly didn't rank.

But Glendale shrugged his little shoulders, a proud smile on his perpetually nervous lips. "Magnetic resonance. A twelve-second shot from our Telstar 9 satellite, enhanced by our computers in Washington. Basically, a small MRI probe in the satellite measures tiny differentials in magnetic force, giving a clear picture of the relative volume of any slab of earth. Would have made Vietnam a cakewalk, if the technology had been available. No more hiding in groundhog tunnels, not from our birds."

Amber watched the man's eyes twitching as he rolled up the blueprint and shoved it back into his coat. He turned toward his side window, glancing anxiously into the darkness. It was obvious he had spent too much time in front of a computer; like a groundhog out of its tunnel, he didn't like being outdoors. But Amber had requested his presence. She would not put herself at risk without seeing the faces of the men on whom her success relied. That was another lesson from her father: the source is always as important as the data. Amber studied her two sources and finally turned away, satisfied.

Barely a second later, she saw the headlights. Her breath quickened as she watched the truck pull along the far side of the rest area. It was a standard, boxcar-style cargo truck, perhaps eighteen to twenty feet long. It grumbled to a stop flush with the rest-area bunker, the engine still running. Amber closed her eyes for a second, coaxing her heart back to a normal rhythm. Then she reached for the car door.

Bader leaned toward her as she unlocked the door, his voice low so the two men in back couldn't hear. "I don't like this. Once inside, you're going to be completely on your own. If something goes wrong—"

"Bader," Amber interrupted, her voice firm but her eyes kind, "I'll handle the situation at my end. You just make sure you're at the pickup point in two hours. And don't use the Mercedes. Choose something small, two-door, green or gray."

Ever since seeing the blue cricket cage outside the shop in Chinatown, she had been cursing herself for using Bader's Mercedes to check out the area. Obviously, his car had been made by the Triad's watchdogs, perhaps recognized from a list of agents' vehicles, or perhaps just spotted thanks to dumb luck. Either way, Amber was certain the Triad had by now traced the car to Bader and the CIA. She hoped they would assume her drive-by was just a routine check of some sort, so it wouldn't set off any internal alarms. If Sheshen and his people knew the CIA was sniffing around, it would make things extremely difficult—and even more dangerous than they already were.

"If there's any sign of trouble, pull out and return an hour later. If I still don't show, assume I've been taken and report my loss to Langley. They'll take over from that point."

She stepped out of the car and shut the door behind her. Bader nodded at her through the glass of the windshield. His face was pale, but his body had relaxed. Mention of Langley had reminded him that they had both chosen their paths long ago. Whatever their personal motivations, they were government operatives, and their mission mattered above all else.

Amber started across the parking lot. She let her arms hang limp at her sides, feeling the strange extra weight of the heavy lead ring on her right hand. She closed the hand, pressing the cold lead into her palm; the ring, another toy from the CIA nonlethal weapons laboratory, was her insurance policy, all she had to rely on once inside Triad territory. She hoped it would be enough.

As she approached the truck, the driver's door opened and a small man in a gray sweatsuit hopped out onto the pavement. He hurried toward the back of the truck, his eyes shifting beneath a wide rimmed golf cap. His face was wide and dark, his features typically Tibetan. His body was short, squat, but well muscled, and Amber could see the edge of a bright green tattoo clawing out from under the left sleeve of his sweatsuit.

Amber reached the back of the truck and stood next to the man, who nervously looked her up and down. Then he nodded, unsmiling, and reached for the latch at the bottom of the metal cargo doors. As he worked open the lock, Amber watched the sweat dripping down the back of his neck. He was taking a bigger risk than she; if his bosses discovered his disloyalty, they would torture him to death, perhaps over a period of months. She would most likely receive a simple bullet to the brain, and a cricket in the back of her throat.

The man's muscles rippled and the cargo door slid upward; darkness led back the length of the truck. Amber could hear hushed whispering from inside, and the shuffle of slippered feet. The man beckoned Amber inside with quick flicks of his hand.

Ancestors, protect me. The thought was involuntary, and Amber quickly pushed it aside, squeezing the ring into her palm. She could protect herself. The Tibetan driver helped her into the back of the truck and slammed the cargo door shut behind her.

It took Amber's eyes nearly a minute to adjust to the darkness. By the time the shapes huddled together on wooden benches bolted to the inner walls of the truck took human form, the truck was rumbling forward, the floor shaking like an aluminum earthquake beneath Amber's slippered feet.

She quickly found a spot on the bench to her left, lowering herself carefully while her eyes remained pinned to the whispering shapes inside the truck. She counted nine of them, five seated across from her, four to her left. All were women, dressed in blue country smocks like hers, with their hair pulled back in similar tight buns. They ranged in age from thirteen to thirty, with the younger girls nestled together at the far end of the truck. Directly across from Amber was a woman who looked to be the oldest of the group. She was tall, with dark skin, full lips, and heavily made-up eyes. Amber guessed she was from one of the more northern provinces. Certainly, she had a touch of Mongolian blood, enough to round her cheeks and jaw. Her hands were cupped together submissively on her lap, her head slightly lowered, her feet pointing inward. Amber guessed it was her natural posture, the result of years of conditioning.

The younger girls, too, sat silently looking at the floor, their hands resting quietly in their laps. Too young to have learned their roles already, they were following the lead of the older women; Amber could see that some of them had even applied their own makeup, garish streaks of red covering tiny, child-sized lips.

She was sickened by the sight of the young girls. Growing up in Taiwan and Hong Kong, she did not see prostitution as something inherently exploitative or sinful; but these were children, this was not a choice they could have made themselves. Though they were not shackled in the back of the truck, they were lost in a foreign country, completely dependent on the Triad flesh-peddlers who had most likely bought them from their poor peasant families. Amber saw how frightened they looked, huddled together, and she sighed, forcing herself to accept what she could not change.

Then she noticed that the woman seated across from her was trying to catch her attention, a tentative but not unkind smile on her wide face. The woman spoke softly, in poorly constructed midland Mandarin: "You don't got to be afraid. It's not so bad after the first week. Not half as bad as the boat that brought you here."

Obviously, the woman had misinterpreted Amber's expression of concern for one of apprehension. Amber decided to play the part, calling up her best peasant accent. "You have been in the U.S. long?"

The woman nodded, something akin to pride in her eyes. "Two months in New York City. Very big city, very lots of people come and go. Officers in army, political people. You smile and make friends, and it goes well for you. Gifts and sometimes parties. Don't know about Boston. Might be different. This not your first time working, though. You old like me."

Amber nodded, struggling to make her grammar as bad as the peasant woman's. "Worked in Shanghai for long time."

"West not much different. Your trip be paid off in one year. You work extra good, you paid off in eight months. Then you send stipend home to family, make good for parents."

Amber knew how the system worked: Triad smugglers bought the young women from their starving peasant families, promising even more U.S. dollars when the women worked off their passage to America. Usually, the promises were false; the longer the women worked in the United States, the deeper in debt they dug themselves, for food, clothing, and even rent for their prison-like accommodations. And the Triad did not have to worry about the women running; most were uneducated, like the woman across from Amber, barely able to speak their own native language, let alone English. And even if they did somehow learn enough English to get by, where would they go? Their world ended at the edges of Chinatown.

The truck swung sharply right, then slowed to a quiet roll. Amber tensed the muscles in her legs, preparing herself; in a few minutes, they would reach their destination. She glanced at the young girls to her left, noticing the fear spreading across their young faces. She tried not to think about the night in store for the poor children. She had to remain focused on her own task.

The truck pulled to a sudden stop and male Chinese voices echoed from outside, some Cantonese, some Mandarin. Amber heard the driver get out and listened to his footsteps as he made his way to the cargo door. Then there was the sound of the metal lock, and the door clanged upward. A gruff male voice shouted at the girls: "Outside. Quickly, now."

Amber rose and shuffled toward the open back of the truck. A callused hand helped her to the pavement. She kept her head down, trying to look like the other women climbing out of the truck behind her. Meanwhile, she took in her surroundings with quick glances.

The truck had stopped in a small dark alley between two rows of boarded-up buildings. From the INS information and the NSA map, Amber knew she was near the center of Chinatown, at the edge of the six-block area controlled by the Triad. To her left was the pawnshop Nestor Paresi had described, though the window was empty and the sign was gone, replaced by two plywood boards nailed together beneath the metal rail of a missing awning. Beneath the boards, the double doors of the pawnshop were held open by two Chinese teenagers in leather jackets, with matching Makarov 9mm machine pistols slung over their left shoulders. Both had longish hair and cigarettes hanging out of their smirking lips. The more gangly one had a tattoo of a crow under his left eye.

Two more men stood on either side of the truck, watching the driver unload the women. One was in his mid-forties, short and stocky, with thick dark hair and wire reading glasses resting on a puggish nose. The other was pudgy and completely bald. Every few seconds he wiped a dirty blue sweat rag across his bulging forehead. Both men were wearing well-tailored blue suits; they looked more like Hong Kong businessmen than Triad flesh-peddlers.

With the women unloaded, the driver nodded at the two older men and headed back toward the front of his truck. The pug-nosed man came forward, ordering the women to line up in single file. Amber stood between two women in their early twenties, keeping her eyes pinned to the tops of her feet. She could feel the eyes of the two suited men as they paced back and forth on either side of the women.

Another moment passed in silence, and then the bald man with the sweat rag cleared his throat. "Ladies, welcome to Boston. I am Mr. Chung. Please follow."

He headed toward the pawnshop entrance. The women trudged after him, eyes still lowered. As Amber passed through the double doors, she felt a hand touch her right hip. She looked up, startled, and saw the gangly teenager with the crow tattoo grinning at her. He flicked his tongue across his lower lip, then said something crude to his partner holding the other door.

Amber quickly lowered her head and followed the other women inside. They entered a poorly lit cement stairwell and ascended three flights. Then they passed through another set of double doors, into a wide, well-lit lounge. The floor beneath Amber's slippers was covered in plush red carpet, and the walls were draped in curtains made of equally red velvet. There were three couches in the center of the room, and a free-standing bar by the far wall.

"Line up facing the couches," Mr. Chung ordered. Amber found herself between the Mongolian woman she had spoken to in the truck and one of the younger girls. The Mongolian woman had a dead look in her eyes, and the young girl was shaking beneath her light smock. Amber stood stock-still, her hand clenched around her lead ring. The next few minutes would determine the success or failure of her mission.

A door opened in the back of the lounge, and four men entered the room. Two of the men were dressed in Chinese military uniforms, both with epaulets marking them as fairly high level officials. The other two were obviously businessmen; one wore a tan suit and a fifties-style hat, and the other was dressed in an Italian leisure outfit, with a high collar and herringbone slacks. The four men took a seat on the closest couch, their eyes on the line of women.

Amber heard the other door to the lounge close behind her, and watched as the two armed teenagers from outside took a seat on another couch. Mr. Chung, his arms crossed against his chest, stood by the last woman in line, while the other Triad man from outside took up a position at the door.

Amber's skin crawled as the room settled into silence. She knew what was coming next. The men on the couches would make their choices, and the *xuan* would begin. Over the next few hours, all of the women would be ranked according to looks, flexibility, and agility. The Triad took its business seriously; visiting officials from the mainland expected the same attention and comfort they could find in Shanghai and Hong Kong, and they paid handsomely for the service.

"Excellency," Mr. Chung said in the direction of the couch, "you, of course, may choose first, as is the custom."

The man in the tan business suit and the rimmed hat rose from the couch. Amber raised her eyes a few inches, studying him carefully from beneath her eyelashes. He looked about fifty, in fair shape except for a slight potbelly and noticeable veins along the sides of his thick neck. From his posture and his suit, Amber guessed he was a legitimate businessman with Triad connections, like the majority of businessmen from the mainland. To outrank the military officials on the couch, he had to be worth at least in the tens of millions, if not much more. He walked slowly toward the line of women, his hands sliding into his suit pockets.

Amber took a deep breath, readying herself. This was the important moment. The high-ranking businessman was her ticket to the best bedroom, the only room with its own private stairwell. If she was going to find and infiltrate Sheshen's base of operations, she had to get to that stairwell. She had to make sure she was his first choice. But she wasn't going to rely on luck or her looks. She had something better under her smock.

As the businessman reached the line of women, Amber slowly moved her hands to the clasp holding her collar closed. Her fingers worked quickly, and the thin material slid open a fraction of an inch. The businessman took another step in her direction, and she undid the next two buttons, shifting her shoulders so the smock opened a few more inches, revealing the tops of her round breasts. When the businessman was directly in front of her, she undid the last three buttons, letting her smock slide open so that it was barely covering the dark dimes of her fear-hardened nipples. The businessman stopped, his eyes widening beneath the rim of his hat, as he looked down the silver of tan skin that ran between her high breasts. Then a hungry smile broke across his lips.

"It's beautiful," he murmured, in upper-class Cantonese.

Amber smiled back, then ran a finger down from the hollow of her throat to the flat muscles of her abdomen. Beneath her finger, a multicolored Chinese dragon writhed with each controlled breath. The tattoo began just beneath the elastic band of her white silk panties and curved upward across her abdomen to the base of her breasts. The dragon's neck rose through the hollow of her cleavage, ending in a snarling, fire-breathing burst of orange and red just below the ledge of her collarbone.

It had taken her three hours to copy the tattoo from a picture she had lifted off the CIA East Asian computer network. Two specialists had painted it on her body with temporary tattoo ink while she studied the NSA blueprint in her hotel room. The dragon would considerably improve her chances of being chosen first. It was more than a beautiful work of art; it was a symbol worn by the most sought-after prostitutes in the Eastern world.

"You wear the Third Dragon," the businessman whispered through his smile. "I pray it is not simply decoration, like the colors on your face."

"I would not wear the dragon without knowing his secrets," Amber whispered. "Choose me now, and you will feel his fire spring from my body into yours."

The businessman stared into her eyes, momentarily stunned. Then he nodded vigorously.

"I have made my choice," he said, taking her hand.

Mr. Chung clapped his hands together, and the young man with the crow under his left eye leaped off the couch. He gestured toward the businessman and headed for a doorway in the corner of the lounge. The businessman followed, still clutching Amber by the hand.

When they reached the doorway at the back of the lounge, the young man with the crow stepped back, waving them through. As Amber passed, he leaned toward her ear, his breath hot against her skin.

"When he's done, I will be next. Maybe I can teach your dragon a trick or two." The look in his eyes was pure lust, tinged with a hint of misogynistic violence. Amber shivered, as she followed the businessman through the doorway.

The private bedroom was gaudily overdone. The walls and floor were covered in purple velvet, the ceiling lined with rectangular mirrors surrounded by tinted miniature spotlights. Most of the room was taken up by an enormous circular bed, a tasteless nightmare of black silk sheets and velvet pillows, like an inky cyclone rising out of the center of the floor. Next to the bed stood a small dresser and a compact wet bar, complete with a gold-plated sink and an accordion-style wine rack. Behind the wet bar were high glass shelves. On them waited row after row of sexual devices, from electronic vibrators to plastic ball gags to rubber equipment Amber couldn't begin to identify.

Five feet behind the glass shelf was a second door with a small window halfway up the stark wood. Through the thick pane, Amber could make out a shadowy cement stairwell, with yellowing cinder-block walls.

"Do you have a name, Third Dragon?"

The businessman took off his hat and set it on the wet bar. Then he turned back to Amber, who was standing at the edge of the round bed. She looked him over, estimating his height and weight beneath the expensive suit. One hundred and sixty pounds; five six; compact, fairly well muscled for his age, which she now placed at somewhere around sixty. Probably with a wife, kids, and grandchildren back in China. His face was not unkind, and the wrinkles around his deep-set eyes reminded her of one of her favorite teachers from the private school in Hong Kong. *Play the part,* she reminded herself. *Become the part.*

"You can call me whatever you want," she murmured, smiling amorously. "And what should I call you?"

The businessman went to work on his tie. Amber could see that his hands were trembling with anticipation, and there was a growing bulge in the crotch of his tan slacks. "Tsung Lo. You are very beautiful, Third Dragon. I am fortunate to have scheduled my visit at this time."

His tie came off, and he set it next to his hat on the wet bar. Then he slipped off his jacket and undid his shirt. Amber watched him from the edge of the bed, every nerve in her body tingling as the moment approached. She glanced at the door to the lounge, making sure it was tightly closed. Tsung Lo folded his shirt and placed it on top of his tie.

"Come closer," she said, seductively. "Stand in front of me so my dragon can taste your strength."

Tsung Lo quickly crossed the room. The scent of strong after-shave mixed with an acrid hint of nervous sweat; his gaze roamed up and down her long body. They were standing inches apart, Amber's head tilted down so she could meet the shorter man's eyes.

Slowly, she moved her hands forward and undid the buttons of his pants. She slid the trousers down over his hips, then let them drop to the floor. Then her left hand crept under the elastic of his white underpants.

Calling on her years of training, she fought the urge to cringe; she was playing a role, like a Hollywood actor.

Her left hand found his small, stiff shaft, and she gently wrapped her fingers around the base. He gasped, his mouth opening as a tiny tear of saliva dripped off his bottom lip.

Amber's right hand came up and caressed his cheek, then settled at the crook beneath his jaw. "This will be like nothing you have ever felt before."

Tsung Lo trembled, pressing his groin forward against her probing hand. "Yes, please. Oh, yes, please."

Amber looked straight into his eyes, leaning forward as if to kiss him. Meanwhile, her right thumb stretched inward to touch a small, almost invisible lever on the band of her lead ring. There was an imperceptible click as the underside of the ring slid back, revealing a millimeter-long titanium needle.

"Pleasant dreams," she whispered, touching her lips against his. Her right hand pressed flat against the underside of his jaw, and the tiny needle jabbed into his skin. His body went completely stiff, his eyes rolling up, his mouth jerking wide open. The muscles of his throat and chest spasmed, and Amber clutched him tight against her, feeling him thrash as his body convulsed. In a few seconds the spasms stopped, and she lowered his unconscious body to the bed. His eyes were still wide open, the whites spotted with burst red capillaries, the pupils completely dilated.

Amber removed the ring and slipped it into the pocket of her smock. It was worthless now, a hunk of lead with fused circuits inside. The burst of electromagnetic energy had lasted less than a second, but it had been enough to set off every nerve in the old man's body. The Myolater had originally been designed as a weapon of self-defense, but Amber found it more useful as a surreptitious first strike that could disable a man silently and unconditionally.

She looked down at the unconscious man on the bed. His pectoral muscles were still twitching; the smell of urine rose from the direction of his underwear. When he awoke in five hours, he would have the worst headache of his life, as well as sore muscles and slightly blurred vision. He would have no recollection of what happened; Myolater victims suffered memory lapses of up to twelve hours. But otherwise there would be no permanent damage. Amber thought it was better than he deserved.

She quickly rebuttoned her smock and headed for the stairwell. The door was unlocked; she shut it quietly behind her. Alone in the stairwell, she took a deep breath, clearing her mind. Then she started down the cement steps.

Her slippers made no noise as she moved, and she kept her eyes straight ahead, fighting the urge to glance back over her shoulder. If someone checked on the businessman before she reached the tunnels, she would be in trouble; there was no way she could fight her way out of Triad territory once the alarm was raised.

She turned a corner and descended the second flight, her pulse racing, her hands sliding along the cinderblock walls for balance. She passed a closed door, bending over to stay below the small window at eye level. Another flight. On the ground floor, a boarded doorway was to her left, and more descending stairs to her right. She continued downward one more flight, and came to a sudden stop facing a wooden door on which swipes of red paint formed a bleeding Chinese character: "Danger." The simple word sent chills up Amber's spine.

She tried the knob but it didn't move. She dropped to one knee, pressing her eye against the crack between the door and the cement wall. It was a standard Yale key lock, steel with interlocking interior gears. Not a problem.

She pressed her thumb against the base of her throat, forcing a reflex halfway between a gag and a cough. A tiny piece of metal touched the back of her tongue. With two fingers, she pulled out a three-centimeter-long blunt pin with a curved, adjustable end. The trick was more dramatic than difficult; her father had taught it to her when she was seven, and she had refined it during her CIA training. She could carry the small lock-picking instrument in the back of her throat for days, sometimes forgetting that it was there. She had once read that Houdini could regurgitate an entire set of handcuff keys, but she hoped she never had to test her own esophageal limitations. Choking to death in a stairwell in Chinatown would hardly bring face to her family name.

She went to work on the lock, and seconds later heard a metallic click. She replaced the lockpick in her mouth, using her throat muscles to ease it back into its resting place. Then she gently pulled the door open.

Dank air hit her nostrils as she stepped through. The ground beneath her slippers was cold, and she peered through the darkness, making out stone walls and a packed dirt floor. She had once interrogated an informant about the Triad tunnels under Hong Kong; supposedly, they had been dug by forced labor right after the English took the territory during the Opium War. She wondered how many indentured immigrants had died digging the tunnels under Boston's Chinatown.

She started forward, keeping close to the left wall. She forced her breathing to remain shallow and silent, controlling her growing claustrophobia by blanking out her mind. In darkness, thought was an enemy, subject to the indiscretions of fear.

After a hundred yards, the tunnel began sloping

slightly to the left, and Amber quickened her pace. She hoped not to run into anyone roaming the tunnels at such a late hour, but she kept her eyes and ears peeled for any sign of motion. A sudden sound sent her into a defensive crouch; but then she saw an oversized water rat scurry across the dirt floor ten feet in front of her, and she relaxed. After about twenty minutes, the tunnel pitched upward, and the walls changed from dark stone to cracked plaster. Another ten yards, and she came to a wooden door in the plaster.

She eased the door open and stepped into another cement stairwell. Here she paused for a moment, catching her breath. Then she climbed the twenty steps to the ground floor.

The Chinese grocery was dark and deserted, most of the shelves empty except for those near the front windows. The dead chickens still hung from metal hooks above the large window that looked out on the alley, but Amber could tell from the visible deterioration and the smell that they had been hanging there for a very long time. The Triad obviously did not feel the need to work hard to keep up the pretense.

Back in the stairwell, Amber padded up the steps, her slippered feet beginning to ache from the long journey. Now that she was in the target building, she had to be even more vigilant. She wasn't sure what she was looking for, but she would know when she found it. She had spent years studying the signs of a Chinese military operation.

At the second floor, she started down a dark hallway with wood-paneled walls and high plaster ceilings. There were doors to her left and right, and she prayed that the floor was deserted. She stopped by the first door she came to, listening. Hearing nothing, she gently pushed the door open.

Inside was an empty cell-like room, with a single cot in one corner. Amber noticed that the cot was crisply made. There was a small duffel bag under the cot, but otherwise the room was devoid of signs of life. She considered checking out the duffel's contents, then decided she did not have time.

She moved to the next room, again waiting outside the door until she was sure it was empty. Inside, she found an identical cell, with an equally crisp cot and a similar duffel, this time tucked to the left of the cot, near a window overlooking the alley down below. She breathed deeply, smelling a combination of scents: foot balm, talcum powder—and an unmistakable tinge of gun oil. Someone had recently cleaned some kind of assault rifle in the second cell. She wondered where the occupant was now.

Cautiously now, she pushed the third door open quickly. This room was slightly different; there was a desk by the wall, and the bed was unmade. At the foot of the bed was a case Amber recognized from her childhood: an acupuncture kit, like the one her grandfather used for his arthritis. The kit was open and the long needles glistened in the moonlight streaming through the half-open window above the cot. They were the firm-style needles used only by professional acupuncturists. Amber's grandfather had believed them too dangerous for amateur use, because of their length and the strength of the unforgiving steel.

Above the desk was a picture of a familiar countenance: Mao. Amber felt a mixture of emotions when she looked at the poster; her father had been born in Taiwan, and although his life, like every Asian's, had been affected by the Communist revolution, he had been removed from the madness that had gripped mainland China during the long years of Mao's reign.

Amber stepped back into the hallway, her expression muted, a solemn feeling in her chest. She was certain now: her target was indeed involved with a hard-line segment of the Chinese military. The matching military-style cells and the poster of Mao confirmed it for her. But she still wasn't any closer to deciphering what her enemy was up to.

Her thoughts snapped away like a rubber band breaking. Behind the next wooden door were noises, metallic, high-tech noises. She ducked low as she turned the knob, not knowing what to expect.

The door swung inward and Amber was bathed in green light. An oversized, high-resolution computer screen stood along the far wall, above a rectangular Pentium processor. Next to the Pentium was a short metal file cabinet, and next to that a long shelving unit filled with small plastic cases. Amber approached carefully, watching the high screen.

The picture was greenish but sharp. It showed a laboratory, filmed from above and slowly turning clockwise. Amber saw a large desk, a row of steel shelves, a small work area with sinks, and then the desk again, as the picture turned. Then the picture suddenly vanished in a wash of green, and a time code appeared in the bottom corner of the screen. It was set to real time.

The screen remained frozen as the seconds on the time code ticked off. Amber guessed the system was set up to automatically record a visual image at preset intervals. She wondered when the picture would return.

She crossed the room and picked up one of the transparent plastic cases. Inside was a small DVD computer disk labeled with a time and a date: three days ago, at four in the afternoon. She wondered what sort of scene she would see if she plugged it into the Pentium processor. She assumed it would be another shot of the lab from above.

She shifted her attention to the small filing cabinet and pulled open the top drawer. Inside was a stack of manila folders, each filled with computer papers. She opened one of the folders and began to leaf through it. Her breath quickened as she realized what she was looking at: equipment request forms from Mike Ballantine's virology lab. Most of the forms contained the same scrawled request: for fully grown, healthy white mice.

Confused, Amber went on to the next folder. Inside were more forms from Mike's lab. These were addressed to something called the National Virus Holding Institute, in Washington, D.C. More request forms—but these were for virus samples, not mice. Mostly for different forms of influenza, with particular properties Amber wasn't familiar with. She saw the word "antihemagglutinin" in a number of places, but had no idea what it meant. The date at the top of this second set of forms was almost three years old.

She put the second folder down. Three-year-old copies of forms from Mike Ballantine's lab—which had been receiving $5 million in secret funding for approximately three years. She looked back at the high screen above the Pentium computer, watching the time code tick off.

Now she had proof that the Chinese military was interested in Mike Ballantine's basement laboratory, although she still didn't know why. This room in Chinatown was the center of an expensive surveillance operation that had been going on nearly three years. She put the two manila folders back in the file cabinet. What else? Squatting on the floor beside the Pentium was a fax machine, connected to a phone line. There was a stack of pages in the receiving bin.

Amber turned the pages over and began to read. By the end of the first paragraph, her heart was racing. By the time she reached the second page, pure shock had set in. She raised her head, her eyes wide.

My God, she thought. *This is pure insanity.* But looking at the computer system and the surveillance equipment focused on Ballantine's lab, she realized it was much worse than insanity.

It was reality.

The air felt brittle against Amber's face as she pushed her way out of the abandoned warehouse on the South Boston edge of Chinatown, her eyes adjusting to the rising light of another metallic New England dawn. The twenty fax pages were pressed tightly against her stomach, held in place by the elastic band of her panties. Beneath the pages, she shivered, not from the cold, but from the excitement of what she had discovered. She had a long way to go before she truly understood—but she knew she was on the right track. The pages against her skin were the clue she had been searching for. As insane as they seemed, they told her the purpose behind the surveillance operation—and, her intuition told her, the real reason behind Governor Kyle's assassination. At the same time, they represented something much bigger than the death of an American politician. Amber didn't yet know all the details, but she knew her mission had now taken on an entirely new importance.

She hurried away from the warehouse, shaking the oppressive scent of the dark tunnels out of her hair with flicks of her long fingers. The journey from the Chinese grocery to the warehouse at the edge of the Triad territory had taken more than twenty minutes, and she knew she was behind schedule. But then she saw the two-door gray Mustang in the far corner of the warehouse parking lot, and a relieved smile broke across her face.

She crossed the lot in quick strides, coming around the front of the car. She reached the passenger side and yanked on the handle, but the door was locked. Irritated, she rapped on the tinted side window, but Bader completely ignored her. His hands remained on the steering wheel, his body facing straight ahead. Then Amber noticed the leather thongs wrapped around his wrists. His hands weren't resting on the steering wheel; they were bound to it.

Amber dropped into a crouch, her mind alert, her eyes shifting back and forth. The sun had risen a bit higher, illuminating more of the wide parking lot. It still looked deserted, so she cautiously moved back around the front of the car, to the driver's side.

She tried the door and found it unlocked. She pulled it open—and staggered back, staring in horror. Bader's face was dark purple, his eyes bulging out of their sockets. A thin line of bright red blood dripped out over the tight noose of piano wire wrapped around his thick throat.

Christ, Bader. Amber looked at him, guilt, anger, and grief rising through her body. Then her gaze shifted to his mouth, and her heart nearly stopped in her chest. Protruding from between his blood-specked lips were the tiny head and thorax of a dead cricket.

CHAPTER EIGHTEEN

Teri had never watched a man sleep before. Well, Brad, her college boyfriend—but she had never thought of Brad in that way. He had been a fumbling, immature, geeky lover. A twenty-one-year-old virgin who had spent most of his senior year at Harvard staring at her across a biology lab, working up the nerve to ask her out.

She looked at Mike Ballantine, curled up on the couch next to her, his head denting the soft material of a down pillow, and she was so swept up she felt like crying. She watched his chest rise and fall, his lips parted, his fingers curled around the edge of the open-weave throw she had put over his shoulders—and she couldn't even remember what Brad looked like.

She reached forward tentatively, and laid her palm against Mike's rough, unshaven cheek. She could feel the heat rise up through her hand. He had been asleep for less than twenty minutes, but already she could see he was in a deep, faraway place. She brushed her fingers through the dark curls that swept down over his eyes, wondering whether he was in pain, whether he was scared, whether he was feeling anything at all.

The exhaustion had hit him suddenly, minutes after they walked through the door to his apartment. He had barely made it to the couch before his knees gave out, and Teri had helped him get comfortable, finding the pillow and throw in a closet by his bedroom. She had watched with concern as his face and arms flushed red, as the beads of perspiration rose on his forehead. But then she had remembered watching her mice go sluggish for hours as the R-E solution turned their immune systems upside down. She had started to explain, but Mike cut her off, his brilliant mind coming to the same conclusion.

"The R-E solution," he whispered, fighting to keep his eyes open. "It's like fighting a hundred different infections at the same time. The hemagglutinin is setting off my T-cell immune response."

Teri nodded. "In my mice, the reaction lasted about three hours."

"I'm a lot stronger than a mouse. But I've been overdoing it the past few days. There's no way I can stay awake until the viroles take effect."

"Mike, I'm worried about this. If your T-cell response is too strong, it could wipe out the viroles before they infect your cells. In the process, you could get pretty sick."

He smiled, touching her hand. "Have you lost any mice so far? Other than the ones you've toasted in that electric thermos of yours?"

"No, but—"

"Then don't worry."

Minutes later, his head had drifted back against the pillow and his eyes had closed. She had found a spot on the couch by his head, watching with concern as the gradually rising waves of fever rocked his sleeping body. Twice, she considered calling off the experiment and taking him to the hospital—but the scientist in her overrode her fears. It was true, none of her mice had died from the R-E solution. And there was no medical reason to believe Mike's body would react differently. Teri had to assume that the experiment was working exactly as they had planned: the R-E solution was assisting the viroles as they infected his hippocampal cells. Slowly, they would begin to reproduce, spreading throughout the central portion of his brain, through all the organs of his memory centers. Carrying with them Andrew Kyle's memories—and a piece of Andrew Kyle himself, his "software," his soul.

Teri gently slid her palm down Mike's cheek. Andrew Kyle's soul. A dead governor's ghost. She looked at her own fingers. They were trembling—but not because she was scared. *My God, what have I done?*

It was a crazy, egotistical question—one Teri imagined Marie Curie asking herself after she had discovered the secret of radioactivity. A question Rosalind Franklin had asked when she uncovered the structure of DNA, months before Watson and Crick stole her glory and banished her to the shadows of history. *What have I done?*

She closed her eyes, momentarily overwhelmed. Three years of research—and suddenly her ideas were springing out of the laboratory, infused with a life of their own. When the work had been only about her mice and a Level Six maze, it had been exciting; now it was something else, something frightening and earth-shattering and impossible to digest.

She had discovered the scientific basis for ghosts. She had proved, in a laboratory, that ghosts exist—and that it was possible to bring images back from beyond death. And now she was participating in an attempt to actually catch a ghost. She knew Mike Ballantine had his own motives; for him, this was less science than a search for answers to his best friend's death and the strange visions that had plagued him for the past few days. But for Teri, it was a new experiment, an exciting next step, building on the success of her work with her white mice. The mystery of Governor Kyle's death paled in comparison to the mystery she had already unlocked—a mystery that would change science and the world, forever.

Teri could still remember the night she had first become enthralled by the idea of ghosts. Nine years old, curled up in her bed, crying, while loud music poured up through the walls of her mother's house—the sound of another drunken party going on in the living room where, five years earlier, Teri's father had collapsed in the throes of cardiac arrest. Curled up with a comic book and a flashlight, humming to herself as she cried, trying desperately to drown out the sound from downstairs. She had stolen the comic book—a cartoon version of *Hamlet*—from her elementary school library, and had reread it a dozen times. The story had been difficult for her to understand, and she had concentrated on each panel, her lips moving as she studied the pages. Even at that age she had known it was a story of revenge, loss, and hatred—all of which she had known firsthand. But apart from the story itself, she had been mesmerized by the scenes depicting Hamlet's father's ghost—especially the opening pages, when the vision first appeared in the tower, demanding to see Hamlet, demanding vengeance, and, most of all, demanding to be noticed, to be seen, to be believed.

Teri had stared at those pages with wide eyes, wondering if it was possible, wondering: was there really such a thing as a ghost?

From that moment forward, she had been obsessed with ghosts, with visions returning from beyond the grave. Through high school and college, she had collected dozens of books on the subject, on haunted houses, on every aspect of the paranormal. At the same time, she had thrown herself into science, learning to think like a scientist because it was a way of controlling the world around her, which had let her down and continued to let her down as she moved into adulthood, shy, scared, and scarred.

Her study of science and her obsession with ghosts had soon led to a frustrating conundrum. The more she read about ghosts, the more she was troubled by the total disregard for facts in the accounts and stories of sightings. She had begun to ask herself: where was the evidence? If people really were seeing ghosts, why was there no scientific proof that ghosts existed? Why were there no theories, no hypotheses, no experiments to be tried and tested and replicated?

The scientific community had chosen the easy answer: there was no evidence because there were no ghosts. But as a scientist, Teri had been unwilling to accept such blind dogma. More than anything, she had wanted to find a way—as a scientist—to believe.

And then, in college, she had discovered virology, and the idea that tiny creatures could travel, invisible, from person to person, from brain to brain. She had read about diseases that could leap, as if by magic, through the air. And she had begun to wonder: maybe there was no scientific evidence of ghostly phenomena because science was looking in the wrong place. The approach was analogous to trying to find a virus by searching the air around a patient. The evidence wasn't in the air; it was in the patient, in his bloodstream, in his brain.

Teri opened her eyes and watched as Mike shifted against the couch, digging his head deeper into the sweat-soaked pillow. The evidence was in his brain.

Teri leaned forward and pressed her lips against his warm forehead. She could taste his sweat on the tip of her tongue. A tremor moved through her chest, tightening the muscles of her stomach. Then she slowly rose from the couch, careful not to disturb his sleep.

She didn't like the idea of leaving Mike alone, but there was no telling how long he would sleep, and she still had work to do. She glanced at the light streaming in through the window on the other side of the charming—if messy—living room, calculating the time. If she hurried, she could be back before Mike awoke, and together they could continue their experiment.

But first, she had to make history. She had already printed up the first twenty pages of her paper, leaving them hidden under the mouse cage on her shelf in the Batcave. She had not yet written in her data, or a section on the R-E dispersion, but she could add the missing sections in a matter of hours. She would drop the paper off at a FedEx office on the way back from the Batcave, and in twenty-four hours the entire world would begin to believe.

She penned a quick note and left it on the cluttered coffee table in front of the couch, took one last lingering look at Mike, then headed for the door.

A thousand sets of teeth bit at Mike's naked flesh as he fell through the darkness; he kicked and flailed frantically, trying to knock the creatures away. But the mice held on with their tiny claws, covering every inch of his body as he hurtled through the air, gnawing at him, tearing through his muscles to the veins beneath. He could feel the blood spilling out of him in a thousand places, drenching the white mice, turning their fur pink. He tried to scream but when he opened his mouth the mice crawled inside and down his throat, and he started to choke. His stomach swelled as more mice found their way into his body, and soon he was full of the frenzied rodents, his body jerking uncontrollably. *My God, my God, leave me alone! Get out of my body! Get out—*

"Dr. Ballantine! You're going to hurt yourself! Mike!"

Mike's eyes flew open and he stared up into concerned almond-shaped eyes. He flinched, gasping, and his head bounced against hardwood planks. He blinked, realizing that he was lying on the floor next to the couch in his living room. The glass coffee table was upside down to his left, one snapped leg jutting out from a sea of unopened mail and crumpled magazines.

"Are you all right? You don't look so good." Amber Chen was kneeling next to him, feeling the side of his neck with her long fingers, checking his pulse. He stared at her, his mouth going dry. She was even more exquisite than he had remembered from the day before. She was wearing a strange blue smock, buttoned to the throat, and there was heavy makeup around her eyes. Her lips were bright red, and her hair was tied up in an odd, but attractive, series of buns resting precariously on top of her head.

"Amber?" he said, using her first name because he didn't know what else to call her. "What are you doing here?"

She put her hands under his shoulders and helped him to a sitting position. There was a strange ache in his stomach, as if he had been flexing his abdominal muscles for the past few hours. His throat hurt, and there was a dull throbbing behind his eyes. But his fever seemed to have broken. Still, his white Brooks Brothers dress shirt was damp with sweat, and the muscles in his thighs spasmed beneath his baggy wool pants.

Amber sat next to him, her back also against the couch. Shoulder to shoulder, she looked at him, and he saw a thick tension behind the high angles of her cheeks.

"It's all coming to a head, and you're the key, Mike. You. Your lab. Your research."

Mike stared at her. There was something strange in her voice—a steady, determined energy, a smoldering tenacity that threatened to erupt at any moment. He coughed into his hand, then noticed that his fingers were trembling violently. He balled his hands into fists, and the peculiar quaking moved up his forearms. He knew it had something to do with the infection inside his body. Like the vivid dream he had just experienced, it was a symptom of the invisible attack on his immune system.

He took a deep breath, letting his arms rest against his sides. He saw that Amber was watching him, waiting for him to respond. He didn't know what to say. Her words made no sense.

"How can my research be the key to anything?" he finally asked. His research? Compared to what was going on inside his body, his work on cytotoxic T cells was an eighth-grade science project. Compared to what Teri had done—

Teri. He realized with a start that she wasn't there. He looked around the room, wondering where she had gone. The bright red oxygen tank with the proper proportion of R-E solution inside sat on the other side of the overturned coffee table; if Teri had left it, she was assuredly coming back. Perhaps she had made a stop at the lab or gone out for something to eat? Almost smiling, Mike thought about how she had helped him to the couch, how she had brought him the pillow and blanket. Over the course of the past twelve hours, a true warmth had grown between them, like the feeling between an older brother and a younger sister.

"Mike," Amber interrupted, "no more games. I know

the truth about your lab. And so do the people I'm chasing. They've been watching you for three years."

Mike stared at her. "What the hell are you talking about?"

Amber undid the middle three buttons of her smock. Mike's eyes widened as he took in the colorful tattoo that ran up her flat stomach. Some sort of beautiful dragon, rising up toward her breasts. He had never seen anything like it. "My God. That's beautiful."

Amber glanced down, as if noticing the tattoo for the first time. Then she reached in and pulled a sheaf of papers out from under the open folds of her smock. She tossed the paper onto Mike's lap.

Mike counted at least twenty pages with his trembling fingers. Then he lifted the top page and began to read.

He had barely gotten through the title when his chest froze: "Viroles: The Transference of Memory and the Existence of Life Beyond Death." There was no name after the title, but he knew who had typed the words.

He skimmed the twenty pages, reading the section headings and the first and last sentence of every other paragraph. The paper was still missing data, but the important ideas were all there, set out in a precise, scientific style perfect for the major journals.

"Where did you get this?"

Amber rubbed her palms over her eyes, then exhaled. "Doesn't matter. Mike, why did you lie to me about your research?"

"I didn't lie. And it does matter. You shouldn't have a copy of this. It's proprietary—"

"One of my colleagues was strangled with a fifteen-inch piano wire, just two hours ago. Your best friend was blown up by means of a high-powered oxygen-compression mine less than a week ago. Both deaths are related to the paper on your lap. So don't give me any more bullshit. I need you to tell me the truth."

Her eyes had gone stone cold. Mike felt like cowering under her gaze. Then he thought about what she had said. Someone had been strangled? And Andrew's death? Because of Teri's research?

"I *am* telling you the truth. I didn't write this paper. This isn't my research. It belongs to one of my graduate students, Teri Pace. This is based on her experiments. She discovered the science behind the ghosts."

Amber looked at him. "Ghosts. That isn't in the paper—but you're right, that's what it's about, isn't it? Transferring memory—through visual images—from beyond death."

Mike nodded. He expected Amber to tell him it was impossible, to laugh, to point in disbelief at the pages on his lap. But the look on her face remained determined. It dawned on him that she didn't doubt Teri's research. She had already accepted it.

"Where I come from," Amber said, quietly, "ghosts are not looked at the same way as here in the West. Our entire culture is built around the existence of spirits from the ancient world. Although in our daily life some of us are as scientific as our Western counterparts, we are less unforgiving when it comes to the supernatural. Personally, I have never seen a ghost. And I don't believe most of the stories I heard as a child. But after reading what your graduate student wrote, I see it's true, isn't it? They exist."

"Something exists," Mike responded. He met Amber's eyes, and suddenly his mouth opened and he started to talk. His words came out quickly, like water from a high-pressure faucet. He told her everything that had happened in the past few days. He told her about the horse, the plume of flame, the gaunt man. Her lips quivered when he described running into the same man

outside Andrew's funeral. And then, finally, he pointed
to the oxygen tank full of R-E solution and told her
about the experiment going on inside his body. "Something exists, and I believe it might be more than just
random images from a dead man's mind. The gaunt man
and the horse might have something to do with Andrew's death. I can feel it, inside."

It was true: something told him he was on the right
track. Some sixth sense—or perhaps a fragment of a
virus attached to a cell wall deep inside his hippocampus, pumping neural information into his cerebral tissue.
He felt a new sheen of sweat break out across his forehead, and he rubbed his right hand against his throat,
feeling his swollen lymph nodes. "You said someone's
been watching my lab for three years. That's about how
long Teri's been working there. But I didn't know about
her research until yesterday. How did they find out what
she was up to?"

"I found some other papers, along with those twenty
pages. Equipment request forms. One of them was dated
three years ago. It was sent to a 'National Virus Holding
Institute' "—

"—requesting hemagglutinin," Mike finished for her.

Amber nodded. He could tell by her face that she
didn't know what the word meant, but it didn't matter.
His question had been answered. When Teri had made
the request for the viral enhancer, "they" had taken notice, because it coincided with whatever project they
were working on. But who were "they"?

"Before, you asked about the Chinese military. Is that
who's been watching my lab?"

Amber was silent, thinking. Mike realized she was
trying to decide how much to tell him. But then her body
relaxed; she let herself sink back against the couch. Her
shoulder brushed his, and he knew that they had just

moved to a new point in their relationship. For whatever reason, she trusted him. And he trusted her. He was drawn by more than her beauty, her air of mystery; he felt something for her he had not felt since Kari's death. The touch of her shoulder against his simply seemed right.

"In some form, yes. I believe the gaunt man you saw in your visions and outside the funeral is an operative named Sheshen, who has been linked to a number of high-profile assassinations over the past twenty years. He has been using the Triad—the Chinese mafia—to run his operation out of Chinatown. He bought off Douglas Stanton, who gave him full access to your lab. But I don't know why, or whom Sheshen is working for, except that his operation has something to do with your graduate student's work. That's why Andrew Kyle died: he was going to expose the Chinese connection to your lab—and perhaps the reason behind that connection."

Mike felt a sudden spike of heat move up his chest, and he shifted against the couch. "What reason could Sheshen have? Why would the military be interested in ghosts?"

"I've been asking myself the same question since I found Teri's paper. One answer came to me when I saw my dead partner. I stood there, looking at his bloodied lips—and I wished he could have told me who had killed him. With Teri's research, maybe one day that would be possible."

Mike nodded. His head swam with the motion. He was feeling worse by the second. "Getting information from the dead. I guess it would have major military ramifications. It would certainly make interrogations easier. You could kill an enemy spy, then take his knowledge after he was dead. But is that application important enough to kill a governor for, on American soil?"

"It might be—" Amber stared at Mike.

"What's wrong?"

"Your face. You're bright red. And your eyes look funny. Your pupils are dilated."

"My pupils—" Mike began, and then his body stiffened against the couch. He stared straight ahead, his mouth wide open.

Andrew Kyle was standing in the doorway.

"Jesus Christ," Mike whispered, pushing himself to his feet. "Jesus fucking Christ."

"What is it?" Amber asked, rising next to him. "What do you see?"

Mike couldn't answer. He stared at Andrew, a dozen emotions filling him. This wasn't the Andrew of his boyhood memories but the real Andrew, the charismatic governor, the man who might have one day been elected president. Dressed in a dark blue pinstriped suit, his hair perfectly aligned over his wire-rimmed spectacles, his chest puffed out, his shoulders back, his feet firmly planted, his hands clasped behind his back. But his smile was the same: friendly, sincere, loving. He was looking right into Mike's eyes, right into Mike's brain. *Andrew. My God, Andrew.*

"You pretty Irish piece of shit," Mike finally whispered. "Even dead you look like a million bucks."

He thought he saw Andrew's smile widen, but he couldn't be sure. Then he heard something and shifted his gaze to the right. As he watched, shocked, the magnificent gray mare sauntered out of his kitchen, hooves clicking against his hardwood floor. *So real, so fucking real.* Mike had to remind himself that the ghostly vision was actually inside his head, not walking across his apartment. The mare stopped next to

Andrew, raising her beautiful head, shaking out her gorgeous black mane.

"Mike?" Amber whispered, touching his shoulder. "Are you okay?"

"It's Andrew," he said, quietly. "And his horse. They're standing right over there, by the door. Andrew is looking at me. The horse is snorting and pawing at the floor. If I didn't know better, I'd think she was scuffing the fucking wood."

Andrew turned and put a hand on the mare's neck. She stepped forward, and Andrew climbed onto her back. It was a strange sight: Andrew in an expensive suit, sitting on a horse in Mike's living room. A strange sight, even if Andrew hadn't been dead for almost a week.

"He just mounted the horse. Now he's taking the reins. He's going for a ride."

The mare leaped forward, straight toward the wall. Her head disintegrated as she hit the plaster, and the rest of her body followed, melting into the wall like butter against a hot frying pan. Then Andrew hit the wall, vanishing instantly. Mike felt a cold wind against his face, and then he heard something, a whisper, in Andrew's voice: "Follow me."

"Follow me," Mike repeated. An eerie feeling filled his body—and suddenly, he knew where he was supposed to go.

"The stable," he said, starting forward. "The stable where he kept his horse. It's in Marblehead. We've got to go there. Right now."

Amber grabbed his arm. "Mike, are you sure?

He turned toward her, his eyes on fire. He was still trembling, but not from fever. He reached forward with both hands and held her by her slender wrists. "I'm positive. Andrew is trying to communicate with me. He's inside my memories, using my hardware—my cells, the neurons in my brain—to tell me what to do."

She paused for less than a second. "All right. Give me five minutes, I can get us a car."

Mike nodded, smiling at her. "I guess that beats trying to chase a horse down the Mass Pike on foot."

CHAPTER NINETEEN

Mike drummed his fingers against the leather-covered dashboard as Amber navigated the BMW roadster through the narrow streets of Marblehead. Beautiful eighteenth-century wooden houses rose up on either side, and salty ocean air wafted in through the crack at the top of the passenger-side window. The harbor was a sliver of blue between the elegant mansions to Mike's right, spotted at irregular intervals by the high white sails of the year-round sailing community.

"American Colonial," Amber said, shifting gears as she took a tight corner in front of a white-shingled church and started up a low cobblestoned hill. "A style that could only have developed in a nation of immigrants."

Mike pulled himself away from the scenery to look at her. She had untied the buns on top of her head, and her long hair cascaded down around her cheeks. Some of the tension had left her face, but her eyes still smoldered. During the scenic hour-long drive out to the North Shore, she had told him about her murdered colleague. She had also told him about the horrible murder and mutilation of her father, and the possible link to Sheshen, the gaunt man from his visions. Shocked by the story, Mike had not known how to react. But she had not been searching for sympathy; she had simply wanted him to understand the emotions driving her forward. She reminded him of some of the athletes he had played with in high school—the ones who had since gone on to professional careers. Absolutely nothing was going to stand in Amber Chen's way.

Mike turned back to the view, noticing the first gray signs of the impending sunset. His eyes roamed across a pair of oversized mansions with high, pointed turrets. "What do you mean? What's wrong with American Colonial?"

"Nothing's wrong with it. But it's a telling architectural development. Everything's made out of wood. This town wasn't meant to last—it was meant to change. In Europe and Asia, you have buildings that were built a thousand years ago—buildings that will still be standing a thousand years from now. But this town was built without an eye to the future. It wasn't meant to outlive its original tenants."

Mike shrugged. He could feel the cobblestones under the BMW's wheels. He thought it was extremely fitting that Amber's phone calls had gotten them the use of Douglas Stanton's car. He wondered who had stolen it off the hospital lot—another CIA agent like Amber? Or had it been much simpler, some sort of confiscation order from the local police? "Well, the town's still here."

"Only because of constant maintenance and rebuilding. Only because the current occupants *want* to keep the past alive. In the East, there is no choice in the matter. Even Mao Zedong, the leader of a rebellion intended to destroy the past, was unable to erase such a solidly built history. But this town, this architecture, was built by a people craving revolution. It echoes a desire for constant, unending change."

They were leaving the town now, starting up the

winding paved road that led into the craggy hills surrounding the bay. Mike nodded. He enjoyed listening to Amber's voice. She was smart and directed, and her accent thrilled him—because it was exotic, and because it was tinged with mystery. He thought about the glimpse of skin and the multi-colored tattoo beneath her smock, back in his living room. Then he chided himself.

Perhaps it was another sign of the differences between their cultural backgrounds. Although Amber's eyes were taking in every detail of the drive through the North Shore, her mind was focused on her mission. But Mike's thoughts were a spinning, jumbled mess, attacked from every angle by emotions he couldn't begin to control. Fear, sorrow, and most of all, a strange exhilaration. Andrew had come to him. Andrew's ghost was with him. Like a flu, or a cold. He wondered how long Andrew would stay. Twenty-four hours? A week? Or would the ghostly viroles act more like hepatitis, or herpes, or HIV? Would Andrew's ghost inhabit Mike for the rest of his life?

He turned to tell Amber his thoughts, but there was a sudden change in her expression. Her lips had curled downward, and her eyes flickered anxiously.

"What's wrong?"

Amber didn't look at him. "Maybe nothing. Mike, when I give you the signal, take a look in the rearview mirror. Don't stare, just glance for a few seconds, then look away."

Mike could hear the tension in her voice. He fought the urge to turn and look over his shoulder. A few seconds passed in silence; then Amber touched his leg with her long fingers.

Without moving his head, he glanced in the rearview mirror. They had just rounded a long, ascending curve, and the blacktop curled backward behind them, an inky snake slithering between two craggy outcroppings of rock. Two hundred yards back, at the point where the two outcroppings nearly seemed to meet, was another car. An expensive-looking brown sedan, hovering just above the pavement.

Mike shifted his eyes back to the road in front of them. "Looks like an Infiniti. The four-door model. With tinted windows."

"It's been with us for the past ten minutes. And I think I saw the same car when we got off the Mass Pike."

Mike's stomach tightened. He remembered what Amber had told him about her murdered colleague. "Do you think they're after us?"

Amber shrugged. But Mike could still see the anxiety in her eyes. "It's possible. Or it could be a coincidence. But remember, your lab is the subject of a very serious surveillance operation. They might have been watching your apartment when we left. There's a chance they might have followed us from Boston."

Again, Mike fought the urge to look over his shoulder. *They might have been watching my apartment?* "What do they want?"

"Well, if it's still a surveillance operation, they probably just want to find out where we're going."

"What should we do?"

Amber didn't answer. Instead, she lifted her foot off the accelerator. The BMW's speed dropped by half. Mike's eyes widened. "You're slowing down?"

She gestured toward the road in front of them. "According to your directions, there should be a sharp fork right around the next curve. If this thing accelerates as well as advertised, we can lose them. Their sedan is much heavier, and the incline will give us an added advantage."

Mike could feel the adrenaline pumping inside him. He imagined the brown sedan closing behind them, the confused driver pressing down on the brake. He nervously checked his seatbelt, making sure it was tightly fastened.

Without warning, Amber slammed her foot against the gas. The BMW lurched forward, the tires squealing against the pavement. Mike was pressed back into his seat, his face frozen. Amber kept accelerating as the rocky cliffs streaked by on either side. Mike saw the yellow flash of a sign to his right, something about a tight curve and a speed limit. Then Amber shouted a warning and yanked the wheel to the left, downshifting. There was a horrible churning as the car tilted precariously into the curve. Mike was thrown forward, the seatbelt digging into his chest. He braced himself against the dashboard, his mouth open, no sound coming out.

Somehow, the tires held to the road, and the car didn't flip. Amber slammed on the brakes, yanking the steering wheel in the opposite direction. The BMW fishtailed, then swung into a full hundred-and-eighty-degree turn. Amber yanked the stick into reverse, and suddenly they were flying backward, smoke billowing out around them. Just as suddenly, they stopped dead. Mike stared wildly through the windshield, the blood rocketing through his head.

He watched as the brown sedan roared past, still heading along the main road. He could see the BMW reflected in the tinted side windows; it sat half concealed in the narrow alley that forked back through the rocky hills.

When the sedan was out of sight, he turned to look

at Amber. Her body was hunched forward, close to the wheel, and there was sweat beading on her forehead. But her hands looked steady, and there was a half-smile on her lips.

"Where the hell did you learn to drive like that?"

When Amber finally answered, it seemed as though she was disclosing an embarrassing secret. "My brother owns a pair of race cars. He keeps them at a track just outside Paris. He taught me during a visit, a few years ago."

"Is he in the CIA also?"

Amber laughed. The sound was forced, a little on edge. It was obvious she was almost as drained as Mike. "No. But Winston knows all there is to know about living fast. You can bet he's tried the same maneuver with a fifth of vodka in his bloodstream."

Amber turned the car around, and they started down the narrow road. They drove in silence, each lost in thought. It was a good ten minutes before Mike's pulse had slowed to a more manageable level. Still, a low-level fear remained inside him. The point had been driven home: this was serious. Andrew and Karl Bader had been murdered—perhaps by the people in the dark sedan.

"This looks like the turnoff," Amber said, easing the car onto a narrow dirt access road. "Emory Stables."

Mike saw the sign to his left, and felt a thrill of anticipation. He remembered his short conversation with Anne Kyle after Amber had requisitioned Stanton's BMW. He had reached her at the spa down the street from the Louisberg mansion, and had struggled to hear her over the sound of steam jets and a half-dozen simultaneous manicures.

"You want directions to Andrew's stable?" Anne had

asked, surprised. "Mike, I told you, the horse died a month ago. There was a fire—"

"I know," Mike had interrupted. "But I'd like to see the place, just the same. Andrew chased his dream there, and I'm in need of that sort of inspiration."

Anne had pretended to understand. She had called him back a few minutes later with the directions. "I hope you find what you're looking for, Mike."

I know I will. Mike pressed his face against the window as the stables came into view. The complex consisted of three rectangular wooden barns, each half a football field long. To the left of the barns was a corral, a glade of brown dust speckled with tufts of grass and low piles of hay. A pair of horses stood in the far corner of the corral, their heads obscured by one of the piles of hay. Both animals were unsaddled and looked overweight, their large bellies bulging.

Next to the corral, at the end of a long, curving driveway, stood a small cement structure with shuttered windows and a bright green door. Amber pulled to a stop ten feet from the green door and turned off the ignition.

"Well?" she asked, raising her eyebrows. It was a fair question. They had driven all the way out here—now what? The problem was, Mike wasn't sure. The vision had not returned since his apartment. But he was certain Andrew was here, somewhere.

He opened the side door and stepped out onto the dirt driveway. The thick scent of drying hay hung in the air, and he kicked his heels, watching the dust billow up around his jeans. Amber crossed around to the front of her car, resting her hip against the hood. A hint of one long leg sneaked out from beneath the folds of her blue smock. "Think we should look around?"

"I guess," Mike started, but before he could take a

step toward the three wooden barns, the green door in front of them swung open.

A short woman with bright red hair stepped out, shielding her eyes from the rising morning sun. She was in her mid-forties, stocky but attractive, wearing a denim shirt, leather riding chaps, and high snake-skin boots. She glanced at Amber, then turned her attention toward Mike, smiling amiably. "Can I help you with something?"

Her accent startled him: decidedly Boston. He guessed she was from Revere or one of the other low-rent suburbs just outside the city. Mike was about to answer when Amber pushed off the car, pulling out her federal ID. The badge glinted in the sunlight. "Are you the manager of these stables?"

The woman looked the badge over. "I'm Anna Emory. This is my father's place. He retired two years ago, moved to Florida. Lot of cops in my family, but I've never seen a badge like that. Are we in some sort of trouble?"

Amber shook her head, her serious expression replaced by a smile. Mike was impressed by the way she quickly took control of the situation. She had a commanding presence. "Not at all, Ms. Emory. I'm sure you're aware of the recent terrorist attack in Boston. We're federal officers, investigating a number of leads into the governor's assassination, and we just have a few questions."

Anna Emory relaxed. "Of course. The governor. A horrible tragedy. Such a nice man. Used to bring me things to brighten up my office. It's like a coffin in there. Just last week, he showed up with a basket of flowers—"

"Last week?" Mike interrupted. "I thought there was a fire a month ago. I thought his horse died from smoke inhalation."

"Oh yes, an awful thing. Fire started during a storm—figure it must have been a lightning strike. Act of God, nobody's fault, but so horrible. We lost three horses, but Black Betty was the youngest of the lot."

"You said Governor Kyle continued to visit," Amber asked, trying to bring the woman back to the point. "Even after his horse died?"

"Every four days or so. The same as the past six months. He and the blond woman went straight into the barn, talked for a bit, then took out two of the younger horses. They were both getting to be good riders, for city folk."

Mike swallowed, his mouth tingling. The blond woman? "Andrew brought Anne with him?"

"You mean that anorexic wife of his?" Anna Emory laughed, a grating sound, like gravel under tires. "I doubt you could get those twigs around a mare if you used a nutcracker—pardon my French. No, this woman was a lot thicker around the middle. And better looking, if you ask me. Dorothy something-or-other. A type of tree. Hold on a minute, it will come to me."

"A type of tree?" Amber asked. Irritation was evident in her voice. Mike felt it too; the woman's meandering style, mixed with her heavy Boston accent, made for a difficult combination. Despite her boots and her riding gear, she reminded Mike of women he had met in the bars around BU—the ones you avoided unless you wanted to spend the night getting your ear chewed with stories that made no sense and went on forever.

"Yes, a tree. Big one, long thin branches, looks like a deflated balloon or a drooping curtain—"

"A willow?" Mike asked.

"That's it. Dorothy Willow. Always showed up a few minutes after the governor, in a little red sports car. Wore a business suit most of the time, blue or gray.

Changed into riding gear in my office. Thick around the middle, like I said, but she had a body on her. Not like that stick the governor married."

"Ms. Emory," Amber put in. "You say the governor met with this woman to go riding every four days, for the past six months?"

Anna Emory nodded, and Amber looked at Mike. He could see the excitement in her eyes. He knew what she was thinking. Dorothy Willow might be connected with Andrew's investigation. Andrew had conducted his investigation into Metro in secret, without the help of his own office. But that didn't mean he hadn't had outside help.

The stables would have been a perfect meeting place. Nobody knew about the governor's passion but Anne, who wouldn't have suspected he was going there because of a secret investigation.

"Ms. Emory," Mike asked, "where was Black Betty kept?"

The woman pointed with a thick finger. "Third barn, the empty stall at the end. Haven't got a new boarder yet. Still some damage to that end of the barn, on account of the fire."

"After the horse died, did the governor continue to go straight to the same barn?"

The woman nodded. "Most of my younger horses are kept together. He said he liked the younger ones, even though they're harder to control. Made him feel more like a cowboy."

"Mind if we look around?" Amber asked, following Mike's lead.

The woman shrugged. "Go right ahead. The barn's unlocked. I'll be in my office if you need me."

*　　*　　*

The heavy smell of hay and horses was nearly over-whelming. Mike stood next to Amber in the open doorway to the barn, letting his eyes adjust to the dim lighting. Hay was scattered on the concrete floor; the walls had been constructed by hand, some of the boards set at odd angles, allowing cracks of light to pierce through. There were ten stalls on either side, closed by latched wooden gates with rounded openings at eye level. Muzzles stuck out through at least half of the openings, heavy feet stamped against the stall floors.

"Sounds like a full house," he said, quietly.

"They're magnificent animals," Amber said, follow-ing him into the barn. She left the double doors slightly open, just enough to let the light in. "My grandfather had a pair he kept near his home in Taiwan. But I was always too afraid to ride with him."

Mike glanced at her, surprised. "You don't seem the type to be afraid of anything."

Amber laughed. The sound was new, and it warmed Mike's ears. "I'm afraid of a lot of things, Mike. I've just learned to control the fear—to use it when I can, and to ignore it when I can't."

A horse to their left whinnied as they walked by, and stamped its hooves. Another horse shoved its muzzle through the gate to Mike's right, nearly touching his elbow. He patted its nose. "So what sort of things scare you?"

Amber's feet made almost no sound against the floor, and Mike wondered how she was able to move so grace-fully. For all his athleticism, he felt like an oaf next to her.

"Well, I'm still a little unnerved by horses, though I think they're beautiful. And I don't like bats." Amber glanced up toward the high ceiling, crisscrossed by dark wooden beams. "Which makes this place just about the least desirable spot on my vacation list."

"What about people?" Mike asked. The walls at the back of the barn were blackened from the fire that had killed Andrew's mare. "In your line of work, I'm sure you meet some pretty frightening people."

"That's true. But terrorists I understand, which makes them much less terrifying. They want something, and they're willing to kill to get it. Some of them even enjoy the killing—revel in it, develop their own style, practice their art over a period of many years."

"Like Sheshen."

Amber nodded.

The empty stall was to their left, blackened by the fire, missing its gate, the floor coated with soot. To the right of the stall was a large bin about a quarter-full of grain. On the other side of the bin was another stall, and a dark brown muzzle poked out through the gate. Mike looked up into the horse's large black eyes, watching as his ears pointed upward, his lips curling back over his large horse teeth.

Mike reached into the bin, pulled out a handful of grain, and held them under the horse's mouth. The horse's tongue tickled his palm, leaving a streak of wetness.

"Sheshen is a professional monster," Amber said, her voice stiff. "If he truly exists, he's worse than anyone I've ever faced before. He's killed more people than any other operative in China's history. He's brutal, he's efficient, and he's smart. And worse yet, he enjoys his work; he mutilates his victims."

She paused, brushing a hand through her hair. "But I'm not afraid of him. If he's a man, I'll catch him or kill him. If he's a myth, I'll still kill him. For my father's honor."

Mike looked at her. There was a tear at the corner of her left eye. But there was no anger in her face, no fiery lack of control. He wished he could be like that. He wished his own father had instilled such power in him, instead of the powerlessness of his own anger, the frantic volcano that waited behind his own emotional walls.

He turned away—and stopped still, his heart coming to life. The corner stall was no longer empty. Andrew was crouching in the far corner, a hand against the charred back wall. He looked up at Mike, smiling.

Mike touched his own forehead, but there were no signs of fever. He touched his lymph nodes, but they felt normal, barely noticeable at all.

No fever, no headache, no nausea—but Andrew's ghost was there, right in front of him. Then he remembered: Teri had explained it at the coffee shop. The vast majority of viruses were not harmful. They lived symbiotically inside their hosts. *Happy viruses living happy lives.*

"The infection is complete," Mike whispered, out loud. "The viroles are reproducing inside my cells. The R-E solution helped them overwhelm my defenses, and my immune system isn't fighting back anymore. My cells have accepted them—"

"Mike, what are you talking about?"

Mike pointed at the stall. "It's Andrew. He's in the corner, touching the burned part of the wall. He's looking at me, and he's no longer smiling."

Mike felt himself drawn forward. He took a small step into the stall. Andrew stared at him, walking his fingers up the charred wooden wall. Mike wanted to grab him by the shoulders, to hug him, to feel him alive again. He reached out, coming closer and closer—and Andrew vanished. Mike toppled forward onto his knees. Amber rushed into the stall after him, touching his shoulder. He looked up at her. "He's gone."

"Did he tell you anything?"

"No, he just ran his hand up and down the wood." Mike looked at the spot Andrew had touched. Three horizontal boards, each about four inches wide. He reached forward, gingerly, and tapped a knuckle against the center board.

The sound echoed through the corner of the barn.

"Hollow," Amber whispered, dropping to her knees next to Mike. "It's hollow."

Mike balled his right hand into a fist and drove it into the board as hard as he could. The charred wood shattered inward, and his hand burst through all the way to the wrist. He slammed his other hand into the wood a few inches away, demolishing another section of the wall.

"It's a cubbyhole of some sort. It goes about two feet, then there's another wall. Wait, there's something in here."

The object was cold and hard; he worked his hands around it. Rectangular, metal, about the size of a laptop computer. He guessed it weighed less than ten pounds.

He used his shoulders to yank the object back through the charred remains of the inner wall. It was some sort of lockbox, black metal that felt like steel held together by a latch with a tiny keyhole in the center. Mike shook the box gently and heard papers rustle inside.

"Andrew must have hidden it in the wall, sometime after the fire. He must have pulled off the burnt planks, then nailed them back in. The fire damage would've made them easy to remove."

Amber was still sitting on the stall floor, staring at the hole in the wall. She rubbed her palms against her knees. "He showed you where to look. His ghost showed you where to go."

Mike nodded. He knew what was going through her mind. She had accepted "ghosts" when she read Teri's research paper—but she hadn't truly believed until he pulled out the box. The enormity of the moment struck Mike, too. Now he knew for sure. Andrew was more than a vision; he was an active entity, *a ghost*. He had used Mike's organs of perception to lead him to the lockbox.

Mike tried the steel latch, but found it locked. "We've got to get this thing open."

He rose, searching the walls and floor of the stall for something he could use to pry the box open. There were two horseshoes hanging from rusted hooks on the wall to his right. The horseshoes were too thick for the job—but maybe one of the hooks? Mike removed one of the horseshoes and twisted the hook as hard as he could. The wood splintered and the hook came free. It was four inches long, tapered to a sharp point.

Hook in one hand, horseshoe in the other, he turned back toward Amber and the lockbox—and watched, confused, as she did something with her fingers against the base of her throat. Her mouth came open and she pulled something off her tongue: a length of shiny metal, curved at one end.

"That's a neat trick," Mike said as she went to work on the lockbox. He looked down at his rusted hook, then at the pick in Amber's hand. Then he laughed, putting the hook in his pocket. "I guess this is a pretty good example of the differences in our cultures. Subtle East meets brutal West."

Amber smiled as she worked on the lock. "There's a time for subtlety, and a time for brute force. Together, we've got both covered."

Mike watched her jiggle the lockpick up and down. "Where did you learn to pick locks? Is there a CIA training course?"

"Actually, there is. But I learned from my father. In truth, it's not very hard. Up and down, back and forth, small, random movements; most standard locks can be beaten by any amateur with the right mix of luck and patience."

The lock came open with a click, and Amber smiled. "See, just a little luck and patience."

Mike cringed as she put the metal pin back on her tongue and eased it down her throat. Then she gently opened the lockbox. He leaned forward to see.

Inside was a small stack of black-and-white photographs. Amber studied the top photograph, her eyes narrowing. She held it out to Mike. "Recognize him?"

It was the gaunt man, sitting in the backseat of a dark sedan. The shot looked as if it had been taken from a long distance with a telescopic lens. Amber turned to the next shot, then the next. She handed them to Mike, and again he was looking at the gaunt man, this time stepping out of the sedan and walking down what looked to be a dock.

The final photograph, also black-and-white, was larger than the rest. It showed the gaunt man standing in the center of a group of similarly dressed Asians, on the bow of a mid-sized cargo freighter. There were Chinese ideograms on the side of the boat, followed by a string of numbers.

"Mao's Revolution," Amber read, quietly. "It's the name of the ship. I don't recognize it, but I'm sure it's registered in mainland China. There's no way to tell where this shot was taken, though. Could be any harbor in any city in the world."

She reached beneath the picture, and pulled out a

typewritten sheet, the last item in the lockbox. Mike moved so that he could read over her shoulder.

The page was printed on official-looking stationery. In the top left corner were three sentences of italic type:

Willow Investigative Services
OP222997
Dorothy Willow, VP

"See the coding beneath the name of the firm?" Amber asked. "That means the company was officially registered with the FBI. Dorothy Willow was either an ex-Fed or a moonlighting agent. Andrew must have been referred to her by one of his friends in the government."

Mike nodded. Since becoming governor, Andrew had made many connections in Washington. If he had wanted help in conducting a secret investigation, he would have had no trouble finding a professional.

The letter was three paragraphs long; there was a palpable fear and desperation behind the words:

Andrew, it's my official opinion that we must hand this investigation over to higher authorities—*immediately*. The longer we keep this a secret, the more dangerous it becomes.

As to the identity of the man in the photographs—the man behind the illegal funds—my evidence is still inconclusive. But there is no doubt that he is connected to Unit 199. My contacts in Beijing have confirmed this fact.

Andrew, we both know what such a connection means. We must hand this information over to the proper agencies. I will return to Washington this afternoon. I expect to hear from you after your inauguration.

Mike took a step back, his stomach churning. He wasn't sure what the letter meant, but he knew it was the clue they'd been looking for. Andrew had known about the gaunt man, and his connection to Mike's lab.

"Unit 199," Amber said, tapping her lips. "I haven't heard that name in a long time."

"What is it?"

"Nobody's really sure, not anymore. Originally, it was the name of a research compound located just outside Beijing, loosely connected to the Chinese nuclear program. In the early sixties, the compound was moved deeper into the mainland, and both the American and British agencies lost track of it. There have been rumors that Unit 199 is still in operation—but it's doubtful that it's still involved with nuclear research."

Mike pointed at one of the pictures of the gaunt man. "Even more doubtful, now. If they've been watching Teri's work—"

A sudden sound stopped him mid-sentence, and he glanced toward the double doors on the other side of the barn. Amber was already on her feet, the lockbox tucked under her left arm. The sound was unmistakable: footsteps, about twenty feet from the barn doors and coming closer. Mike was praying it was just Anna Emory—when he heard male voices from outside. They weren't speaking English.

"Shit," Amber whispered. "I guess we didn't lose them after all. They must have doubled back, and now they're coming for us. That means this isn't a surveillance operation anymore."

She looked at Mike. Her face had gone cold, and that

scared him more than the voices outside. "What do you mean?"

"Somehow, they've gotten what they needed. Now they're here to clean up the loose ends. They're here to kill us."

CHAPTER TWENTY

In one fluid motion, Amber reached beneath her smock and pulled out a small, gleaming pistol. Although Mike was no expert on guns, this one was unlike anything he had seen on television or in the movies. It fit entirely in Amber's hand, and the barrel was no wider than a Canadian dime.

Amber saw the look on Mike's face. "It was about the only thing that would fit under this smock. I strapped it to my thigh before I came to your apartment. After Bader, I had a feeling I might need it."

The voices were getting closer, and Mike counted at least three different timbres. Still, he did not doubt Amber's abilities. "Can we take them?"

"Doubtful. Chances are, they've got some real artillery with them, especially if they've figured out who I am."

"Then we're dead."

Amber didn't respond. Instead, she pushed him toward the stall to his right. "Hide in there, beneath the horse."

"What about you?"

She grabbed the edge of the grain bin and eased herself inside. Crouching, she was just barely hidden by its low sides.

Mike trembled as he quickly crossed to the occupied

stall. The brown horse stuck its muzzle through the gate. Mike placed his palm on the horse's shoulder and gave a gentle shove. The horse backed away from the gate, and Mike undid the latch.

The horse stamped its feet and Mike had a sudden fear that the creature would whinny or leap forward. But he had no alternative hiding place, and the voices were getting closer. He pulled the gate open, holding his breath. The horse stood there, staring down at him with dark, curious eyes.

Mike exhaled softly, then placed his hand against the animal's flank. He could feel the packed muscle beneath his palm. He stepped forward, his hand still on the horse, and quietly shut the gate behind him.

The horse began to paw nervously at the floor, and Mike clenched his teeth, about to panic. But then a strange thing happened. A calmness moved through him, and suddenly he knew what to do. He leaned close to the horse's ear and began to whisper. He told the horse that he was a friend, that he was just going to crouch down for a few minutes, that he wasn't a threat. Then he ran his hand down the horse's side.

The horse stopped pawing the floor. Mike was amazed—and then a thought hit him: Andrew would have known how to calm a frightened horse. Was it possible that Andrew had shown him what to do?

Anyway, it had worked. Mike slowly lowered himself to the floor and crouched next to the horse's legs. He concentrated on the ground in front of him, trying to keep the fear from taking over.

The air beneath the horse was so thick with the animal's scent, Mike had to take shallow breaths to keep from gagging. A discarded horseshoe lay a few inches from his feet, half covered by straw. Thinking it might make a last-ditch weapon, Mike reached for it, careful not to startle the horse.

His fingers had just closed around the heavy iron shoe when a loud creak reverberated through the stall and the barn grew lighter briefly. Someone had opened the door and entered the barn.

Mike shifted his weight forward, finding a crack at the edge of the gate three feet off the ground. By pressing his eye against the crack he could make out a five-foot section of the barn directly in front of his stall. He could just barely see the edge of the grain bin.

The seconds passed like dripping glue. Mike clenched and unclenched his hands around the heavy horseshoe. His knees had started to ache from the crouched position, but he pushed the pain away. If he had to move, he knew his body would compensate. If he had to fight, he would.

Not just for himself—but for Amber. In the short time they had been together, he had grown attached to her. Even though he still knew very little about her, his intuition told him that they *worked.* He wanted the chance to see what would develop, given time and opportunity. It had been so long since he had cultivated a real connection with a woman—

There was a sudden shuffle of feet directly in front of the stall, and the horse snorted next to Mike, bobbing its head. Mike squinted through the crack and saw the first man come into view. He was of average height, thin, with slicked-black hair and a round Chinese face. He was wearing a white smock and had a cruel-looking automatic rifle in his hands.

Just behind him walked a second man, also Chinese. He was stockier than the first, with a completely shaved head and thick, arching eyebrows over his narrow eyes. He was wearing a similar white smock and had a pair of sunglasses perched on his head. In his hands was another automatic rifle, with a sharp bayonet attached.

Mike heard a voice from behind the two men; both stopped in their tracks, standing completely still. They were directly in front of Mike's stall, their hands tightening against their rifles. The third man was still out of view, but Mike guessed he would be similarly armed. Three men, carrying assault rifles, at least one with a bayonet. Amber had a small pistol. Mike had a horseshoe. Not great odds.

Mike swallowed, his throat chalk dry. In another moment, the men would discover Amber in the hay bin. She would come out shooting, and it would all be over. She and Mike wouldn't last a minute. He had to do something to even out the odds. He looked at the horseshoe in his hand, then cursed inwardly and started searching the stall for something better, something that would give them a fighting chance—

His gaze settled on the muscular brown flank to his right. *The horse.* A plan formed; he reached into his pocket, and his fingers closed over something rusty and sharp.

He pulled the hook out of his pocket. He hated to do this, but he didn't have a choice. If he lived, he'd have a vet come see the horse tomorrow.

The man out of view said something in hushed Chinese, and the first two men continued forward toward the hay bin, their rifles rising. Mike knew he had no more time to think. He pressed himself hard against the wall of the stall, and jabbed the hook into the horse's left flank.

The horse screamed and reared, kicking wildly at the air. Then it leaped forward, hitting the gate with full force. The gate slammed outward and the horse burst through, hooves spinning like helicopter blades. The two men on the other side looked up, their eyes wide with fear. But before they could move, the horse was on top of them. The closer man took a kick to the direct center of his face, and there was a sickening crunch. His body crumpled like a rag doll.

The second man spun, trying to lift his rifle. But the horse came at him too fast, and he barely had time to scream before the animal's front hooves crashed into his chest. He flew back into the empty stall, his head hitting the charred wall and bursting through.

Then there was a burst of gunfire, and the horse jerked like a marionette. Bright red splotches of blood appeared across its right side, and its head twisted upward in agony. Mike's mouth went wide and a sudden, uncontrollable anger filled him. Out of the corner of his eye he saw Amber rising from inside the hay bin, her gun in front of her—but Mike was already moving forward, the fire inside spurring him on. His fingers whitened against the horseshoe as he leaped through the open gate.

He landed solidly on both feet, facing the front of the barn. The third man was standing three feet in front of him, his automatic rifle still trained on the convulsing horse. The man was tall, with wide, muscular shoulders and a thick neck. His head was square, his hair graying at the edges.

The man saw Mike and recognition flashed across his dark face. He swung the rifle, but Mike was a step ahead of him, diving forward, the horseshoe flashing through the air in a tight arc. It caught the man full on the right shoulder, and there was a loud crack. The rifle clattered to the ground, and the man staggered back, holding his shattered arm.

Mike kept coming, the horseshoe whizzing through the air. He hit the man in the other shoulder, and there was another crack. The man screamed, both arms hanging useless at his sides. Mike swung the horseshoe a third time, catching the man full on the jaw. The man's eyes rolled up and his knees buckled. His body crumpled to the ground.

Mike stood there, chest heaving, staring down at his broken enemy. Then he saw the horseshoe in his own hand, and his fingers went limp. The horseshoe hit the ground a few inches from his feet.

He dropped to his knees to check the unconscious man's pulse. Thankfully, it was strong. He leaned close to the man's chest, listening to his steady breathing. Good. The man probably had a concussion—but he would survive. Mike rose to his feet, relieved.

He heard Amber coming up behind him, but he didn't turn around. *I could have killed him. I could have shattered his skull.* He still felt remnants of the fiery anger that had rocked his body. And he could still hear the sound of the man's shoulders cracking as he swung the horseshoe. Shame washed through his body as he realized what he had done—the violence of which he was capable. What kind of man was he? How was he different from his father?

Finally, he looked past Amber toward the wounded horse in the corner stall. It was lying on the ground, spasms rocking its tattered body. Its eyes were half open, its lips curled back in anguish. Amber touched his shoulder with her left hand. In her right she held one of the assassins' assault rifles.

"Mike, that was quick thinking. Another second, and they would have found me."

Mike shrugged, barely listening, his gaze pinned to the dying horse. His body felt numb. *Quick thinking.* He hadn't been thinking at all. He had been acting like an animal, driven by his anger. Murderous anger. "I didn't mean for this to happen."

"You saved both our lives."

"Two people dead," Mike murmured. "Another with broken bones and a concussion. And this poor horse. I know it was self-defense—but that doesn't make it any easier. I'm a doctor."

He said the words, but they didn't mean anything. His education did not change who he was. Like his father, he had the potential to hurt. The potential to kill.

Amber stepped in front of him, the rifle low at her side, and looked him in the eyes. "Mike. Listen to me. I know it isn't easy. It shouldn't be easy. But remember—you didn't ask for this. They came here to kill us both. They killed Andrew, and Bader. They tortured a Secret Service man to death."

Mike felt her strength running into him. The thought of those murders pushed away some of his shame. And Amber was right: he hadn't asked for this. He had to try to forget the rage and violence that had gripped him, and think about the consequences of his actions. He had saved their lives.

He squeezed Amber's hand, then turned back toward the horse. The horrible sight tugged at his heart. "What about him? We can't leave him like this."

"You're right," Amber said. She blinked, hard; then her mouth became a thin line. "Mike, turn away."

"What are you going to do?" But it was a stupid question. He saw her raise the automatic rifle, and turned away.

A burst of fire echoed through the barn. Mike swallowed, his knees quivering. He felt like throwing up. There was death all around him. Because of Teri's research.

He remembered what Amber had said, right before

the men had entered the barn: "This isn't a surveillance operation anymore. They've gotten what they needed. Now they're here to clean up the loose ends."

A sudden, horrible thought struck Mike. His eyes came wide open.

"Mike," Amber said, "it was the right thing to do. He was suffering."

Mike didn't respond. He wasn't thinking about the horse. He was thinking about the person who had started it all. If they had come after him and Amber, then that meant . . .

Teri. *Teri!*

CHAPTER TWENTY-ONE

Teri felt as if she were back in college. The smell of coffee, the buzz of caffeine inside her veins, the *click click click* of her fingers against a computer keyboard—all she needed was a stack of loan-payment notices and Brad leaning over her shoulder, and it was senior year all over again.

Somewhere between noon and late afternoon, she had lost track of the time. Her shoulders and neck ached from leaning over her laptop, and her eyes burned from concentrating too hard on the screen. Dr. Ballantine's swivel chair felt like a medieval torture device beneath her hips, and her elbows were bright red where they leaned against the hard mahogany desktop. But she was minutes away from printing, and she had no intention of stopping until she was done.

Somewhere in the back of her mind, she was aware of the phone in the corner of the lab ringing. Her fingers paused over the keys. The phone call could be from Mike; by now, he would have awakened to his empty apartment. Maybe the visions had returned, or maybe he had seen something new, something more concrete.

Teri hit the Save key and rose, the swivel chair creaking beneath her. But before she could get out from behind the desk, another sound joined the intermittent ringing. A heavy, metallic whir.

The elevator. Someone was descending toward the basement lab. Teri looked at the laptop screen, filled with her data and the last half of her conclusion. *Shit.* She didn't want any of the other graduate students seeing her work. She knew she was being paranoid—but science was a competitive field. People stole research all the time.

She quickly flicked the screen off, leaving the processor going. Then she snatched her small pile of notes off the desk, sending a few of Mike's souvenirs crashing to the floor. She spun and headed toward the shelves along the back wall.

She reached her mouse cage just as the elevator buzzed, signaling its arrival in the basement. The phone was still ringing, and the mixture of sounds echoed off the cinder-block walls, a noxious cacophony. Teri put her notes on the top shelf, lifted the wire mouse cage—and went pale.

The first twenty pages of her paper—gone. Sometime in the past few days, someone had removed them from her hiding place. Teri's throat constricted and she felt like crying. Someone had stolen her work—

The elevator doors *whiff*ed open behind her, and she turned, still holding the mouse cage. She watched in shock as two men walked into the basement lab. Both were wearing long white doctor's coats, surgical masks, caps, and latex gloves.

Teri stood against the shelves, tightly gripping the mouse cage. She could feel whiskers against her thumb, and tiny mouse fingers tickling her palm. The elevator doors slid shut behind the two men, and the only sound left in the lab was the incessant ringing of the telephone.

"May I help you?" Teri asked, her voice cracking.

The two men stepped forward. The closer of the two reached up with two long fingers and pulled down his white surgical mask. Teri's mouth opened as she saw the hand-shaped acne scar running down the right side of the man's face. His dark eyes narrowed. His lips curled back, his teeth sharp and yellow.

"We no longer need your help, little girl." He had a heavy Chinese accent.

"You're the ghost," Teri whispered, remembering what Mike had told her. Her fear was so intense she no longer felt the floor beneath her feet. "You're the one from Andrew's memory."

The gaunt man raised his eyebrows. Then he nodded. "You're a very smart little girl. Know that my nation is grateful for all you've done. Know that your research will change the world."

His arms moved beneath his long white coat, and there was a glint of metal. Teri lowered her eyes, and her stomach turned over. The gaunt man was holding a scalpel in his right hand. And a cruel-looking bone drill in his left. His finger tightened against the drill's trigger, and the long steel bit tore at the air.

"Please," Teri whispered, "don't hurt me."

The gaunt man glanced at the man behind him. He, too, pulled down his mask, and Teri saw that he had a tattoo of a bird beneath his left eye. The second man laughed.

"If you knew who you were talking to," he said, his accent even heavier than the gaunt man's, "you'd understand why that makes me laugh."

The gaunt man took a step forward, and Teri's hands tightened against the mouse cage. There was no doubt in her mind: the gaunt man was going to kill her. He was going to cut through her skin with the scalpel—or even worse, tear through her body with the awful bone drill. She imagined the pain she would feel, the terrible agony of the seconds before death. The sheer horror of the thought was nearly overwhelming. She felt faint, and struggled to stay on her feet. She knew she couldn't overpower the gaunt man. But she had to do something.

She looked wildly around the lab, searching for help or an escape route. A polished glass bulb hung from the wall ten feet to the left of the mahogany desk. A fire alarm. If she could get to it, she might have a chance.

The gaunt man was moving forward, the drill and the scalpel steady in his hands. She waited until he was right on the other side of the desk, so close she could see the scalpel rising, the razor-sharp blade sparkling beneath the fluorescent lights—

In one sudden motion, Teri hurled the mouse cage across the desk and dove for the fire alarm. The cage crashed into the gaunt man's chest, sending him stumbling backward. The cage door snapped open and the tiny mice spiraled into the air, their tagged tails fluttering behind them.

Move, Teri screamed at herself, *move, move move!* Her shoes skidded as she rushed toward the alarm. She was still a good three feet away when there was a flicker of motion behind her. She glanced back, her body still barreling forward. The gaunt man had recovered; he was sliding around the desk behind her. Before she could turn away, his arm twitched upward, and there was a sudden flash of metal.

Something touched the bare skin of her throat, right below her jaw. A warm feeling moved down her neck to her chest, and her mouth opened, but no sound came out. She looked down—and saw the hilt of the gaunt man's scalpel sticking out of her throat.

She crashed into the wall, her hand inches from the fire alarm. Blood was spraying out of her carotid artery, and her dress had already turned a shade darker. She stared down into the growing pool of crimson beneath her feet, and her knees buckled.

She hit the ground shoulder first and lay there, sprawled against the wall, her eyes wide, the blood gushing out of her. She felt no physical pain, but her mind was in agony, gripped by the sure knowledge that her life was pumping out of her with every heart beat. She could still hear the phone ringing from the other side of the lab, but the sound had begun to melt at the edges. Then she heard the two men speaking in Chinese, their voices echoing through her skull, as if suddenly her ears were miles apart. The language sounded beautiful and horrible at the same time, the tones winding together like dancing strands of silk.

Footsteps reverberated through the floor beneath her head. The gaunt man's legs came into view, and she fought to shift her gaze upward. He was looking down at her, the bone drill hanging ominously from his left hand. His right hand reached into his white doctor's coat, and pulled out a small cell phone.

He punched in a number and put the phone against his ear. His voice trickled down like rain. "Everything is going as planned. After we finish with the lab, we'll retrieve the final object from the doctor's apartment. Then we'll head straight for the Charlestown Navy Yard. Make sure you delay any potential response."

Teri watched as he shoved the phone back in his pocket. Through her agony, a sudden question entered her mind. Why had she been able to understand the gaunt man's phone call? *He had been speaking English.* The man on the other end was not Chinese. She knew that was significant, but was too weak to figure out why. The truth was, it didn't matter anymore. Nothing mattered anymore. She was dying.

She thought about Mike, sitting in his apartment wondering where she was. A sob caught in her pained chest. Now he would never know how she had truly felt about him. *He'll never know* . . .

She had nearly lost consciousness when a sound grazed the back of her mind. A loud hiccup, followed by a gentle, familiar humming. Something about the sound comforted her, and her body finally relaxed, the agony vanishing. Her muscles turned to liquid, and her eyelids fluttered shut.

CHAPTER TWENTY-TWO

As the BMW careened between two ambulances and skidded toward the receiving circle, Mike exhaled, glad Amber was behind the wheel. If he'd driven in his frazzled state, they might never have made it to the hospital—and certainly not in under forty minutes. His hands shook against the BMW's car phone, as the metallic ringing echoed through his skull. He had let the phone ring for most of the ride, each passing minute magnifying his fear. He had also tried Teri's apartment and his own, but no one had answered in either place, and he was beginning to dread the worst.

"Mike," Amber said, pulling into the receiving circle, "just because they made an attempt on us, doesn't mean they went after her. They may not want her dead."

"What do you mean?" Mike could barely hear her over the sound of the tires screeching to a stop against the pavement. "You said their surveillance operation is over. They've got what they needed."

"But maybe what they need is Teri, alive. If Unit 199 has been conducting parallel research, using Teri's results to bolster their own, they may need her help to get to their goal."

Mike pushed open his door and leaped out onto the sidewalk. It was dark outside, and growing darker by the minute. He raced toward the glass double doors, Amber two steps behind him. No matter how fast he ran, he felt he was moving in slow motion. "If their goal is getting information from beyond the grave, they don't need Teri. They just need her notes and her R-E solution."

The entrance doors flew open and Mike narrowly avoided a stretcher carrying a pregnant woman across the ER. Both knees cried out at the motion. *Stay calm,* he told himself, *stay in control.* Amber caught up to him near the admission desk.

"But what if their goal is something bigger than a new, seamless method of interrogation?"

"Like what?"

"I'm not sure. But it's got to be something huge. Mike, they killed a U.S. governor. Now they're running around Boston with assault rifles. Remember, Unit 199 was originally a part of the Chinese nuclear program. It was Mao's brainchild. My guess is, whatever they're up to, it's as big as the nuclear bomb. If not bigger."

The nurses sitting behind the admission desk looked at them with wide eyes as they barreled past. Mike ignored them, heading straight for the elevator to his basement lab. He hit the button with the heel of his hand, his chest heaving, his muscles electric. "Amber, I don't care what they're up to. They killed my best friend. They tried to kill us. If they've hurt Teri—I swear I'll kill them. Whatever kind of an animal that makes me."

Amber looked at him. Her expression was unreadable. "It makes you human, Mike."

The instant the elevator doors slid open, Mike knew something was wrong, that the place had recently been violated. The flickering sound of the fluorescent lights was somehow different, the dim glow against the cinderblocks subtly off. Then Mike saw the empty shelves at the back of the room, the cabinets hanging open, the vacant equipment racks, the cleared-off surface of his mahogany desk—and his heart sank.

"Christ," he whispered, stepping into the lab. "They took everything. My PC *and* the laptop. All the equipment. Everything from Teri's shelves. Even the mouse cages—"

Something ran past his shoes. A white mouse, heading for a corner at breakneck speed. Amber followed his gaze. "Is that one of Teri's?"

"Must be. See the tag on its tail?"

"Mike," Amber said, stopping him with her hand, "I need you to prepare yourself. I know you're a doctor—but this might be much worse than anything you've seen before. If you fall apart on me, I'm going to have to finish this on my own."

Why was she telling him this? Then Mike saw that Amber was no longer looking at the scurrying mouse. Her eyes were trained toward the floor next to his mahogany desk. A thin pool of red was seeping across the green tiles.

Closer up, Mike saw a pair of high-heeled shoes sticking out from behind the desk corner, then Teri's stockinged legs. Then the rest of the body came into full view—and Mike stopped, his face sheet white. He covered his mouth with his hand, forcing the bile back down his throat. Then he slammed his hand against the desktop, the sound reverberating through the lab. The pain echoed up his arm, and he slammed his hand again and again, trying to clear his mind. "Mutilated. They mutilated her. Her ears. They cut off her ears."

Amber came around the other side of the desk, her face drawn, and dropped to her knees to look over Teri's body. "She was dead before he started. Stabbed in the throat."

Mike couldn't tear his eyes away. It was unthinkable—unbelievable. He was a doctor, had seen hundreds of dead bodies, but this was horrible. Teri's face was drained of blood. Both her ears were missing, and there was a deep opening in the left side of her skull.

"It's his signature," Amber whispered. "He removes the central portion of the brain."

"The same thing he did to your father," Mike said. An idea tugged at him, but he ignored it. Teri, murdered and mutilated. Her research, gone. Everything he had gone through paled against what they had done to an innocent young girl. "She was just a kid. The bastard. She was just a child—"

"Mike, stay in control. We have to try and figure out where they're headed next."

"Stay in control? How the fuck can I stay in control? Look what they did to her!" Mike lowered himself to the floor, his eyes still pinned to Teri's porcelain face. Her eyes were closed, her lips flecked with blood. Still, she looked like an angel. Mike had barely known her, but her death was affecting him as much as anyone's ever had. She had been a genius. A child genius. She had been on her way to the acclaim and respect she deserved. Her death was unfair.

He reached forward, and touched her outstretched left arm. He ran his fingers down her cold skin. *Teri, I'll make it right. Somehow, I'll make it right.*

"They came for her equipment," Amber continued, half to herself. "But did they get everything they needed?"

Mike was barely listening. He could feel the anger building inside him. This time, he let it build. *Teri. My God, Teri.* He wished that she could rise out of her body like Andrew, that she could somehow communicate with him, tell him where to find the bastard who had killed her. He tried to imagine her viroles in the air, leaking out of her hippocampal cells—and then his gaze settled back on her mutilated skull. What sort of animal could do this? What sort of monster? His teeth came together as his fingers reached Teri's hand. He remembered the tender way she had covered him in a blanket, back at his apartment. How she had watched him fall asleep.

"Mike, is there anything else they're missing? Anything that wasn't in the lab?" Amber was standing at the high shelves at the back of the room. Teri's shelves. Mike remembered how she had kept them so cluttered, to hide her work. In three years, he had never noticed her equipment. The mouse maze. The electrifying cylinder. The R-E solution.

He paused, raising his eyes. *The R-E solution.* "The oxygen tank, containing the aerosolized R-E solution—and the proper disbursal ratio that made Teri's experiment work. They'll need the tank to calculate the ratio and recreate her work. It's the key to Teri's success—and it's still in my apartment."

Amber met his gaze. A second later, they were both moving toward the door.

CHAPTER TWENTY-THREE

Commonwealth Avenue was lit up like an amusement park at midnight. Mike counted three fire engines, two ambulances, and at least half a dozen police cars. He stared at the chaotic scene in shock as Amber pulled the BMW in behind a network news van. Then he saw the black smoke billowing out through the shattered third-floor window of his apartment building, and his chest constricted. Teri's death wasn't the end of the horror; it was just the beginning.

He tore out onto the sidewalk, almost upending a television cameraman filming a woman he recognized from the five o'clock news. Amber was right behind him as he pushed through the growing crowd of spectators. A police officer tried to stop him, but he shoved right past, heading straight for the front steps to his building. He nearly slammed headfirst into a fireman in bright yellow protective gear.

"Hold up!" the fireman shouted, yanking a soot-covered gas mask off his face. He was African American and huge, built like a linebacker, with wisps of gray hair and bloodshot eyes. "You can't go in there. We're just barely getting the damn thing under control!"

Before Mike could respond, he felt a hand come down on his shoulder, and he was yanked sideways. A red-faced police officer shouted something at him, and then Amber broke free of the crowd, waving her federal ID. The cop backed off, leaving Mike and Amber alone with the fireman.

"What happened?" Amber asked, taking the words out of Mike's mouth.

"Pipe bomb," the fireman answered, lifting his angled hat to wipe sweat from his forehead. "At least that's what we think. Attached to the door of one of the apartments on the third floor. Set to blow when someone put a key in the lock. The sucker went off about ten minutes ago."

Mike felt his knees weaken. They had destroyed his apartment. He tried to picture his living room blackened by fire and filled with thick smoke. The furniture he and Kari had painstakingly picked out, the home they had created together—now it was all gone. His world was turning upside down, the way it had after Kari had died—worse, because now it wasn't fate that was fucking with him, it was a real live enemy. A violent, hateful enemy who had attached a bomb to his door, no doubt hoping to kill him when he came home. But someone else had gotten there first, someone else had set the bomb off.

"Mike," Amber whispered, not wanting the fireman to overhear, "who else has a key to your apartment?"

Mike shook his head, bewildered. He had lost Kari's keys long ago and had never made a spare set. The one time he had locked himself out, he had needed a locksmith to get in. Maybe the bomb had just gone off on its own—

Mike turned and looked past the gathering crowd to the curb, across the fire engines and police cars—and an anguished noise escaped his throat. The gray pickup truck was parked twenty feet away, on the other side of the street.

Mike spun back to the fireman and grabbed him by the arm. "Where is he? Is he alive?"

The fireman looked at him, confused at first. Then he read Mike's expression. He pointed toward one of the ambulances.

Everything seemed to blend together in front of Mike's eyes as he ran down the sidewalk. *No, please, no, no!* He could still hear the sirens and the shouts, could still smell smoke and the exhaust from the emergency vehicles, but he was somewhere else, somewhere far away. Somewhere the pain and the fear couldn't reach.

The back of the ambulance was open; Mike counted at least three paramedics hovering over the stretcher. His heart sank: one of the paramedics had the defibrillator paddles attached to his hands. Mike took the last few steps as one, and jumped up into the ambulance just in time to hear the shout of "Clear!"

The paramedic pressed the paddles against the body on the stretcher and sent three hundred joules of electricity into his patient's wounded heart. The half-naked man spasmed upward, then crashed back against the stretcher. There was a brief silence as everyone turned to look at the heart monitor in the far corner of the ambulance. The line was flat.

Mike pushed past one of the paramedics and leaned over the stretcher. He barely recognized his father beneath the blood and bruises. Both arms seemed to have been twisted three hundred and sixty degrees at the shoulders; they were hanging limp over the sides of the stretcher. One leg had been severed at the knee, and white gauze covered most of the lower half of Flannery's body. His face was partially obscured by the intubation tube, but his bright blue eyes were wide open, the pupils fixed and dilated.

Please no. Please, God, no!

The paramedics backed away from the body, defeated. Mike stared at them, then at his father. *No. It can't be true.*

He slammed his palms down against his father's chest, and started pumping. He counted off the compressions the way they'd taught him in medical school, the way he had done a thousand times before. *One one thousand, two one thousand, three one thousand—*

"Sir," one of the paramedics said, startled. "He's gone. Sir!"

"I'm a doctor!" Mike shouted. "I'm not letting him die!"

One one thousand, two one thousand, three one thousand. Mike clenched his teeth, ignoring the ache in his arms and shoulders. He could see the paramedics staring at him, bewildered. But they didn't understand. He didn't care what the heart monitor said. His father couldn't die yet. Not like this. Not after their last conversation. Not before Mike had a chance to get past the hate, the anger—

"Mike, stop. He was gone before they got him to the ambulance. He died when the bomb went off. They were just going through the motions."

Mike looked up and saw that the paramedics were gone. Amber shut the ambulance doors behind her, leaving them alone with Flannery's body.

Mike fell back from the stretcher. He squeezed his hands together, looking at his father's shattered body. He felt tears on his cheeks. He didn't understand why he was crying. He hadn't cried when Andrew died. He hadn't cried for Teri, either. He hadn't cried since Kari. "They killed my father."

Amber didn't say anything. Mike lowered his head.

"I hated him so much. But I never gave him a chance to show me that he'd changed."

"Mike, we have to keep going. We can't let Sheshen get away."

Mike knew she was right, but his father looked so frail and broken. Tatters of his forest-green windbreaker still hung down around his twisted arms. . . . and something was clutched in the gnarled fingers of Flannery's right hand.

A tiny screwdriver, less than four inches long. Mike gently removed it. The handle was still warm, the blade covered with tiny grooves. Flannery had used the screwdriver a dozen times to pick his way into Mike's apartment. To ask for forgiveness. To offer help. To spend time with his son the only way he could—by breaking into his life.

Amber was speaking: "They'll take Teri's research and the oxygen tank back to China and Unit 199. We don't have much time. If they go by boat, the way they came, they'll be difficult to trace. No flight plan, no cargo checks, no customs. There are a hundred places to dock a boat in this city."

Mike clutched the screwdriver. The muscles in his forearm contracted as he squeezed harder and harder. He couldn't let them get away with what they had done. He looked at his father's face, at the glazed blue eyes. For an instant, his pulse rocketed—he thought he saw them flicker—but it was the reflection of some bright light. He looked upward, and saw something he didn't understand.

The air above his father's stretcher was shimmering, as if a glowing dust cloud were drifting down from the roof of the ambulance, carried by an odd, unexplainable draft of air. Mike gasped. The glowing particles began to coalesce.

"Mike, what's happening?" Amber's voice was soft, but a shiver moved up Mike's spine.

"I don't know," he whispered, staring at the shimmering above his father's body. Then a sound reached his ears: an anguished, horrible moan. It was the voice of a woman. A young woman.

Mike watched, shocked, as the glowing particles slowly took form. The moaning grew louder, the anguish more palpable. Mike found himself staring at an angelic, beautiful, tragic face—with bright green eyes. The face was nearly transparent; Mike could see the other side of the ambulance through the gaping mouth. He felt a strange wind against his cheeks as the green eyes stared at him.

"It's Teri!" Amber's voice was tinged with fear.

Mike whirled toward her. "You can see it, too?"

"It's so real. So vivid! My mind doesn't want to believe—but it's there, in front of me!" Amber's eyes were wide, her face the color of ash. Her back was pressed up against the inside wall of the ambulance. "How can this be?"

Mike didn't answer. He turned back to the apparition, and noticed that the glowing, disembodied lips had begun to quiver. A low whisper echoed in his ears: "Stop them."

"How?" he whispered back, staring into Teri's ghostly green eyes. "We don't know where they are."

The lips moved again. Just four words, but they were enough. Teri's face began to flicker, like a neon light struggling to stay lit. Then it vanished. Mike slid across the ambulance to Amber's side, and touched her arm.

"Mike, how is this possible?"

Mike paused, thinking. There had to be a scientific explanation. Now, even the paranormal followed hard and fast rules. "Teri died, violently, in the basement lab.

The same lab where she had spilled the R-E solution into the ventilation cabinet. Traces of the solution must still be in the air. So the atmosphere was right, our susceptibility high."

"But it's been less than an hour."

Mike nodded. "True. Maybe that has something to do with Teri herself. She's been working with the R-E solution for a long time: inhaling it, probably spilling it on her skin, perhaps swallowing fluid particles by mistake. Maybe her viroles have developed elevated binding capabilities. Then again, there's also another possibility."

Amber ran her fingers through her hair. Her face had returned to its normal color. "What's that?"

"She wasn't ready to die. She had something she needed to tell us, so she came back." A few days ago, the idea would have seemed ridiculous to Mike. But his mind was no longer closed. "Amber, Teri's experiments and my experience with Andrew prove the existence of ghosts. With Teri's R-E solution and a controlled environment, we can create and re-create ghosts in a laboratory. We can study them, document them, perhaps even manipulate them. Just as we experiment with viruses, bacteria, and other agents of disease."

He looked back at his father's body. "But this isn't the laboratory. We don't know yet how the process works out here. Maybe there are things that enhance susceptibility but have nothing to do with R-E solution. Maybe people catch ghosts the way they catch diseases, for reasons we don't always understand, at times we can't always predict. The key is to keep an open mind. The science demands that we be willing to believe."

Amber nodded, squeezing his hand. Mike's gaze remained on his father; rage lingered inside him. With the help of Teri's message, he would find an outlet for that rage.

"We don't have much time," Amber said, reaching for the ambulance doors. "They have a good head start."

"But now we know where they're going," Mike responded. Teri's final words echoed in his ears, but it was Amber who spoke them aloud:

"The Charlestown Navy Yard."

CHAPTER TWENTY-FOUR

Mao's Revolution rocked beneath Sheshen's feet as he watched his men loading the wooden crates of equipment into the cargo bay. It was a cloudless night; swaths of moonlight laced the waves as they crashed against the sides of the eighty-foot freighter. Sheshen pressed the portable oxygen tank to his chest, feeling the cool metal through his thin smock. He breathed deep, tasting the strong salt air. It was over. He had won. In a matter of days, all China would honor his victory. Even his hateful father would applaud the success of his mission.

He looked off to the right, toward the dark opening where the navy yard met the ocean. Somewhere out there, moving closer by the minute, was a sleek Cigarette-style speedboat. The speedboat would carry him and the oxygen tank in his hands to a second freighter with a specialized long-range helicopter on board. From the helicopter, Sheshen would travel to an island with a small airstrip—and from there, straight home to Mogue De Ghong and Unit 199.

Sheshen turned back to the shrinking pile of crates on the dock. He did not like the idea of leaving his men in charge of the cargo while he traveled the faster route back to China; but there was no other choice. He intended to deliver the oxygen tank to his father—to personally accept the honor and respect he deserved. The oxygen tank had been the clue they were looking for all along, the secret to the young girl's success. The aerosolized R-E solution inside had made her experiment work; now Gui Yisheng could easily recreate the aerosolization ratio of the gas. The minute Sheshen had told his father about the tank, Gui Yisheng had agreed: the time for action had come. With the girl's notes and the tank, Gui Yisheng could move his own work to the next phase—and a step closer to the ultimate goal. The ultimate revolution!

Nothing could stop Unit 199 now. The girl was dead. Although the mercenary Triad team Sheshen had sent after the doctor and the traitorous Chinese woman had failed, his sources had confirmed that the explosive trap set on the doctor's apartment had indeed gone off, claiming at least one victim. Even though the CIA traitor had survived, she had no way of tracing Sheshen's escape route.

Sheshen still wasn't sure how she had gotten involved with the doctor in the first place. But after his inside source spotted the Mercedes passing the Triad headquarters, it had not been difficult to identify her as another federal agent. When Sheshen saw her enter the doctor's apartment building, wearing a traditional Chinese smock and an enormous amount of makeup, he immediately suspected she had taken part in some undercover scheme aimed at the Chinatown headquarters. Once this had been confirmed, her mystery had evaporated. She was nothing, a whore in the pay of the *yang gui,* a traitor to her own kind. He would have liked to go after her and the doctor himself, but the girl had been more important to his mission. His successful mission.

Sheshen's chest swelled with pride. *Great Father Mao, it won't be long now!* He looked over his shoulder at the huge two-century-old sailing ship, the U.S.S. *Con-*

stitution, that rose from the water a bare ten feet from his freighter. Above the two-hundred-foot center sail was a fluttering rectangle of fabric. Sheshen could not make out the Stars and Stripes in the darkness, but he could imagine the bloody strips waving at him in the stiff ocean wind. He grinned at the impotence of his enemies. The ship next to him had once been a symbol of the young Western nation's strength. Now it would watch, helpless, as Sheshen sailed off with a secret as powerful as anything in the history of war.

A secret that would sweep across the world, devouring China's enemies in tongues of bright red flame.

CHAPTER TWENTY-FIVE

The Freedom Trail looked extremely different at ninety miles per hour. Mike pressed his face against the trembling side window, imagining the crowds of tourists following the painted red line on the blur of sidewalk to his right. Once, he and Kari had walked the three-mile route; from the Commons to the State House to Faneuil Hall to Bunker Hill, they had laughed and hugged and joked, wishing that life could freeze and never change. But life hadn't frozen—it had shattered.

Mike turned away from the window as Amber slammed the car's cell phone back into its holder. Irritation was evident on her face. "It's going to be close."

"What do you mean?" Caught up in his own inner turmoil, Mike had barely listened to her phone conversation. The death of his father made it difficult to concentrate on anything beyond his growing rage.

"That was Dick Leary on the line. He's in charge of the investigation into Andrew's death. I've convinced him to get a squad over to the navy yard, but I'm not sure how many officers he's going to bring, or whether they'll get there in time. Sheshen might already be on his way back to China."

"Why do we have to go through Leary? Why can't you scramble some Coast Guard boats, or alert the navy yard itself? Don't you have the authority?"

Amber glanced at him, then back at the road. He hadn't meant the statement as a challenge; he was simply a stranger to the politics of her work. "It's not a matter of authority. It's a matter of confidentiality. Mike, this can't turn into a military exercise. And I can't afford risking major media attention. If the media make a connection between Governor Kyle's death and the Chinese military, what do you think would happen?"

Mike paused, staring out the window as they turned onto the bridge that separated Boston's North End from the waterfront community of Charlestown. "I guess things could get a little crazy."

"Things could get a lot crazy. Wars have started over much less. China is backward in a lot of ways, but it's a nuclear power. And there are many hard-line factions inside Beijing that would not mind an open confrontation, as insane as that sounds. A confrontation would give them the political power they need to resolidify China's Communist dictatorship. Push the drift back in the direction of Mao's revolution, erase all the footsteps toward democracy and capitalism made in the years since Tiananmen Square."

Mike didn't know much about Chinese politics, nor did he care. But he understood Amber's point. If Sheshen's actions in America became public knowledge, there would be an enormous outcry against China. Perhaps even a call to war. And even apart from the nuclear threat, an armed skirmish with China would mean countless deaths. Still, Mike hated to think that Sheshen might get away because Amber had to keep her mission a secret. At the moment, he didn't care about international relations; he cared about getting his hands on the man responsible for his father's death.

"If we *don't* stop them," Mike countered, "who knows what the ramifications will be? Maybe it will be worse than war. With Teri's research, they'll be on the cutting edge of a brand-new area of science. You said it before—they're probably already working on something as big as the nuclear bomb."

"True," Amber said, gunning the BMW past a pair of taxis and nearly touching the side rail of the massive bridge. Through the darkness to Mike's right, he could just make out the *Constitution*'s center mast, far above the choppy waves of the bay. "But my superiors won't take the chance of opening this operation up, not without some real proof of what Sheshen and his people are up to. To them, all we've got so far is a bunch of ghost stories."

Mike nodded, rubbing the backs of his hands against his eyes. Over the hum of the BMW's engine, he could hear the dark water lapping at the base of the bridge. Ghost stories. He thought back to the moment in his lab when Teri had floored him with a single question: "Do you believe in ghosts?" In the past twenty-four hours, his entire belief system had changed. He was still a scientist, but he could no longer call himself a skeptic. There were still hard-and-fast rules—but a new logic, one without barriers.

"So we've got to do more than just stop them from leaving with Teri's research," Amber continued. "We've got to find out what Unit 199 is really up to. We've got to find out where Teri's research is going to lead them. And we've got to rely on Dick Leary and whatever backup he's bringing."

Mike swallowed, watching the end of the bridge grow near. In another few minutes, they would be at the entrance to the navy yard. He closed his eyes and tried to remember what the yard looked like during the day. It had been more than five years—one of his first dates with Kari, months before their wedding. He remembered being tired from the long walk across the bridge; he remembered sharing an ice cream sundae as they strolled across an open field to the dock. He remembered seeing the enormous, ancient sailing ship standing alone in the water, set off by a long wooden ramp, surrounded by low spotlights. He remembered the navy boats on the other side of the dock, the guard posts and the huge howitzers trained, for show, toward the ocean.

"It seems an insane place to park a Chinese freighter," he said, his nerves on edge. "It's too late for any tourists to be hanging around, but there's such a large navy presence. And I'm sure the *Constitution* is well guarded, even at night."

Amber shook her head. "It's not as crazy as it seems. The navy yard has open access to the ocean. With radar jammers and sonic cloaking, the Chinese could get in and out with relative ease. But I doubt they even need the high-tech equipment; navy and Coast Guard ships secure their radar when they reach port. In fact, navy yards are notorious for poor seaward security. And from what I understand, the *Constitution*'s anchorage is actually separate from the navy yard proper. So there's the same ocean access, but without the same level of danger. The area right around the *Constitution* might be guarded, but the guards won't be expecting anything. Not at this hour. They certainly won't be expecting Sheshen."

Mike rubbed his sweaty palms against his slacks. He felt something in his right pocket, but it took him a second to recognize its shape. His father's screwdriver— the lockpicking tool that had cost Flannery Ballantine his life. Mike exhaled, lowering his eyes. His father had only wanted to be there for his son. To seek forgiveness for a lifetime of alienation. To seek forgiveness for a thirty-year-old mistake.

Amber touched Mike's shoulder as the BMW exited

the bridge and curved toward the entrance to the navy yard. "Mike, you and I can beat Sheshen."

Mike put his hand on top of hers, and the warmth of her skin sent vibrations through his body. They were separated by race, culture, and history—but inside, they weren't all that different. He squeezed Amber's hand as she shut down the BMW's engine and let the car roll silently into the navy yard parking lot.

A few minutes later they were on foot, skirting the far edge of the asphalt lot. Mike's pulse raced as he hunched next to Amber in the darkness, his mind skittish but alert. There was a familiar clenching sensation in his lower abdomen, the same excited feeling he used to get during lacrosse finals. Now the stakes were much, much higher—but his body didn't know that; his body simply reacted to the stimuli in his brain. The fear, the adrenaline, and, most of all, the anger. The overwhelming anger.

"Careful," Amber whispered, motioning him down. He saw the cylindrical guard station at the corner of the parking lot, and immediately crouched low. Amber drew her small gun out of her smock.

She nodded at him; together they approached the guard station. A small triangle of orange light spilled out of the cylindrical booth into the parking lot, and Mike could make out a shape in the open doorway—something lying across the threshold, half in, half out. A few feet closer, and the shape began to take form—two forms, to be exact, awkwardly intertwined together. Mike swallowed hard as Amber slowed to a stop next to him, her eyes narrowing to determined slits.

"It looks as if Teri's ghost was right," she whispered, looking down at the two bodies. "He's here."

Both men were wearing white naval uniforms, and were sprawled nearly on top of each other in the open doorway. It looked as though they had been on their way out of the booth when they were hit. Mike quickly dropped to one knee, checking the nearer man's pulse. Nothing, of course. There was a bright red splotch across the center of his chest. The other man was missing most of his upper skull.

"Close range," Amber said, looking at the wounds. "A low-caliber weapon, probably silenced. You can tell by the impact creases around the head wound."

Mike could not believe how rational and controlled she sounded. Two innocent young men were lying dead in front of them. He slowly rose to his feet. How many more people were going to die tonight?

He followed Amber around the guard station, and out of the lot. A long sidewalk ran along the harbor; below, the triangular, foamy tips of the waves glowed in the high moonlight. To the right was a civilian docking area, lined with small day-trippers and a few mid-sized yachts. About a hundred yards ahead, across an empty area of water, loomed the great sailing ship. The flag at the top of the center mast was barely visible. The *Constitution* itself was vast, more than forty feet wide and almost five hundred feet long. Mike remembered strolling along the deck with Kari at his side, marveling at the enormous determination of the young nation that had dared build such a leviathan.

"Isn't it supposed to be lit up?" Amber asked, pointing at the spotlights that hung from the dock in front of the great ship. Mike nodded. Usually, half a dozen spotlights illuminated the ship's detailed black walls and colorful circuit of flags and rigging. But the spots were out, and the ship was blanketed in darkness.

"Looks more like a ghost ship than a tourist attraction," Mike whispered back, his fear rising. "They must have cut the spotlights. Won't that draw attention?"

"It's a surgical operation," Amber said, gesturing toward the guard station now thirty feet behind them. "They don't expect to hang around long enough for anyone to notice. They cut the lights in case someone from the navy side of the yard walked by; better that someone should think there's a power outage, than see a group of armed Chinese loading lab materials onto a hundred-foot freighter."

They continued forward in the near blackness, even more cautious than before. They were barely fifteen yards from the *Constitution*'s stern when Amber held out her hand, stopping Mike in his tracks. She pointed past the great ship to a shadowy outline beyond its triangular bow. "There's the other boat. It looks like it's parked right up in front of the *Constitution*."

Mike felt the sweat break out across his back as he looked at the floating, dark shape, still more than a hundred yards ahead. To his left, across the empty dock, he could just make out the huge navy ships behind the *Constitution* museum. He knew there were barracks somewhere nearby, and at least a dozen gunships. But despite the military presence, the area seemed deserted, the darkness uninterrupted. Until Leary and his backup arrived, Mike and Amber were on their own.

They continued forward, reaching the long ramp that ran up around the *Constitution*'s stern. Mike was so focused on the dark shape in the water ahead that he nearly tripped over something lying on the dock in front of him. He gasped: another body. This corpse looked more like a boy than a man in his gleaming white naval uniform, sprawled against the ropes that ran across the ramp's entrance. There was a bloody hole in the center of the boy's forehead, surrounded by a black powder burn. Someone had placed a silenced pistol right up against his skin.

"Chinese Type 59," Amber whispered, looking at the powder burn and the size of the hole in the boy's skull. "It's a modern copy of the Russian Makarov. Nine millimeter short, with a suppressor. Goes hand in hand with the Type 56 assault rifle we saw in the stable."

"They're leaving behind a lot of bodies," Mike said, his voice dull. He wondered if beneath her outward composure, Amber felt the same numbing sorrow at the sight of so much death. "They don't seem to care what happens after they're gone."

Amber nodded, thinking. "You're right. They don't care. Maybe it's because once they get away, it won't matter anymore. Maybe Unit 199's goal is so momentous, they don't have to worry about consequences. Mike, there's no question—we have to stop them. Whatever it takes."

They crept forward, using the *Constitution* to shield them from the Chinese boat. When they reached the bow they crouched low, peering into the darkness.

Fifteen feet below the long bowsprit of the *Constitution*, Mike could make out the front of the other boat. The freighter was ugly and small compared to Old Ironsides, with an open deck area, a square cabin that took up most of its center, and a rectangular cargo bay. The cargo bay was flush with the dock, and Mike could see movement in and out of the open doors that led down into the hold. He tried to count the moving shapes. At least five, maybe six. They were shrouded in darkness, but Mike could tell that three had rifles slung over their backs. The odds seemed enormous, the situation hopeless. Mike tried to keep his voice from betraying his despair. "Do you see Sheshen?"

Amber shook her head. Then she pointed at something in the water, just to the right of the Chinese freighter. A low, rectangular object hidden by shadows. "Is that another boat?"

Before Mike could respond, a muffled engine coughed to life. The low rectangle slid forward across the water, rapidly gaining speed. Amber cursed, half rising out of her crouch. "It's a Cigarette boat. Very fast, very hard to follow. It's heading toward the ocean. We have to do something."

She started forward. Mike reflexively grabbed at her arm. She was enormously brave, but the men on the freighter would cut her to pieces. He couldn't bear to lose her like that. Not even to stop Sheshen.

"Hold on. There's got to be a better way."

He was interrupted by the sudden crunching of tires as a car rolled quietly to a stop on the sidewalk behind them. Mike let go of Amber's arm and whirled around— and was relieved to see a souped-up cruiser with a colorful police department seal across its hood. The driver's door swung open; a short, squat man stepped out onto the sidewalk. He was balding, with puffy, oversized lips, a huge nose, and thick chest hair that poked out from beneath the collar of an ill-fitting, rust-orange shirt. A heavy service revolver hung from his right hand, loosely pointed at the area in front of Mike and Amber's feet. Mike's despair trickled away. Help had arrived. Sheshen wasn't going to escape.

"Leary." Amber's voice was elated. "We've got to move quickly. How many men did you bring?"

Leary looked from her to Mike. There was a horribly long pause, and then his lips curled in what only could be described as a sneer. "Just two. But they're more than enough."

The back doors of his cruiser swung open, and two men leapt out onto the sidewalk. Both carried assault rifles trained directly at Mike and Amber. Mike's jaw slid open, as he looked from barrel to barrel, then up to the two grinning faces.

Both men were Chinese.

CHAPTER TWENTY-SIX

Amber stared at the two Chinese men in complete shock, her head pounding. This couldn't be happening. Leary had betrayed them. He had been working with the Chinese government all along.

Since the beginning of her investigation, Amber had wondered if they had someone on the inside. But she had never suspected Dick Leary. He had completely fooled her, from the moment they had first met. His own paranoia about a betrayal scenario had been a shrewd, effective disguise. His racism, his oblivious, hardheaded determination, his thuggish exterior—all had worked to camouflage his duplicity. Amber shifted her eyes from the assault rifles to Leary's thick-lipped sneer. Rage filled her, and her fingers tensed around her Walther P9 snub-nosed pistol. She wanted to ram the barrel down Leary's throat. She wanted to go at him firing—to risk everything, and take him down with her. Then she glanced at Mike, standing confused at her side.

Alone, she might have taken her chances and opened fire. At the very least, the noise would have raised the alarm at the nearby navy barracks. But there was no way she and Mike would both survive a firefight. And she could not watch him die. It was as simple as that.

Cursing inwardly, she lowered her pistol. Leary winked at her, then pointed to the ground. "Set it down at your feet. Slowly. And don't try any of that tricky spy shit on me. You know how far that crap got your buddy Bader."

Amber's teeth came together, revulsion sweeping through her. But she forced herself to comply, carefully setting the gun on the ground. "So you killed Agent Bader?"

Leary grunted. The sound was more pig than human. "Not personally. But I did run a make on his car for my wealthy friends here."

"They bought you off," Amber said, squaring her shoulders. Scorn dripped from her tongue as she spoke. "You sold out your investigation. Not to mention your country."

Leary laughed as one of the Chinese men strolled forward and retrieved Amber's gun. "Coming from a CIA chink with an English accent, that doesn't mean very much. And listen, honey, for three million over three years, I'd have fucking killed the governor myself."

Leary cupped his hand around his mouth and called out in the direction of the freighter. It took Amber a second to realize he was speaking in poorly accented Chinese. She heard a muffled response from the freighter, then the sound of running feet.

Her pulse quickened as she watched Leary's cold eyes. The situation was unraveling around her. She had been so focused on Sheshen—on the idea that she was chasing the Chinese Jackal himself—that she had clearly misjudged the schoolyard bully. In retrospect, he was the perfect plant. He had access to every level of the investigation, and probably connections throughout the city's administration. And although outwardly he seemed like a stereotypical racist, he was obviously not as ignorant as he seemed.

Amber remembered him saying something about being stationed in Korea. He could easily have picked up enough Chinese to negotiate a financial deal with the Triads, even before Sheshen and his operation had come into the picture. When the governor had been murdered, Leary was probably already in the Triad's pay, positioned perfectly to keep the investigation from focusing on the true culprits. It was directly in line with the cautious habits of the Chinese; even a perfect crime could be more perfect, even the best plans needed insurance. Dick Leary was that insurance. But perhaps he didn't realize the extent of his betrayal.

"Leary," she said, keeping her voice calm, "maybe you don't know who you're working for—"

"Quiet," Leary ordered, yanking a pair of police handcuffs out of his pocket. "I don't have time for a lecture. I'm still in the middle of an assassination investigation, after all."

He jabbed a thick finger at Mike, and Amber's heart jumped in her chest. "Step forward, arms behind your back. And don't get any ideas, Doc; I've cuffed guys a whole lot bigger than you."

Mike didn't hesitate. He stepped forward and turned around, his blue eyes focused on Amber. She saw bewilderment, fear, but also fury and determination. Despite the situation, he had not given up. She felt her own resolve growing as she looked at him. *Mike, you're right. Too many people have died for this to end here.*

Leary pulled Mike's arms together and slammed the handcuffs down over his wrists. "Sorry, kids, but this is where you part. See, Doc, I know a little bit about how these spies work. With Bader out of the picture, I doubt there's anyone keeping close tabs on Ms. Chen. Once my Chinese friends get her aboard their freighter, she'll as good as vanish into thin air. And nobody's gonna ask questions about a missing CIA spook on some sort of secret mission. Even if they come looking for her, they certainly won't find her in the middle of the fuckin' ocean."

He grabbed Mike by the hair and yanked his head back. "But you're a little more difficult. You can't just disappear without people getting suspicious. So I came up with a little plan on the way over here. Something nice and creative."

Suddenly, he started to drag Mike toward his police cruiser. Amber was about to lunge after him when someone gripped her by the shoulder and spun her around.

She recognized the crow tattoo immediately. It was the teenager from the Triad headquarters, the one who had clutched at her thigh. Her heart sank as he leered at her from behind the long barrel of a bayoneted assault rifle.

"Time to take a little boat ride, Third Dragon."

He laughed, forcing her forward with quick jabs of his bayonet. She threw a final glance back in Mike's direction. Leary had him facedown against the hood of his cruiser, his service revolver pressed tightly against Mike's cheek. Then the two Triad men closed ranks behind Amber, obscuring her view as they prodded her toward the waiting freighter.

CHAPTER TWENTY-SEVEN

"You're a smart guy," Leary hissed into Mike's right ear. "So I'm only gonna say this once. Hard or easy, this is already a done deal. I suggest you opt for easy."

Leary slammed Mike's head against the hood of the cruiser, then took a step back. Mike tasted blood; streaks of pain moved up his jaw. His head was spinning, not only from the blow, but from the unthinkable situation, the knowledge that everything had again turned upside down. A moment ago he had thought they had a chance. Now that chance had been yanked away. He and Amber had been separated, perhaps for good. And now he was in the hands of a vicious, traitorous cop.

Mike forced himself to concentrate on the shiny hood beneath his face, fighting the paralyzing fear spreading through his body. *Come on*, he told himself, *it's not over yet. It's not over yet!* He clenched his teeth, his wrists straining against the cold handcuffs. He had only been cuffed once before in his life, during his freshman year of college. Drunk and disorderly, urinating in public: a foolish evening after his first lacrosse victory. He remembered being more embarrassed than scared as he tried to explain himself to an angry police officer. He had been young and stupid, and the officer had let him off; but he had always remembered the feeling of helplessness, the feeling that someone else was in control.

Now he had that feeling again, only a thousand times worse. This time, the officer was an accomplice to multiple murders, hiding behind a badge. He could hear Leary moving around, and he shivered, the despair momentarily taking over. Certainly, it was a desperate situation.

He had to accept the facts: Amber was gone, probably already aboard the freighter. There was no one else around, and Leary was a trained professional with a gun. He was also a mean, ugly bastard, an Irish tough like the kids Mike had known in Southie, growing up. At least that, Mike understood. A badge and a gun didn't make Dick Leary any different from the delinquents who ruled the Southie parks and playgrounds.

"You shouldn't have gotten mixed up in this," Leary finally continued from somewhere to the left, his voice halfway between a whisper and a grunt. "You got yourself in way over your head. Your friend the governor was already dead; what did you think, you were gonna bring him back?"

Mike wondered whether Leary knew how ironic his statement was. He doubted it; he guessed that Leary knew very little about the men he was working for except the color of their money. Mike slowly turned his head to the left, ignoring the pain in his jaw. It took him a moment to focus his eyes. When his vision cleared, he saw that Leary still had the gun balanced in his right hand, while he worked a small object between the fingers of his left. Mike squinted through the darkness and made out a large syringe connected to a vial of clear liquid.

"Dead is dead, Doc. Didn't they teach you that in med school?"

Mike watched as Leary pulled back on the syringe with two fingers, filling it with the clear liquid. A new terror broke through his body when he saw the needle flash in the moonlight. The muscles in his forearms clenched involuntarily, pressing his wrists tight against the handcuffs. Doctor or no doctor, he was viscerally effected by the sight of such a long needle.

"So what did all your running around get you?" Leary continued, discarding the empty vial. "Maybe a little bump and grind with the chink superspy? Hey, I'm sure she's pretty good—but was it worth your father's life?"

At the mention of his father, Mike forgot about the pain in his jaw, the fear, the needle, the despair. He thought about Teri, mutilated on the laboratory floor. His father, broken and lifeless in the back of the ambulance. And Amber. Maybe still alive, maybe already dead. His rage grew and his hands turned into fists. *Leary, you damn bastard.* Handcuffs or no handcuffs, he was going to hurt this cop.

He tensed his thighs, preparing for what would most likely be his suicide—and felt something between his right leg and the cruiser hood. A small, cylindrical object in his front pocket. His father's screwdriver.

His pulse rocketed, as he realized what that meant: a fighting chance. Slowly, carefully, he inched his hands toward the pocket. Despite the handcuffs, he knew he'd be able to reach. He just needed to stall Leary long enough to get the screwdriver free.

He cringed, as Leary shifted the syringe to his right hand and stepped forward. "This won't hurt a bit, Doc."

"Hold on," Mike sputtered, making his voice as frightened as possible. "Maybe we can work something out. You're in this for the money, right?"

Leary paused, his head cocked. Then he smiled. "Sorry, Doc. I've seen what that skinny Chinaman does to the guys who piss him off. No amount of money's worth a rod up your cock. Or an empty bowl for a skull."

He started forward again, the syringe raised in the air. Mike reached the screwdriver and started to draw it out of his pocket. *Stay calm,* he told himself. *A few more seconds.* "You won't get away with this. I was Andrew's best friend. They'll make the connection. My murder will start a whole new investigation."

Leary jerked his head toward the syringe. "Who said anything about murder? A syringe full of Demerol ain't a murder weapon, Doc. You should know that as well as anyone."

Mike exhaled, glancing again at the clear liquid inside the syringe. Leary was right: a syringe full of Demerol didn't point to murder, it pointed to suicide, especially when the victim was an MD. Demerol was the self-medication of choice for doctors who had gone over the edge. A Demerol OD was quick, relatively painless, and easily traceable. All Leary needed to do was forge Mike's signature on a prescription pad and plant some fingerprints on the syringe.

"You made it real easy for me, Doc. Freaked out in the hospital during rounds. Ended up checking in for tests the next day. Even spent time with the chief of psychiatry. But who could blame you? First your wife gets it in a plane crash. Then your best friend gets blown up by terrorists. That would drive anyone crazy."

Leary had stopped a few feet away, waving the gun and the syringe like a pair of conductor's batons. It was obvious from the gleam in his eyes that he had given this some thought. "Not just crazy—paranoid, schizo, delusional, and whatever else the psych boys can come up with. Got so bad, you started thinking the terrorists were after you. So you came up with a plan to get them. You planted a booby trap in your own apartment. Rigged the door with a high-load pipe bomb."

Mike glared at Leary, the bile building in his throat.

Leary was going to blame Flannery Ballantine's death on him. *My own father's murder.* Mike ground his teeth. He had the screwdriver out of his pocket now. Carefully, he pushed the chiseled blade toward the keyhole at the base of the handcuffs. He remembered what Amber had taught him back in the stable. Up and down, back and forth. Small, random movements. A lot of luck and patience. Luck and patience . . .

"When your father died," Leary continued, too consumed by his mental fabrications to notice what Mike was doing with his hands, "it pushed you over the edge. You wrote yourself a prescription for Demerol, and jacked yourself right to hell. The only question left is where to dump your body. Somewhere significant, like maybe the back of your father's pickup truck."

Mike heard a tiny click and the right handcuff suddenly came loose. The screwdriver slipped from his fingers and spiraled toward the pavement. Mike shuffled his feet to mask its clatter. He gripped the open handcuff with his free hand, pretending it was still locked around his wrist. He fought the immediate urge to go after Leary at full throttle, telling himself that he had to wait for the right moment. The advantage of surprise was all in the timing.

Unaware, Leary sighed, turning his concentration back to the syringe. "If only my job was always this easy."

Luck and patience, Mike repeated to himself as he watched Leary flick the air bubbles out of the syringe. *Just a little more luck and patience . . .*

CHAPTER TWENTY-EIGHT

Amber tasted her own sweat running heavily down her nose and over her upper lip. She could sense the point of the bayonet inches behind her back. One misstep, and the steel blade would drive right through her body. She imagined the agony she would feel, the blood running down her skin, the sharp point crackling through her spine—and then she collected herself, banishing the horrible thoughts, demanding that she remain in control.

"Down the stairs. Quickly."

A hand shoved her forward, and she nearly toppled down the narrow stairway that led into the belly of the freighter. She navigated the steps carefully, listening to the footsteps that followed. She had counted at least five men in the cargo hold of the freighter, in addition to her three-man escort. Eight total, all armed with assault rifles. The odds were numbing. Once the freighter left the dock, Amber knew, she was finished. Leary had been right; no one was keeping close tabs on her investigation. Her mission demanded total autonomy, so that her superiors could not be held accountable if something went wrong. America, and more specifically the CIA, would not be held responsible for the actions of a lone-wolf agent.

That meant Amber would have to face the situation entirely on her own. She pressed her lips together, con-

juring up a dozen memories of her father, of his strength
and his serenity. She needed his spirit, his voice whispering in her ear. She needed to see the situation through
his eyes.

She reached the bottom of the stairs and came to a
stop facing a closed door. Just when the fear threatened
to overwhelm her, her father's words suddenly spun
through her memory: *Liliang. Jongyu. Zizhi.* Strength.
Honor. Control. A new sense of calm moved through
her, and she barely trembled as the teenager reached out
from behind and turned the knob. Then she was shoved
forward, stumbling, into a long stateroom.

The room was twenty feet across, lined on one side
with four sets of three-high bunk beds. There was a desk
against the opposite wall, and a small, open bathroom
with a shower stall off to the left. A damp red-brown
rug covered most of the floor.

"Wait outside while I deal with the traitor," she heard
the teenager tell the two other men. Then he shut the
door behind him. The hair on Amber's neck stood up.
They were alone in the room. Any second, she expected
a bullet in the back of her head. That was how traitors
were dealt with in China: quickly and efficiently. Amber
clenched her hands, repeating her father's mantra in her
head: *Liliang, jongyu, zizhi.* She counted the seconds,
not daring to move, her body braced.

The waiting became agony, as she stood in total silence. She could feel the teenager's warm breath against
the back of her neck, and she sensed the tension inside
him, the nervous energy growing as he worked himself
up to finish her. Perhaps he expected her to beg for
mercy; perhaps he was waiting for her to cower in front
of him. Instead, she squared her shoulders and looked
over the interior of the stateroom, searching for anything
she could use as a weapon.

She saw six military-style duffel bags sitting on the closest three bunk beds, but she had no way of knowing what was inside. Then an object on the bottom bunk nearest to the desk caught her eye, and excitement filled her. It was the acupuncture kit from the Triad headquarters in Chinatown. The polished teak case was closed, but she could imagine the long, sharp needles inside—

Without warning, the teenager grabbed her arm and spun her around. The butt of his rifle slammed into her lower abdomen. She toppled backward, slamming into the stateroom wall. Pain shot up her back and she gasped, losing her breath.

The teenager came at her, bringing the bayonet up toward her chest. Its tip stopped right between her breasts, inches from her smock. The boy smiled at her, the crow tattoo rising beneath his left eye. The bayonet hovered between them, and now Amber saw that the boy was savoring the moment, a sadistic, nearly sexual pleasure overwhelming him as he dominated her. She could see the beads of sweat above his eyebrows, the tip of his tongue flickering across his lips. This was a high for him, like cocaine or heroin, a vicious, violent high. In a few seconds he was going to open her up with the bayonet and watch her die in front of him. Unless she did something to stop him. Unless she took his high away.

She forced the terror back and met the boy's dark eyes with her own. Then she smiled. He stared at her, shocked. She laughed, the sound cruel and mocking. "Look at you—foolish little boy. You have me here all to yourself, and you don't even know what to do with me."

The teenager's surprise turned to anger, and his lips curled back from his teeth. She was baiting him, taunting him with her bravery. She was turning the situation into a matter of face. He hadn't dominated her; he was nothing, a child, a little boy. She could see his anger growing as she pulled her shoulders back, the derisive smile still on her lips. "Such a big gun for a child. I'm sure your friends outside think you're so brave—in here alone with me, and all you have to defend yourself with is that big gun."

The teenager snarled, his eyes narrowing. He jabbed the bayonet toward her, pressing the sharp point against her smock. She involuntarily drew away, and the boy laughed, his crow jerking with the motion. He ran the bayonet down between her breasts, tearing through the material to the skin beneath. Amber felt the sharp edge cutting into her skin.

"You think I'm a child," the boy said, focusing on the tattoo that ran up her stomach. "Maybe I should show you that I know how to deal with a whore like you."

He paused for a moment, his lips trembling as he looked her over. Then he jerked his head toward the bunk beds. Amber dared to hope. She moved in a slow circle toward the beds, watching the assault rifle still aimed at her chest.

When her back was to the beds, the boy pulled a small automatic out of his belt and checked its ammo cartridge. Satisfied, he aimed it at Amber's head, sighting down the short barrel. "Lie down with your hands behind your head."

Perfect, little idiot. Amber finally let her shoulders droop, as if she had acquiesced. She backed up to the bed closest to the desk and lowering herself onto it. She put her hands behind her head, letting her torn smock fall open, and lay back, feeling polished teak beneath her wrists.

The boy leaned his assault rifle against the wall and

came toward her, the small pistol aimed at her bare chest. He reached the edge of the bed and went to work on his belt with his free hand. As his buttons came open, Amber moved her fingers beneath her head, finding the clasp of the case. The case came open as the boy's pants dropped around his hips, revealing his engorged penis.

"I'll show you what a man is, whore," he hissed as he leaned over her, his left hand grabbing the elastic of her panties. His eyes left her face, and in that instant she reached with both hands into the case.

Her arms whipped forward simultaneously, one on either side of the teenager's head. The needles reached his ears at the same time, the long, sharp points driving straight through his eardrums and into the cartilage beneath. There was a loud pop as the needles hit bone, and the boy staggered back, the pistol dropping out of his hand. Amber grabbed another pair of needles from the case, fury sparking behind her eyes. She leaped off the bed, moving toward the boy at lightning speed.

The boy had reached the center of the stateroom, his pants around his knees. His eyes were wide, his hands pulling at the needles jammed deep into his eardrums.

Amber reached him in two steps, her lips curling back from her teeth. "This is for Bader." Her left hand swung forward and shoved the long needle upward between the teenager's testicles. Blood sprayed toward the floor. His mouth opened, but before he could scream Amber's right hand flashed forward, driving a needle right through the center of his throat, impaling his voice box. "And this is a gift from the Third Dragon. For all the young girls you've destroyed."

The teenager collapsed, a gurgling sound rising from his speared throat. Amber stepped over him, retrieving his pistol. It had taken her less than two minutes to overcome the teenager—but in combat time, two minutes was forever. She thought about Mike, alone with Leary, and her stomach flipped over. There was a good chance that Mike was already dead.

She raced to the door, the pistol clutched in her right hand, and pressed her ear against the wood, listening. She couldn't hear the other men; perhaps they were loading the last of the cargo. She was still vastly out-numbered. But she had no choice except to try—for Mike's sake, if not her own.

She was about to open the door when she caught sight of something jutting out from the corner to her left. A wooden crate, about four feet high, running flush with the wall. The crate was open, but Amber couldn't see inside without getting closer.

She glanced back at the teenager in the center of the room, making sure he was no longer any threat. Then she stepped forward and leaned over the open crate. What she saw made her eyes go wide. Five silver-colored cylindrical plastic objects, each three feet high and a foot in diameter. Amber could see the English markings across the top of each cylinder.

She was looking at the five remaining Valhallas, the oxygen-compression mines, still in the same crate that had been lifted off the back of the truck in South Korea.

Amber shook her head, cold anger rising inside her. She knew that Andrew Kyle was dead partly because she had failed in her surveillance of these stolen mines. She had lost face—but now she was determined to re-gain her family's honor. She was determined to bring Sheshen down.

Certainly, she was not going to die in a shootout on a Chinese freighter. The Valhallas were going to help her get out, alive.

She gently lifted the five cylinders out of the crate. Each weighed about twelve pounds. The top cover of each Valhalla consisted of a round timer with a digital display, a compression valve, and a detonator panel.

Carefully, Amber took one of the cylinders and placed it against the wall to her left. Then she turned her attention back to the remaining four. She steadied her nerves and reviewed what she remembered from her research into the mines.

A key feature of the Valhalla was the fact that one could control the explosive payload—and even disarm it entirely. That goal in mind, Amber went to work on the compression valves of the four mines in front of her. Each twist of a valve was followed by a soft hiss as the cylinders released oxygen and decompressed. In a matter of seconds, she had reduced all four mines to harmless plastic shells.

Then she retrieved the fifth mine from the wall. It was all she needed to turn the Chinese freighter into driftwood. She leaned over the detonator panel and hit a series of plastic keys. The timer blinked once; then glowing red digital numbers appeared: "2:00." Amber hit another key, and the timer began to tick down toward zero. In two minutes, the explosive would go off, swallowing the freighter in a plume of bright orange flame.

Amber replaced the active Valhalla in the wooden crate, then retrieved one of the impotent Valhalla shells. Moving quickly now, she crossed back to the door, the disabled Valhalla braced between her hands. She put her left hand over the detonator panel, her fingers centimeters from the ignition trigger. She counted softly to herself until thirty seconds had gone by; then she steeled herself and gently pushed the door open.

The stairwell was empty. Cautiously, Amber crept upward, keeping the Valhalla in front of her, her finger right up against the detonation trigger. At the top of the stairs, she heard Chinese voices from the deck of the freighter, followed by a mechanical growl. The freighter rocked beneath her feet, and she realized they were pushing away from the dock.

She raced up the last few steps and burst out onto the deck. She counted five men ahead of her; the other two were probably in the freighter's control cabin on the other side of the boat. One of the five saw her and shouted, and suddenly all of them were turning toward her, their automatics rising.

Amber held the Valhalla up so they could all see what she was holding. The men froze, fear evident in their eyes.

Amber sidestepped toward the railing closest to the dock, keeping the Valhalla between herself and the men. She could see them angling their automatic rifles toward her legs—but they couldn't risk a shot with her finger near the detonation trigger.

She reached the railing and put one leg over the side. The dock was now more than ten feet away, separated from the freighter by the choppy dark water. In her head, she was still counting down. Less than thirty seconds left. She took a deep breath—and, in one motion, hurled the disabled Valhalla at the men and lunged over the edge. She heard shouts of fear turn to shouts of relief as the Valhalla clattered uselessly against the deck. When the real Valhalla went off twenty seconds later, the fools would never know what hit them.

As Amber struck the cold water, she prayed that the ancestors protecting Mike Ballantine had been as powerful as her own.

CHAPTER TWENTY-NINE

Leary kept his gun trained between Mike's eyes as he closed the distance between them. Meanwhile, Mike's focus remained on the syringe and the clear liquid inside. Twenty ccs at least, which translated to as much as a thousand milligrams of Demerol. Intravenously, it would overwhelm his system in a matter of minutes. His skin would go cold and clammy, his breathing and heart rate would slow, he would collapse in a somnolent stupor. Another few minutes, and his breathing would stop entirely. Then his heart would stop, and he would die.

Even if Leary missed the vein and injected the Demerol into muscle, the killing liquid would reach Mike's bloodstream and eventually his heart. Mike squeezed the open handcuff tight in his free hand as he watched Leary approach, preparing himself. He would take a bullet before he let Leary empty the syringe into his body. Better a painful death that would draw an investigation than a silent, if painless, "suicide."

Leary moved behind him and briefly out of sight. Mike experienced a moment of pure terror as he listened, blindly, to Leary's final few steps, and then he felt the gun against the side of his head.

"That's right, Doc. Nice and easy."

Mike felt the point of the syringe against his left inner arm. He only had a few more seconds to react. But the gun was still pressed against the side of his head.

There was a prick as the needle slid into his skin. Panicked, Mike jerked upward. Leary cursed as the needle missed the vein. Mike could feel the tip tearing into his lower bicep, just above his elbow. *Christ, do something!* But the gun was still against his head.

"Hold still," Leary ordered, jamming the needle in deeper. "Just another second—"

Suddenly, an immense noise tore through the darkness. The air turned white and searing heat hit Mike from the direction of the water. His eyes widened at what he saw reflected on the cruiser hood in front of him: a plume of bright orange flame.

Then he realized that the gun was no longer pressed against the side of his head. Leary's concentration had broken, and he had half turned toward the fiery explosion.

Mike spun around, the sudden motion tearing the syringe out of Leary's hand. The open handcuffs slashed through the air, catching Leary's gun arm just above the wrist. He yelped in pain as the gun clattered against the cruiser hood. Then Mike was on top of him, and they both crashed backward to the pavement.

Flaming chunks of the Chinese freighter rained down around Mike as he slammed his right fist into Leary's face. There was a crunch; then Leary sagged, unconscious. *The traitorous bastard didn't even have the decency to put up a fight.* Still pulsing with anger and adrenaline, Mike lifted his fist for a second shot—and heard coughing behind him.

He turned. Amber was stumbling toward him from the direction of the explosion. Her smock was torn open, and she was soaking wet. Mike instantly forgot about Leary. He reached her in five steps and swallowed her body in a full, protective embrace. Her knees gave out. Together they sank to the ground.

"I'm okay," Amber whispered. "I'm okay."

Mike was too overwhelmed to respond. He couldn't believe they were together again. A few seconds ago, he had thought she was already gone. He himself had been moments from death. He pulled her tighter against him, his eyes burning with relief and shock.

They remained like that, silently clamped together, watching the plume of flame disappear as what was left of the Chinese freighter sank into the bay.

"My God," Mike finally whispered, looking at Amber, at her torn clothes and her drenched hair. "You make quite an entrance."

Amber's chest heaved as she fought to catch her breath. "That water's fucking cold. But a lot better than the alternative. I see you managed to take care of Leary."

Mike nodded, glancing with distaste at Leary's supine body. Blood trickled from the stocky man's crushed nose. There was a sharp tug in Mike's right bicep. He looked down and saw the syringe sticking out of his skin.

He grabbed the syringe with his other hand, yanking it free. Thankfully, it was still full of clear liquid. *Another second, and he would have depressed the plunger. Just like that, it would have been over.* Mike wished Leary had lasted a few more punches.

"We were almost killed," Amber murmured, staring at the syringe and the handcuffs hanging off Mike's wrist.

"We're alive," Mike responded, and the words seemed hard to believe. It was the second time they had narrowly avoided death, and so many others had been less lucky.

There were shouts coming from the other side of the

navy yard; soon the area would be swarming with people. But for the moment, he and Amber were alone, watching the last sparks raining down around them.

"Sheshen got away," Amber said, breaking the silence. "We didn't stop Unit 199."

"Does it matter?" Mike whispered. He noticed that it hurt to talk too loudly. He grimaced, remembering how Leary had slammed his head against the cruiser. "Most of Teri's work is gone. Her data, the laptop computer—"

"Sheshen wasn't aboard the freighter, at least not that I saw. He probably got away on the cigarette boat. He might have escaped with enough to continue Unit 199's work. And even without Teri's research, they won't stop until they've reached their goal. Not unless we stop them. Which we can't do, unless we can find Unit 199."

"Then I guess we lost and Sheshen won." Mike's shoulders sagged. He hated to think it had all been in vain—his father's death, Teri's mutilation—but what could they do? Sheshen had an enormous head start. "Is there any way to track the Cigarette boat? Or are you still trying to keep this thing secret?"

Secrecy seemed a moot point, at the moment. The shouts were closer now, less than fifty feet away. And there were sirens in the distance.

"The Cigarette boat could be miles from here by now, and Sheshen could have switched modes of transport a dozen times. As for secrecy, we'll come up with a story for this." Amber gestured toward Leary and the burning pieces of the freighter. "Escaping terrorists; an inside job involving Leary—we certainly won't need to mention the Chinese connection, and my people will bury Leary so deep he'll never get a chance to open his mouth. But none of that will help us stop Sheshen."

"Then we really have failed."

Suddenly, Amber stiffened, as if struck by a thought. She pushed to her feet. "Maybe not."

Mike watched as she trudged toward Leary's cruiser and yanked the front door open, both shoulders bared by the motion. Then she leaned inside. "It's a hunch— but I've seen him with it once before. If we're lucky . . . Here we go."

She crawled back out of the cruiser, a slim metal briefcase in her arms. The briefcase trailed curls of wire.

"A satellite receiver," she said, as the sirens grew louder. "Originally, I thought Leary was using it to keep in touch with people at the Pentagon. But now we know he wasn't getting all his orders from Washington."

She looked at Mike, her eyes alive. "Maybe we can trace this back along the satellite route. Maybe we can find Unit 199 after all."

CHAPTER THIRTY

"Time elapsed: three hours, two minutes."

Sheshen trembled as the metallic female voice reverberated through the glowing green control room. He pressed his face close to the cold black Plexiglas, his attention affixed to the steel-walled experiment chamber on the other side. The transparent cylinder that stood in the center of the chamber was empty now, the pink mist already settling to the wire-covered floor. To the right of the cylinder, the six test subjects were lined up against the back wall of the chamber. All six were young and male, their naked bodies glistening under the bright fluorescent lights. The terror was obvious in their round peasant faces.

Sheshen watched them carefully, his body alive with anticipation. His muscles felt abnormally charged, and there was no trace of the long journey from Boston in his posture. He understood the importance of the experiment he was watching. This was the first test since his successful return.

The test subjects had been chosen carefully. All were young, healthy, and male, with strong immune systems and no history of serious viral disease. They represented the cream of China's peasant population, the healthiest examples of the near-billion Chinese who lived in villages across the mother country. They were scared, stupid, and confused—but they embodied the revolution past and the revolution still to come. They were China, and today was the true moment of their rebirth.

Three hours ago, each of the six men had been placed inside the huge transparent cylinder and forced to breathe in the pink mist. The source of the mist had also been chosen carefully: another representative of China's past and future, an aging Red Guard hero recently shipped to Mogue De Ghong from an invalid hospital outside Shanghai. Gui Yisheng had chosen to use the comatose general instead of another peasant as his test source, because this way the situation mimicked more closely Unit 199's final goal. The Red Guard hero had been a close companion of Mao Zedong during the Cultural Revolution, a visionary who had led thousands of Chinese peasants against the enemies of the revolution. He had been a powerful man, who would have continued to lead China against its enemies inside and out—save for the inexorable tyranny of his own mortality. His flesh had given up, even though his mind had remained pure. *His weak, mortal, insignificant flesh—*

Sheshen's thoughts froze as he noticed the sudden change in the experiment chamber, the shiver that moved through the six test subjects standing against the back wall. It was beginning. He focused on the young peasant closest to the transparent cylinder; he had been the first to breathe the pink mist. Tall, naked, his head completely shaved, his young, wide eyes staring straight ahead. Sheshen guessed he was no more than twenty, a farmer who had spent his entire life in the fields of an agricultural collective. He was terrified, bewildered; he had no idea what was happening around him. What was happening inside him.

Suddenly, his round face began to jerk back and forth. His mouth opened, and his right hand came up, pointing at a spot of air ten feet in front of him. He started to scream in shocked Chinese: *"Juedui bu keneng! Weida de cuxian—juedui bu keneng!"*

It cannot be! Great ancestor, it cannot be! Sheshen watched in awe as the naked peasant dropped to his knees, covering his face with his hands. A few seconds later, the next peasant dropped to the ground next to him, his face sheet white. Then the next, and on down the line. Soon all six subjects were on their knees, prostrating themselves in front of the blank air. Their shouts of fear and subservience echoed through the steel chamber. As two doctors in white lab coats entered the chamber and began administering an intravenous tranquilizer to the hysterical peasants, Sheshen heard one phrase over and over again, a phrase that drove into his ears like a searing hot spike: *"Huo gui! Huo gui!"*

Living ghost! Sheshen closed his eyes as his head began to spin. The experiment had worked! The first step was complete! He looked down at the portable oxygen tank he still carried—the same tank that had allowed his father to recreate the young girl's work. It had taken less than an hour for Gui Yisheng to analyze the tank and duplicate the oxygen–to–R-E solution ratio; it had been equally simple to pump a similar aerosolized concoction into the transparent cylinder.

Now that the experiment had worked, the real preparation could begin. Huge steel drums were already being readied in a storage facility on the far side of the laboratory; soon they would be filled with the aerosolized solution and prepared for shipment to points across China. The largest drum would be on its way to Beijing within twenty-four hours for the first—and most important—demonstration.

Sheshen opened his eyes and turned away from the window. The control room stretched out to his left. It was shaped like a half-moon, approximately three hundred meters long from tip to tip. The back wall was sheer and steel, marred by numerous jutting plastic panels covered with dials, knobs, and digital readouts. The curved front wall where Sheshen stood was spotted at regular intervals by the circular black Plexiglas windows; in front of more than half of the windows stood single three-legged stools, complete with foot stirrups and heel-operated pedals to raise or lower the seat. Only the stool at the far end of the room was presently occupied.

Sheshen's throat went dry as he watched his father lower the stool, then rise and slowly turn to face him. Squat, armless, his face covered in deep wrinkles, his eyes sunken black pits surrounded by purplish bags of dying skin. The ancient face of a million Chinese nightmares, of myths that spread like raging infections through villages thousands of miles away. The face that had haunted Sheshen every day of his life.

"Brilliant Father," Sheshen said, struggling to keep the hatred out of his voice. "The experiment was a success. The moment has arrived."

Gui Yisheng stood in silence for a long moment, his black eyes locked with Sheshen's. Then his mouth broke into a wide, toothless smile. "You are right, Sheshen. You have served me well. You have brought honor to me—and to Chairman Mao."

Sheshen's knees weakened and he leaned against the window. It took all his concentration to keep from dropping the oxygen tank to the hard stone floor. In all his life, he had never seen his father smile. And the words he had spoken . . . Sheshen's stomach trembled as he realized what they meant. His father had confirmed what he already knew: with the successful experiment, the last phase of Sheshen's mission had finally arrived.

Sheshen watched in silence as Gui Yisheng started

forward across the control room, still beaming with pleasure. His shaved head glowed in the green light as he moved, his useless white sleeves flapping at his sides. For the first time, Sheshen noticed how old and fragile he seemed. Perhaps it was the smile that still spread across his ancient face, perhaps it was the new stoop in his rounded shoulders—but, for once, Gui Yisheng appeared human.

An idea struck Sheshen, and he realized instantly it was correct: Gui Yisheng was dying. Three months past ninety-two years old, his body had finally accepted that it was mortal. Sheshen had witnessed the same transformation before, when the Great Leader himself had finally succumbed. It was the one certainty of life: Even gods and devils died.

Still, Sheshen was surprised by the feelings inside him as he watched Gui Yisheng's labored steps. He had always believed that his hate was pure, brought on by years of emotional and physical abuse, capped by an abandonment he had never understood. But now, awash in the success of his mission, awed by his father's obvious mortality, he wondered: did this dying soul deserve his hate? Was his hatred fair?

"Come," Gui Yisheng gasped as he finally reached Sheshen in the doorway. "Accompany me to the storage cell. We can talk along the way."

Sheshen bowed his head and followed his father out of the control room and into a long steel corridor. Scientists in sterile white lab coats and paper slippers scurried out of the way, their eyes averted, as Gui Yisheng hobbled past. Like Sheshen, they understood their master's power—and their own expendability. Certainly, they did not need myths to make them tremble at the sight of the armless doctor; they had all witnessed his rage before.

Sheshen remembered the day two years ago when Gui Yisheng had decided to teach the scientists at Mogue De Ghong a lesson about loyalty and duty. At his command, his guards had rounded up twenty-five Mongolian programmers who had failed to meet their work quotas. He had locked them in a basement chamber in the mountain laboratory and had pumped in aerosolized ether, rendering them unconscious. Then he had slowly filled the chamber with wet cement.

He had televised the entire proceeding, and had forced the other scientists to watch. From that moment forward, all work quotas at Mogue De Ghong had been met well ahead of schedule.

"Your arrival, and our success, could not have come at a more critical moment," Gui Yisheng said. They turned a sharp corner and entered another steel corridor. "Only this morning, I received a call from General Dhou."

Sheshen grimaced, picturing the overweight, pasty Dhou in his mansion in Xining. Dhou was the governor of Qinghai province, the most powerful man east of the Yellow River. He had been appointed by Deng Xiaoping shortly after Mao's death, and he represented the democratic, capitalistic infection that was slowly making its way toward Beijing. "And what did the fat piglet want?"

"He called to discuss the rumors again. Nothing surprising, of course. Stories of whole villages rounded up, never to be seen again. Corpses found floating in the Yellow River, or half buried at the edge of the Gobi."

Sheshen nodded, slowing his pace as Gui Yisheng leaned against a steel wall, struggling to regain his breath. "Does this concern you, honorable Father?"

Gui Yisheng sneered, still using the wall for balance. "Of course not. But this time he was insistent—much more so than usual. I believe he's receiving pressure from Beijing. Since the handover of Hong Kong, the battle lines are being drawn."

Sheshen knew all about the change in Beijing. It was the result of the horrid disease that had gripped the party since the Great Leader's death. During the Tiananmen incident in 1989, the rest of the world had reacted in shock at what they had considered a resurgence of hardline fascism in China; but Sheshen had shuddered at the relative peacefulness of the crackdown against the democratic traitors. Had Mao been alive, the streets of Beijing would have been piled high with the corpses of the brash, unfilial protestors.

And since the handover of Hong Kong, the situation had grown dramatically worse. In Sheshen's mind, there were now two Chinas: the old world of Mao and his unfinished revolution; and the new, softer world of liberalism, capitalism, and even democracy. For the moment, Dhou and his kind still feared and respected Gui Yisheng, and the past Unit 199 represented. But that, too, was changing. The tide had turned; the slumbering giant now had a white man's right eye.

In Sheshen's view, only one thing could save Mao's revolution: Unit 199, the work his father was doing. Sheshen held the oxygen tank like a holy child and thought about the experiment he had just witnessed. Then he imagined Dhou and the other liberals in Beijing, gathered together in a similar steel chamber. Waiting patiently, unknowing, as a canister was rolled in front of them and a valve opened. Sheshen pictured Dhou dropping to his knees, the same awed look in his eyes. *Huo gui! Living ghost!*

"In any event," Gui Yisheng interrupted, finally moving forward, "it does not matter. Dhou and his liberal brethren can stamp their feet and blow smoke out of their ears. It will make no difference. Beginning tomorrow morning, they will no longer matter. China will be reunified—forever."

They turned another corner and came to a round hatch carved into the rock wall of the mountain. The hatch door was smooth and white, covered in pure marble. Next to the door, less than two inches off the ground, was an oval groove about the size of a mailbox.

Gui Yisheng kicked off his left slipper and shoved his foot into the groove. A red light touched the tops of his gnarled toes as magnetic rays read the twisting signature of the veins beneath his skin. There was a low whistle, then the sound of immense gears. Slowly, the great hatch creaked inward.

Sheshen breathed deeply, tasting the cold, slightly refrigerated air. He followed his father through the massive hatch, his shoes whispering against the smooth marble floor.

Gui Yisheng cleared his throat. "Lights."

Suddenly, the room was bathed in blue. Not a fluorescent or neon blue, nothing you would see on the streets of Tokyo, Las Vegas, or Hong Kong. This was a pure, oceanic blue, the blue of children's marbles and tropical bird feathers. Sheshen let his eyes adjust, then followed his father into the room.

The storage cell was a perfect circle with sheer marble walls thirty feet high. It was lined with two hundred identical, opaque blue cabinets. Each cabinet consisted of ten stacked shelves, with pull knobs and tiny color-coded labels.

Gui Yisheng ignored the cabinets along the side walls and headed straight for the back of the room. When he reached the back wall he paused, waiting for Sheshen to take his place at his side. The back wall consisted of a single cabinet, set off from the sheer marble by twists of plastic tubing and electrical wires. The cabinet contained only one shelf, oversized, with no label and no pull knob. When Sheshen had reached his side, Gui Yisheng leaned close to the cabinet and spoke solemnly: "Cabinet One."

There was a slight pause, and Sheshen felt the hair on his neck rise up. It was a ritual they had performed many times over the past three years, but today it had awesome significance. The moment was growing near.

Finally, a mechanical whirring filled the blue cell. The single shelf rolled out, nearly hitting the oxygen tank resting in Sheshen's arms. Sheshen took a step back, then leaned forward so he could see inside the shelf.

The container inside the shelf was spherical and filled with clear liquid. Two tubes ran up out of the center of the sphere, twisting into the back of the cabinet. Oxygen bubbles sputtered in a constant stream where one of the tubes touched the clear liquid. The effect was of a high-tech fishbowl.

Sheshen took a deep breath, wincing at the sharp scent of the clear liquid. Gui Yisheng had explained the ingredients many years ago, and Sheshen had dutifully memorized them: 4 millimolar potassium, 140 millimolar sodium chloride, 1/1000 of a millimolar calcium, 100 millimolar glucose, and a touch of magnesium. The liquid was perfused with oxygen and filtered with natural sea salt.

"As you can see," Gui Yisheng whispered, inclining his head, "the timing is fortuitous. The level of cellular death is still minimal, but growing every day."

Sheshen squinted past the stream of bubbles. He could just barely see the small, ovular mass sitting at the bottom of the tank. It was a little bigger than a human thumb, with cordlike twists coming out of both ends. Over the years, it had changed color from pink to a light brown. Even Gui Yisheng's modified Ringer's solution couldn't keep the entire mass of organic tissue alive indefinitely.

Sheshen glanced at his father, alarmed. "So we are not too late?"

Gui Yisheng smiled for the second time in Sheshen's memory. "No. There is enough living tissue left to breed a billion viruses—as many as we need. We are not too late. We are right on schedule."

He took a step back, his eyes boring into Sheshen. Sheshen felt suddenly uncomfortable, caught in his father's gaze. He did not know what to do with the emotions rising inside of him. He had always thought of himself as a living weapon, a tool created by Gui Yisheng's hate and Mao's love.

"Sheshen, I am a hard man. But everything I have done has added up to this day. And you, Sheshen—you have been my arms. Together we will inflame China!"

Sheshen watched as his father retreated to the center of the storage cell and turned his bald, ancient head up toward the ceiling. The ceiling was rounded, like the inside of a sphere. His father's toothless mouth opened wide, and a guttural command escaped.

Suddenly, the ceiling of the storage cell turned snow white, and a colorful image appeared across the center. Sheshen recognized it immediately; it was a detailed map of China, with every city and village marked with a tiny black circle. Sheshen stared in wonder, his neck bent back as his eyes roamed from the eastern shoreline to the great Yangtze River to the mountains in Tibet, the roof of the world. He saw Mogue De Ghong marked with a tiny yin-yang symbol near the far side of the map, and Beijing thousands of miles away, represented by a tiny Chinese flag.

"It's spectacular," he whispered, surprised by his own

sentiment. But the image was overwhelming: China laid out in all its geographic beauty. The mother country. The center of the world. "It almost shimmers."

"My programmers outdid themselves. It is the product of two hundred high-density lenses, controlled by a dozen microchips. It is more than a map, Sheshen. It is a living representation of China. Wind, temperature, weather patterns, even population density and the resulting changes in heat and oxygenation."

Sheshen's mouth opened, as he realized what his father was saying. He stared at the image more carefully and saw that the shimmering was focused around the marked urban areas, more conspicuous where the population density was greater. He also saw sweeping spirals of white around the mountains in the East, and patches of green that must have symbolized rain across areas of the eastern shore. "I don't understand, Father. It's beautiful—"

"Wait, Sheshen." Gui Yisheng cleared his throat, then shouted another command. Suddenly, a bright red swirl appeared over the yin-yang symbol that represented Mogue De Ghong. The swirl grew, sweeping outward in ever larger circles. Another swirl appeared over a black mark on another part of the map and was joined by half a dozen others. In a matter of seconds, the red swirls had enveloped the entire eastern corner of the map. A minute later, half of China had turned bright red, numerous intermingling swirls flickering as they danced through the shimmering weather patterns over the great Yellow River. By the time the swirls had finally reached Beijing, most of China had turned the color of a pulsing, living heart.

Sheshen stared, not knowing what to say. He knew what the swirls represented, but he was overwhelmed by the image, now so clear in his head.

"The Revolution," Gui Yisheng whispered. "The Revolution that will sweep across China once again. This time, it will be immortal, total, and unstoppable. And it will not end at China's borders. One billion men and women with one mind—one soul—cannot be stopped by borders!"

Sheshen was shocked to see tears in the corners of his father's eyes. Then he realized that he, too, felt the emotion burning inside him. He thought again of the six peasants cowering on the floor of the experiment chamber. He thought of the liberal leaders in Beijing, cowering in the streets of the Imperial City. He thought of the steel canisters being filled with the aerosolized R-E solution—and the millions and millions of virole particles that would be carried, along with the solution, to every corner of the great nation.

Then he imagined all of China on its knees, accepting, once and forever, their immortal destiny! One soul—a billion bodies! One revolution, eternal and unlimited!

Sheshen bowed, showing true deference for the first time since Mao's death. Gui Yisheng stepped forward and kissed the top of his head. "Come, Sheshen. I will show you how it will happen."

Sheshen followed him out of the storage cell, overwhelmed by emotion. The monster of his memories was gone, replaced by an old man with the true power to change China, and the world. Forever.

CHAPTER THIRTY-ONE

The air in the small basement office was unusually cold, and Amber fought the urge to cross her legs against the draft resonating off the cement walls. She did not want to appear any more tense than she already felt; nor did she want to risk distracting the man sitting on the other side of the glass desk. Instead, she concentrated on the thick manila folder open in his hands, the folder she and Mike had painstakingly prepared during the short shuttle flight to Washington.

As the seconds ticked by in silence, Amber tried to imagine the thoughts running through Daniel Hutchins's head. She had known Hutchins for nearly ten years, but only professionally. She had met him only in carefully orchestrated circumstances. In many respects, he was as unreadable as his sparse office; the nondescript cement walls, the thick beige carpeting, the glass desk with its inlaid flat-screen computer, the black leather couch on which Amber sat. There were no pictures on the walls, no framed photos on the desk, and Hutchins's chiseled rectangular face and cool gray eyes divulged little about his personality. He was tall, handsome, with carefully cut blond hair and gently weathered skin. He was the kind of man whose appearance demanded respect, and perhaps a little fear—especially in the basement hallways of Langley. But the respect and fear came without a knowledge of the man himself.

Amber could only pray that Hutchins's character allowed him an open enough mind to believe the notes inside the manila folder: the carefully chosen sections of Teri Pace's paper, the detailed account of Andrew Kyle's assassination, the links and educated guesses she and Mike had produced through their own experiences— in other words, the bulk of Amber's investigation, distilled into a half-dozen sheets of computer paper. To Amber, it was immensely important that Hutchins believe, because unless she had his help, her mission had truly ended in the Charlestown Navy Yard.

Amber had gone through it a dozen times in her head; she and Mike could not have continued without the short trip to Washington. Daniel Hutchins was the CIA's executive chief of Asian affairs, and Amber's direct superior. His turf included most of the Eastern world, and he in turn reported to the director of the CIA himself. Hutchins's bio was impressive, his accomplishments legendary; a top graduate from West Point, he had served in the field for twenty-five years, and had been personally responsible for over two hundred successful intelligence missions. Since his appointment to Washington, he had revamped the sector under his control, bringing in younger agents with deeper connections to the East; Amber had been one of his first recruits, and she owed much of her own success to his unwavering trust in her abilities.

She watched as he finally set the folder down on the desk in front of him, and gazed at her with those immeasurable gray eyes. "This is quite a story, Ms. Chen."

Amber fought the urge to look away. "It's more than a story, sir. Many people have died because of this— including the governor of Massachusetts."

Hutchins rubbed a callused hand across his jaw. "The scientific basis for ghosts. The power to reach beyond death. If anyone else had brought this to me—"

"I've seen it with my own eyes," Amber interrupted, her voice low. "It's not a trick or a fabrication. It's an experiment that can be reproduced—inside *and* outside the laboratory."

Hutchins paused, turning back to the folder. He shook his head, a low whistle escaping his lips. "The Chinese Jackal here in the United States, responsible for the murder of Andrew Kyle and a young Ph.D. student. A Chinese operation on American soil that stretches back at least three years."

Amber nodded. "This is a powerful new science. It warranted the enormous risks. Teri Pace's work will force open up an entirely new era of scientific investigation. It is a monumental discovery."

Amber thought about adding more, then decided to let the facts speak for themselves. Hutchins wasn't a scientist, but it didn't take a scientist to understand the historic nature of Teri's work.

As Hutchins contemplated her words, Amber pictured Mike waiting for her in the hotel near Dulles. She had thought about bringing him along to the meeting, but Mike was a civilian, and she hadn't been sure how Hutchins would react to his presence. Her own feelings for Mike were based as much in instinct as anything else; she certainly couldn't expect the same level of trust and confidence from her boss.

Finally, Hutchins leaned back in his chair, his fingers spread out against the folder. "But is this new science a weapon? Is it a geopolitical threat?"

Amber exhaled. It was a question that did not yet have a definite answer. "There's no telling what this research will lead to, in the wrong hands. But we both know the conjectured history of Unit 199—its basis in China's nuclear weapons program. Personally, I believe the danger is real, and immediate."

"And you've managed to locate Unit 199?"

Amber nodded, drawing a small sheaf of photos out of the inside pocket of her black nylon jacket. The photos had been waiting for her at the airport when she and Mike had arrived in Washington. As she had hoped, Tarrance Glendale, the NSA satellite specialist, had been able to use Leary's receiver and a well-known Chinese military satellite to triangulate a coordinate deep inside eastern China; from there, it had been simply a matter of rerouting a U.S. Telstar satellite, and snapping the handful of magnified photos.

Hutchins took the photos and looked them over. Amber watched his blond eyebrows rise as he examined the enormous yin-yang symbol cut into the base of the mountain, and the boxlike structure that stretched deep into the ancient stone. "Looks formidable."

"Every structure has its flaw, sir. I believe you were the one who taught me that."

Hutchins allowed himself a half smile. "And every platitude has its exception."

Amber shrugged, undaunted. "I've already made preliminary arrangements in the target area. Sources I've used before—extremely capable sources. Most of the details have already been worked out."

Hutchins nodded. He didn't know all of Amber's sources, but he had overseen most of her previous missions, and he was aware of her extensive contacts within the Eastern sphere. He cupped his hands over his chest, and Amber was surprised to see a pensive look wash across his weathered face. There was something else he was concerned about, something beyond what Amber had just shown him. "The timing of your discoveries may be more significant than you realize, Ms. Chen."

"How do you mean?"

Hutchins leaned forward. "Over the past twenty-four hours, we've been receiving reports of unconventional construction projects in areas across the Chinese mainland. A special core of engineers has been assigned to these projects by an unknown, hard-line division of the Chinese military—very possibly the same people who sponsored the activities you've related in your file."

Amber's skin prickled as she looked into Hutchins's eyes. "What sort of construction projects?"

Hutchins pushed the manila folder off the center of his glass desk and opened a panel just beneath his palms. The built-in computer flickered to life. He hit a series of buttons on the control panel, and an image appeared in the center of the screen. He played with another pair of buttons, and the image revolved so that it faced Amber. She had to rise a few inches off the leather couch to get a proper look.

She had never seen anything quite like the structure pictured on the screen. It was some sort of tower, made up of interlocking steel beams. Running up the center of the tower was a huge, rubberized tube, with a series of gaskets and vents near its rounded top. Amber couldn't be sure from the picture, but the structure seemed enormous.

"Each tower measures nearly a thousand feet in height," Hutchins continued. "And all of the structures— close to eight hundred that we're aware of so far—have been constructed in high-altitude locations, within a few miles of dense population centers."

Amber leaned back from the computer picture. "It looks like some sort of radio tower, except for the rubber tube in the center."

Hutchins ran a hand over the computer screen, his

palm glowing green in the reflected light. "Actually, our best guess is that it's some sort of ventilation system. The rubber tube seems designed to carry highly pressurized gas up to the gaskets and vents, where it can be released in a controlled fashion. But we have no idea why these things are being built. Do you think they might be related to Unit 199?"

Amber finally crossed her legs against the cool basement air. "I don't know. But there is a way we can find out for sure."

Hutchins nodded, resting his hand against the flat computer screen, his long fingers obscuring the strange tower. "For obvious political reasons, I can't authorize a major operation. And I can't pass your file upward for higher authorization—"

Amber jumped in before he could finish the sentence. "Mr. Hutchins, I'm not asking for a major operation. It will be a surgical strike; I'll arrange the team myself. If all goes as planned, there won't be a single shot fired."

Hutchins paused. Finally, he turned away, his gray eyes focusing on a spot on the cement wall to his left. "Finish your investigation, Ms. Chen. With discretion— and expedition."

Amber smiled inwardly as she rose from the leather couch. Her thoughts were already focused halfway around the world.

A little over sixteen hours later, the twin-propeller cargo plane lurched nauseatingly through the low cloud cover, rising and falling with the drafts of night air sweeping up from the Gobi. Amber's arms were looped around the leather seat harness, and her heels tapped nervously against the rumbling steel floor of the cargo hold. Across from her, Mike Ballantine looked as if his eyes were about to pop out of his head. He clutched his harness with both hands, his fingers curled together in tense organic knots.

Amber still wasn't certain why she had let Mike come along. She knew Daniel Hutchins would see it as a case of emotion clouding judgment. But after their meeting in the basement of Langley, everything had happened so quickly; she had not paused to think Mike's presence through. It had been a gut decision—and, until now, one she had not had a chance to analyze.

She watched Mike's nervous fingers, wondering what her father would have thought about bringing a civilian along on such a sensitive mission. Certainly, it was an unorthodox move; but perhaps it wasn't entirely unjustified. This wasn't technically a combat mission and, as she had told Hutchins, if all went well, there wouldn't be a single shot fired. Mike's expertise, along with his knowledge of Teri's research, made him an invaluable partner. Without him, Amber might stumble right past the truth, ending her operation in as much mystery as it began.

Furthermore, the more time she spent with Mike Ballantine, the deeper her respect for him had grown. Respect—and more complex feelings of affection and trust. The cultural chasm between them seemed to add more than it took away. Although she and Mike had not yet had a chance to move beyond the dockside embrace, she knew they were a match, emotionally and intellectually.

Mike caught her eyes and a weak smile crossed his lips. The small cargo prop—the Chinese markings on its fuselage identified it as belonging to the Xinshan Collective Peasant Farm located just beyond the city of Xining—was the fifth plane since they had left Washington on their trip around the world. Amber had spent most of the time on an air phone, making sure the operation was moving forward as planned.

In truth, the operation itself was quite simple—and even relatively safe; as she had promised Hutchins, a silent, surgical strike. She and Mike would be in no danger, and the entire action would take less than two hours.

"I think there's something I forgot to tell you," Mike said, shouting so his voice could be heard over the plane's engines. "I hate to fly."

Amber glanced at her watch. "We'll be on the ground in less than twenty minutes."

"The way this thing is shaking, we might be on the ground much sooner than that."

Amber laughed, relieving some of her tension. She was not worried about the old airplane. She had used it seven times before to get in and out of the Chinese interior. The outside of the plane looked like an outdated grain carrier, but the engine had been overhauled and refitted with state-of-the-art parts. It was as safe as any military plane. "Haven't you learned to trust me, Mike?"

Mike looked her over with cynical eyes. She followed his gaze down her black bodysuit, to her gloved hands, then back up to her tightly wrapped hair. She looked like the CIA "black" operative that she was. She smiled, eyeing Mike's BU sweatshirt and red lacrosse-team sweatpants. She had tried to get him into a bodysuit like hers, to no avail.

"I think I'm too scared of you to answer that question," Mike joked. Then his expression turned serious. "I hope this goes off as cleanly as you've described. I know I probably shouldn't be here."

"Don't worry. The setup couldn't be better. My people on the ground will have the situation secured before we even touch down."

Mike nodded. "I hope you're right."

"If all goes as planned," Amber explained, although she had already explained it a dozen different ways during the long flight, "it will happen so fast, they'll never know what hit them. Their mountain complex was built with an enormous security flaw. A self-contained filtration system, like your lab's, but on a much bigger scale. The system is fed through a network of fans on the east side of the mountain. It's extremely vulnerable to an aerosol 'accident.' "

"And I'm guessing you've already figured out what sort of 'accident' we're talking about?"

Amber nodded. With the aid of inside information from an extremely reliable, and angry, source, she had been working on the plan for the past twenty-four hours. "Aerosolized ether. According to my contacts, Unit 199 keeps a large quantity on hand, stored in a special facility."

She didn't add that the gas had been used on at least one occasion in the past, to sedate a large number of Mongolian computer programmers slated for a brutal execution. Nor did she add that her main source was the brother of one of the murdered Mongolians, and the leader of a Mongolian terrorist group funded by the CIA. Ono Tang had a copy of his dead sibling's notes to work from, and a need for vengeance that would spur him to wonderfully creative levels.

"Aerosolized ether," Mike commented. "Everyone inside will be rendered unconscious in thirty or forty seconds. They'll remain sedated for at least twelve hours."

"It will look like an accident," Amber continued. "And the gas will dissipate quickly. We'll be able to move in, look around, set our detonation charges, and get out without anyone knowing what happened."

Mike raised his eyebrows. "You've done this sort of thing before."

It wasn't a question. Amber nodded. Her accomplishments were a matter of neither pride nor conceit; they were a matter of fact. "A few years ago, I 'liberated' a Mongolian terrorist out of a North Korean army base. It was a similar operation. No shots were fired, no alarms raised. I went in alone, came out with my target."

"So we're just going to walk right in?" Mike asked, the tension evident in his voice. The plane bounced over a wind draft. "As easy as that?"

Amber nodded. "We crossed over the border through a radar hole in their air defense three hours ago. In another twenty minutes, we'll land on a deserted strip three hundred yards from the exterior ventilation access. We'll meet up with a small, highly trained assault team, and follow them inside." She pointed toward a pair of chemical gas masks hanging from the wall behind her. "Those masks will protect us from the lingering ether. We'll be in and out in two hours, then back in the air."

Mike nodded, but his face was still serious, his lips a tight line above his square jaw. Amber knew that he was scared, that this was beyond anything he had done before. But she also knew he would hold up. He was solid. He had proved himself twice already.

The plane hit another patch of turbulence and jerked sideways; Mike let out a gasp. Amber saw the sweat beading above his eyebrows and felt a tinge of sympathy. She felt fear, too, but it was far outweighed by another, more intense sensation.

She remembered her father's name for it: *shengsi cienwuan*, the edge. The acute, nearly erotic feeling an agent experienced right before action—a time when the world was suddenly broken down into seconds, where primal instincts dominated over everything else. It was an incredible feeling, one Amber wished she could share with Mike.

Maybe one day, she thought to herself, as the wonderful sensation swept through her body. Then her thoughts turned again to the operation ahead. In a few more minutes, she realized with a thrill, Unit 199 was going to have an overwhelming experience of its own.

CHAPTER THIRTY-TWO

It was nearly three in the morning when Sheshen finally returned to the storage cell to collect the hallowed specimen in preparation for the final phase of his father's work. His nerves fired off as he approached the open shelf at the front of the spherical room. Gui Yisheng had spent the past three hours showing him the details of his brilliant plan: how the freed mirror viroles would multiply in the specialized canisters as they traveled across the country; how the viroles would mix with the aerosolized R-E solution, ready to infect an unsuspecting nation; how the revolution would spread in swirls of red, exactly like the vivid geographic image that still flickered across the curved ceiling above Sheshen's head. A magnificent, earth-shattering moment—and it was now only hours away.

His head whirling with anticipation, Sheshen was just about to disconnect the tubes and lift the spherical tank out of the shelf when a strange sound pricked at his ears. A steady hiss—familiar, but alarming at the same time. Reflexively, he stepped back from the drawer. His eyes narrowed as he searched for the source of the sudden noise. Then he looked up, focusing on the steel vent in one corner of the storage cell's ceiling.

A cloud of shimmering air was spilling out of the vent. Sheshen's heart jumped: he had seen such a cloud before. Years ago, when his father had made an example of the Mongolian programmers.

Impossible! This can't be happening! Sheshen struggled for control of his senses. *Not so close to our victory!* His mind was on fire, panic surging through his veins. Then, suddenly, his body clenched tight—and a single, peculiar thought ripped through him: *Rats eat the souls of failed little boys!* His father's threat, from so many years ago; it was enough to banish the panic. He was Sheshen, the snake spirit, the living weapon. Failure could not touch him here!

His hands balled into fists, the muscles in his legs becoming steel wires. He forced his mind into that special, heightened zone; he knew he had only seconds to react. Whoever his enemies were, they had the advantage of surprise—but he had his training and his natural ability.

He tore off a piece of his sleeve and clamped it over his mouth and nose. He could hold his breath for two minutes, perhaps more. But he needed closer to ten, and even for him, that was impossible. He had to find a way to breathe—

He looked across the room, to a spot near one of the many cabinets that lined the curved walls. The portable oxygen tank was still where he had set it when he had first arrived back at Mogue De Ghong; he had left it in the storage cell as a reminder of his successful mission abroad. Now, perhaps, it would salvage the mission it represented.

Sheshen quickly retrieved the tank and unrolled the long yellow tube. He placed the nose plugs in his nostrils and reached for the gauge.

Cool oxygen swirled down his throat and into his lungs. He knew the oxygen was laced with Teri's R-E solution, but he also knew the solution would not affect him for many hours. By then, this would all be over, one way or another. He shut the gauge, his eyes narrowing; a new calm filled his body. The tank would work. He could breathe.

But the ether was just the beginning. Some sort of assault would soon follow. Whether Sheshen had any real chance depended on the nature of that assault. What sort of enemy was he going to face? Who would dare go after Unit 199?

Two possible answers came to him immediately. Either General Dhou had decided to take things into his own hands, and had arranged an attack on the laboratory. Or somehow, Sheshen's enemies in the West had traced him back to Unit 199.

If it was Dhou, Unit 199 was finished. Hundreds of armed assassins would swarm inside. Dhou would kill everyone he found without pause. Sheshen would have no choice but to escape, and return to take revenge some time in the future.

But if the enemy came from the West, Sheshen still had hope. It was doubtful that even the CIA could bring a large force over the border into China without risking immense repercussions. They would instead have planned a quick, surgical strike with a handful of professionals.

Sheshen's teeth came together, his body coiling. His shock and surprise had completely vanished. He could not change the horror that was happening, he could only react. Taking rationed breaths from the oxygen tank as he went, he exited the storage cell through the circular hatch and raced down the long steel corridor. The steady hiss followed him as he went; by the time he had turned the next corner, he could feel the cool ether against his skin.

His teeth clenched as he passed gasping scientists and

lab assistants, most already on their knees as the ether numbed their minds. By the time he had reached the control room and experiment chamber at the center of the complex, everyone he passed was nearly unconscious, some curled up on the floor, others braced against the steel walls.

He bypassed the control room and headed straight for the experiment chamber. The door to the chamber was open; he could see Gui Yisheng lying in the center of the room, just a few feet from the Plexiglas cylinder. Two assistants lay collapsed on the other side of the room, next to one of the specialized canisters.

Sheshen's rage grew as he hurried to his father's side. All the preparations had been made; Gui Yisheng had only been waiting for him to return from the storage cell with the specimen. It would have taken mere minutes to free the mirror viroles, than transfer them to the waiting canister for multiplication, and transportation to Beijing.

Sheshen dropped to his knees next to the prone body and realized with a start that his father was still conscious, his mouth clamped tightly closed, his dark eyes wide open. Gui Yisheng was holding his breath against the ether, struggling to stay conscious as his life's work collapsed around him.

Sheshen knew he had to do something for his father, but what? The Plexiglas cylinder gave him an idea. He slid his hands under his father's squat body and lifted him gently off the floor. Armless, helpless, quivering with fear—his father seemed so fragile in his hands. Was *this* the monster from his memories? This little, feeble, dying man?

Sheshen crossed quickly to the cylinder, and opened the curved hatch. He carefully placed his father inside, then secured the hatch behind him. The hatch automatically sealed itself.

His father's eyes glistened, and his mouth came open. A small fog appeared on the inside of the Plexiglas as he breathed deeply. The airtight cylinder contained enough oxygen for many hours, easily enough time to outlast the ether.

Sheshen watched as Gui Yisheng leaned close to the curved wall of his sanctuary. His mouth moved, and muffled words reached Sheshen's ears: "Stop them."

The words were unnecessary. Sheshen nodded, then turned away from the cylinder. His eyes brightened as he saw a familiar object in the far corner of the experiment chamber. The small leather briefcase he always kept nearby—the specialized tools he had carried all the way around the curve of the world. The tools of his trade.

Soon, he knew, he would have a chance to feed his rage.

CHAPTER THIRTY-THREE

Mike followed Amber across the packed sand. The stars were strange above his head. Back in Boston, he had hardly ever noticed the stars, but now that he was on the other side of the earth, he could see that everything was out of place. It gave his surroundings a surreal feeling. When he glanced back, he could see dust clouds rolling low over the moonscape of sand and stone, curling through the darkness like waves over a Pacific beach. Just ahead rose the mountains of the East, craggy cliffs and rock outcroppings blacking out the stars. This was truly the rim of the world.

Somewhere in those mountains lay the front entrance to Mogue De Ghong, the Heel of the Demon. Amber had told Mike about the vast yin-yang symbol from the NSA satellite photos, and he had been awed by the idea that such a place could exist. But after the events of the past week, he had lost the ability to be truly surprised by anything.

Something small and dark skittered past his left foot, and he watched it disappear in a puff of sand. Some sort of lizard, he assumed, indigenous to this inhospitable place. Mike's sense of unreality increased as he watched the sand settle back down. Teri, his father, the violence at the stable and again at the navy yard—this was not his life. A part of him wanted to curl up and shut down, to close his eyes until it all made sense again.

Then he caught sight of Amber's long body striding across the sand ahead of him, her heavy backpack slung over her right shoulder. She would never erase Kari from his thoughts; but Amber Chen had begun to fill a void in his life. He could no longer imagine his life without her—and if curling up and shutting down meant erasing the closeness they had developed in the past few days, the price was much too steep.

"Up ahead," Amber called back over her shoulder, her voice riding the desert breeze. "Right where they're supposed to be."

Past her, Mike made out three shapes standing in the shadows of a high gray boulder, just at the base of the mountains. As he moved closer, the shapes came slowly into focus. All three were short, stocky, wearing dark green uniforms. Mike did not recognize the uniforms, but assumed they had something to do with the Chinese military.

He caught up to Amber as she reached the men. All three were armed with automatic pistols and carried gas masks over their shoulders. The men had wide faces, elongated narrow eyes, and thick dark hair. Two had beards, the third a wispy gray mustache. The man with the mustache stepped forward, a wide smile on his lips. He spoke rapidly in Chinese, and Amber nodded. Then the mustached man pointed at Mike and said something else; all three men laughed loudly, the guttural sound lifting across the sand.

Amber turned to Mike. "This is Tang. He's going to lead us inside. He and his men have been combat trained by the CIA, and have run many missions inside northern China. They're very good at what they do. They'll move on ahead, making sure it's secure, and we'll follow a few minutes behind."

Mike looked at Ono Tang. He had a kind face and sparkling eyes. "Why were they laughing at me?"

Amber smiled. "Because of the way you're dressed. They want to know if you think you're here to play football."

The three men broke away, heading around to the other side of the boulder. Amber and Mike followed slowly. Mike could see his own breath in the darkness in front of him; he shivered from the cold. He guessed the temperature was close to freezing and wondered how hot it got during the day. It was hard to believe he was standing at the edge of a desert in the middle of China. No visa, no passport, no official red tape. He knew Amber was used to working outside the rules, but it was strange to him, a parallel universe he had never imagined before.

They came around the other side of the boulder, and Mike watched as the three Mongolians hovered around a rectangular metal grate in a slab of thick granite set right into the sandy ground. Tang pulled a long steel lever out of a pack slung around his waist and went to work on the grate. His partners added their weight to his, and soon there was a loud metallic snap as the grate popped free. The sound echoed through the night.

Ono Tang said something to Amber; then all three men slid their gas masks over their faces. Ono Tang pulled out his automatic and climbed through the opening. His men followed, and a second later Mike and Amber were alone.

Amber must have noticed the expression on Mike's face. She reached forward, running a gloved hand across his cheek. "I know this seems insane to you. But we're here. This is real."

"Nothing seems insane to me anymore. I've seen ghosts, remember?"

Amber smiled. Then she gestured toward the open access tunnel. They moved forward carefully, stopping when they reached the granite slab.

Through the dark opening, Mike saw rungs leading down a vertical corridor for what looked like forty or fifty yards. His nerves crackling, he turned away and watched Amber put on her light, rubbery gas mask. With its hose and transparent faceplate, against the panorama of the desert, it made her look like some futuristic insect, or a soldier in an invading alien army.

Mike rubbed his hands together; cold sweat covered his palms. He reminded himself that Amber would not have let him tag along unless the operation was relatively safe. She had told him everything about her meeting with Daniel Hutchins, so he knew that one condition of the mission was that it not turn into combat. As long as things went smoothly, he was in no real danger.

Amber helped him strap his own gas mask over his face, fastening the clasps behind his neck. He took a deep breath, tasting the carbonized air. The faceplate fogged slightly as he exhaled, then cleared. The world looked even more surreal through the plastic shield.

"Ready?" Amber asked, donning her backpack. Her voice echoed through her mask. "No turning back?"

Mike nodded. He felt slightly ridiculous in his college sweats and the gas mask, yet he was about to climb down into a laboratory that had ordered the murder of his best friend, a young woman, and his father. He reached forward and squeezed Amber's hand.

Then he followed her over the edge of the ventilation access and started down the metal rungs. His tired knees cried out, but he clenched his teeth against the pain, refusing to let his ancient injury slow him down. Amber had called him solid; Mike didn't know if the description fit, but he certainly liked the way it sounded. It was the complete opposite of every adjective he had ever heard used to describe Flannery.

A solemn feeling moved through him at the unfairness of the thought, but it still rang true. The feeling was replaced by anger as he remembered that he'd never have a chance to work things out with Flannery Ballantine, he'd never have a chance to forgive—

Thoughts of his father vanished: he felt Amber's hand against his ankle. He looked down to a stone floor bathed in fluorescent green light. He dropped off the last rung, next to Amber, and saw they were in a long access tunnel that led deeper into the base of the mountain.

Amber started forward, her feet silent against the stone. Mike had still not figured out how she could walk so quietly, and he concentrated on keeping his own heavy steps as hushed as possible.

The tunnel ended in an open metal hatch. There was no sign of Ono Tang and his two men; Mike assumed they were somewhere deep in the complex by now, making sure no one had escaped the ether. Mike hadn't asked Amber any questions about the Mongolians; in truth, he didn't know much about Amber's job, her past, or the people she worked with. When they got out of this place, there would be time for such questions—if he ever decided to ask.

The hatch opened into a long, well-lit, steel-lined hallway. Amber pointed toward the floor, and Mike gasped into his gas mask, startled to see a man in a white lab coat lying right in front of the open hatch. The man was on his back, his hands limp at his sides. His chest was rising and falling, and Mike felt relief. The Mongolians hadn't been overenthusiastic with the ether. Although he understood the seriousness of their mission, he would not have been able to stomach the wholesale murder of an entire laboratory full of people.

Now the hallway curved to the left; Mike was stepping carefully over more unconscious bodies. Although his adrenaline was still pumping, his nerves had begun to relax. So far, the mission was an obvious success. Now it was up to Amber and Mike to find out what Unit 199 was about—and put an end to whatever that was, for good.

"Mike." Amber's voice echoed back through the hallway. She stepped over two lab workers curled up next to each other in a wide doorway. "I think I've found something."

Mike rushed to her side. The doorway opened up into a vast, brightly lit room with curved walls. "Shaped like the blade of a scythe. Or a half-moon."

"It's some sort of computer control room." Amber pointed toward the back wall, which was covered with dials, levers, knobs, and digital readouts. "There's a lot of power in here. I wonder what it's for."

Mike stepped past her. On the other side of the curved room, he counted six huge black windows behind strange-looking three-legged stools. The stools had what looked like foot stirrups attached to their bases. "What the hell is this place?"

Amber turned, approaching one of the stools. Then her body went rigid. "Mike."

He followed her gaze through one of the circular black windows. It looked out on a huge rectangular chamber with steel walls. In the center of the chamber was a narrow, transparent cylinder. Inside the cylinder stood a man. At least, Mike thought it was a man. He had never seen such wrinkled skin, such deteriorated features. The man was hunched forward, breathing hard. Then Mike noticed his sleeves: they hung empty at his sides, covering nothing more than puckered stumps. The old man had no arms.

"Amber—"

"It's Gui Yisheng. The Devil Doctor. That cylinder must be airtight. That's why he's still conscious."

Mike looked at her. Her face had turned pallid. Behind her gas mask, her eyes were as wide as he had ever seen them. "Gui Yisheng?"

"Another legend. Sheshen's father. Supposedly, he runs around eastern China, sucking up peasants' brains—"

She stopped suddenly, looking up. Mike had heard it, too—a muffled shout from somewhere up ahead.

At the far end of the long control room was an open hatch that led into another steel corridor. It was impossible to see what was happening down the corridor but Mike guessed the Mongolians were somewhere nearby. Perhaps they had found something important.

He and Amber started toward the open hatch, but a new sound stopped them dead. Mike's stomach churned when he realized what it was: the unmistakable pop of a suppressed automatic.

Minutes before, Sheshen had crouched in a screened equipment alcove, watching as the three Mongolians left the control room and entered the steel corridor. Sheshen's eyes had narrowed as he recognized the ethnic features behind the gas masks: the three men were undoubtedly mercenaries, which pointed to an antagonist from the West, not from within China's borders. Sheshen's rage had grown exponentially as he considered the audacity of his enemies. To come after him here, of all places! To dare challenge him inside his father's laboratory!

He had watched the Mongolians move down the corridor in a classic scouting formation—two in front, bent low to the ground, while the third covered the rear, his automatic sweeping the air as he turned back and forth. Sheshen had waited until the first two were directly in front of him, their weapons at the ready, their attention still on the long corridor that stretched out ahead. Then he had carefully set the portable oxygen tank down, trading it for the two instruments he had retrieved from his leather briefcase. The air had tasted dull against his tongue, but, as he had predicted, the ether had already settled and that danger had passed. He had given the Mongolians a few more seconds, letting the advancing pair move another meter beyond the unconditional range of the rear man's automatic. And then it was time to strike.

He burst forward through the cloth screen, his slippered feet churning against the stone floor. His right arm whipped upward as he moved, the surgical scalpel flashing through the air. The rear man saw him and shouted, his automatic rising—but he was too slow, off-balance. The scalpel caught the closest man in the side of his neck, slicing straight through to the carotid, releasing his life in a spout of bright red.

The rear man finally got off a poorly aimed shot: Sheshen heard the bullet ricochet off the wall behind him. Before the man could fire again, Sheshen had his right arm around the other lead Mongolian, yanking him up off his feet. He spun the man around, using him as a shield. Meanwhile, his left hand drove upward, toward the center of the man's back.

The bone drill caught the Mongolian directly in the midpoint of his spine. The sharp bit tore upward through his skin, then on through the protective bone beneath, instantly liquefying the man's spinal column and the nerves inside. The spinning tip continued through, piercing the back of the man's lungs and tearing straight into the base of his heart. A spray of dark blood erupted out of the Mongolian's lifeless mouth, knocking the gas mask half off his face, then splattering across the steel walls of the corridor.

Sheshen yanked the drill free as he peered over the dead man's shoulder. He could see the horror in the remaining Mongolian's eyes as he stared at his lifeless, gutted comrade. The damage to the corpse's spinal column had left his facial muscles limp and flaccid, hanging like a melting waxen mask from his cheekbones and jaw. A horrid, paralyzing sight. Exactly as Sheshen had intended.

Finally, the Mongolian came to his senses and screamed, firing off three wild shots in the direction of the human shield. But by that time, Sheshen was no longer behind the corpse; he was sweeping along the wall of the corridor at full speed. He twisted at the last minute to avoid the arcing automatic, and then he was on top of the last remaining man, the scalpel flashing back and forth. Blood sprayed upward in a savage fountain, but he kept slashing, again and again.

He did not stop until he had completely severed the man's head. He tucked the scalpel into the sleeve of his smock, then gripped the Mongolian's head tightly by its thick dark hair and lifted it up in front of him. The Mongolian's gas mask dropped to the ground with a clatter. Sheshen could see himself reflected in the man's dead eyes. His chest heaved, the wonderful thrill of the moment evident in his blood-spattered, gaunt visage. But the violence wasn't over yet. He knew he still had work to do.

The three men had been a scouting party, which meant there were more invaders somewhere nearby. Sheshen crept forward, the Mongolian's head still hanging from his right hand.

He paused as he reached the hatch at the end of the

corridor. He could hear hushed breathing from somewhere deep inside the semicircular control room. He pressed himself flat against the corridor wall and slid the last few inches in complete silence. Careful to keep from being seen, he stole a quick glance through the open hatch.

He stifled a gasp as he recognized the Western doctor and the female traitor, standing in frightened shock in the center of the long control room. He pressed himself back against the corridor wall, momentarily stunned. Both alive—and they had dared follow him all the way back to China! Perhaps they had figured out Unit 199's true mission. Or perhaps they were simply seeking revenge for the young girl's death.

Either way, it didn't matter. They had severely underestimated him. And now he had a chance to do what he should have done a long time ago. He looked back down the corridor. The headless Mongolian still clutched his automatic in his lifeless right hand. Sheshen promised himself he would use the gun only to incapacitate, not to kill. He glanced down at the heavy bone drill in his left hand, still dripping blood and spinal fluid to the cold stone floor. Then he smiled.

Mike watched in silence as Amber slipped her gun out of her backpack and motioned him back in the direction they had come from. She was staring at a spot in the corner of the open hatch, as if she had just seen something that scared the hell out of her. "We've got to get out of here. Now!"

"But what about—"

Mike was interrupted by a flash of motion. Something round and heavy arced through the air of the control room, landing with a thud on the floor. The object rolled to a stop a few yards from Mike's feet and he stared down. He recognized the mustache and the narrow eyes. It was Tang's head, rudely severed.

Amber shouted something in Chinese and fired three wild shots, simultaneously pulling Mike back. There was brief return fire, and Mike ducked as he felt something whiz by his right ear. Then there was a sickening sound as a bullet connected with flesh, and he saw Amber crash backward, clutching at her shoulder. Her body slammed into the steel wall and crumpled, her gun clattering to the floor.

"Amber!" Mike almost forgot where he was as he dropped to his knees at her side. She was dazed but breathing, her face pallid behind the gas mask and her pulse rocketing through her wrist. The wound to her shoulder was messy but not critical. It looked as though the bullet had just missed the bone. Still, she was bleeding badly, and there was still the danger of more gunfire. Mike applied pressure to the wound, meanwhile dragging her as far out of range as he could, then he yanked his sweatshirt up over his head. The sweatshirt caught on the straps of his gas mask, and he cursed, making a quick decision. It had been at least ten minutes. The ether had probably dissipated to a harmless level.

He yanked off the gas mask, tossing it to the floor. Thankfully, the air tasted fairly clean. His sweatshirt came free, and he tied the sleeves tightly around Amber's wound, trying to get as much pressure as possible. It wasn't great, but it was the best he could do.

"Amber," he whispered, "can you hear me?"

Her head lolled back, her eyes closed. She had hit the wall pretty hard; Mike worried that the blow had given her a concussion. He started to undo her gas mask when something flickered at the edge of his vision.

He turned and saw a nightmare come to life. The gaunt man was standing at the other end of the control room. Blood spattered the front of his white smock; there were specks of red in his hair and in the scar under his right eye. He saw Mike crouched next to Amber and started forward, his movements sleek and easy.

Mike looked at the gaunt man's hands, expecting to see the deadly barrel of a gun. But Sheshen had exchanged his gun for something worse. In his left hand was a surgical scalpel, six inches long and razor sharp. In his right hand was a cruel-looking drill of a kind Mike recognized. Designed for orthopedic surgery, it had a special bit that could cut through bone in seconds. The bit was bright red, dripping heavy drops toward the control room floor.

Christ. Sheshen could have shot them both. But instead, he intended to use a drill and a scalpel. Mike remembered the liquid violence he had seen in the man's eyes outside Andrew's funeral, and his mind felt suddenly disconnected.

Suddenly, Sheshen sprang forward, the drill tearing through the air in front of him. Mike reacted without thinking, bringing Amber's gas mask up like a shield. The drill struck it and the faceplate shattered, pieces of plastic flying in every direction. Mike rolled to his right, away from Amber, and vaulted to his feet. He was standing with his back to a black-tinted window, and directly in front of him was one of the stools with the unusual foot stirrups. Mike glanced down at the heel pedal, then put his hands defensively out in front of him, wishing he had a gun although he knew it probably wouldn't have made any difference.

Sheshen turned to face him, jerking the drill through the air. There was a frightening moment as he looked down at Amber, still semiconscious on the floor; but then he refocused on Mike, his eyes glowing in the strange green light. He paused for a moment, relishing his obvious, impending victory. "I will enjoy this, *ang mo.*"

He dove forward at nearly inhuman speed. Mike slammed his foot down, hitting the heel pedal attached to the stool in front of him. The stool hopped upward with a pneumatic hiss, catching Sheshen's hip and spinning him off balance. Mike twisted, barely dodging the drill as Sheshen collided with his body. Together they toppled backward, crashing into the window.

There was a loud cracking as the window fractured like a pitch-black spider web; the pane sagged inward, but somehow didn't break. Daggers of pain shot through Mike's skull and neck, the breath knocked out of him by the force of Sheshen's body. He saw the bone drill whip out of Sheshen's left hand and spin across the control room. In the same instant, the scalpel flashed from above his shoulder and he reached out, catching Sheshen by the wrist.

There was a frozen moment as the scalpel hung in the air. Then Sheshen's right knee came up and Mike suddenly found himself flying. His spine twisted like a corkscrew as his hands came free from Sheshen's wrist, and then he was tumbling upside down, the room spinning around him.

The back of his head hit the stone floor in the center of the control room, and green light sparked at the corners of his eyes. He tasted blood; there was a dull throbbing in his head. Then he opened his eyes and realized that he was still conscious—barely.

He tried to lift his head, but sparks of pain ran down his neck, and his fingers clenched together. Sheshen had thrown him with some sort of martial arts move. He had hit the stone floor hard, maybe hard enough to crack his skull.

Slippered footsteps crossed the cold stone, and

Mike's stomach lurched. *Oh my God, he's coming.* He struggled to sit up, but his head spun with the effort. He closed his eyelids, the tears welling behind his eyes. *He's coming, he's coming, he's coming!*

"Mike," he heard from a few yards to his left, "get up! *Quickly!*"

It was Amber. He could hear her struggling, injured, along the wall, searching for her gun. Mike tried to respond, but before he could speak, he felt something straddle his waist. He forced his eyes open and saw the horrible gaunt face staring down at him. Then he saw the surgical scalpel, poised in Sheshen's right hand. Mike clenched his teeth, waiting helplessly for the killing stroke. It was over. He had lost; his nightmare had won.

"Mike," he heard again, this time even closer. He realized, with a start, that it was a man's voice. A familiar voice. With all his might, he turned his head to the side—and saw Andrew's ghost standing in front of Amber, just inches from her feet. Andrew pointed toward the floor in front of him. *The bone drill.* It had landed barely a yard from Mike's outstretched hand. Mike stared at his best friend, his eyes full of sorrow. *I'm sorry, Andrew. I can't reach. I can't reach—*

Then Andrew's foot swung out. The drill slid across the stone floor and smacked into Mike's hand. Stunned, Mike grabbed it. He saw Sheshen rearing up, grinning, the scalpel arcing through the air. Without thought, Mike focused all his strength and brought the drill up, his finger on the trigger.

The drill caught Sheshen in the direct center of his rib cage. Sheshen's mouth came open and a scream ripped through the air. Mike pressed as hard as he could, feeling the bit tear deep into Sheshen's body, splintering bone and shredding the organs beneath. Sheshen toppled backward, but Mike held on, dragged forward as he pushed the drill deeper and deeper. There was a sudden pop as the bit ripped out through the other side of Sheshen's body, gnawing at mere air. Finally, Mike let go, crashing back against the floor.

He watched as Sheshen teetered across the control room, his hands waving in circles, his face a mask of agony. Sheshen screamed something in Chinese; then his back slammed into the switches and levers that covered the control room wall. His knees crumpled and his lifeless body slid down the wall, hitting more switches and levers. A digital panel above the switches lit up and started counting downward in bright red numbers: *10. 9. 8.*

There was a rumbling from somewhere beneath Mike's feet. *7. 6. 5.* The lights flickered; Amber shouted, pointing toward the black windows. *4. 3. 2.* Mike turned, fighting the pain in his back and neck.

1.

The armless man inside the cylinder in the adjoining room was leaping up and down, terror in his dark eyes. He slammed his ancient body against the cylinder wall, but he was trapped inside, and his terror grew as the rumbling below the floor increased. His toothless mouth opened, and he screamed familiar words in Chinese. Then there was a flash of light—even through the black Plexiglas, it burned Mike's eyes—and the rumbling stopped. Mike lurched forward, staring through the window at the cylinder in the other room.

"My God," he whispered. "Oh, my God."

There was nothing left inside the cylinder but a billowing, pinkish mist.

CHAPTER THIRTY-FOUR

Twenty minutes later, still numb, Mike huddled next to Amber in front of a massive circular hatch dug into the very center of the mountain complex. Soothing, oceanic blue light poured over them, and Mike could taste the refrigerated air as it moved down his throat.

They had stumbled silently through the complex, searching every cell-like room. Amber's shoulder wound and the growing stiffness in Mike's back and neck made for slow going. But Amber's wound had stopped bleeding, and she had assured Mike she was strong enough to keep moving. She wouldn't even let him carry her backpack, which she had slung over her good shoulder. She knew her own body, and its limitations.

As for himself, Mike needed an X ray and maybe even an MRI, but he didn't think there was any permanent damage. Like Amber, he would recover. The same could not be said for Sheshen. Mike had destroyed his living nightmare with the bone drill—and a little outside help.

Mike looked at Amber standing next to him in the circular hatch, and again considered telling her about Andrew and the drill—but then decided to keep that to himself. After all, he couldn't be sure what had really happened. Andrew's ghost had been standing right in front of Amber; she might have hit the drill with an outstretched leg, making it seem like a ghostly intervention.

That had to be it. No matter how willing Mike was to believe in ghosts, the other alternative made no scientific sense. Not even under Teri's new rules. In any event, Sheshen was finally gone—for good. Mike turned back toward the blue light.

"This looks promising."

"Let's hope so," Amber responded, and he could hear the strained anticipation in her voice.

So far, they had found nothing to tell them the purpose of the laboratory. But the instant Mike had seen the enormous circular hatch, he'd known: if they were going to find anything in the sleeping complex, it was here.

"I think that's a foot scanner." Amber pointed to a curved hole in the wall near the floor. "If so, then this room had restricted access. That's a good sign."

She stepped forward, into the blue light. Mike followed, his eyes widening as he surveyed the impressive room. "Fantastic."

The place was a perfect circle, its high marble walls lined with polished blue cabinets made up of identical stacked shelves. Each shelf had a knob and a colorful label. At the far end of the room stood a single enormous cabinet, made of the same material as the rest but with only one shelf, unmarked. The shelf was open, but Mike couldn't see inside from that distance.

"My God. It's beautiful."

Mike turned and saw that Amber was pointing toward the curved ceiling. With difficulty, he craned his head—and was astonished at the colorful image covering most of the area above him. It took him a moment to realize it was a computer-driven map of China, covered in strange swirls of bright red. As he watched, the swirls seemed to pulse outward, enveloping more and more of the Chinese mainland. Within the swirls, Mike could make out dark circles that might have represented cities; smaller marks, perhaps, were villages and farms. The swirls seemed focused around the larger marks, and Mike wondered what the image meant. Was it significant, or just decorative?

"Mike, take a look at this." Amber had shifted her attention to a cabinet on the left side of the room. One of the central shelves bore a Chinese label and a numerical date: 3/6/79. "I recognize this name. He was a Taiwanese diplomat. He was murdered and mutilated by Sheshen, in 1979."

Carefully, Mike pulled the shelf open. Inside was a round glass tank about the size and shape of a three-gallon fishbowl and filled with clear, strong-smelling liquid. Two plastic tubes ran out of the center of the tank, and a stream of tiny bubbles rose from the end of one of the tubes.

Mike took a deep breath. He knew that smell. "Ringer's solution. I've used it in my lab many times. It keeps organic tissue alive."

Organic tissue. He peered into the tank—and his stomach froze. At the bottom of the tank, was a small, rubbery object about the size of a finger. Stringlike cords twisted out of both ends of the object. Mike staggered back, his face pale.

"What is it?" Amber asked.

"A human hippocampus. The cords are the related ganglia. It's the human memory center. The central portion of a human brain."

Amber looked at him, then back at the object in the fishbowl. She began reading over the other colored labels. "If these labels are accurate, he's been collecting them for twenty years. Since the late seventies.

Sheshen's signature—it wasn't just for the violent thrill, it had a purpose. They were collecting human memory centers. Why?"

Mike swallowed. He tried to make sense of the clues in front of them. The Ringer's solution. The strange cerebral mutilation. The interest in Teri's work. He began to think out loud: "It's where the mirror viruses live. The tissue in this fishbowl—it contains Teri's mirror viruses."

Closer. Clearer. He grabbed another drawer at random, and yanked it open. He looked down into an identical fishbowl. Then he opened another shelf, and another. His head swam. He was still trying to understand. "Souls. Dead people's souls. They've been collecting ghosts. Why?"

Amber moved down the cabinets, reading the labels. Mike could see what she saw: the labels were in chronological order.

"It's not just a new interrogation technique," she whispered, still reading the dates, her face determined. "It's got to be more than just stealing secrets from the dead. This collection spans a generation. So many captured souls."

She stopped in front of one of the shelves. Mike moved next to her, and read the date on the label. Roughly seven years ago. The name next to the date was in Chinese, but he could guess what it said. Amber's fingers shook as she pulled open the drawer. "That's what it's about—capturing ghosts!"

Christ. It was even more astounding than Teri's own ambitions. Gui Yisheng had obviously begun his work decades earlier. Using the same scientific principles, he had set out to devise a way to capture individual spirits. But why? What was his purpose?

There had to be more. Mike thought about the ancient, decrepit, armless man in the cylinder. What had he been chasing? Immortality?

"Amber, Gui Yisheng shouted something in Chinese before he died. Sheshen shouted the same thing as he crashed into the control room wall. What was it?"

Amber was still staring into the fishbowl in front of her. "He shouted two sentences: 'Ancestors, protect me. Mao, protect me.' The first is a common phrase. In the East, we believe that our ancestors' spirits follow us around, keeping us from harm."

She paused, looking at Mike. Suddenly, her eyes flashed. "That's it! That's what this place is about!"

Mike nodded, Gui Yisheng wasn't just out to capture the spirit world. He intended to bring it back. He had the ghosts of his enemies to experiment with—but his goal was not to raise his dead enemies.

Mike crossed the room to the main cabinet against the far wall. He looked inside the open shelf, at the fishbowl inside. The organic tissue in the bowl was deteriorating at the edges—aged, like Gui Yisheng himself. Still, there was no way to know for sure. They would never know for sure.

"He was going to raise a ghost," Amber whispered from across the room, "powerful enough to change the world."

"That's only the beginning," Mike said, suddenly staring up at the image on the ceiling. Finally, it all became clear. "He was going to infect the entire nation with that ghost. He was going to spread it—like a disease—to every corner of China."

Amber followed his gaze. The reflection from the red swirls glowed across her upturned cheeks. "But how?"

Mike's thoughts coalesced as he spoke. "Every hippocampal cell contains millions of mirror viruses. Once they're released in virole form, there are numerous ways to help them proliferate, and to suspend them within an aerosol. That's exactly what happened when Andrew died: his viroles became airborne, ready to infect a new host. The only difficult step is to spread the airborne solution over population centers—but I think we already know how Gui Yisheng planned to do that."

"The ventilation towers."

Mike nodded. Amber had told him about Hutchins's discovery—the hastily constructed towers in high-altitude locations all across China. Hutchins had also mentioned that all the construction sites were near dense population centers, the dark spots beneath the swirls of red. It was a simple, elegant, and horrifying plan. "An airborne viral infection that carries with it a ghost from China's past. An immortal ancestor."

Amber's face had gone ashen. She understood even better than Mike, because she was Chinese. She knew the history—and the possibilities. The ramifications. "Imagine what would have happened. An entire nation unified—and hurled backward fifty years. A living infection inside each and every person, guiding, controlling, ruling. An unstoppable tyranny, from inside."

Mike could feel her emotion from across the room. "It would have created a nation of Sheshens, following the same immortal vision. It would have sparked a revolution that would never have stopped at China's borders."

Mike shivered, moving away from the main cabinet. He saw Amber wincing as she struggled to unzip her backpack. She pulled out a handful of black disks, each the size of a hockey puck. Mike knew, from what Amber had told him during the flight into China, that each disk had the explosive power of twenty sticks of dynamite.

He crossed back to Amber's side, looking at the open shelf in front of her. "Amber, what about—"

"My father died seven years ago. My brother and I cried at his funeral. He lives on in my memory, and that's where he should remain."

She stopped, her throat clenching. Mike understood. *Oh, God, I understand.* Amber shut the drawer and placed one of the black disks on the floor at her feet.

Quickly, they moved through the vast blue-lit room, placing the other disks randomly next to the cabinets. They saved three disks for the main cabinet at the back of the room, placing them all inside the open top shelf, right next to the fishbowl.

Then Amber pulled a small plastic box out of her backpack and positioned it in the center of the room. She hit a switch on the box, setting the detonator. Then she grabbed Mike's hand.

"Let's get out of this place."

The propeller plane was a thousand feet above the low clouds when the explosion went off. Still, the shock waves reverberated through the plane, and Mike gripped Amber's hand tightly.

It was finally over. Unit 199 was finished. Gui Yisheng's terrifying dream would never reach fruition. His laboratory had been destroyed—and along with it, his collection of stolen souls. Still, the moment was bittersweet.

Mike would never forget the plume of fire that had taken Andrew, or the sight of Teri, murdered and mutilated on the floor of his basement lab. And he would never forget the sight of his father, lying broken in the back of an ambulance. But now he could begin to put the pieces of his life back together.

Teri's research was gone, but her ideas were alive inside Mike. One day, he swore, he would recreate her experiments and she would take her rightful place in the pantheon of great scientists. One day, her ideas would truly change the world.

As for Mike's world, it had already begun to change. He looked at Amber, at the glow in her beautiful dark eyes, at the angle of her high Asian cheekbones—and he felt a wonderful excitement move through him. No one could ever replace Kari, but Amber would do honor to Kari's memory.

It was time, Mike told himself. To mourn. To begin again. He turned to face the open hold of the cargo plane.

For a brief second, he thought he saw Andrew sitting across from him, grinning. Then the vision disappeared.

TURN THE PAGE FOR A

SNEAK PREVIEW OF

THE CARRIER—

HOLDEN SCOTT'S ELECTRIFYING NEW NOVEL

—COMING IN HARDCOVER IN MAY

FROM ST. MARTIN'S PRESS!

Seven-thirty A.M., maybe closer to eight. Tiny electrical pulses travelling through braids of copper as thin as a human hair, bouncing from the ground to the sky to the ground, finally surging like an infection through a dormant patchwork of circuits, diodes, and minuscule mechanical gears.

Then the shrill, metallic cry of a portable phone.

Jack Collier's eyes came open on the third ring, sleep a swirling fog across his vision. He was still wearing his clothes from yesterday, light blue scrubs and a white T-shirt. His sneakers were on the edge of the bed by his feet, and his lab coat was curled into a ball a few inches from his shoulders, a makeshift pillow that smelled vaguely of formaldehyde, sweat, and stale junk food.

Slowly, resentfully, achingly, he turned toward the table by his bed. Twists of his unkempt, dirty blond hair fell in front of his eyes, as he fumbled for the phone that peeked out from beneath a pair of dog-eared oncology textbooks. Usually, he kept the damn thing unplugged. But last night, he had returned early enough from the lab to make an attempt at a delivery dinner. The unopened pizza box was still sitting on top of his dresser, grease bleeding through the cardboard and staining the antique oak.

The plastic phone felt cold against his palm, and Jack shivered, casting a glance toward the window on the far side of the room. As usual, the weather was a color, 'gray, and the deeper the calendar slid into November, the grayer it was going to get. The tree in front of his dorm building had already turned skeletal, its limbs casting daggered shadows across the piles of dirty laundry covering his floor.

Jack brought the phone to his ear, pretending he didn't feel a pang of hope as the fourth ring spasmed through the oblong chunk of plastic. *She hadn't called, she wasn't going to call.* He should have chucked the phone in a vat of battery acid months ago. He hit the answer key with his thumb, finally quelling the electric infection. Then he cleared his throat.

"If this is a special offer from a phone company— *any* phone company—I'm going to kill you."

There was a brief pause on the other end, then an angry, young, male voice.

"Jack, where the hell have you been?"

It took Jack a moment to place the mild Southern accent. Daniel Clayton, a Ph.D. student who worked part-time in the office of the Dean of Students. A tall, gangly kid about Jack's age, with a shock of bright red hair and wire-rimmed glasses. When he wasn't filing papers for the Dean, Clayton worked in a lab four floors above Jack's own, chasing a neuro Ph.D. In a way, that made them brothers under their scrubs.

"Hey, Clayton. Is this about tuition again? Tell the Dean to relax. My grant check was late last month—"

"Jesus, Jack, this isn't about your goddamn tuition. Haven't you read the letters from the Dean's office?"

Jack paused, disturbed by the frantic edge to Clayton's voice. He glanced toward the pile of unopened mail on a shelf by the door.

"There's been a problem with my mail."

"And your phone? I've left you at least ten messages."

Jack raised his eyebrows.

"I haven't had time to check my machine. I've been spending a lot of time in the lab."

Jack winced at the understatement. Twenty-hour days, seven days a week. Nearly an entire year secluded in a cinder-block coffin, where time had as much authority as an unplugged phone. Jack had completely lost touch with the outside world—but it had been a necessary sacrifice. He was within days of completing his project. *His miracle.*

He did not expect Daniel Clayton to understand.

"Is it something important?" Jack asked, chafing now that he was fully awake and wasting valuable lab time.

"Important? Jack, the proceedings started twenty minutes ago."

Jack's mind moved somewhere else—a refrigerator in a corner of his lab. Second shelf from the top, a plastic petri dish filled with tiny specks of bacteria. One more day, two at most. He closed his eyes and saw Angie, her long dark hair and her crooked, fragile smile.

All for you, Angie. I did it all for you.

Jack's hands trembled. He wanted to hang up, but Clayton's voice continued to dribble into his ear.

"Did you hear me, Jack? You better get your ass over to Sackler Hall, the third-floor auditorium. Dean Cryer's already there, along with Professors Landry and Ballacroft—the chairs of the Judiciary Committee. Oh, and Dutton, of course. I'm sure he's in your corner—but there are specific guidelines for this sort of thing. Even Professor Dutton doesn't have enough pull to challenge the university charter."

Jack blinked, something beginning to register. A cold feeling moved through his chest. "Clayton, what the hell are you talking about?"

There was a hiss of frustration on the other end.

"OPEN YOUR FUCKING EARS AND LISTEN TO ME."

"I *am* listening. Say it again so I'll understand."

Clayton spoke slow enough for Jack to taste every word.

"Jack, you're being expelled."

*   *   *

By the time Jack stepped through the double doors at the top of the bowl-shaped auditorium, his shock had transformed into a dull, throbbing fear. In his dorm room, amidst the stench of old pizza and even older laundry, the word "expulsion" seemed laughable. But here the word was as heavy and real as a pendulum above his throat.

Sackler Auditorium smelled like Harvard—and not the diverse, glossy, laminated Harvard from the brochures. The semi-circular room was vast, poorly lit, and tiled in Italian marble. Strips of crimson carpeting ran down the aisles, and huge oil paintings of long-dead alumns hung from the excessively polished walls. A pair of chandeliers dangled over the raised, wooden stage, trickles of orange spilling down through matching bouquets of triangular crystal. In the center of the stage stood a long steel conference table, incongruously set between stone statues of the first two presidents of the university. The four figures seated behind the conference table seemed ghostly from Jack's distance, and the only thing he could tell for sure was that they were all men— and that they, too, smelled like Harvard.

As Jack began the lonely trek to the stage, he felt himself whirling backward to his first day as an undergraduate, nearly seven years ago. Fresh from the long bus ride from New Jersey, he had sat on a hard wooden bench along the back arch of this same theater. Drowning in a sea of strangers, waiting for the president of the university to speak, to tell him that he was privileged and chosen and bright—that he belonged.

He had looked up at the portraits on the walls, and the bearded, aristocratic faces had stared directly back at him, lips curling into mocking smiles.

Jack didn't belong. He had never belonged.

The ghosts at the conference table turned real as he reached the bottom of the crimson aisle, heading for the stairs that led to the stage. He recognized Dean Cryer immediately, a towering man with harshly combed hair and thick, black-framed glasses. Next to Cryer were the two heads of the Judiciary Committee, Landry and Ballacroft. Landry was Harvard's oldest English professor, and looked the part: frizzy white hair, sagging, bloodhound eyes, skin like crumpled canvas. His clothes came straight from central casting; tweed jacket, red bow-tie, striped blue shirt, and an ever-present handkerchief gripped tightly in his gnarled, trembling hand.

Ballacroft was more of a mystery. By title he was an anthropologist, but Jack doubted he had ever left the Ivory Tower long enough to worry the dry cleaner who managed his tailored khaki suits. Ballacroft's family was one of the richest in Boston, and there had been a family member involved with Harvard since the late seventeenth century.

Jack's feet became heavy as he reached the first step; if this was his jury, what chance did he have? Then he caught sight of Michael Dutton, at the far corner of the table. Dutton was leaning forward over a stack of white paper, his windswept, auburn hair glowing in the light from the chandeliers. As usual, he was wearing an impeccable suit, and his weathered face emanated calm and control. Jack felt a surge of hope: with Dutton's help, maybe he *did* have a chance. Dutton was one of the most respected professors at the university, twice on the short list for the Nobel Prize. He was also a campus favorite, with his rugged good looks and his easy smile. Most important of all, he was Jack's advisor. He had chosen Jack as his protégé, and that made Jack his investment.

Dutton looked up just as Jack stepped onto the stage, and their eyes met. Jack saw sympathy in those pools of green—but also something else, something that sent his hope spiraling away.

Pity.

"Jack," Dutton said, and immediately every face at the table shifted toward him. "Maybe you can help us understand what's going on here. I've done my best to come up with an explanation, but I'm truly at a loss.''

Jack could feel the sweat dripping down his back. He was wearing his only dress shirt, a white Oxford that Angie had bought him a month before she had left. The shirt was a size too small, but he hadn't had the time to exchange it. Once Angie had run, he hadn't had the time for anything outside of the lab—because nothing outside the lab mattered. Nothing was as important as his project.

At least, that's what he had thought.

"I'm sorry," Jack said, as Dean Cryer beckoned him toward an empty chair at the head of the long steel table. "But I'm not even sure why I'm here. I haven't gotten my mail or my phone messages in some time."

Dean Cryer raised his eyebrows. "You expect us to believe that you don't even know the charges against you?"

Jack lowered himself into the chair, his face turning red. He didn't like the tone of Cryer's voice, and he had the immediate urge to lash back. Instead, he did his best to remain in control.

"Your assistant told me it had something to do with my qualifying exam."

Ballacroft pointed a manicured finger at a pair of folders on the table in front of Jack. "Why don't you take a look for yourself?"

Jack glanced at Dutton, but his advisor was looking the other way. Jack turned his attention to the folders. He opened the closer of the two and read through a paragraph of typewritten text. He stopped himself half-way down the page. He didn't need to read more—because he had written it himself.

"This is from the exam I took when I entered the biology Ph.D. program two years ago. It's an essay on the human immune system. Specifically, on the activity of Killer T Cells."

Jack could have rewritten the essay in his sleep. Certainly, he knew more about Killer T Cells than anyone at the table—except maybe Dutton. Well, even Dutton. As brilliant as Michael Dutton was, he couldn't have come close to achieving what Jack had accomplished in the lab over the past year. When Dutton found out what his charge had done—Jack wasn't sure how he'd react. Jack had been very careful to keep his work a secret for that very reason. In truth, there was no way to tell how a man like Dutton would take being upstaged by a student.

"A fine essay," Dutton commented, still not looking at Jack. "I remember telling you that I was proud to have you in my lab—in part because that essay distinguished you from the rest of your classmates."

"Ironic," Professor Landry croaked. Then he wiped his mouth with his handkerchief, and Jack couldn't tell if he was embarrassed or amused. "If you'll take a look in the other folder, Jack, you'll see what I mean."

Jack nervously reached inside the second folder and withdrew another sheet of paper. The back of his neck burned as he read the entire page. Although the words were different, it was almost the same essay. *His* evaluations of T Cell behavior, *his* innovative description of immune system response. But someone else's words.

He shifted his eyes to a banner at the top of the page. There was a name he didn't recognize, followed by a date. It was a qualifying exam from seven years ago.

"This is impossible," Jack said, his voice soft. He again looked at Dutton. "Professor Dutton, I wrote this essay."

"Yes," Dean Cryer interrupted. "But someone else wrote it first. A bright student who finished his Ph.D. two years ago, then went on to teach at Stanford. His name was Albert Finsey. Unfortunately, Finsey died last year in a car accident, so we were unable to speak with him. But our records are quite clear; Finsey submitted it to Professor Minton, the previous Chair of Biology, who has since retired. Minton can't quote the exam word for word, but he remembers Finsey and has already testified that this was his exam.''

"The bottom line,'' Ballacroft added, his jaw tight, "is that this was not your own work, Mr. Collier. And the university has very clear rules about this sort of thing.''

Jack felt his throat closing. This was insane. This was bullshit. He looked down at the two exams on the table in front of him. Then back at the Dean, and the two old men seated next to him. Then, finally, at Michael Dutton.

This was worse than bullshit. This was *deliberate* bullshit.

"Someone faked this old exam,'' Jack hissed. "There's no other explanation. Finsey's dead, so he can't corroborate. And Minton's as old as this fucking building—''

"Watch yourself,'' the Dean admonished. "There's another explanation, and it's much simpler. The qualifying exam takes place in Widener Library. We don't police our students, because we don't usually need to. It would have been easy for you to use the library's computer system to search previous exams. It was just that sort of search that alerted Professor Dutton to your violation.''

Jack's stomach turned over. He glanced toward Dutton. Dutton shrugged, a tired expression on his handsome face. "I'm sorry, Jack. I was checking through the literature on T Cells for a paper I'm reviewing. Both your exam and Finsey's old exam came up. I couldn't ignore what I had found.''

The room had suddenly become an echo chamber. Dutton's voice was everywhere, and Jack felt like he was going to slip out of his chair. Dutton was supposed to be his supporter. But Dutton was the one who had aimed the gun at his head. Dutton was the one who had called this meeting.

Dutton was the one who was getting him expelled.

The sick truth was, Dutton could have ignored the two papers. Or he could have come to Jack, first. But he had chosen to go straight to the Dean. Maybe it was proper procedure—but every lab rat in the world knew that procedure was a tool you bent to your needs.

Jack rubbed his hand over his eyes, not wanting to believe.

"Give me another fucking test. Give me ten tests. I didn't cheat. I didn't *need* to cheat."

But his words were little more than air. He kept his eyes covered as the Dean rattled on about the appeal process, about Jack's rights as a student, about the notification that had already been sent to his grant committee. He kept his eyes covered as the two Judiciary Committee members told him how hard this was for them, how they regretted the severity of the university charter, how he still had a chance to make something of himself. He kept his eyes covered as the chairs pulled back from the table, as three of the four men filed away.

He kept his eyes covered until it was he and Dutton left alone at the long steel table, the orange light trickling down from the chandeliers like blood.

The silence didn't last long.

"I *am* sorry," Dutton finally said. "You were a brilliant protégé. You might have made a wonderful professor."

"Why did you do it?" Jack asked, moving his hand so he could look Dutton in those fucking green eyes. There was no reason to play games, now. It didn't take a *brilliant* mind to figure it out. "Why did you set me up?"

Dutton leaned back, momentarily stricken. Then a dangerous smile touched the corner of his lips. "I resent the accusation. I was your biggest supporter at this university. Despite your background, I knew you had potential. It's always sad to see potential wasted."

Jack's hands shook. He wanted to grab Dutton by his fancy suit and throw him to the floor. He wanted to tear one of the oil paintings from the wall and bash Dutton's handsome face with the frame. "You doctored the old exam. You added my paragraph to the old test to make it look like I cheated. Why?"

Dutton rose from the chair, smoothing his sleeves. "This isn't getting us anywhere, Jack. I've got work to do—and you've got to pack."

Jack wanted to throw up. He tried to tell himself that it was going to be all right, that somehow it was going to be all right. He didn't need Harvard. He didn't need a Ph.D.

He had his project. *His miracle.* Even Harvard meant nothing in the face of his miracle.

"Oh," Dutton added, turning away from the table with a sweep of his jacket. "Don't bother heading to the lab for your things. Your privileges have been revoked. The lock has already been reprogrammed to reject your ID."

The words hit Jack and he doubled over, gripping the edge of the table. His face paled as he finally realized the truth.

He had been such a fool. A naive, fucking fool.

"My project. You know about my project."

Dutton paused, his back still turned. He could have ignored Jack, he could have simply walked away. But that wouldn't have been in character. Jack was no threat.

"It's a university lab, under my supervision. You were careful, but not perfect."

"You're going to steal it from me. You're going to pretend that it's yours."

Dutton raised his arms out at his sides, palms up. His face was turned toward the chandeliers. "It's the miracle that matters, Jack. Not who takes the credit."

Jack slammed his fist against the table. The sound reverberated off the marble walls. "You can't do this!"

Dutton turned to face him. For a brief moment, there were wolves in his grin. "Why not? You going to blow the whistle on me? I was on the short list for the Nobel. You're here on financial aid. And now you just got kicked out of school for plagiarism."

He stepped away from the table and moved down the steps. He waited until he had reached the crimson aisle before pointing a finger at Jack's face.

"Your word against mine, Jack. Who do you think they're going to believe?"

Jack leaped upward. The chair crashed to the floor behind him. "You can't do this!"

Dutton continued up the aisle.

"You're a smart kid. I'm sure you'll land on your feet."

"It was my idea! It's my cure! It's my miracle!"

Dutton laughed, shaking his head. His auburn hair danced against the nape of his neck.

"You're already gone, Jack."

Jack wanted to race after him. But as he moved across the stage, he felt the eyes of the oil paintings burning into him from the marble walls. Dutton was right. Nobody would believe him. This was Dutton's world, not his. Against a man like Dutton, he'd never get justice.

Even after seven years, Jack didn't belong.

READ ALL THE HEART-POUNDING MEDICAL SUSPENSE NOVELS OF

DAVID SHOBIN

THE CENTER
In the most advanced hospital in the world, medical computers ensure perfect care. But machines have no scruples, no compassion—no mercy. And now they have a mind of their own...
0-312-96167-7___$6.99 U.S.___$8.99 Can.

THE PROVIDER
A string of tragic, senseless deaths has struck the babies of the neo-natal unit of University Hospital—and one young doctor is determined to uncover the truth about a killer who operates with startling brutality...
0-312-97185-0___$6.99 U.S.___$8.99 Can.

TERMINAL CONDITION
A promising young doctor at New York's most prestigious hospital finds out that the hospital is run on greed and malice, rather than compassion. Horrific human experiments are taking place; people are being robbed of vital fluids; and for some reason, no one seems concerned with healing the sick...
0-312-96622-9___$6.99 U.S.___$8.99 Can.

Publishers Book and Audio Mailing Service
P.O. Box 070059, Staten Island, NY 10307
Please send me the book(s) I have checked above. I am enclosing $_____ (please add $1.50 for the first book, and $.50 for each additional book to cover postage and handling. Send check or money order only—no CODs) or charge my VISA, MASTERCARD, DISCOVER or AMERICAN EXPRESS card.

Card Number_____

Expiration date_____Signature_____

Name_____

Address_____

City_____State/Zip_____
Please allow six weeks for delivery. Prices subject to change without notice. Payment in U.S. funds only. New York residents add applicable sales tax.   DSM 11/99